MIST

DANITA CAHILL

IN MEMORY OF JUDY JEFFERSON

I love you, Mom. You will always be with me.

MIST

Copyright © Danita Cahill 2012

Ridge Publishing

First Edition

This is a work of fiction. Names, characters, places and incidents were created in the author's imagination, or were used fictitiously and are not to be construed as real. Any resemblance to actual events, locales, organizations, or persons – living or dead – is entirely coincidental. All rights reserved. The republication or utilization of this work in whole or in part in any form by any electronic or mechanical or other means, not known of hereafter invented, including xerography, photocopying and recording, or in any information storages or retrieval system, is forbidden without the written permission of the publisher. The scanning, uploading, and distribution of this book via the Internet or via any other means without permission of the copyright owner is illegal and punishable by law.

Cover design by Christy Keerins – christykeerins@yahoo.com. Cover photograph by David Romanini/Dreamstime.com.

PART ONE: THE SIGHTINGS

CHAPTER ONE

Wednesday, 11:44 AM

The only super natural thing in this salt-water town is the crazy lady on Center Street who claims she can predict the future. So, when I whip into a parking space at the speedy mart, almost hit a black dog roughly the size of a Dodge Neon, and it turns and stares at me with glowing red eyes, I say to myself, "Ridiculous, Dianne. You must be seeing things."

I fumble through my camera bag. No one will believe this story without photographic evidence. Before I can pull out my Canon, the dog trots off into the November fog. With a trembling finger, I punch down my window and yell, "Go on, get lost!" Oh yeah, I'm big and tough all right, yelling at a retreating dog's butt. I jab up my window. "And good riddance," I add through the glass, to demonstrate I'm not afraid of any stupid stray dog.

I stay inside my Blazer for a few minutes, waiting for my hands to stop shaking. When I'm sure the stupid stray dog is really gone, I step outside, unload Megan from her car seat and hug her close. I try to forget about the scarlet eyes I thought I saw glaring at me through the mist.

I hike with Megan across the rutted lot and around a dark-colored sedan. The stench of sulfur hovers near the store entrance. Weird, I don't see anyone striking a match or setting off smoke bombs. I shrug, swing open the glass door, and go on inside the Coast Town Speedy Mart and Fuel Station. I need a Diet Coke to lubricate my courage. My next stop is the newspaper office to drop off Grandma Austin's obituary. Facing Grandma's departure in black and white print terrifies me more than I'd like to admit.

Inside the store, a blast of warm air dries the clinging sea mist, making my hands and face prickle. I check Megan's skin for dampness, but she's dry. Good. My body shielded hers from the fog. Standing at the checkout counter with his back to me is a tall, lean man. He's wearing a blue dress shirt and snug-fitting gray slacks. His sandy-blond hair is military short. He stands with feet planted broad-shoulder width apart, his posture crisp. Kevin McCoffey? I'm almost sure of it. I imagine a set of sparkling golden eyes in the face I can't see.

The Kevin look-alike and the store clerk talk in tones so low I can't make out what they say. The man nods and appears to write something down. Kevin is a detective now. Professional clothing and note taking are right in line with that.

I duck behind a Coors Light display to spy, jiggling Megan up and down to keep her quiet. I'm hoping the man turns so I can get a look at his face, see if it's really Kevin. But danged if he doesn't continue to focus his full attention on Miss Cashier Girl and his notebook. Jealousy stabs me. Oh, brother. Kevin, or whoever, is just doing his job. He's not flirting, and even if he were, and even if it is Kevin, so what?

I've seen Kevin many times over the past year from afar. Funny though, living in the same town with a population of less than 10,000, I haven't come face-to-face with him in months. I tread back to the soda machine, wondering with every footfall if it really is Kevin. And if so, why is he here? Does it have anything to do with the two recent Roseland disappearances? Maybe someone held up the speedy mart. Or – I swallow at the knot of apprehension – maybe another customer saw the big, black dog with the freaky red eyes and called the Roseland police.

I try to delete that last ridiculous thought.

I'm still busy ejecting evil-eyed dog visions out of my head, bouncing Megan and struggling one-handed to fill a cup with ice when I catch a whiff of sporty, clean-smelling aftershave.

"Hey there, Dianne. Need a hand?" a voice drawls behind me.

Kevin moved to Oregon from New Orleans when he was twelve, but he never managed to shake the southern accent. Chicks find his drawl alluring, and I suspect Kevin hasn't tried real hard to lose the slow, sexy speech pattern. I'd recognize that accent and aftershave anywhere.

"Kevin McCoffey." I whirl around to gaze up into a pair of vibrant golden-brown eyes.

Kevin. My Kevin.

Throughout high school, he was there when I needed him, holding my hand, listening, making me feel secure. As trusty and safe as his cologne.

Longing bubbles up from some inner domestic spring – the wish to live life as part of a whole, happy family. Me the mother, Kevin the father, and baby Megan makes three.

The longing bubble surfaces and pops. Where did it come from anyway? Kevin isn't Megan's father. Her father is gone. He died almost a year ago – I sprinkled his ashes out to sea. And blended families rarely work. Besides, Kevin is afraid of commitment. I found that out the hard way. The night I was sure he'd propose, he dumped me instead. For the third time.

So much for trusty and safe.

"Hey," I say. Regardless of our past, it's still nice to see his familiar warm gold eyes and hear his charming drawl. "You smell good, as always." Did I just say that? I can't believe I just said that.

"Thanks," Kevin says. He puts his nose close to my hair and takes a whiff.

Delight tingles down my spine.

I am so pathetic.

"You don't smell bad, yourself, ma'am," he says.

When anyone else calls me ma'am, it makes me feel middle-aged, instead of twenty-four. But hearing Kevin say it with his sexy twang makes me feel hot. I wish I really were hot – a tall, svelte blonde with a perfect smile. In reality, I'm average height and packing an extra ten pounds. My hair's plain brown, and my bottom teeth are a little crooked.

Reality bites.

Megan squirms and kicks her feet. She's slipping. I give her a little jounce to reposition her on my hip.

Kevin takes my fountain cup. A warmth radiates from where his hand brushes mine, and his fingers linger there a moment longer than necessary. I suck in a lungful of his clean, familiar scent and fight the urge to sigh. It's been months since I sniffed a man.

What am I thinking? I don't have time to be sniffing and sighing over a guy like he's The King, and I'm a lovesick Elvis fan or something. My priorities are different now. I glance down at Megan bundled in her pink romper. I've got a baby to raise.

Kevin fills my cup half full of ice and points an index finger my way. "Diet Coke. Top it off with a shot of Sprite and a squirt of root beer." I imagine him giving me an Elvis lip lift, a pelvic thrust and saying: "Hey baby, that's what you like."

I grin and nod. He remembers.

What else does he remember?

I'd heard Kevin earned Roseland officer of the year, and the chief promoted him to detective, but I will always think of him as the first boy I ever kissed. The first boy I ever did a lot of first things with…. "What brings you in here?"

"Just doing some follow-up on a case. Sorry, I really can't talk about it."

Figures. I'm still just as curious as when I ducked behind the cases of beer a few minutes ago. Well, not quite. At least now I know the man at the counter talking to the cashier was Kevin.

He focuses his attention back to the stream of brown liquid and fizz sputtering out of the fountain spout. My cup's only half-full, but he releases the button and shifts his weight from one foot to the other. "How're you doing anyway? I meant to stop by, or send a card after Matt's accident, something. You hanging in there?"

I glance at the floor. My marriage to Matt was brief and none too happy. He wasn't the love of my life, but when he proposed, I said yes. I couldn't spend a lifetime waiting for Kevin. I figured if Kevin hadn't proposed after all that time, he was never going to. I was ready to settle down, start a family. So, I became Matt's wife. I wasn't crazy in love with him, but I was committed. Till death do us part. Although him dying certainly wasn't what I planned for, or wanted, especially not after I'd just found out I was pregnant with his baby. Tomorrow is Thanksgiving. With Grandma gone, I'll be spending the holiday without adult companionship. And I have eighteen years yet to raise Megan on my own.

"I'm okay," I say anyway. No one likes a whiner.

Kevin shoots me a look that tells me he's not totally convinced. His chin crinkles, grooving the dimple there into a cleft.

It makes me smile again. Smiling is good. I've had death slap me around too much this past year. I don't want to think sad thoughts anymore at the moment. We need to talk about something different. Something more upbeat. "Congratulations on your promotion. That's wonderful."

Kevin gives me a smile. "Thanks." He tops off my soda with a foamy squirt of root beer and reaches for a lid. He scans my face, as though to check and see if I'm truly okay nearly a year after my husband's death. "Congratulations yourself. I'd heard you had a baby girl." He peels the paper off a straw, and studies Megan, who's snuggled against my shoulder. "How old is she now?"

"Three months." Megan is a beautiful baby. I'd think so even if I weren't her mama. I shift so Kevin can get a better look at her face.

"She's a cutie. Got your brilliant blue eyes."

I beam. At least it feels like I'm beaming.

Kevin beams back, pokes the straw through the lid and hands me the cup. "There you are."

My fingers graze his. The contact gives me a nice tingly knuckle buzz. "Thank you." The knuckle buzzing disconcerts me, but Kevin's chivalry is touching. Good men need to be heroes. Kevin more than most.

He studies the baby again. "What did you name her?"

"Megan Austin Harris." My tongue stumbles over her middle name.

"Austin, after your Grandmother?"

"Yes." Tears burn the back of my throat and well up in my eyes.

Kevin lays a big hand on my shoulder and peers down into my face. "You sure you're okay?"

"Yes," I say again. But this time I can't hide the lie. Two tears slide down my cheek. I look at the floor, sniffle and shake my head. "I mean no. Grandma passed away Monday night." Grandma Austin was more like a mother than grandmother to me. One of my few unconditional-love people. No more of her sage advice, her homemade apple crisp, the lavender scent that filled her home and clung to her clothes.

I shut my eyes and draw in a breath. The air smells like lavender. Ridiculous. Grandma isn't here. She's gone from my life forever.

Not forever, Dianne. We will be together again someday.

Okay Grandma. That's good to know.

Wait a minute…Grandma? Is that really you? I look at Kevin to see if he heard the voice. If he did, he gives no indication.

Am I going nuts here?

"Ah, Dianne, I'm sorry," Kevin says. "Adelle was a great lady."

I nod in whole-hearted agreement. Grandma Austin was an amazing, wise and generous woman.

I'm relieved when the voice doesn't chime in with two bits of her own.

Kevin's cell phone rings. He snatches it off his belt, looks at the screen. "I'm sorry. I have to take this. You take good care of yourself. And that baby girl."

"Okay." I hug Megan a little tighter. "I will."

Kevin already has the phone to his ear and he's three strides down the aisle before I can holler, "Have a good Thanksgiving!"

He holds up a hand and glances back before pushing out the door. Through the glass storefront, I watch him jump into the dark sedan, phone still to his ear, lips moving. He flips on flashing red and blue lights hidden in the car's grill and visor. Then he's gone, like a cowboy riding off into the sunset. Only he's driving. He's not a cowboy. And there is no sunset, just the endless autumn fog.

Even with an infant held to my shoulder and a store smattered with late-morning customers, I feel instantly, and completely alone. A foreboding wave of homesickness splashes over me, which is ridiculous with a capital R. I've got only two more errands to run – drop off Grandma's obituary, then zip by her house and feed Bubba dog. I'll be home to my own little warm apartment in an hour. Two hours tops.

The smell of corn dogs and chicken drifts from the market's backroom deep fryer, reminding me I skipped breakfast. My stomach rumbles a complaint, but greasy deli food isn't what my stomach needs. I grab an energy bar before stepping into the checkout line. The red-eyed glare of the parking-lot dog flashes through my mind. I force away the distracting thought. I'm next up in line.

Without uttering a greeting, the same cashier who earlier spoke to Kevin rings up my stuff. I want to ask her what she and Kevin talked about. The disappearances? A robbery? The dog? But up close the cashier's appearance stops me short. She's got a stud screwed through one cheek and a hoop jabbed through each eyebrow. Beneath the hoops, her eyes are dull, almost lifeless. Tattooed around her wrist is an angry-looking rattlesnake. It's head, open-jawed fangs and split tongue color the entire back of her hand.

Ouch, that must have hurt. I hate needles. I can't imagine volunteering to get poked with one over and over, let alone feeling the desire to permanently sport a serpent bracelet. The only thing worse would be a bracelet of spiders. I'm not wild about snakes, but spiders send me packing. Packing and screaming like a sissy girl, if you want the truth. A chill walks on eight hairy little feet all the way up my backbone.

The cashier looks to be five or six years older than me, which would put her at about thirty. There's something unusual about her face, besides the extra holes, I mean. Something I've seen before, but can't quite put my finger on.

I reach into the pocket of my jeans for money and lay the crumpled bills in the cashier's outstretched snake hand. She clips the dollars into the cash drawer, awkwardly digs out some change, and with a limp-wrist motion slams the till shut. She tosses the coins into the cup of my palm, as though I am a leper and touching me might give her the disease. A quarter and a dime bounce out of my hand and onto the floor. I let out an exasperated breath and stoop to retrieve them.

What's her problem? A jumble of insults tumbles through my head. I open my mouth to let the cashier know what I think of her lack of customer-service skills. The scent of lavender overpowers the smell of deep-fried chicken.

Give her the benefit of the doubt, Dianne. You never know what might be going on in her life.

It's the voice again.

I draw in some air, count to three and let out a sigh. The voice is right. After plucking the thirty-five cents off the floor – no easy feat while balancing an infant – I stand up straight, smile, look the cashier in the eye and say, "Thank you. Happy Thanksgiving tomorrow."

Ms. Cashier's expression doesn't happy up one tiny bit, and she doesn't say a word in return.

Oh, well. There's no such thing as miracles.

Grandma, er... I mean the voice, should still be proud of me.

I've had songs stuck inside my head before. Annoying jingles. Useless bits of trivia. But never voices. Can this voice really belong to Grandma Austin? Is that possible? Or is it just my conscience's way of letting me down easy – creating an inner voice that sounds like Grandma so I don't feel as alone?

Could be I'm just plain loco.

After Matt died, I felt lost and somewhat off-kilter. I took my pregnant self to group grief-counseling sessions. The general consensus among the grievers was that feelings of insanity are natural after losing someone close.

At least I'm a normal nut.

Fresh grief seeps into my heart. I miss the comfort and security of marred life, even if they weren't my happiest days. I miss a father for Megan. But right now, most of all, I miss Grandma. She's only been gone a couple days and how many times have I thought of her already? Twenty? Fifty? Seventy-five? Maybe more.

I grab my purchases off the counter, tuck my change and protein bar into my purse and turn to leave. Megan starts to fuss. The overhead fluorescents hit my eyes like a hundred camera flashes. A dull throb beats at my temples.

I trudge, none too willingly, towards the front door. I'm not excited about my next stop – delivering Grandma's obituary. Announcing the end of her life to the community seems so… permanent. So final. So damn sad.

Although I'm positive it was my imagination working overtime before, I don't want to stumble across any dumb black dogs with stupid, red-looking eyes on the way to my SUV.

"Be careful," a hollow voice says behind me.

Chapter Two

Wednesday, 12:01 PM

I spin around to see who warned me. The slurred words must have come from the cashier. She still wears a blank expression. One side of her mouth pulls down in an unnatural grimace, but she's the only one staring at me. Three other customers stand in line but none do more than casually glance my way.

Butterflies the size of dragons thump inside my stomach. "Be careful of what?" I ask.

Apparently, I don't ask loud enough since the cashier doesn't act like she heard me. She's already ringing up the next person. Oh well, I try to convince myself, look at her, she's not the type to put a whole lot of faith in anyway.

Don't judge a book by its cover.

"Okay," I say, responding both to the cashier's warning and to the moral Grandma compass vocalizing inside my head.

The huge butterflies continue their awkward stomach thumping. Megan continues to cry. My head continues to throb.

Outside the front doors, I pause by the newspaper box and scan the misty parking lot. Thank God there are no dogs in sight. The butterfly-dragons slow their flight.

Until I notice today's headlines:

Roseland's Third Mysterious Disappearance

The gut thumping starts in again. Poking two quarters in the coin slot, I tug at the paper box handle, pull out a newspaper and tuck it under my arm. I carry Megan through the now empty space where Kevin's unmarked car was parked before. Warmth spreads through the soles of my feet.

Ridiculous. I must be imagining it.

I cross the postage-stamp-size parking lot to my Blazer, keeping an eye out for stray dogs. My clogs and boot-cut jeans plow a path through the low-lying fog. My blood whooshes through my arteries. Megan fusses louder when I load her into her car seat.

A nagging feeling of forgetfulness drifts over me, as if I'm spacing something important. For the life of me I can't think what it could be. I climb inside the SUV and try to figure it out. Nothing pops into my mind. This sort of brain stumble drives me crazy, and seems to come more frequently since Matt died and Megan was born.

I unfold the newspaper and scan the lead story:

ROSELAND – Three people in two weeks have mysteriously disappeared, according to Police Chief Ken Donning. "We're working on these cases day and night," Donning this morning said.

Three disappearances now? In my cozy, safe, nothing-out-of-the-ordinary-ever-happens-here-little Oregon town – well , except for a dog whose eyes appeared to glow red, a deceased grandmother who's started conversing with me, and an eerie warning from a creepy cashier....

Nevertheless, I still don't believe in any supernatural, otherworldly, woo-woo crapola.

A knot of tension the size of a grapefruit lodges in my craw. This is all starting to freak me out.

Like a ticker tape, my mind spits out questions: How are these people disappearing? How many more will vanish? What if someone I know disappears next? What if it's Megan? Or me? What would become of Megan if something happened to me? Is it a serial killer taking these people? If so, where is he taking them? What does he do with them once he gets them to where he gets them? Before he kills them, that is. And hides their bodies.

I stretch an arm back over my seat and give Megan a little pat. "Don't worry little one. Mama will keep you safe."

It's hard to swallow around the lump in my throat. Who's going to keep me safe?

I'll bet Kevin is working these cases. They probably have top priority at the police department. Maybe that's what he got called away for, something in connection with the disappearances. Did it have anything to do with why he was here at the market talking to the cashier?

I read on:

Daniel Merle Archer, 33, disappeared Monday, according to a police report filed Tuesday afternoon by Archer's wife, Audrey. This morning Audrey told a Roseland News reporter that she wanted to file a missing person's report earlier, as soon as her husband disappeared. "The police made me wait until Dan had been missing 24 hours," she said. "But I knew something was wrong when he didn't come home from work Monday. That's not like him."

Mable Owen, a homeowner on Mason Avenue, where Daniel Archer was last seen, called The Roseland Sanitation Station Monday afternoon. Owen told the receptionist that one of their drivers left a truck running in front of her house for over an hour, with her garbage can still suspended in the truck's dump claw.

The sanitation station owner, Blair Nydell sent another employee to pick up the truck as soon as Owen contacted his company.

According to Nydell, Archer punched into work at the sanitation plant at 4:45 Monday morning. But he never punched out. Nydell told a Roseland News reporter that Archer had never before skipped out in the middle of a shift. Nydell said Archer was a dependable worker with a solid, 15-year employment record with the company.

Archer's disappearance comes on the heels of the death of his young daughter. Christina Mae Archer, age five, passed away Oct. 1 of this year, after a long battle with Leukemia.

As for the vanishing cases, police remain tight-lipped about any possible leads, but Chief Donning urges the public not to panic:

"Go about your lives as usual. Just use common sense and be aware of your surroundings."

"Easy for him to say," I mumble.

That poor Archer woman. First she lost a child and now a husband. I know how hard it is to lose a spouse. But a child? I can't even go there.

Two photos illustrate the news story. The main shot is of Audrey Archer. She's standing in front of the garbage truck her husband was last seen driving, holding a photograph of her husband out toward the camera. Her face is drawn, the expression reminding me of the tattooed cashier's at the mini-market – shocked, empty, dull. The secondary photo is a detailed close-up of Daniel Archer's time card with its last punched entry from Monday morning.

The news story goes on to recap the other two disappearances: A nine-year-old boy last week; a young woman the week before that. There is a gray breakout box asking for the public's help in solving the disappearances:

An anonymous source has offered a $2,000 reward for information leading detectives to solve the case. The Roseland Police Department is asking that anyone with information contact them.

Under the story in bold letters, it says "RELATED STORIES ON A5". But I've read enough for now.

The young woman who disappeared was twenty-four. Same age as me. The tension knot in my throat drops to my stomach and rolls around. I press a hand over my midsection and try to drive the disappearances out of my head, and out of my gut. It's too much for me to deal with at the moment.

Right now I need to stay focused on Grandma.

I open the newspaper to page A2 and search over the names in the obituaries. Thankfully, I don't know any of the people listed. I'm not sure I could absorb any more grief into my life right now. I scan through the obits for style and content, making sure I got Grandma's correct.

Yesterday, when I made arrangements at the funeral home, the director offered to write Grandma Austin's obituary for me. He called it "part of the package". But I wanted to make sure Grandma's obit was written with love. I stayed up until 2:30 this morning, laboring to finish it. Being a photographer by trade and not a writer, the process was painful in more ways than one.

After comparing Grandma's obituary to the others, I feel satisfied I did an okay job. I refold the paper and toss it onto the passenger seat.

I still can't remember what I'm forgetting.

"Sometimes Dianne, you can be so spacey," I mutter. I slip the key into the ignition and give it a twist. The Chevy sputters and dies. "What the heck?" I try again. The motor fires. "That's more like it." I click on the windshield wipers to clear the liquid fog settling on the window. After hesitating, the wiper arms groan into motion.

Okay. Ready for action. I back out of the parking spot and point the Blazer north, towards the newspaper office to deliver Grandma's obituary. I can't put it off any longer.

Maybe after Grandma's obit runs, and her service is over, the voice inside my head will go away.

Perhaps, Dianne.

Grandma?

Yes, dear.

I think I'll miss that voice.

It feels as if the damp fog layering the street is seeping into the vehicle and inside my bones. I shiver and dial the heater up a few clicks. Reaching behind me, I make sure Megan hasn't kicked off her Winnie the Pooh blanket. But she's still securely covered.

Riders wait at bus stops along Center Street. They huddle inside bus shelters and under umbrellas against the drenching fog. I pass the crazy fortuneteller's house. Hanging from two posts anchored near the sidewalk, her wooden shingle blows in the wind. In plain block letters, the sign simply states: FORTUNES TOLD.

Oh, brother.

A storm brews from the west and darkens the layer of ground-hugging fog. The mist above it condenses into drops. To my left the Pacific Ocean looks like a stirred hornets' nest with white caps. The rain beats an eerie staccato on the windshield. I suppress a shudder and crank the wiper speed up a notch. The wipers slow. Pause. Stop all together.

The fog-rain quickly collect on the window, blurring the street in front of me. I grip the steering wheel tighter, let up on the gas. "Come on, come on. This is no time to quit." The wiper motor groans and pushes the wiper arms halfway across the windshield, where they stop again. I turn the wiper knob off and back on. This time the motor catches. The arms flash back and forth.

"Thank you." I breathe a sigh of relief and relax my white-knuckle grip on the wheel. The check-engine light pops on. Something is going haywire. Maybe it's my electrical system. I should have a mechanic look at it. Like I can afford that.

Contorted coastline trees stoop lower under a rush of wind. The stench of rotting sea kelp leaks in around the window seals. A bumper sticker on the rusted red and white pickup in front of me says, "Honk if you've been rude to a tourist today." I haven't, but I laugh and toot my horn anyway.

Around here, we locals have a love/hate relationship with out-of-towners. It's true they propel our coastal economy, and for that the chamber of commerce folks are grateful, but tourists spend too much time gawking at the ocean instead of paying attention to their driving. They're notorious for lurching this way or that without using turn signals. And they travel twenty miles below the speed limit because, apparently, even they don't know where they'll be veering off to next. Tourists don't think about us poor schmos who actually live here. We schmos aren't operating on vacation time. We schmos need to get from point A to point B, daily, in a timely fashion.

The owner of the bumper sticker, a middle-aged dude in a ball cap, gives me a friendly backwards finger wave out the rear window of his pickup. I give my horn another tap, and hold up a hand in a return salute – the coastie version of a secret handshake.

A section of newspaper whips across the lane between my Blazer and the salt-corroded pick-up in front of me. A swirling gust lifts the paper and slaps it flat against my windshield, blocking my view.

"Holy…" I stomp on the brakes and pray no one is riding my tail.

Chapter Three

Wednesday, 12:07 PM

ROSELAND'S THIRD MYSTERIOUS DISAPPEARANCE

The headlines scream at me for the second time in five minutes. An eerie silence echoes through my core. It bounces off the inside of my rib cage, rattles its way up through my sinuses and settles behind my eyes. The blood exits my head and my vision floats on tiny white dots.

The sympathetic reaction surprises me. I'm not generally one to feel faint. For Heaven's sake, I don't even know any of the people who disappeared. So why would the newspaper choose me?

'Choose' me? That's a ridiculous thought. The paper would have landed against whatever vehicle happened along at this particular instant.

Right?

"Right," I say.

But it didn't land on any other car. It pasted itself to *my* window. Front page first.

The glob of silence drips from inside my head, slides down the path to my stomach, and trickles to the bottom of my large intestine, where it rustles around for awhile like a frightened wild animal trying to burrow into a pile of dead leaves.

Is this gut wriggling what people mean when they speak of premonitions?

Doesn't matter. I don't believe in foreseeing things to come. This isn't a Christmas Carol. I'm not Scrooge. And today's newspaper is not the ghost of Christmas future. I mean, really. Come on.

A corner of the newspaper lifts and flaps against the front glass, laughing at me.

Ridiculous. Ridiculous. Ridiculous. Newspapers don't laugh.

I remind myself of who I am: Dianne Harris – mother, photographer, widow, grounded realist.

Blinking my eyes to get rid of the annoying floaty dots still drifting through my line of vision, I roll down the window, stick out an arm and rip the paper off my windshield.

Enough is enough.

The newsprint tears in half. It takes another swipe to remove the rest. I'm not usually one to litter, but the paper feels slimy and restless in my hand. Instinctively, I drop the pulpy mass to the street. A cold sweat breaks out on my forehead.

Twisting around, I peek over at the infant seat and touch the top of Megan's head. I hope I didn't whiplash her when I stopped so fast. "You okay, sweetie?"

Sweetie seems fine.

I romp on the accelerator and get the heck out of the middle of the foggy lane. Idling there any longer is a good way to get us rear-ended, then Megan *would* get whip lashed. Keeping her safe is my number-one priority.

I look in the mirror. I don't like what I see. My face is ashen and covered with sweat beads. I swipe at the moisture under my bangs. My skin there feels clammy under my fingers. Like the wet newspaper. I can't stop the shudder that rocks my entire body.

A contented coo drifts up from behind me.

Megan.

What would I do without her? My heart flutters and my worries scoot to a back corner. She's only three-months old, but already I know I'd lay down my life for her. Without hesitation.

The sun breaks through the fog layer and the ocean turns brilliant blue – the color of Megan's eyes, and the color of mine too, as Kevin so gallantly pointed out. I sing a few bars from "Over the River and Through the Woods" to cheer myself up. When I get to the part about "to Grandmother's house we go" it makes me sad and I stop singing the Thanksgiving song. It's not like I can carry a tune anyway.

Patches of foggy clouds roll back over the sun and the water changes from aqua, to murky green, to serious gray. Again the waves appear churned and stirred. As if by a giant, angry hand.

Or maybe a huge, monstrous paw.

Ridiculous. Where did that thought come from? Slowing down, I enter the middle turn lane, then dart across traffic through the fog to enter the Roseland Daily News parking lot. I skirt a big, dark-colored dog that lopes out of nowhere. I don't believe in Deja-vu. But if I did, I might be sensing it right now.

I score an empty parking space near the main entrance. Before I have a chance to entertain more than a flickering, uncomfortable niggling about the coincidental dog, my cell phone rings. The musical tones make me jump. I grab up the phone and check the screen. The number is unfamiliar. I answer anyway, "Hello?"

"Hi, Dianne." A slow, sexy drawl.

I can't believe it. Kevin! I hadn't seen him for months, then I bump into him and he calls me, all in the same day. I try not to let my pulse race. But when I imagine his crooked smile, his dimpled chin, his long, thick fingers and the things they used to do to me…my heart speeds up anyway.

"It was great to see you," Kevin says, "and meet little Megan. What a cute kid." I feel all warm and fuzzy hearing him praise my baby girl. "Sorry I had to rush out on you like that," he says.

"No need to apologize I totally understand it was nice seeing you too. Been a long time and thanks for helping me out with the soda and everything." Whoa, Dianne, slow down. Take a breath, girl. He's going to think you contracted brain damage – I check my watch – in the sixteen minutes since you last saw him."

"You bet." He hesitates. "So, where are you? Is this a good time?"

"I'm at the newspaper office…" my voice catches, "…dropping off Grandma's obituary."

"I really am sorry about your grandma, Dianne. You're busy. I won't keep you…but, I was thinking, maybe we could get together sometime. Talk about the 'good old days' of Roseland high." Kevin chuckles, low and slow and delighted.

That particular laugh of his, deep and easy going, has always made me tingle in certain places. Today is no exception. I tingle and giggle. Oh brother, what am I, seventeen? No. I'm closing in on twenty-five. I'm a mother now. A widow for Pete's sake. Granted, I've only been with two guys – Kevin, and then Matt. I'm not exactly a woman of the world, but I am a mother and not a virginal schoolgirl anymore either. Besides, those "good old days" for the most part didn't seem so good back then, and we both knew it. I guess we could laugh about it now, though. Nothing wrong with that. I could use a few good laughs. What could it hurt to get together with Kevin, for old time's sake?

Me. That's what it could hurt. And Megan.

I'm no fortuneteller but I can still foresee it all now: The Future. Laid out in front of me plain as day. Kevin and I would start out again as friends. I'd get attached to him all over. Megan would grow attached. Kevin and my friendship would turn into something more.

I've sauntered down this stretch of beach before.

There would be kissing. Heavy breathing. Promises whispered in the dark. We'd make love, our naked bodies entwined, writhing with passion and ecstasy.

My heart races triple-time at that visual.

Then Kevin would get scared and break up with me. Like he did three times before.

Megan and I don't need the extra complication in our lives.

"I don't think that's a good idea, Kevin."

"Oh." Pain sharpens his voice. "Well, you take care. I'm sorry to have bothered you. Have a good Thanksgiving."

For a brief moment, I find myself wishing I could travel back in time to those lazy summer afternoons spent with Kevin near the jetty. We hung out for hours there. I miss our long talks. I miss my bare toes touching his under the warm sand. I miss Kevin.

That was then. I'm not a teenager any more. I have Megan and her needs to think of now. I decided months ago, after Matt's accident, dating and raising a baby wouldn't mix. I'm parenting alone for the long haul, like my mother before me.

Only I plan to do a hell of a better job of it.

"You aren't bothering me…" I start to say, wanting to lighten the rejection, but Kevin's already hung up. Too bad things can't be different.

But they can't.

How'd he get my number anyway? I shrug and tuck my cell phone back into my purse. Scanning the parking lot, I spot no dogs – big, little, red-eyed or otherwise.

What a coincidence it was to see two big, dark-colored dogs, running loose in separate parts of town on the same day. That's all it was. Just a coincidence. Nothing more. No sense getting worked up about it.

"Don't borrow trouble," Grandma always used to say. I wouldn't be too surprised if she said it now. Wait for it…wait for it….

Grandma doesn't say a thing.

Of course she doesn't. Grandma is dead and gone. I hold back the tears.

Grabbing my purse and the file folder with Grandma's obit inside, I climb out of the SUV and pull open the back door to get Megan. But Megan's crashed. Just like that. She had a rough time sleeping last night. I hate to wake her, but I shouldn't leave her in the Blazer. Should I?

No, it's against the law in Oregon to leave a young child unattended in a car. What if a cop happens along, writes me a ticket? What if the cop is Kevin? How mortifying would that be? Especially after I just turned him down. Maybe he'd haul me in to the Lincoln County Jail just for spite.

No. He wouldn't. Kevin's not the spiteful type.

I gaze at my precious baby. My heart swells. She looks like a cherub when she sleeps, her rosebud lips parted, and her fuzzy blonde halo of hair going every which way. I watch her chest rise and fall in perfect rhythm. I unstrap and lift her out of her car seat.

I lock the Blazer, cross three empty handicapped parking spaces and heave open the front door of the newspaper office. This shouldn't take long. Drop Grandma's obit at the front desk. Piece of cake. With an electronic jangle, the door swings shut behind me.

There's no one in sight. I glance at the wall clock, 12:16, mid-lunch hour. I didn't think about that. After two full minutes, which feels like two full days, I'm about to leave when a wooden door to the left of the front desk creaks open. A woman with cropped salt and pepper hair peeks around the door.

"I'm so glad to see you. It was starting to feel like a ghost town in here," I joke.

My attempt at humor seems lost on the woman. "How may I help you?" she mumbles.

All business now, I swallow against the endless tide of tears that try to surface. "I have an obituary I'd like run in tomorrow's paper." I hold the file folder above my head and give it a little shake to show the importance of what's inside before I place the folder on the desk.

"Oh, dear." The woman's head disappears and the door creaks closed behind her, leaving me on my own again.

Was it something I said?

When the woman reappears a few moments later, a set of reading glasses wobble on the tip of her long nose. She shuffles through a stack of papers on the desk. "Oh, dear," she says again.

Two "Oh, dears"? This doesn't sound promising. My headache flares again. Megan starts to fuss. "Is there a problem?" I ask. It comes out louder and sterner than I intended.

"Well, er…no. Not really. It's just that…I'm filling in for Thelma and I was hoping no one would come in with anything too difficult while she was at lunch."

"This isn't difficult. It's an obituary. Your paper runs them everyday." I try hard to curb the impatience creeping into my voice. "Surely there's a file there for you to slip it into. Or someone in particular you should give it to?"

This is Grandma Austin's final tribute. Her last hoo-raw.

This is damn important.

The woman aimlessly shuffles more papers around. "Wait here, please. I'll be back in a moment." The woman disappears around a corner.

Megan's fussing turns into a full-throttle howl. I jounce her this way and that. It's not helping. To heck with this. I'm done waiting. I pick up the obituary. I'm taking it with me. There's no way I'm leaving something I worked so hard to write – my last gift to grandma – in the hands of a fill-in receptionist who doesn't know how to deal with the public. She'd probably misplace it anyway. I'll go feed Bubba and come back in an hour when lunchtime is over and the real receptionist is staffing the front desk.

The door jangles as I leave. Outside, salt-laced moisture settles on my face. It's sticky and uncomfortable. I wipe a hand over my cheeks to get rid of the briny mist. Ten yards away, two dark shadows slink through the wall of fog surrounding the parking lot. The two shadows converge into one. The fog parts around the entity and the image once more splits. Two forms creep low-slung along the mist, edges still blurred by the vapors of moisture. The shadows turn organic, then beastly as legs and heads appear.

My heart thuds loudly inside my ears, echoing, as if both my heart and head are trapped inside a tunnel. At first I think I'm seeing things. After all, it's between the covers of comic books, or up on the big screen where large beasts sneak through cities, half hidden in shrouds of fog, not in downtown Roseland.

The shadows emerge like dark ink blots.

Dogs.

The beasts are ordinary, domestic dogs. One is probably the mutt I avoided hitting on the way in. Yes, I'm almost sure of it. The front dog looks like a black

German shepherd cross. Judging by its size, maybe a little grizzly bear thrown in the mix. It looks strikingly familiar. Like the giant black dog I almost hit at the speedy mart.

Impossible. This black can't be the same dog. The other was halfway across town. A dog couldn't travel this far so fast.

It has to be two different black dogs. Maybe they have the same father. A traveling salesman stud dog who roams around town, getting stuck together with a female dog here, another there, stamping out identical pups all over Roseland. Identical pups that grew into identical black dogs. Gigantic hairy bookends. One on either end of town. What's the likelihood of that?

No matter. What does matter is the owners need to keep their pets inside fenced yards. Unless they want Bear and Fido here to get run over. Animal control should get off their duffs and enforce the city leash law.

The second beast is long-haired. Grey, I think. I can't quite tell. Can't make out its color too well, or individual features on either animal. The fog still obscures the dogs' faces. Both crouch low to the ground, as though stalking an unsuspecting rabbit along the blacktop.

I grip Megan tighter. My heart tells me to run. My instincts warn me to move slowly. Try not to bring attention to Megan and myself with any sudden movements.

Too late. The dogs are looking directly at me. And their eyes don't seem right. There's a ruby glint to them. Feral. Like the eyes of nighttime wild creatures caught in a floodlight. Coyotes, maybe. Or wolves.

One of the dogs crouches lower, as if getting ready to pounce. An unexpected realization drops my stomach to the blacktop. These dogs are not stalking a rabbit. They are hunting me. And I'm holding Megan.

Chapter Four

Wednesday, 11:58 AM

With lights spinning, Kevin sped his unmarked sedan the few blocks to where the latest "vanishing vic" – as the police department called the three missing persons – was last seen. Headquarters directed Kevin to the site because twenty minutes ago a man found a work boot in the ditch.

Footwear showing up two days after the disappearance seemed…well, it seemed off to Kevin. Not completely impossible, but highly improbable. Two days before, Kevin thoroughly searched that ditch himself. There had been no boot near the area the driver left the garbage truck running. He was sure of it.

Kevin swung his unmarked police car into an older, established neighborhood. The houses were rambling ranch style. Yards were tidy. Streets were clean. The pine trees shot massive trunks up through the fog.

He pulled over alongside the road where a female officer talked with a bearded man. The pair stood next to a bicycle with half-filled, lumpy plastic bags strapped to the rear fender. A small American flag hung limply from one handle bar. On the ground nearby was a mud-encrusted work boot.

Kevin stepped from his car. "Hello there," he addressed the two. "What did we find?"

"This is LeRoy Swank," Officer Sharon Brown said. She bent slowly and picked up the muddy work boot by the lace, giving both men a peek-a-boo shot at her cleavage in the process. Kevin couldn't help thinking the peep show was for his benefit. Of course he looked. So did Mr. Swank. Dangle fruit in front of men and they're obligated to look. Sharon's fruit were pears. Not bad, except Kevin preferred peaches. Dianne's were peaches. Round and firm. He felt a little smile play around his lips.

Sharon gave him a come-hither glance.

Oh, shit. I hope she doesn't think I'm smiling at her pears.

Kevin brushed at imaginary lint on the front of his shirt and cleared his throat. What Sharon needed to do was finish buttoning her uniform. Leaving the top two buttons undone like that was against code. It was also unprofessional. And damn distracting.

"Mr. Swank found this in the ditch." Sharon pinched a lace between her thumb and index finger and dangled the filthy boot at arm's length. "He thinks it might be from the truck driver who disappeared."

"Thank you, Officer Brown." Kevin didn't dislike Sharon. He just felt no real attraction towards her. Dianne's bright blue eyes flashed through his mind – fun, feisty, sometimes sarcastic. Sharon's eyes were murky hazel. Sarcastic yes, but also cynical. Besides, she wore too much black eye makeup, like she was trying to look like a porn star or something.

Kevin's partner, Buzz kept trying to fix him up with Sharon. Kevin didn't encourage either one of them. "I'll handle it from here." Kevin gave Sharon a little nod before he pulled out his notebook and a pen. He glanced at his watch and jotted down the time: 12:02 PM.

Sharon released the boot string, letting the boot clunk to the ground. She huffed off in the direction of her patrol car. Kevin tried to ignore her, turning his attention instead to the man who claimed discovery of the footwear.

"This boot could be a clue. Don't you think?" LeRoy asked.

"First let me take down some information," Kevin said. "Full name? And spell it for me please."

"LeRoy Terrance Swank." Slowly the bearded man spelled out the name.

"Address?"

LeRoy shifted his eyes skyward, as though straining to remember. "Two-three-nine Maple Boulevard."

Kevin recognized the address. He scribbled Mission/homeless.

"Telephone?" Kevin asked.

LeRoy shook his head.

Without a permanent address or phone number, the man would be hard to contact if Kevin needed to question him further. In his notepad, he jotted a few abbreviated words describing LeRoy, in case he later needed help locating him: Lft. eye droop. B & W beard-mid chest. Dirty orng. cap. Crooked lttle finger on rt. hand.

He didn't smell too great either, but Kevin didn't write that down.

At the sound of a car door slamming, Kevin looked up. Sharon had stomped her way to her patrol car. She revved the motor and spun the back tires, spitting gravel as she whipped the sedan from the shoulder onto the street.

Kevin scowled and shook his head. Guess he'd really pissed her off. Oh well, it wasn't the first time. Probably wouldn't be the last. He wondered what ticked her off more – that he didn't take advantage of her advances, or that he outranked her. Didn't matter. Even if he'd felt more physically attracted to her, she was too hot-headed for his taste in a date. She was his subordinate anyway. Even if he were interested, it would be against regulations and unethical to go out with her. Buzz knew that too.

Kevin turned back to LeRoy, his pen poised above his notebook. "Alright Mr. Swank. Tell me how you happened to find this boot."

"Well, I was riding my bike along this road, see, looking for pop cans. Beer cans. You know, for cash."

Kevin nodded.

"I saw something shiny down there." LeRoy pointed at the bottom of the muddy ditch.

"I got off my bike and went down there and it was this here boot."

Kevin glanced at the filthy boot lying on the ground. "This boot?"

LeRoy bobbled his head up and down.

"The boot was shiny?" *This man is a terrible liar.*

LeRoy glanced at the patch of dandelions near his feet and verbally backpedaled. "Well…uh….the boot…uh, wasn't exactly shiny. It must have been a can or something like that was shiny. When I went to investigate, I found this here boot."

Kevin checked out the indents in the ground leading down into the ditch and back out. Muddy water filled the footprints. As he watched, a blade of bent grass popped into upright position.

Fresh tracks.

Kevin looked at LeRoy's shoes. They were black, Converse-type, high-top tennis shoes. Old and battered, but not muddy. Kevin figured after LeRoy went down into the ditch – probably initially after a can – the idea to plant "evidence" popped into his head. So he'd changed foot wear, tossed one of the boots he'd been wearing on the ground, stashed the other, then flagged down Patrol Officer Brown with a story about finding the boot in the ditch.

For this Kevin got called away from Dianne?

"What made you alert the police?" Kevin asked.

"Well, I thought I'd heard this was where that last guy – that garbage-truck-driver dude – disappeared from."

Kevin nodded. LeRoy took the gesture as a green light.

"I thought the boot might be that guy's and it could help you detectives and all."

"There's a reward for anyone who gives information in these cases that leads to a conviction."

LeRoy widened his eyes. His mouth formed an exaggerated "Oh".

It was obvious the man was feigning surprise.

"Is that right?" LeRoy asked. "I'll be. So you telling me if this boot somehow helps you catch the killer, I get some cash?"

"We have no evidence that the missing persons were killed. But yes, Mr. Swank, if this boot leads to a suspect, and he or she is arrested, AND convicted, you will receive some money."

LeRoy grinned. He was missing a bottom bicuspid and a neighboring molar. It left a dark, miniature cave in the bottom left side of his mouth.

Kevin made a note of the missing teeth.

"Of course if I find out you planted this boot, or are lying to me in any way," Kevin explained, "I could arrest you for giving false information to a police officer."

LeRoy looked at the ground and kicked at a rock. "Yes, sir," he mumbled.

"Do you have anything else to add?"

"No, sir." LeRoy shuffled his ratty high tops. "Can I go now?"

Kevin nodded. "Yes, Mr. Swank. You're free to go."

Kevin went to his car and got a paper bag out of the trunk. He picked the boot up by a lace and carefully lowered it inside the bag. He initialed the sack, and wrote down the time and date before carefully folding down the top. He set the bag on the backseat, shaking his head at the amount of paperwork this single boot was going to cause him. He knew it was a false lead, but he was helpless to do anything but follow it to the end of the trail. This meant he had to call the missing man's grieving wife. Again. How many times had he already called her? Three? Four? The poor woman. She couldn't even grieve in peace.

From the front seat of his squad car, Kevin watched LeRoy peddle a crooked path until he disappeared into the fog. This left Kevin with a misty image of the American flag whipping from the handlebars. *Let freedom ring.* No one could be much freer than Mr. Swank.

The homeless man was lying to him, but Kevin didn't intend to haul him in for further questioning. LeRoy Swank might be free to come and go – no mortgage, no car payments, no taxes – but Mr. Swank had enough to deal with just living day to day. At least the mission provided nightly shelter and one hot meal a day. If Kevin was in LeRoy's battered high tops, he might fabricate evidence for a shot at a stack of cash too. A couple thousand dollars would drastically change the quality of Mr. Swank's life. At least for a while.

Kevin glanced at his watch. It had taken him four minutes to drive from the speedy mart to this spot. Seven minutes to interview LeRoy Swank and bag the boot, and three minutes to put off calling Archer's wife. He hated making calls like this. He remembered how he felt when people back in Louisiana continually brought up his father's accident. It was like pouring vinegar into an abscess. He detested being the one to do the same thing to another grieving person.

Kevin took a deep breath. Let it out. It was part of his job. Like it or not, it had to be done. He looked up Mrs. Archer's number in his notebook, picked up his cell and punched in the ten digits.

The line was busy. He felt relieved. But his relief was short lived – all a busy line meant was he'd be calling the number again in a little while. He had a few minutes to kill. He didn't want to leave the scene until he knew if the boot might belong to the Archer man or not. If it turned out to be a real possibility, Kevin would comb the area again for clues. As much good as that would do. The scene was old, cold and contaminated.

He could start filling out the paperwork pertaining to the interview with Mr. Swank and the piece of filthy "evidence" sitting in a sack in the back seat.

Kevin filled his cheeks with air and blew the breath out. "Hoo, boy." He hated the paperwork end of this job. He was next to certain there was no more evidence to find here. So, instead of a futile search and filling out non-urgent paperwork that could wait until he was back in his office, he picked up his cell again.

His palms grew damp.

Eight months ago, when Kevin heard Adelle Austin wasn't doing so well, he'd called to check on her. He admired Dianne's grandma. She was a tough old bird. A tough old bird with a tender heart. Kevin also had ulterior motives in calling the elderly woman. He wanted another chance with Dianne. Adelle had adored Kevin since he and Dianne were kids in high school, and Kevin adored her right back. When he'd asked, Adelle gave him Dianne's number without hesitation.

Kevin scrolled through his cell phone contacts, found Dianne's name and hit the send button before he could talk himself out of it, as he had so many times before.

She picked up on the third ring.

Chapter Five

Wednesday, 12:13 PM

When Dianne turned down Kevin's offer of a date, he hung up without asking her why. He already knew why. And he couldn't blame her. Not really. He'd broke it off with her three times in the past. It was surprising she still talked to him at all. For the first two breakups, they'd still been kids in school. But he'd been a fool, a damn fool, to have let her go that last time six years ago. That time he'd lost her for good. She'd hooked up with Matt soon after.

Ah, but that was water under the bridge now. Water that had come and gone, left a baby and washed out to sea.

Baby and all, he still wanted Dianne. He'd always wanted her. He didn't even know for sure why he broke up with her back then. Just wasn't ready to go through all the steps a woman expected, he guessed. The promise ring. The engagement ring. The wedding vows. It wasn't that he didn't love her enough. He did. There was something else holding him at arm's length. A termite gnawing at the back of his heart, telling him he wasn't man enough. Wasn't hero enough.

Just plain wasn't enough.

He didn't have time to dwell on any of that right now. He had things that needed doing. It was time to try calling Audrey Archer again. First…he grabbed his flashlight and climbed out of the front seat. He opened the rear passenger door and peeked inside the sack sitting on the back seat, being careful not to touch the boot inside and leave fingerprints, on the off chance it did prove to be an actual clue. Maybe he'd read LeRoy Swank wrong. Maybe the man hadn't been lying to him. Maybe a bit of DNA clung to the muddy boot – a hint in the right direction that could crack the baffling case wide open. Kevin spread the mouth of the bag with one hand and shined the light down into the back of the boot. The number nine was stamped inside.

He called the missing man's wife again. This time the line was clear. Audrey Archer answered on the fifth ring. "Hello?"

"Mrs. Archer?"

"Yes."

Kevin could hear fresh tears in her voice. He felt deep pity for this woman. Several weeks ago she'd lost a child to leukemia. Now her husband was missing. Sometimes life really wasn't fair. Kevin discovered that cold, hard fact himself at the tender age of twelve.

"This is Detective Kevin McCoffey, ma'am. I'm sorry to bother you, but there's been a boot found at the location where Mr. Archer was last seen."

"I see." Her voice held a glimmering thread of hope.

"We're trying to determine if it could be Mr. Archer's boot. What size shoe does he wear?"

DID he wear was more likely, but Kevin didn't want to say that. Not yet. Not when there were no definite clues pointing to foul play. Not when there was still that glimmer of hope.

"Daniel wears an eleven."

Kevin puffed out a frustrated breath. "I'm sorry to get your hopes up, ma'am. This boot is a size nine. Thank you for your time."

Audrey Archer's voice cracked as she said good-bye.

Damn. He'd shaken the woman up again for nothing.

He'd been right about LeRoy Swank. Sometimes he hated being right. In this case, he was also right back to square one.

Kevin fired up his car, radioed in to headquarters. "This is seven-four-three, headed back in."

"You bringing us something good?" the dispatcher asked. Word traveled fast. He imagined most everyone in the department had heard about the boot in the ditch. They were all anxious over the vanishing vic cases.

"That's a negative."

The dispatcher's voice dropped half an octave. "Roger that."

On the drive back to the office, Kevin's thoughts wandered again to Dianne. Over the past ten months he'd often wondered how she was doing, what she was doing, if she was seeing anyone yet. He kept hoping to bump into her. Kept thinking in a town the size of Roseland, running into her sooner rather than later would be inevitable. But it had been months since their paths had crossed.

The last time he'd seen her she'd been nearly full-term with the baby and glowing with the bloom of pregnancy. Today, at the market – before she'd spoken of her grandmother anyway – she'd glowed with something new, something even brighter. Was it motherhood? Kevin didn't know becoming a mother made a woman glow. Of course he'd never noticed details about any other woman the way he seemed to hone in on little things about Dianne: Her shiny, clean-smelling hair, her beautiful smile, those playful blue eyes. Her body.

Don't even get him started on her body.

It had changed since before the baby. Filled and rounded out – in all the right places, he might add. A little smile played around his mouth as his mind's eye lingered on those places. Her body had gone from a girl's thin form to a woman's lush figure. The baby he had to thank for Dianne's delicious new curves was sure a cutie. When little Megan had looked at him with the same big blue eyes as Dianne, his heart warmed towards another man's child.

A baby he wished was his.

He cringed again at the thought of the child's last name, Harris – Matt's last name. But of course Dianne had given the baby Matt's last name. It was Matt's baby, and Harris was Dianne's last name now too. Maybe she'd take her maiden name back now that Matt was gone. No. Of course she wouldn't. She was a widow, not a divorcee.

Kevin never cared for Matt, he was an arrogant son of a bitch. Kevin swallowed the bitter pill lodged in his throat. He needed to think of some way to show Dianne he really cared. Maybe it wasn't too late to win her back again. There hadn't been a day gone by that he hadn't regretted breaking up with her that last time. He wished he could explain that to her. Just like the vanishing vic cases, letting Dianne go wasn't something he could easily explain.

Even to himself.

Whether she'd ever take him back or not, he still intended to send Dianne a sympathy card. When she told him of her grandmother's death, the sadness in her brilliant blue eyes was almost more that he could take.

Kevin could spare a few minutes. There was no hurry in getting the bogus boot back to the evidence room. He'd stop off at the drug store and pick up a card right now, while it was fresh in his mind.

He steered into a drugstore parking lot. Inside the store, he shuffled through card after card. Read them – too sappy, too religious, too boring – and placed them, one-by-one, back on the rack.

It wasn't an easy task, finding the perfect card. Adelle had been a fine lady, willing to give up much of herself to benefit others – like taking Dianne in when Dianne's mother moved away. Adelle was a determined, sometimes sarcastic woman, with a stubborn streak running thick through her veins. In Dianne's case, blood was definitely thicker than water. The proverbial chip off the old block skipped a generation and reappeared as Dianne. Kevin smiled at the thought. Now, to find a card to match that sentiment….

Finally choosing one with the perfect greeting – sympathetic but not too mushy, he didn't want to scare her away with too much sentiment – he paid for his purchase and strode out to his unmarked cruiser. He fought the impulse to drive straight to the Roseland News office, assuming Dianne was still there, and hand the card to her in person. But he decided not to press his luck. At least not yet. He didn't want to scare her away forever. He needed to move slowly with Dianne. She was going through a lot right now. He put the sedan in drive and steered it towards the police station.

Once there, he pulled into his designated slot and stepped from the car. He retrieved the paper bag from the back seat and strode into the building through a side door. He greeted coworkers he met in the hall.

"What did you find?" The officer who asked the question was fresh out of the academy – green, eager, and still sporting a face full of acne. The kid reminded Kevin of himself – minus the zits – when he joined the force seven years ago.

"Nothing but an old cast-off boot."

"Evidence?"

Kevin shook his head. "Nope. Wrong size."

The young officer scowled. "That's a hell of a bummer."

"And how."

"Damn. I was hoping you were onto something."

Kevin nodded. "You and me both."

This case had the whole department on edge. Department? Hell, it had the entire town spooked. And all the little towns up and down the Oregon coast. Kevin laid a hand on the kid officer's shoulder. "We'll figure this thing out. Whoever's grabbing these people is bound to screw up soon. Then we'll nail his ass to the wall." Kevin wished he felt as confident as he sounded.

The young officer gave him a tight-lipped smile and a nod.

Kevin made his way down the hall, through a short corridor and into the evidence room. He scribbled out a tag, stapled it to the bag and left the dirty boot in the hands of the evidence officer. Kevin still felt as hopeless and confused about the vanishing vic cases as he had an hour ago. At least an hour ago he'd been sharing conversation with a beautiful woman. Kevin's pulse quickened at the thought of Dianne's clean scent, her full, ripe peaches. And those blue, blue eyes.

At his desk, Kevin spun his rolodex to the Js, for Jacobs – Dianne's maiden name. He never could bring himself to enter her in the Hs, under her married name. Against his will, he printed her current name, Dianne Harris, across the face of the envelope and copied down her SE Daffodil Lane address from his card file. He dug through his top desk drawer for a stamp. He'd drop the card in the mail on his way home.

Buzz, Kevin's senior partner, breezed into their tiny, shared office. The fifty-one-year-old detective set his hair clippers on the next-to-bald setting before buzz cutting his own silver hair, hence the nickname. With a real name like Chester, Kevin totally understood his partner's desire to go by Buzz.

The older detective tossed a gossip-type pulp magazine on Kevin's desk. "Lookie here."

"What's this?" Kevin looked at his partner before he reached for the magazine.

"Seems we're famous," Buzz said.

Kevin read one of the front-page teasers out loud: "Alien abductions in Oregon?"

"Yeah." Buzz smirked. "Check it out." He crossed the cramped room in two long strides and plopped onto a creaking office chair behind a desk piled high with papers and files.

Kevin flipped through the magazine until he came to the article near the middle. He read the story headline out loud:

Are aliens snatching people from this coastal town?

Kevin raised his eyebrows and shot Buzz a look.

Buzz thrust his chin Kevin's way. "Keep reading. It only gets better."

"I'll bet." Kevin turned back to the story and again read aloud:

Two people have vanished from the quaint seaside town of Roseland, Oregon, in less than a two-week period.

Kevin paused. "Guess the reporter didn't hear about Daniel Archer's disappearance." At least not before this weekly rag went to press. He continued:

The first victim, a 24-year old woman, was last seen jogging along a popular exercise path nearly two weeks ago. The second person to disappear was a 9-year-old boy the following week. The boy crossed the street in front of his house to pick up his family's mail on a Thursday afternoon.

He never returned home.

What is causing folks in this coastal burg to vanish? No one seems able to answer that. No one that is, except John Whitmore, one of the 9,952 citizens populating Roseland.

Whitmore has a theory.

"Alien John?" Kevin asked Buzz. "The National Interrupter interviewed Alien John?" Kevin slapped a hand on his desk, sure now this stupid gossip magazine would make everyone in Roseland look like idiots. "That's just great."

Buzz dropped his chin to his chest and rotated his hand in a "Go ahead, go ahead" gesture.

Kevin went ahead:

We caught up with Whitmore on the corner of Center and Walnut Streets, near downtown Roseland. Whitmore was busy wrapping the bottom five or six feet of phone poles with sheets of household aluminum foil.

"The foil messes with the alien's brains," Whitmore explained. "It fouls up their communications."

Kevin and Buzz looked at one another. Buzz rolled his eyes. Kevin shook his head.

The 38-year-old man claims he has worked at warding aliens away from his hometown for years:

"I saw my first UFO when I was twenty-two, so I've been at this mission for, what is that now…" Whitmore paused to count on the fingers of both hands, "…sixteen years, I guess." He grinned. "I've gone through a lot of foil." He grabbed another roll and started a silver wrap up the next phone pole.

Holding onto the bicycle helmet perched on his head, Whitmore tipped his face to scan the skies, apparently searching for alien spacecraft.

Kevin couldn't help but chuckle. He had to grant the reporter this – she'd captured the essence of John Whitmore's unique personality. Kevin kept reading:

Whitmore's plan apparently fooled the extraterrestrials for over a decade and a half. So, why then did the foil suddenly stop warding off the body snatchers?

"Them aliens is getting smarter. Either that or the foil barriers quit working when they get old. I'm not sure which."

And what do Roseland authorities have to say about the missing persons?

Police Chief Ken Donning said, "We've got our best people working these cases. We'll get to the bottom of it."

And the possibility of the disappearances being alien abductions?

Roseland Mayor, Ilene Brenson said, "Not to call anyone a liar, but I'd have to see something like a UFO with my own eyes to believe it."

As for ordinary citizen John Whitmore, he's determined to move forward with his life's mission – keeping the phone poles along Roseland's streets wrapped in fresh tin foil; doing his part to keep the citizens of this friendly little Oregon town safe from the grasp of unfriendly aliens.

The reporter labeled Whitmore "an ordinary citizen", but Alien John was far from ordinary. If he missed a few days of his schizophrenic medication, he was downright dangerous. Kevin knew this from experience. In his patrol days, he'd hauled Whitmore in a time or two for menacing and assault. When Alien John – as he'd dubbed himself – wasn't on his meds, his amazing strength made it hard to slap the cuffs on him, let alone get him loaded into the car to transport him downtown.

Kevin lowered the paper. "I'll be damned. Looks like Whitmore got his fifteen minutes of fame."

"And Roseland got its fifteen minutes of shame." Buzz said with a wry grin.

Kevin spread the pulp magazine out on his desk and studied the photo. The illustration showed John Whitmore wearing his trademark bicycle helmet, shaggy hair poking out chaotic, chinstrap hanging loose and one pant leg tucked inside the top of a hiking boot. He stood near a foil-wrapped phone pole, several cartons of aluminum foil scattered at his feet. In the background was the fortuneteller's house. Kevin didn't have to strain hard to make out Delta's little cottage, or read the words "FORTUNES TOLD" on the sign hanging near her sidewalk.

"I'll be damned," Kevin said again.

A grave look settled over Buzz's craggy features. "We may all be damned before this is over."

Chapter Six

Wednesday, 12:21 PM

These dogs can't really be hunting us. Can they?

"Stay!" I shout, the way I'd yell at Grandma's old lab if he refused to mind. "Go home!"

The dogs glare at me with their glinting red eyes.

These dogs are nothing like Grandma's sweet, ancient Bubba dog. Bubba might be nearly deaf, but if you shout loud enough, he minds. Most of the time anyway.

Both the black and the gray dogs turn their bodies into the path between my Blazer and me. As if in planned, defiant teamwork.

My blood turns to ice water. How am I going to get past these beasts?

Confidence, Dianne. Confidence.

"Right, Grandma," I say under my breath. Pulling back my shoulders, I suck in a big lungful of sea air tinged with lavender, hoping to draw in some courage.

A third beast, brown and brindled, creeps out from between two parked sedans. It joins the black and the gray.

The icy water running through my veins turns to slush.

I exhale. My throat does a weird clenching thing, making a strange little strangled sound.

Time to come up with a new strategy. A couple of menacing dogs I could almost face. Three? No way. It's all I can do not to panic and run screaming into the street for help. In this fog, all I'd accomplish is getting myself and Megan run over.

I can't let these dogs know I'm afraid. It's not like I'm usually afraid of dogs. I like dogs. Man's best friend, right? Like good old loyal Bubba. Only these brutes creeping up in front of me don't fit into the man's-best-friend category. These three look like a mad scientist's experiment gone awry. Like Frankenstein – add a couple legs, some fur, take away a few scars, bloody up the eyes.

Six red-tinged eyes look right through me, as if I'm part of a rival pack. Or a walking side of beef. The ice in my veins condenses in the chili air and pops out on my skin as droplets of cold sweat.

What is a small pack of large dogs doing running wild in the middle of town anyway?

Maybe yelling at them again will do the trick. You never know. They could suddenly decide to become obedient.

"Go on, Get!" I say in the most commanding voice I can muster.

The three sets of glowing eyes continue to stare my way.

Where's the dogcatcher when you need him? My tax dollars pay his wages. He needs to make his rounds and get his dog-catching butt here pronto. I could call the dog pound. If I knew the number. And if I didn't have to make a big production digging around inside my purse for my cell phone. Right now, I'm afraid to move. Hollering at the dogs doesn't seem to cause any problems – or any results, for that matter. Motion of any kind might attract too much unwanted attention. Like a game of cat and mouse.

Or as in this case, a game of dog and rabbit.

I can't twist and jump like a rabbit, but I think I could still make it back to the newspaper office door if I sprint. The path to the door is clear. Despite giving birth three months ago, I've been doing my exercise tapes at home. I'm still in good shape. What good would hiding inside the paper office do me? The only person I'd seen in there during the short-handed lunch hour was the timid,

I-don't-know-how-to-do-this-job woman. What could I expect her to do, whisper the dogs into submission?

I could step inside the door and call someone on my cell phone. Maybe the police.

Maybe Kevin.

What would I say to a cop? Help me, please? There are three stray dogs in a parking lot and I'm afraid of them? Oh and by the way, the dogs all have red, glowing eyes. I don't think so. I just have to calmly, slowly move around the dogs. No big deal. Right?

The three beasts watch me as if they have all the time in the world. All the time in the world to do what? Rip me apart? Chew me into little pieces? My stomach clenches. I feel like little red riding hood. Only I'm wearing green and blue instead of red, carrying a baby instead of a picnic basket. And these are dogs, not wolves.

Aren't they?

The black and the gray dogs are in front of me, to the right of my vehicle. The mottled brown is slightly behind the others and to the left. Three tongues move in and out over sharp, yellowed canine teeth. In and out with slow, controlled pants. Saliva hangs from the black dog's mouth. A glistening string drips off the end of its tongue, hits the ground, and melds onto the wet surface of the parking lot.

Oh my. What big teeth you have.

The better to EAT you with my dear!

The panicked feeling rises inside me again. Terror clings to my skin like oil. I hope the dogs can't smell it, sense my fear. I breathe deeply, in and out, in and out, trying to control my panic.

Whether the beasts smell my fear or not, from seven or eight yards away, I can smell them. The powerful stink of wet dog, mingled with something else. Something worse. Something sinister. The smell of a giant's match, lit and plunged into water. The stench of dank sulfur.

Just like the smell in the convenience store parking lot.

The scent travels through my nasal passages and squirms through my brain's filtering system. Ridiculous, my reasoning program scoffs. Dogs don't smell like sulfur. The photographer's side of my brain takes over the ridiculing. No such thing as glowing red eyes in such dim light. Only a flash of light could create such a red glow.

I wish I could believe my brain. I try to listen. Try to let it reason me into a calm state. But the doubting Dianne inside me is not strong enough to overpower the danger signals zinging though my adrenal glands.

A question old as time zips to my core like an arrow: Fight or flight?

I can't run very fast while carrying Megan. Besides, let's face it – the dogs would be on me in three seconds. They have the advantage of two extra legs each. That's five extra sets of legs working against me. Plus who knows how many extra teeth. And all those claws.

Facing them is my only choice.

The black's hackles rise to the occasion. A growl vibrates in his throat. I feel the growl vibration deep inside my bones, as if I'm in the passenger seat of a semi truck rumbling over grooved pavement.

Carefully, so as not to ring the dogs' alarm bell, I reach in my purse for the Blazer keys. I tippy toe my fingers around inside the bag. Shit. I can't find my keys.

Can't. Find. The damn. Keys. Oh, God. No.

I didn't lock the keys inside the Blazer. Did I? I shake my head. I know they're here. If I dump my purse out on the pavement and dig through the contents, I know I could find them. But all that motion would really draw the dogs' attention. Wouldn't it?

Desperate now, cold sweat clamming my palms, I claw inside my purse for the keys, never letting my eyes leave the dogs. The purse slides from my damp hands, drops to the black top and spills. There are my keys, on top of the jumble.

As though the fumbled purse is the unspoken signal they're waiting for, the dogs move closer. They creep to the last handicapped space between the Blazer and me. The black and the gray slightly in front of the brindle, their three dark bodies now completely blocking the route to my car.

There is no time for fear, only action.

Crouching, I hold Megan tight, never letting my eyes stray from the approaching dogs. I flash back to high school, to the state softball play-offs, and the importance of each pitch I threw during those three empowering days. Focusing on my mark, pushing all other thoughts from my mind, I run my hand along the tarmac, blindly trying to get a grip on my heavy leather purse. Locating it, I grasp the bag and in one fluid motion spring from my crouched position, draw it back and let it sail.

My arm is rusty. My muscles cold. The throw pulls to the right. My bag hits only the gray dog's shoulder.

I'd meant to biff both front dogs. Still, there was some power behind the throw. The gray yips in surprise, cowers and retreats. The brindle brown joins him. The solid black beast stands his ground, hackles and top lip raised. The lip quivers but the dog is silent.

Leader of the pack.

The black takes one last glowering look my way before turning on his haunches to regroup with the other two. All three trot away, tails held low – coyote fashion – to the edge of the parking lot, where they disappear into the foggy drizzle.

I let out the breath I'd been holding for who knows how long, snatch up my keys, jog to my purse, back to the pile of purse contents. I slam my purse on the wet pavement and with two quick scoops shovel my cell phone, wallet, lip gloss and the rest of the stuff inside and then hustle to the Blazer. The keys jangle together with my shaky effort to single out the door key.

"If you'd gotten a new battery for the keyless entry you'd already be in," I chastise myself.

A point of the key catches, cockeyed in the lock. My hand is shaking so badly, I have to pull it out to reinsert it. "Come on. Come on. Get in there all ready. Unlock."

Two Chihuahuas dash out from under a nearby van. They yap madly and snap at my ankles. I let out a nervous laugh, glad for a moment of comic relief.

I push at the mouse-colored dogs with my foot, trying to nudge them out of the way. The tiny dogs snarl and charge my heels.

What is it with the people in this neighborhood letting their dogs run loose? These are old lady lap dogs – the sort of pet that could get hit and killed by a bicycle. A tricycle for that matter, let alone any one of the cars I hear streaming by.

"Go on." I smile at the hilarity of the tiny dogs acting so macho. "Get out of here." I stomp my feet at them like "I'm gonna get you."

The little dogs don't back down. Instead, they stare at me. Their round eyes change from shiny black buttons to seething red lasers. The acrid scent of sulfur fills my nostrils.

So much for comic relief.

One tiny dog grips my clog in its mouth, lets go of the shoe and sinks its teeth into my ankle. The other dog rips into the leg of my jeans, making teeth-to-skin contact.

"Get out of here you worthless mutts!"

I take aim and kick at the dogs in earnest. The lighter-colored one recognizes a size-eight threat when it sees one. It lets go of my leg, cowers and retreats. I hear a soft "whump" as my foot makes contact with the darker one and sends it skittering over the pavement. I yank open the driver's door, dropping my purse again in the process. This time I also drop the file holder with Grandma's obit. I bail inside and slam the door.

I drop my head back against the head rest. Hug Megan to my chest. I've still got my keys in hand. I drop them into the consol tray. Sitting on my knees, I turn around backwards and carefully place Megan in her car seat.

There's no sign of dogs out my window – big or little. But I'm still afraid to open my door wide enough to retrieve my purse and Grandma's obit. The Chihuahuas could be lying in wait under my SUV.

This whole unbelievable nightmare sweeps me back on waves of childhood terror. Back to the fear of letting an arm or leg dangle off my bed at night. Imaginary crocodiles lived beneath, snacking on dust bunnies, biding their time until I made that one hapless move. Then they'd chomp off one of my hands or feet.

As a first grader, I'd lie awake for hours, too afraid to fall sleep lest I relax and let a limb dangle. My wide-awake, seven-year-old mind swam with visions of Dad bursting back into my life. In these fantasies, he'd rush through my bedroom door, and throttle the crocs with his big, strong Dad hands.

Then he, Mom, and me would live happily ever after. But Dad never came back. As an adult, I know better than to waste time fantasizing about someone rushing in to rescue me. Didn't happen then. Not gonna happen now.

You can count on yourself.

Right, Grandma. I have only myself to count on. And you. Except you're dead. I can't really count on you anymore, can I? I'm the only one who's really here to keep me and my baby safe.

If I stick a hand out my car door for my stuff, these little dogs might not chomp off a whole hand like my imaginary crocs, but I'll bet money the little assholes would make a serious effort to gnaw off a finger or two.

My driver's license, debit and credit cards and $178 in cash are in my wallet. My wallet is in my purse. I have to get my purse. And I have to get Grandma's obit. It still needs to go in tomorrow's paper. I check out all my windows and my rearview mirrors.

No ember eyes burn through the mist.

I suck in some courage, open the door as quietly as possible and stretch my hand out to feel for my purse. My fingers close around the handle. I quickly pull the bag inside the door. I whip my hand back out to snatch up Grandma's obituary. My fingers close around the folder. A sharp pain rips through my thumb. I jerk my hand back and watch the blood pour from the wound and run onto the manila-colored folder.

A snarl resonates under my Blazer. Sulfur burns my nose. A small, dark gray head and ears, along with a bulging set of ruby eyes, appears near the door opening. The dog pushes and claws at the door, trying to get in.

Blood dots its muzzle. My blood.

I kick at the dog and slam the door.

The scent of damp matches wafts through the door seals. Do these dogs sweat sulfur or what? I thought dogs couldn't sweat, that's why they pant. Isn't that right? I'm sure that's right. So if the smell isn't seeping from the dogs' pores, where is it coming from? Their mouths? Does rabies cause rotten-egg breath?

My thumb is bleeding profusely. My ankle throbs, but I don't feel blood running down my leg, so I must be all right there. I rifle around in the glove box with my good hand for some napkins and wad them around my thumb. Bright red blood immediately seeps through. "Stupid little dogs," I mutter.

What is with these dogs anyway? Are they rabid? They bit me. Three times they bit me. That means a three times chance I might have rabies. Right? Will I have to get a series of painful shots through the navel? Isn't that what happens when someone contracts rabies? What if doctors can't stop the disease in time and I go Cujo crazy? What if I turn into a slobbering, vicious beast like poor Old Yeller?

What if I bite Megan?

CHAPTER SEVEN

Wednesday, 12:40 PM

Kevin rolled up the pulp gossip magazine and speared it into the trashcan beside his desk. *Aliens. Hoo boy.*

Born in Louisiana, Kevin lived in New Orleans until he was twelve. He'd seen black magic at work. Voodoo he could buy. But aliens? For God's sake, what will the press think of next? They'd print anything to make a buck.

Then again, *someone* was grabbing people from Roseland. If not aliens, who?

Kevin was as stumped now as when the first victim disappeared twenty days ago. The vanishings came out of nowhere. No rash of crime first. No gang activity in the area. Nothing out of the ordinary happening on the streets. Shoot, Kevin even went as far as checking out the lunar cycle on the nights of the disappearances. None of the vanishings happened during a full moon, when the crazies tended to venture out.

In the meantime, the kidnapper/killer continued to strike, averaging a hit a week.

Who was doing this? Where was he taking the people? Or more likely – and Kevin hated to have to think this way – where was he dumping their bodies?

This was Kevin's hometown, damn it. He'd taken an oath to uphold law and order here. The not knowing, and the helpless-to-do-anything-about-it feelings were eating him alive.

His stomach rumbled. Hunger was eating at him too. He looked at his watch. He needed food. He'd meant to grab something at the market after he finished taking the cashier's statement. But he'd bumped into Dianne, got preoccupied talking with her, then dispatch paged him and he'd had to leave.

To pick up the infamous work boot in a ditch. "Hoo boy."

Buzz looked up from behind his desk. "Huh?"

Kevin hadn't realized he'd hoo-boyed out loud. "I'm going to grab a bite."

Buzz nodded.

"Care to join me?"

Buzz shook his head. "I don't have much of an appetite just now."

Kevin was hungry, he needed to eat, but lately his appetite hadn't been normal either. These damn cases were wearing on all of them.

Out in the parking lot he warmed up his car and cranked the heater against the damp cold. He cruised up Fifth Street between the police station and downtown. A nagging worry about Dianne mingled with his overabundance of stomach acid. He didn't know what the worry was, exactly; he just knew that he couldn't shake it. Dianne looked great, as always. It wasn't her health that concerned him, although the sadness he'd seen in her eyes when she told him about her Grandma's death was hard to handle.

Dianne and Adelle were close – closer than most Granddaughter/Grandmothers. Adelle had taken Dianne in when her mother remarried and moved to Malaysia. Dianne was a high school sophomore that year. Kevin was a junior, still struggling with the circumstances surrounding his father's death.

Kevin and Dianne had each lost a parent. They turned to each other for emotional support.

He thought back to the high-school Dianne – vivacious, a star pitcher on the state-champion softball team. She was the sweet, funny girl everyone liked – jocks, hoods, preps, brainiacs – she blended in with all the cliques. Kevin hadn't only liked her. He'd loved her. More than he'd ever loved anyone outside his own family. She was his confidant, his best friend, his lifeline.

He couldn't trust himself with that much love.

That funky sensation hit him in the gut again – an uncomfortable rumbling not caused by lack of food. An unexplainable worry about Dianne. And it was about more than the sadness he'd seen in her eyes.

He wanted to check in on her. Make sure she was all right. He didn't want her to think he was stalking her…but could he help it if the newspaper office was on the way to the Burger Barn where he planned to grab a sandwich? She probably wouldn't even still be at the paper office. It depended on how long it took to arrange for an obituary to run. He'd never been in charge of the details of a family member's death. When his dad died, his mom took care of all that.

The fog grew thicker the closer he got to downtown. He turned his low beams on to try to shine light underneath the dense curtain of white. It didn't much help visibility.

Kevin cruised past the Roseland News office, slowing his car to a crawl in order to see through the fog and into the lot. He could barely make out her Blazer.

Across the street at the Burger Barn, the line was three cars deep at the drive through. Kevin pulled in anyway. He was glad Buzz had turned down his offer to join him for lunch. Buzz was a health nut. He wouldn't eat anything from the Burger Barn's menu anyway, and Kevin didn't want to explain to Buzz his dire need to come to this particular restaurant because of its close proximity to the newspaper office and possibly Dianne.

Inching forward in the order line, he kept a watchful eye on the parking lot on the other side of the street, but he couldn't see anything through the blasted fog. He couldn't even make out the outline of Dianne's Blazer anymore.

"Damn."

"Pardon me?" A voice asked through the intercom system.

Oops. His turn to order. "Excuse me. Double cheeseburger and a medium root beer."

"Would you like fries with that?"

Kevin's stomach churned. "No thanks." He wasn't sure he'd be able to get a burger down, definitely not grease-drenched fries. He idled up to the take-out window.

With the burger in a sack beside him on the seat, he drove slowly back past the newspaper building, straining to see through the misty fog. An uneasy little voice nagged at him to cruise through the lot. Check on her. Make sure she was all right.

He didn't listen to that voice.

Dianne was a big girl. She was inside the Roseland City News office. Why wouldn't she be all right? He didn't want to heap too much attention and concern on her all in one day and he didn't want to come across as a stalker. He had to play it cool with Dianne. She'd been through a lot, and she'd been hurt. By him. By her parents. By death.

On one hand, Dianne was independent and strong-willed, but on the other, she was skittish. Like a frightened rabbit. He didn't want to scare away her bunny side. He loved that part of her too.

Kevin returned along the Fifth Street route to the police station. Buzz wasn't in their tiny, shared office. Kevin ate alone at his desk, surrounded by photographs of the three missing persons.

He took a big bite of cheeseburger and studied the three headshots. Each photo represented a huge chunk missing out of their family's lives. He knew what that was like – first he lost his father, then Dianne. He knew how it felt to miss special people. It burned a hole straight through the heart.

He had to put a stop to the disappearances. Find the perp before he struck again.

Before he left more holes in more Roseland hearts.

As for the gaping spot in his own chest cavity, the one that only Dianne could fill, Kevin hoped to patch that hole soon. He took another bite of his burger. Chewed. Swallowed. The masticated beef dropped to his stomach like a rusted steel ball. He couldn't shake the uneasy feeling that hit him like a sucker punch every time he thought of Dianne.

He wanted to do something for her. Something to let her know he really cared, regardless of her turning him down. He'd mail the sympathy card later this afternoon on his way home. She'd get it in a day or two. But he wanted to do something for her today. Right now.

He wrapped up the half-eaten burger and dropped it in the trash. Reaching into a desk drawer, Kevin pulled out a phone book. He flipped through the yellow pages, found the number he was looking for and picked up the receiver.

A perky, female voice answered, "Good afternoon, Betsy's Bloomers."

"Yes, hello. This is Kevin McCoffey. I'd like to place an order."

"Okay, Mr. McCoffey, what can I get for you today?"

"I want a big bouquet of flowers that say, 'I'm sorry about your loss…' " Kevin paused, took a deep breath and let the words tumble out. "…and I'll love you forever.' "

"That's sweet," the perky woman said. "We can do that. How about some yellow carnations for the loss… maybe red roses to express your love? Of course some greenery – a few ferns, some salal, a palm frond and some filler. Baby's breath is a classic filler, and it always looks so pretty with roses."

Salal? It grew wild in the woods around here. Kevin always thought of the evergreen shrub as food for elk, not greenery for flower arrangements. No matter. As long as Dianne liked it. "Uh…sounds fine. Could you deliver those today to SE Daffodil Lane, Apartment 209?"

"We can do that."

"And can you put them in a real pretty vase?" The kind a woman might want to keep, Kevin thought, and remember the sender by.

"No problem, Mr. McCoffey. And what would you like the card to say?"

Kevin recited the words he wanted the perky florist to write, then gave her his credit card information. He smiled as he hung up the phone. Flowers should do the trick. Don't flowers always get to a woman's soft spot? Flowers, jewelry and babies.

Hmmmm…babies. That got him thinking. He'd take care of that thought later. Right now, he needed to focus on the baffling cases sitting in front of him. The files waited six-inches deep on his desk.

Chapter Eight

Wednesday, 12:34 PM

Rabies.

I shudder and roll up my pants leg. My ankle burns. I push down my sock to inspect the damage. Four small holes pierce the skin, two on each side of my Achilles tendon. There's no blood, but the area is starting to swell. Aren't puncture wounds the most susceptible to infection? Especially if they don't bleed?

I'll think about all that later. Right now I just need to get my baby out of this parking lot, far away from these hideous, rabid dogs. I'm shaking hard, but I manage to use my good hand and get the key in the ignition. I anticipate the blast of warm heat washing over us. Drying my mist-dampened clothing, lulling Megan back into a contented sleep. The Blazer has an excellent heater. I turn the key.

The motor whines, but doesn't fire. "Huh?" I give the key another crank. Nothing.

In the near distance a howl sounds, low and plaintive. Another canine voice joins in. And another. Followed by several high-pitched, excited yips.

The dogs. The evil, awful, rabid, feral dogs.

The dogs stop howling. Now they're yipping. Like a pack of coyotes hot on the trail of an injured animal.

Guess I know who the wounded prey is. My heart hammers so loudly inside my head for a moment I can hear nothing else.

The yips grow louder. Louder than my pounding heart. The yips grow nearer. Twelve yards away, three big puffs and two smaller puffs of vapor rise, denser than the fog. The puffs move closer. Closer. Hot-breathed, demon steam engines. Chugging straight for us.

The dogs emerge from the mist and plant their paws firmly on the blacktop in front of my vehicle. They stare up at me with their red, surreal eyes.

I knock on the window, shake a finger at the brutes. "Go away! Go home!" I yell, as if the beasts are obedient, backyard pets and I am their trainer.

Yeah, right.

I press the master lock in my door panel, locking me and Megan in. Locking the dogs out. A welcome calm lights on my shoulders. I embrace the feeling of safety, even while sensing it may be very temporary.

Ridiculous. I can't "sense" things like that. I'm no fortuneteller. Fortune telling is a big bunch of hooey anyway. The dogs can't get me in here. I'm safe. Megan's safe. My engine will start soon. I'll drive away and leave the dogs behind. There's nothing temporary about our safety. Of course there's still the stitches-in-my-thumb, rabies-shots-through-the-navel, major-needle-phobia thing…but I'll think about that later.

Megan starts to fuss.

The black dog rears up and plants his front feet on the driver's window ledge. From my vantage point he looks roughly the size of Idaho. Only hairier and scarier. His face is inches from my window, his wild, glowing eyes are even with mine. He snarls, bares his teeth and barks ferociously.

Flecks of dog saliva pepper my window.

I scream and turn the key again. RRRrrr, RRrrr, RRRrrr, RRrrr. The engine won't turn over. I bang my forehead on the steering wheel.

Megan's cries turn to agitated wails. "It's okay, baby," I say in the calmest voice I can muster. But my voice sounds shaky. Terrified. Not calm at all.

I turn the key again. Rrrrr, Rrrrr, Rrrrr. The motor still won't fire. "Come on. Come on. Start already." I give the key another crank. And again. Rrrrr, Rrrrr, RRRrrr. Once more. Nothing. No spark. Gasoline fumes waft back from the motor compartment and filter inside the SUV. I've flooded the engine. "Wonderful."

The black dog is still standing guard at the driver's side door, his two massive paws on my outer window ledge. His lips pulled back in a snarl.

Like a maniacal grin.

My fear level rises a couple notches. My intestines quiver and a sour taste floods my mouth. Megan squalls from the backseat. I have to stay calm, reason my way through this. I'm inside my vehicle with Megan. We're both safe. The dogs can't get us in here. So my truck won't start. No biggie. Things could be worse.

"Oh, yeah, Dianne, like how could things be worse?"

I can't believe I'm arguing with myself. Out loud.

Look for the bright side.

"We could be outside. With the dogs."

See? Things could be worse.

Yeah, okay. Things could definitely be worse. "Thanks Grandma."

Grandma doesn't say you're welcome, but the scent of calming lavender fills the Blazer interior.

The brindled dog raises himself on his hind legs, front paws on the Blazer's hood. He glares at me through the windshield with eyes that look blood-soaked.

"You stinkin' mangy dog!" I yell and lay on my horn. It doesn't phase the stinkin' mangy dog one bit.

"Where's the gray?" I ask no one in particular while checking my rearview mirror. He's not behind me.

A gray blur flashes past the corner of my eye, followed by the screeching sound of sharp claws against metal, and a tinny thump on the roof.

The roof?

The gray is on my roof.

How did he get up there? He must have gotten a toehold in the tire tread and hauled himself up over the hatch. How could a dog the size of a double XL German shepherd pull his bulk up such a steep, slippery slope?

Because these are not ordinary dogs, Dianne. These are dogs of death and despair.

"No joke, Grandma."

I immediately feel bad for snapping at her. "Sorry. No disrespect intended."

None taken.

"I love you, Grandma. You always were forgiving."

Again I lay on my horn. I'm not usually one to cuss, but I aim a few choice words at the freakin' dogs. I'm turning into a regular potty mouth here. "Sorry, Megan. Mommy shouldn't say those things." But Megan is crying so loudly, I doubt she heard me anyway.

You'd think someone else would hear my horn though and come out from the paper office. But no one so much as sticks a head out the front door of the building. I jerk my full attention back to the dogs. The giant black one snarling inches from my face is hard to ignore. But then so is the big brown dog halfway onto my hood. I can't exactly pretend away the huge gray dog banging around on my roof either. Let's face it. I'm surrounded. The only clear path from my SUV to the paper office is from the passenger side door.

I could use a good cry about now.

There's no time for tears, Dianne. Take care of yourself so you can take care of Megan.

What should I do, Grandma? My blasted car won't start.

Call someone.

Duh. Call someone. Why didn't I think of that before now? I guess my brain is on overload. But then I have been a little preoccupied, haven't I? I forgive myself for being a space cadet, dig my phone out of my purse and stare at it. Who should I call? Do I dial 911 or just call directly to Kevin's line?

Call Kevin.

Here I am, in a helluva pickle, having trouble working my way out of it and

I'm thinking of Kevin as a lifeline. Like I'm back in high school, having family troubles. And the voice of my dead grandmother is shoving me in Kevin's direction.

"Ridiculous," I say.

Ridiculous it may be, but who am I to go against Grandma Austin's wishes? Assuming, of course, the voice is Grandma's. But who else's voice could it be?

Is the voice right? Should I call on Kevin for help? His answer might be something like: "No. You turned me down and hurt my pride." But then his cop/public servant side would kick in, wouldn't it? And he'd want to know the details so he could plan his strategy of attack and save us.

I'd have to give it to him straight: "I'm locked inside my vehicle with Megan. We're surrounded by crazed, red-eyed dogs. My vehicle won't start. But don't worry, we're not in any real danger at the moment."

Kevin would keep the conversation professional. He'd ask about the dogs. How many are there? What are they doing now?.

"What are the dogs doing now?" I'd say. "Oh, they're snarling and drooling and making asses of themselves. One is on my hood. One's outside my window. Oh, yeah, and there's one on my roof. You'll be right here? That's great, Kevin. I knew I could count on you."

But I can't really count on him, can I? I can only count on myself. Whenever I start counting on someone else, they leave me.

Or even worse, they die.

Besides, I'm doing all right here. Yeah, the dogs are big, freaky, and totally ticked off. They're snarling and flashing three-inch yellow teeth. They're scratching my paint, denting my roof and sliming up my windows. But at least they can't get to me. And most important, they can't get to Megan. Soon they'll tire of this game and leave to go terrorize somebody else. Right?

Problem is, I can't bet on it.

"Okay, Grandma. Kevin it is." I'll just check my recent calls for Kevin's number. But wait, my phone's not turning on. No lights. No bars. No signal.

The screen is completely dark. Dead battery? Shouldn't be, I left it on the charger overnight.

"What the…" I give the phone a shake. Nothing. Bang it against my thigh. Nope. Rattle it over my head like a maraca. Still nothing. It's definitely dead. I flip it over. A crack runs along the back of the case.

Chapter Nine

Wednesday, 12:51 PM

"Oh no…." My phone must have broken when I threw my purse at the dogs. It probably got moisture inside from all this thick fog and the wet parking lot.

"Now what am I going to do?" I'll roll down the window and yell for help. That's what I'll do. Help? Help from who? It's still lunch hour and there's not a soul in sight in the newspaper office parking lot. Except for the ghoulish dogs clambering all over my SUV. Besides, I don't dare roll down my window. The dogs would be on me and Megan in an instant. And my windows are electric. I'm not sure if they'll still roll down since my car won't start. Doesn't matter. I'm not willing to chance it anyway. Not with Megan in the car.

What I really want is for a handsome knight to come galloping up on a sleek black horse and swoop me up behind him. I'd hold onto the knight's waist, which would be covered with armor, but he'd be sporting a ripped six-pack underneath.

How could he swoop you up? You've locked yourself inside an SUV. And what about Megan? Is the knight going to swoop a three-month-old baby up onto his horse, too?

I know it's ridiculous, Grandma, but this is my fantasy.

Anyway, where were we? The knight would seek out the wicked dogs and slay them with his sword. I'm no wimp, except when it comes to red-eyed dogs. And rabies. And needles and spiders. And death. So, I'd bury my face against the knight's broad back so I wouldn't have to watch the red-eyed dogs die. Although inside I'd be shouting a cheer of victory.

Megan and I would be safe. I'd breathlessly thank our rescuer for saving our lives. The knight would help me dismount from his glossy black stallion and bow deeply from the waist. He'd open the faceplate on his helmet and reveal his identity…

Kevin.

"How did you know, Grandma?"

I know.

Okay, okay. You're right. The knight would be Kevin. He'd ravish me with his sparkling golden eyes. And even though I wouldn't be able to see his chin, which would still be hidden under the helmet guard, I'd know it was dimpled and wrinkled with concern for Megan and me. He'd be shocked at the narrow escape we had, and so relieved he didn't lose us to a pack of rabid dogs that he'd encircle us both in his arms. Carefully though, so he wouldn't bruise us with his armor.

He'd dip his face close to mine…I'd lean in close to my brave knight and press my lips against his and…my fantasy bubble bursts as the black dog takes his front feet off my window, drops to the ground and throws himself against my door. The force of his weight rocks my Blazer. The dog jumps at the door again, feet first. His claws screech against the sheet metal.

My pulse skips some beats and my head feels light, but I am not going to panic. I repeat, I am not going to panic. There is no way the dogs can break into my car. And even though I can't call Kevin, it's probably just as well anyway. He's not really a knight. And he's not coming to rescue us. I know if you want something done right, you have to do it yourself.

"Damn," is all I can say about that.

I need the dogs to go away now so I can make a plan. Stop to think about it, I should make a plan right now. That way I'll be ready when the dogs do leave for greener pastures.

Or easier pickings, as the case may be.

A tow truck. If I could only get my phone to work, just once, just for a few minutes, I could call a tow truck. Except a tow bill is an expense I can't afford if I can help it. I have precious little left of Matt's life insurance. And freelance photography jobs barely cover my basic bills. But If I can get through to a towing service, I'll figure out some way to pay for it. I need to get Megan out of this parking lot and away from these dogs.

I check my phone again for any sign of life. The screen is still blank.

Megan has quieted. I reach behind me, rub her tummy, pull the blanket more securely over her and settle back into my own seat. I lean my head against the headrest and close my eyes so I don't have to look into the menacing faces of the two dogs. I try not to think about the one crawling around on my roof either.

Just a couple more minutes to let the gas fumes die down. Then I'll try the ignition again.

A chortle drifts from the backseat. I twist to check on Megan again. She kicks her little feet, waves her arms, and lets out another adorable baby sound, as if nothing out of the ordinary has touched her day.

I stroke her soft cheek, still wet with tears. She nuzzles my hand and starts to fuss. "You're getting hungry, aren't you, little one?"

I don't want to nurse her here, in a cold, foggy parking lot, surrounded by crazed dogs. It just seems so…so wrong. I'm not even sure I'd be able to relax enough to let my milk down. "Let's get out of here, baby, and then Mama will feed you."

A loud thump sounds from the roof, as if the dog up there just threw itself down on its belly. Smaller thuds now, as though it's crawling. Two paws appear at the back window. Then a face. A big, gray, upside-down face with a mouth full of sharp, yellow fangs. The mouth is snarling and stringing saliva. The monster is looking straight in at Megan. Growling at her. Drooling. Making her cry.

The son of a bitch is scaring my baby!

Who am I kidding? The son of a bitch is scaring me.

The motor's gotta start now. I grasp the key in a pincher hold, close my eyes, tip my face parallel with the headliner and exhale a quick prayer. "Please, dear God. Oh, please let it start."

If the engine doesn't fire this time, I'll…I'll….I'll make a break for the newspaper office. Use their phone to call a tow truck. I have to get Megan out of this situation, before it causes her emotional scars. Before the freakin' dogs figure out how to tear their way through the sheet metal. Or break the glass. Or turn into vapors and leak in around the window seals.

Ridiculous. Ridiculous. Ridiculous.

I turn the key. The motor turns over but still won't fire. Tears of frustration and fear burn my eyes.

The passenger side doesn't have a guard dog posted. I could climb over the console, slip out the passenger door, and sprint. I used to make double, sometimes triple-base runs in softball. From here to the newspaper office front door isn't as far as two bases. Maybe only like a dash to first. I could do it.

No. I can't do it, even if I could muster up the courage to try. I can't open the door and make a run for it with Megan in here. What if the dogs charge past me, get inside and attack her? And there's no way I can take her with me. Even if I wait until the dogs have vanished into the mist again, they could still lie in wait, just out of sight. Just past the fog bank. They could be on top of us in seconds. I can't chance it.

But still…there is a clear path, out the passenger door, it's a straight shot to the building… .

A yapping sounds from the rear of my vehicle. I look in the passenger side mirror just in time to see two mouse-colored Chihuahuas, one light, one dark, round the back of the Blazer and trot along the passenger side. I'd almost forgotten about the miniature mutts. Apparently, they hadn't forgotten about me. It's as if they read my mind. As if they knew I was thinking of exiting that side of the vehicle.

But how ridiculous is that? Dogs aren't mind readers. There's no such thing as mind readers, human or canine.

The small dogs hang out near the rear door of the Blazer. I can see them in the side mirror. Their eyes glint like rubies. The scent of a lit match thickens the air inside the vehicle. The stench roils my stomach.

So much for my escape route. Now I really am trapped. The five dogs have us completely surrounded. If I can't get the SUV started, we're here until the fog lifts and someone finds us. I'll give the engine one more try. If it won't fire, I'll just feed Megan here. Right in front of these evil, nasty, good-for-nothing, possibly rabid dogs.

Look at the bright side.

There's a bright side?

There is always a bright side.

Could you help me out with that, Grandma?

Grandma doesn't help me out.

Okay. Fine. I'll help myself out. The bright side is…okay, I got it. Megan and I are only temporarily trapped inside a vehicle. It's not like we're stranded on a desert island without food or anything. We're not going to wither away and slowly perish. For heaven's sakes, we're in the middle of a city. We're not going to starve. I have a big fountain drink, an energy bar, and plenty of breast milk for Megan. Eventually the fog will lift and someone will find us. Lunch hour is almost over. The employees are due to come rolling back in to work any minute now.

See? There is always a bright side, if you look for it.

Things would seem a lot brighter if only my SUV would start. I turn the key. The engine sputters. Dies.

One more turn. The motor catches. Fires.

"Yes!" I squash the gas pedal to the floor, give it a good rev so it doesn't have a chance to die.

Power. I have my power back, in the form of a six-cylinder, internal combustion engine. I give the motor another overdose of RPMs.

The black and the brindled brown dog drop off the SUV onto all four paws and stare blankly. The bright ruby glare of their eyes dulls and fades to a dark red.

They look dejected and confused. And I am loving every minute of it. "Stupid dogs. Like you've never heard a motor run before."

I throw the transmission into drive, hit the gas, then plow on the brakes. The gray slides off the roof, down my windshield and over the hood. He hits the blacktop hard, landing on his side.

My satisfaction is intense.

The dog flails his legs like a sow bug flipped on its back before he rolls and staggers to his feet.

"See if you scare my baby again, you son of a bitch."

Wait a minute, a female dog is a bitch, right? So calling a dog a son of a bitch is only calling it what it is. It is no insult. And I mean to insult this son of a bitch.

"You ugly gray asshole!" I yell through my closed window. There. That's better.

Oh my. I've turned into such a potty mouth. I've got to learn to curb my language around the baby. "Sorry, Megan. Mommy said bad words."

Megan doesn't seem concerned.

The five dogs are all behind me. I put the car into reverse to pull out of the parking space and romp on the gas again. The dogs dodge out of the way, tails tucked. They don't look so menacing now. I entertain thoughts of chasing the defeated beasties around the parking lot with my S10, squashing them one-by-one into the tarmac. I'll start with the black. Yeah. The lead dog. He'd be my first choice to see die. He's the one who started this whole thing this morning at the market. This is all his fault.

But it would be better to curb my parking-lot rage and just get the hell out of here. I don't want to chance the engine stalling, stranding us again. Besides, I love animals. Before today, I never would have entertained thoughts of killing a dog.

Before today you had never met dogs like these.

You can say that again.

Before today you had never met dogs like these.

"Funny, Grandma." I giggle. It comes out high-pitched, nervous, and I gotta admit, borderline insane. I flip on my headlights and gun the accelerator. "Hang on Megan." I put the transmission in neutral and rev the engine again. I don't want it to die. "You hang on too Grandma." Another crazy giggle escapes me.

Ready to turn onto the main road, it feels so good to be almost free. I punch the gas pedal harder than necessary. My tires chirp on the wet pavement as I exit the parking lot.

"Bye-bye, doggies." I look in my rearview mirror, expecting a foggy vision of three big dogs and two little ones standing in the parking lot, heads hanging, eyes dull red, sheepish looks on their faces.

But I don't see sheepish looks. What I see behind me sends barbed chills jabbing up my spine.

Breaking through the mist come three large, loping forms.

Part Two: The Chase

Chapter Ten

Wednesday, 12:59 PM

The three big dogs lope down the middle of the lane, following only a car length behind my Blazer. They leave inverted, beast-shaped shadows and three sets of red tracers in their wake.

Panic bile rises in my throat. I romp the gas. The burst of speed leaves the dogs behind, out of sight in the settling fog.

Out of sight, but not out of mind.

How far back there are they? How long can they keep chasing me before they get tired? Do evil dogs ever tire?

"Ridiculous, Dianne. Don't even go there," I tell myself. "They're just stray dogs. Persistent, yes. But still just stray dogs."

A red beacon of light rises overhead through the mist. Shoot shoot shoot. I don't have time for a stop signal. I grip the wheel tighter. "Ouch." I'd momentarily forgotten about the dog bite on my thumb. I should go to the hospital. For rabies shots. The thought of injections through my belly button makes my head light and my stomach woozy. I'll think about the dog bites later.

How long will this light stay red? I could blow it. Traffic isn't heavy. At least I don't think it is. The fog's so thick, though, I'm not sure. If a car came from either direction, I wouldn't see it until it was right on top of me – especially if it didn't have its lights on. I can't take the chance. Who cares about the possible ticket – I can't chance getting in a crash with Megan in the car.

I glance from the red light to my rear-view mirror. The dogs are catching up. I can barely make out puffs of their hot breath, rising through the fog half a block back.

Or maybe I'm just seeing things.

The light turns green. Thank you, God. I speed off, leaving the dogs blocks behind me again.

At least I hope they're blocks behind me.

Without thinking, I point the Blazer north, in the direction of Grandma's house. Towards familiar comfort. Towards Bubba, Grandma's sweet old dog who needs food and attention.

Realizing where I'm heading, I rationalize the decision: No sense driving home, all the way across town. And Bubba's gotta eat. I'd just have to go back to the newspaper office and then to Grandma's later if I don't go now.

A trip to Grandma's has been a daily ritual for months now. Ever since Grandma got so sick. We had in-home health care for her and hospice towards the end, but I still made it a point to go everyday to visit, check in with the nurses, and take care of Bubba. I still go everyday to take care of Bubba. Now I need to start packing Grandma's things. My mom is executer of Grandma's will. I'm sure she wants to list Grandma's house for sale as soon as possible. But with Mom out of the country, I can't count on her to help much.

I haven't been able to count on Mom since I was in high school. That's when she married Gene and moved seven-billion miles away. I mean, Malaysia? Who up and moves to Malaysia?

I smash the gas to the floor. It doesn't ease the hurtful memory. The fog is still thick as forest-fire smoke, making visibility almost nil, so I ease up on the accelerator.

When Mom finally remarried, I was glad. My new step-dad seemed like a decent guy. And I thought Mom getting remarried would be a big improvement over the string of losers she dated for as long as I could remember. I thought my home life would stabilize when she finally settled down. I didn't figure on Gene getting offered an electrician's job in a Malaysian paper mill. And I didn't figure on my mom moving away with him before I graduated. I had only two-and-a-half years of high school left to go. Gene already had a good job here. Couldn't they have waited?

Abandoned by my father at four. Left behind by my mother at fifteen. Widowed at 23, and now I've lost Grandma too – my last beacon of family connection. I feel like an orphan. I squash down on the gas pedal.

I take a quick peek behind us, past Megan's car seat, out the rear window. I see no signs of the dogs. No puffs of dense vapor, no sets of piercing red lights. I keep accelerating as fast as I dare through the thick fog. Forty. Forty two. Forty-six miles an hour. If I just keep the pedal to the metal, I should easily stay ahead of the dogs and lose them.

Right? "No problem," I say in a tone way more confident than I feel.

Keeping my mind busy with something other than the freaky dogs is good. It's holding the panic at bay. Straining my eye muscles to see the road ahead of me, I let my mind wander where it will.

It returns to my mom. She's the reason I decided not to date after Matt died. I don't want to sift through dusty piles of man coal like Mom did, hoping to extract a diamond. It would be a waste of my time. Precious time I can spend instead with Megan.

Time I wished my mother had spent with me when I was growing up.

People say I look like my mom. I can't really see it, but I take it as a compliment, I guess. Mom was…still is, a good-looking woman. When I was growing up, there'd been plenty of men interested in her.

Not wanting to disappoint a single one of them, she dated them all.

That sort of unstable lifestyle is not for me. Not now that I'm an adult and have a choice in the matter. I look in the rearview mirror at the backwards facing infant seat and the active pair of waving hands and smile. "And it's not going to be the sort of lifestyle for you either, is it Megan?"

Out the back window, I see no hot clouds of dog breath rising through the foggy air. No glowing red pinpoints of light.

"Woo-hoo. Looks like we lost them for good this time, Megan."

I focus on the road in front of me, obscured at the edges by clinging mist. My hands start to tremble against the wheel. The shakiness crawls up my sleeves, along my neck and sets my teeth to chattering. What is this, some sort of delayed shock reaction? I've ditched the dogs, why would I start shaking like a leaf now?

Keep your mind busy.

Right, Grandma. Busy. So I don't freak out and have some sort of nervous breakdown.

Home. I'll think about home. Yeah. Won't it be nice to get back to my own warm, cozy apartment? Except, wait, I'm going to Grandma's. Her house won't be so warm since I turned the heat way down yesterday. Still, Grandma's place is filled with years of warm memories.

But no Grandma.

A wave of sadness engulfs me. "I miss you so much, Grandma." My voice quivers. I sniffle back tears.

That's enough. I can't cry. Not now. I don't need liquid emotion blurring my vision. Fog. Crazed dogs. A baby in the car. There is too much going on to give in to a blinding wave of grief. Or pity, because that's exactly what it is.

I don't feel sorry for Grandma. I know she's in a better place. She's no longer locked inside a shell of a body with only a smattering of her mind left. It's not Grandma I feel pity for.

"Enough, already," I pep talk myself. "Stop feeling sorry for yourself, girl. Think about Grandma. Think happy thoughts to honor her memory."

Yeah, speaking of honoring her memory, what about her obituary? The main reason I left my warm, safe apartment this morning was to drop Grandma's obit off at the paper. It has all the information about her service. With all her volunteer work and community involvement, she was well known and well liked. There will be a lot of people attending her service, I bet. Those wishing to pay their last respects need to know when and where the service is going to be so they can plan for it. I have got to make sure it makes it into the paper by tomorrow.

When I die, I want a big service, with lots of flowers, and happy songs, and tons of people packing the place. Then my loved ones left behind will feel honored that so many others loved me too.

I want the same things for Grandma.

But the obituary is sitting in a folder on the seat beside me instead of at the newspaper office where it belongs. Even if I do shake the dogs, and get Bubba fed, I don't know if I can force myself to go back to the newspaper parking lot again today. Or anytime soon. If ever.

But if I don't go back, how am I going to make sure Grandma's obit runs in time? When I get home, I could zip the newspaper an email with the obituary attached. I thought of doing that this morning, except my server was down. Last time that happened, it was down for several days. Small, dial-up internet providers – slow and unreliable. I wish I could afford high-speed cable.

I wish I didn't have to go back to the paper office and face the dogs in the parking lot again, that's what I wish. How am I going to make myself brave those snarling, slobbering, red-eyed dogs again? Especially with Mcgan.

A drive-through newspaper window! That's what this town needs. Maybe I'll write a letter to the editor and suggest it. Something like:

Dear Newspaper Editor,

Due to the snarling, drooling, red-eyed dogs who seem to have taken up ambushing innocent people in your parking lot, I'd like to suggest a drive-through window. This would allow customers to drop off obituaries and other important news items from the safety and security of their vehicles.

While I'm making suggestions, I'd also like to see a friendlier, more experienced receptionist manning the front desk during the lunch hour.

Sincerely,
Dianne Chenille Harris

Yeah. Right.

I smile at the imaginary letter I'll never actually write. I'm trying to entertain thoughts of anything else except the damn dogs running along somewhere in the mist behind us. Hopefully somewhere far, far behind us by now. I haven't caught a glimpse of them in the mirror for several blocks. Hard to say exactly where they are, but they aren't right behind us. And that's something.

There is no way the dogs will be able to keep up with me the whole five or six miles to Grandma's. Especially if I don't hit anymore red lights.

As if on cue, another red light veers out of the dark fog. I press the brakes and drum my fingers on the wheel, staring in the mirror at the road behind me for any sign of glowing eyes. I see nothing but a sheet of fog. The light changes to green. I let out a huge sigh of relief and press on the gas.

I travel three more blocks. Still no sign of the canines. I swing onto the main coast highway and let out a small whoop of victory. I'm home free now. There is no way a trio of dogs can run along this narrow, winding, busy, oceanfront road and stay alive. A tourist would run over them for sure. Tourists are here to look at the ocean, and that's just what they do. They don't watch out for things like small packs of wild dogs running down the center of their lane.

God bless the damn tourists.

I look at the ocean to my right as though through the eyes of an outsider. It is an immense, awe-inspiring, constantly changing body of water. However, today, that's where the beauty ends. Hanging mist obscures the line where sea meets sky, turning both into a mass of gray. The curtain of fog casts a shadow that reaches dark tentacles beneath the surface of the ocean, as if something living and sinister writhes just below the frothing white caps.

Ridiculous. The only things living in the sea today are the same things living in the sea everyday – plankton, kelp, fish. A few sea mammals. What is with all these evil-laced thoughts today? As if something *is* out to get me.

I check my rear-view mirror. Two car lengths back, three chugging puffs of vapor rise in the air.

"Holy mother of God." Something is out to get me.

Chapter Eleven

Wednesday, 1:13 PM

Kevin drummed his fingers on his desk. Gnawed the end of his pencil. Rearranged the files of the missing persons.

Where were these people disappearing to? Who was taking them? It's as if they were vanishing off the face of the planet.

Damn it. These weren't junkies who'd chosen to leave society behind and were dying with a needle in their vein. Kevin chomped harder on his pencil. These were contributing Roseland citizens: A schoolboy; a family man; a young, professional woman.

A young woman the same age as Dianne.

His heart dropped. He couldn't stop thinking about Dianne. Couldn't shake the unexplainable uneasiness he felt every time she crossed his mind today. He wondered what she was doing right at that moment. He remembered the sadness in her eyes at the market earlier that day, when she spoke of her grandma Austin.

Her life must have been going great before Matt's accident. She was young, beautiful, married. Kevin frowned. She and Matt were expecting a baby. Kevin imagined Dianne had everything she'd ever wanted.

Before her dreams were shattered.

Her husband died and she lost her Grandma both in less than a year. No wonder Dianne's eyes flickered with such deep sadness.

Kevin wished he could take Dianne and her baby girl under his wing. But how could he take care of them? He couldn't even take care of his own father when his father needed him most.

What if something happened to Dianne or her baby? What if they got hurt and he couldn't help them? The going would get tough and he'd choke. That's what. He'd seen himself do it before. He needed to quit living in fantasyland and concentrate on his work.

He put his head down and puzzled over the cases some more. He had to stop whoever was taking these people before they took anyone else. He couldn't allow whoever was doing this to keep seizing citizens of his town. It would only be a matter of time before someone close to him disappeared.

Someone like Dianne.

Kevin shoved the thought from his mind. He scooted his notes and the photos around on his desk. He tried to make sense of the jumble of papers in front of him, but nothing slapped him in the face. With little or no evidence, there was nothing to slap him in the face. No fingerprints. No suspects. No clues to support foul play.

For perhaps the first time in his career, Kevin felt completely and totally at a dead end.

He picked up the three headshots of the vanishing vics and walked over to the bulletin board covering the south wall of his office. He stuck the three photographs up with pushpins, each beside his or her own timeline. Kevin stood back and studied the faces.

The latest, Daniel Archer, was a thirty-four-year-old man with dark, thinning hair, thick eyebrows and a lopsided grin. A father of two – well one now. The Archer's were in the news a few months back when doctors diagnosed their five-year-old daughter with Leukemia. The whole town rallied around the family, raising money to help with the mounting medical bills. In the end, all the rallying in the world couldn't save the little girl. He felt sorry for Mrs. Archer. First she lost a daughter. Now a husband. Of course Kevin, along with the rest of the department, would do his best to find Daniel, but his hopes were not high.

They hadn't found the other two vanishing vics.

Kevin's gaze settled on the photo of the nine-year-old boy who disappeared nearly three weeks ago. Little Radley Smith. A set of brown eyes peeked mischievously from under a mop of blond hair. Radley had a definite Dennis-the-Menace thing going on.

The boy's family was heartbroken, of course. Desperate for any news, any sign that Radley was still alive, the family called Kevin's line often. Daily now, though, not the three-or-more-times a day like when the boy first disappeared. Kevin didn't discourage them from calling. The family members needed someone to talk to, vent their frustrations to, and share their hopes that any day now little Radley would turn up. Alive. Although after nearly three weeks, even finding the boy's body would give the family closure so they could grieve properly and move on with life.

It was usually the boy's father or aunt who called Kevin. Earlier in the year, Radley's mother suffered a stroke. Her doctor was hopeful she'd eventually make a full recovery. Right now, she had limited use of the right side of her body and trouble with her speech. When Kevin had questioned her this morning at the market, he'd had to strain to understand what she'd said.

Then there was the first vanishing vic, Emily Cater. Her eyes and smile shone bright in the photograph her mother had supplied the police department. A studio photographer took the photo just weeks before Emily's husband served her with divorce papers. Emily's mother said the portrait was an anniversary gift from Emily to her husband, something for him to frame and keep on his desk at work. Something Emily hoped would keep her husband's attention focused on her.

Emily's mother told Kevin the husband had cheated on her daughter. More than once. But Emily still didn't want the divorce. She wanted to iron out the problems and try to make the marriage work.

The husband was a suspect in his wife's disappearance. But Kevin and Buzz could find nothing to link the husband to a crime. The guy was a certified ass for what he'd put his wife through, but he had no motive to kill her. Well, almost no motive. Estranged spouses always have a motive – hatred, loss, the feeling that if they couldn't have the other person, no one else should either. In this case, the husband's motive could be the desire for a quickie divorce that his wife wouldn't willingly grant him.

But, according to Emily's mother, and other family members and friends, things between Emily and her estranged husband never turned violent or ugly. Besides, the husband had an air-tight alibi. He was at an afternoon awards ceremony, given in honor of his marketing team during the estimated time of Emily's disappearance. Twenty-seven people vouched for his presence there. When Kevin and Buzz served a search warrant at ABC Marketing and obtained the ceremony attendance sheet, there was Dudley Cater's name, in alphabetical order, near the top of the list. So, unless the ex-husband hired a hit man or a kidnapper to do his dirty work, there was no way he'd had a hand in his wife's disappearance.

Kevin couldn't figure why the husband wanted to divorce Emily in the first place. She obviously loved him, flaws and all. And not that looks were everything, but they sure didn't hurt – Emily was trim, fit and pretty. Her smile, shining from the photograph, seemed warm and sincere. Her brown hair was long and shiny – like Dianne's.

Dianne.

His heart hammered with dread.

What were these feelings haunting him? He'd talked to Dianne in person less than ninety minutes ago, called her on the phone an hour ago, driven by her location to make sure she was all right. He'd spotted her vehicle in the newspaper lot – seen nothing out of the ordinary there. He'd bought her a card and sent her flowers. He already felt like a borderline stalker. Short of calling her again, or following her, there was little else he could do to insure her safety.

He tried to push aside the uneasy feeling, as he'd been trying to shove it away all afternoon.

Again, he studied the photos, looking for something, anything, to link the cases. A thirty-four-year-old man, a nine-year-old boy and a twenty-four-year-old woman. No link in age. They weren't all the same sex, so no link there either.

The vics had each been occupied right before they disappeared. The man was driving garbage truck in a suburban neighborhood. The boy was crossing the street to get the mail – also in the suburbs. And the woman was jogging along a suburban bike path.

A connection in location. Sort of. At least in the type of area. It wasn't much to go on, but it was something. Not that it was a new thought. He and Buzz had already combed over this distant connection. Kevin studied the Roseland city map hanging on the wall near where he'd stuck the photographs. A map he'd already pored over countless times. There were three stickpin flags, one for the spot where each victim was last seen.

The pin representing Daniel Archer was stuck in a southeast neighborhood. Radley Smith's pin hailed north of city center. Emily Cater's flag was in the southwest corner of Roseland. Not much connection there. It's not as if the perp were concentrating his efforts on a certain section of town or anything.

There was no typical suspect signature – no note or sign of a perpetrator thumbing his nose at authority. That's what stumped Kevin the most. Who was this perp? They didn't have a single legitimate suspect. They'd interviewed everyone within a three-block radius of all three disappearances. Not one of the interviewees had seen or heard anything out of the ordinary on the days the victims disappeared.

Roseland Police Chief, Ken Donning, had called in an expert profiler from Portland to give his detectives clues as to who they might be looking for. No one of interest fit the psychological profile the big-city, so-called expert drew up.

According to the profiler, Kevin and Buzz were looking for a male. A loner. Someone angry at society in general, but not at a certain slice in particular. Not a person who hated only women, or only married men, or who targeted only young boys. The completed profile pointed to a man who hated humanity across the board. A sick and twisted sociopath. The sort of person who learned to blend in with society by studying the actions and reactions of those around him. A chameleon, if you will.

A Ted Bundy.

Expert profiler or not, there were a handful of things in the report which Kevin questioned: The suspect is probably a snappy dresser; he may be obsessive compulsive – otherwise known as a hand washer. He's the sort of man who has to feel in charge, although he probably has a nasty temper and people aren't likely to turn to him for fair leadership. He probably considers himself a lady's man and can't accept his own shortcomings. He may suffer from road rage.

So, to sum it up, they were looking for a man with a temper and dry, chapped, over-scrubbed hands. He'd be wearing neatly pressed, stylish clothing. His home and car would be immaculate. He'd come across as arrogant and controlling.

Hoo-boy. No problem. Not to lesson the skill of criminal profiling, Kevin was sure there was something to it, but he was a strong believer in going with gut instinct. That willingness to listen to premonition is what had made his dad such a good cop. And it's what carried Kevin so far up the police food chain in such a short time.

Besides, even if the criminal profiler knew the suspect ate oatmeal with brown sugar, cinnamon and raisins every morning; brushed his teeth with fluoride-enhanced, tooth-whitening toothpaste and colored outside the lines left-handed, it didn't much help. At this point they had no suspects who fit even the general profile of an angry, sociopath able to blend in with society, let alone someone with a particular way of dressing, and fastidious grooming habits.

Kevin wearily rubbed his forehead. He went back over the details of each case again. There had to be something more here. Something tying these cases together.

Something. Anything.

The three vics all came from middle-class backgrounds. Not too poor, certainly not too rich. All the families had mortgages; the breadwinners held down decent jobs. Any children still living at home attended public schools.

They'd checked out the school connection and turned up zip. But there was one more connection – the families all shopped at the same grocery store chain. Kevin couldn't remember how he stumbled across that tidbit of information. Unfortunately, he didn't think it was relevant anyway. The families all shopped at the same grocery chain, but they didn't all shop at the same store.

There were two Kash N Cart Grocery stores in town. The Archer family shopped at the north store. The boy's family shopped at the south store. So did Emily, until her husband kicked her out of their home. She moved across town then to a small apartment and began shopping at the north Kash and Cart. It seemed a shaky connection at best.

What about church? Community activities? Kevin returned to his desk and jotted down ideas. Club and gym memberships? Where did the families shop for clothing? Where did they buy their vehicles? Where did they do their banking? Kevin wrote down anything he could think of that might link the three together. He would have to interview the grieving families again. Ask them a bunch more nosy questions which probably had nothing to do with anything. But he could leave no stone unturned.

A serial killer had never struck in Roseland before. Kevin still fervently hoped this wasn't one striking here now. There was no proof the vics were dead. There was no blood, no signs of a struggle, no bodies. And most convincing of all, no serial killer's signature. Most repeat killers had a mark, or a brand to label their crimes.

To them it was sport, and the game was to outfox authority. After a while the perpetrator felt invincible, infallible. And he flaunted it. There was usually a note left at the crime scene. Or a certain type of location where he dumped the bodies. Or a particular way he tied his victims up. Or tortured them. Or killed them.

Sometimes a serial killer would get so cocky he'd leave bodies in public places – stuffed under vehicles inside a parking structure, crammed inside city dumpsters, or dropped in wooded areas just off a busy highway – someplace the killer could easily access to revisit and mentally relive the crime over and over. But so far with this case, there was none of that.

No signs. No signatures. No bodies. No suspects.

Shit. There weren't even any crime scenes to speak of. There were no footprints or fingerprints, no bits of fiber. No hair, cigarette butts, chewing gum or other DNA clues from either the suspect or the victims.

There was nothing. It was as though these three vics had simply vanished into the mist. It was damn baffling. Kevin crinkled his chin. He once more scanned the photos, the map and the timelines covering the wall before he shook his head, stepped outside his office and pulled the door closed behind him.

Chapter Twelve

Wednesday, 1:07 PM

I blink my eyes and squint, sure I'm seeing things.

Three vapor clouds hang like white helium balloons in the afternoon mist.

My heart beats a drum solo. My panic rises to a new level. I make an involuntary mewling sound.

No way.

There is no way the dogs can still be following me. Not this far. Not this fast. Not down the middle of Pacific Coast Highway 101, for heaven's sake.

But what else would make three puffs of condensed steam like that?

I'm not taking any chances. I press my foot firmly down on the cold steel of the gas pedal, effortlessly taking the familiar corners at speeds not meant for foggy driving.

I enter the passing lane and blow past two Fords and a Dodge, whip around a station wagon in a no-pass zone and whiz past a double-trailer semi gearing down to climb the last incline before the turn ahead to Grandma's house.

Over the crest of the hill and halfway down the other side, I slow, click on the left turn signal, by-pass the turning lane and shoot directly onto Otis street. I glance out my side window. No dogs in sight. I see no steams of breath puffing behind me.

There is no way the dogs could have made it around three vehicles and a semi without getting run over. They're stupid stray dogs, not race cars. Besides, they couldn't have seen me turn. The fog is too dense and they were too far away.

Shoot, they aren't even out there, are they? No way. Can't be. The puffs of vapor I keep thinking I see? Just my imagination, I'm sure. Like the knight I imagined coming to my rescue earlier. Like I imagined my dad wrestling the crocs under my childhood bed.

Imagination is a powerful liar.

Besides, no worries now, I'm almost to Grandma's house. Almost as good as home. I let out a big breath of relief and try to change the red-eyed movie reeling through my mind.

"Over the river and through the woods, to grandmother's house we go. …" I sing a few lines of the song to reassure Megan and myself.

Again, the Thanksgiving tune leaves me melancholy. It's sad to think of spending tomorrow without Grandma. Maybe I'll take Megan with me to the mission and help serve Thanksgiving dinner as I used to do with Grandma. Grandma would like that. "Wouldn't you Grandma?"

Grandma doesn't answer.

The green road sign looming out of the fog ahead says Mill Street. The yellow diamond-shaped road sign below it says Dead End. I veer left. Checking my mirror again, I still see no dogs.

"We lost them again, Megan."

Megan, bless her little heart, is not as relieved as I am. She starts fussing at the sound of my voice. Or maybe my singing dialed her mood to cranky. She's getting hungry, poor thing. "Hang on, sweet pie. We're almost to Grandma's and then Mommy will feed you. Promise"

Life seems so comfortably normal at the moment. I'm on my way to my favorite childhood place. My baby's with me. I don't even mind that she's fussing. The Blazer is running well. The wipers are doing their wiper thing.

There are no dogs in sight.

Were there ever really dogs?

I start double-doubting myself. Not only doubting the vapor puffs I thought I saw, now I'm doubting the whole thing – dogs with eyes glowing, teeth snapping, and breath smelling like a doused campfire. It all seems so…so far fetched.

I wiggle my toes inside my left clog. The movement shoots a pain through my injured ankle. I glance down at my thumb, still wrapped in shreds of blood-soaked napkin. There's no way I can talk myself out of believing this. It's real all right. At least the little dogs and their teeth were real. Flesh-ripping, jean-tearing, ankle-biting real.

The Blazer sputters. I press down harder on the accelerator. *What the heck?* The SUV lurches forward. Hesitates. Coughs and dies.

Okay, this is getting old. I turn the key off and back on. No spark. I try it again. Nothing. I check the gages. The red arrow on the fuel gage points below E.

I slam a fist into my thigh. "Bingo, stupid. You're out of gas."

Now I remember what I was forgetting earlier at the Speedy Mart. The Coast Town Speedy Mart *AND FUEL STATION*. I can't believe I forgot to gas up. Duh. Nothing like a memory hiccup to really throw a wrench in things. Now I have no choice but to call a tow truck.

At least it's fall and high school senior portrait season. If I can pick up a few extra sittings this month, I should have enough to pay for a tow service bill and still buy groceries. I could always charge it to my Visa. I try to avoid using the card, except for emergencies.

This definitely qualifies as an emergency.

You're right Grandma, it does. I pull my cell phone out of my purse. The screen is dark. Double duh. "It's broken, remember?" Wonderful. Maybe the battery is getting old and it isn't holding a charge well anymore. Might as well plug it in and see what happens. I revel for a moment in my brilliant level of deduction. Anything to make myself feel better after stupidly running out of gas.

I do a quick check out the windows for the dogs. There's no sign of them.

I plug the cell into my phone charger. It shouldn't take long to zap in enough power to make a quick phone call. The little light on the charger doesn't light up so I check the screen. Still blank.

The car motor doesn't have to be running for the charger to get juice, does it? Nah, I don't think so. The phone must be switched off. That's it. I press the power button. Still nothing. I try pressing down longer this time, desperately longer. Nada. I check the port connection. It's pushed in all the way.

Is there no signal here? I've never noticed a cell-tower dead zone by Grandma's before. Besides, even with no service, I should still have a picture, just no bars, right? I unplug the charger, plug it back in. Wiggle it around. I turn the slim phone over in my hand. Of course, the crack hasn't miraculously healed itself. The hairline facture still runs the length of the case. A drop of liquid seeps out of the back of the phone. What is this, cell phone blood? Gross.

Why oh why didn't I think to take the phone out of my bag before I heaved my purse at the dogs?

Like I'd had time to think through something like that at the time.

I rap the phone in my palm. It sends a pain shooting through my injured thumb. I check the phone screen. No bars, no picture, no time. "Don't panic, Dianne. Things could be worse." I don't know how, exactly. But I'm sure they could be worse.

Count your blessings, Dianne. You know things could be worse.

"Maybe there's enough gas fumes to coast as far as your house, Grandma. Then I could use your phone." I try the car ignition again. The motor doesn't fire, and Grandma doesn't reply.

Not that I really expected either.

We're only five or six blocks away from Grandma's. I could walk the rest of the way, carry Megan.

Walking is not a good idea. What if the dogs come again? What if they attack Megan instead of me this time? Besides, my ankle is throbbing.

Shall I call the wambulance?

Very funny, Grandma. First the dogs, then my Blazer and then my phone.

Now, even my 71-year-old deceased grandmother is conspiring against me. Isn't anything, or anyone, on my side today? I whap the cell phone on the dashboard. "Cheap piece of crap. Can't even throw a cell phone these days and expect the friggin' thing to work anymore."

Megan cries harder.

"Sorry baby. Mama's just having a little temper tantrum here."

The phone screen comes to life. Bars appear. If there were such a thing as dumb luck, this is totally it.

Quick, before the stupid cell decides to die on me again, I dial 911. It rings through to county dispatch. "Nine-one-one," says a weary-sounding female voice. "What's your emergency?"

"Well, I'm not sure if this exactly qualifies as an emergency."

"Ma'am, this number is reserved for emergencies only." I can tell by the tired finality in her voice she's about to hang up on me.

"Wait!" I've got to keep this woman on the line. "I'm on Mill Street near Otis, in North East Roseland," I spit out the info quick, before she disconnects or my cell phone pukes out again. "I'm out of gas. My baby's in the car with me and I'm being chased by dogs." My voice is surprisingly calm. I'm proud of my voice.

"Chased by dogs?"

"Yes, Ma'am. That's right."

"But you're in your car?"

"Yes. Well, technically it's a truck. It's an SUV."

"And you're inside your *truck*, right?" The dispatcher sounds exasperated.

"Yes, that's right."

"And you're out of gas?"

"That's what I said."

"So you're not moving, right?"

"Right." It's my turn to sound exasperated. What is this, twenty stupid questions? How can I be moving if I'm inside my car/truck and its out of gas?

"So why are you worried about dogs chasing you?"

Now I see where she was going with this line of questioning.

I have to make her understand the desperation of my situation. "Because there's something wrong with these dogs."

"Something wrong?" The dispatcher no longer sounds tired. Now she sounds dryly amused.

"They have red eyes."

"I see." She pauses. "What color are their noses?" She snickers, snorting on the intake.

Very funny. I'm wasting my time here. This snickery, snorty, sarcastic woman thinks I belong on Center Street, living in a halfway house next door to the crazy fortuneteller lady. Regardless, I can't let her hang up. It may be my last shot at a phone call. Who knows if my damaged cell will ever work again.

"Could I speak to Detective McCoffey, please?" Even with his wounded pride, I'll bet Kevin will still speak to me. And help us.

"Is he city or county?"

"Roseland Police Department."

"That's city," the woman says smugly. "Hold, please. I'll put you through." She's probably happy to get me off her dispatch line and out of her phone jurisdiction.

There's a long silence and I feel panic rise in my throat. Oh no, has my call been dropped? But when I hear a ring tone on the other end, relief washes the panic back down. When Kevin doesn't picked up by the third ring, my short-lived relief shrivels. "Three. Four," I count out loud. "Five rings. Six." His answering machine picks up. Damn. He's not there. The warm, Louisiana tones of his voice instruct me to leave a message.

"Kevin? It's me, Dianne. Gee *(Gee? Did I really just say Gee?)* I'd hoped to catch you in person. See, the thing is, I'm stranded out here on Mill Street. This is really embarrassing, but I ran out of gas. And Megan's with me. And there are these d... ." I decide to skip the part about the dogs. I don't want to get into that right now. The last person I want thinking me crazy is Kevin. "So, anyway, I guess

I'll call a tow truck. Which is probably what I should have done in the first place." I'm rambling. I know I'm rambling.

"And about turning you down before? It's really not anything personal." *Okay Dianne, shut up now.* "I'm just not doing the dating thing." *I thought I told you to shut up, girl.* "Okay. Well, maybe I'll run into you at another soda machine sometime."

I hang up and smack the heel of my hand to my forehead. I'm such a ditz. I must have sounded like a bad commercial for a movie premiere – drum roll, please…Dianne Harris, coming soon to a soda machine near you!

I gather my wits for a moment. Pretend anyway, that I have wits to gather and try to forget about leaving such a stupid, stupid, idiotic message.

Time now to move on to the next problem.

First I send up a prayer. "Please, dear God, let my cell phone work just one more time." I look down at the phone in my hand. The screen is black as a starless night. Crap! I give the cell a sharp smack on the dash. Once. Twice. Three times. I'm either gonna get it to work or break my dash trying…. One more good, hard rap and….I can't believe it – the picture of a snowboarder appears on the screen. It's almost enough to make me actually believe in luck. I check the online Roseland yellow pages for Roseland Tow and Rescue Service, repeat the number to myself over and over as I quickly punch it into the keypad and pray my phone doesn't decide to go belly up again.

"Tow service," a man answers.

I give him my location.

"I'm on a call on the other side of town. It will be a half hour, maybe longer."

Wonderful. That should just about give the pack of dogs enough time to catch up and find me. If there really are dogs.

"Okay," I say. What other choice do I have? It's not like I can say, "Oh, well. That's too long. Never mind. I have crazed dogs on my trail and I have to be on my way sooner than thirty minutes. I'll just call another towing company."

No. I can't say that because I can't chance my phone will work again. That and Roseland only has the one towing service.

So instead I say, "I'll see you as soon as you can get here. I've got my infant daughter with me. Please hurry."

The tow truck driver makes a noncommittal grunting sound.

Reluctantly, I press "end call." It was comforting to have someone on the other end, even a grunting stranger. I'm not sure I could face the dogs again alone. I check the mirrors and windows. No steaming puffs lift through the fog.

I should feed Megan while we wait. I unbuckle myself, twist around and unharness Megan. Now I have to maneuver her over the seat. How much easier it would be to get out, open the back door and lift her out of her car seat like any other normal mother.

But today is not normal.

Boy, Grandma, you can say that again. Today is anything but normal. And there is no way I am getting out of this vehicle right now. Those dogs are still out there, somewhere. I'm not chancing that they're just figments of my imagination.

I finally manage to hike Megan into the front seat with me. I expose a breast and snuggle Megan in close. She latches on, tugging gently. My mammary glands tingle as my milk lets down. A tender warmth spreads through my body as I look down at the infant in my arms. "Isn't she precious, Grandma?"

Grandma doesn't answer, but I detect a hint of lavender. I imagine Grandma smiling down at me and her great granddaughter.

After several minutes, Megan's suckles decrease. Her eyes close and her lips part, leaving my nipple slack in her mouth as she drifts off to sleep. I tuck my breast back into its corral. Slowly and carefully, so as not to wake her, I return Megan to her car seat.

A year ago, when I peed on a pregnancy test stick and it turned blue, I was nervous and happy, excited and scared. But nothing prepared me for how much love I could feel for someone so tiny and helpless – she's like an extension of my own body.

I take a sip of my now flat, watered-down soda and glance at my watch, 1:35, eleven minutes since I called the tow company. That means at least nineteen minutes to go.

I check my rearview mirrors. No pinpoints of red light approach through the mist. No hot puffs of breath rise in the air. No dark, loping shadows appear out of the fog.

I need to keep my mind busy, or I'll go nuts here worrying about the dogs finding us. What to do to pass the time? I pick up the newspaper in the passenger seat. At the end of the lead story about the third disappearance, it says RELATED STORY ON PAGE A5. I leaf open the paper to the fifth page.

Neighbors Recall Missing Persons

Daniel Archer's next-door neighbor of four years, Rob Lundy told a reporter from the Roseland Community News that Archer was "a good neighbor. A good guy." Lundy said Archer was friendly, quiet, and kept his grass clipped and his yard tidy.

Lundy said that Archer seemed "sort of distracted and depressed lately" but the neighbor called it understandable. "His five-year-old daughter died of Leukemia two months ago," Lundy said. "She was a real sweet little girl too."

I gather the paper to my chest. It crinkles in sympathy for poor Audrey Archer. First her daughter dies, now her husband has disappeared. It's devastating to lose a husband – it feels like God has denied your future. But to lose your child? That would be like having a piece of your own soul torn out and shredded into a million strips.

I read on:

Across town, Deb Bunk, 36, a neighbor of the Smith's, whose nine-year-old son, Radley disappeared nearly three weeks ago, said, "Radley was a typical boy."

"He spent a lot of time riding his bicycle," said Mary Welks, another Smith family neighbor. "He'd set up jumps over there with blocks of wood and a sheet of plywood." Welks, 48, pointed to the end of the cul-de-sac she shares with the Smiths.

"Sometimes he'd tease his little sister and make her scream," Welks said, "but what older brother doesn't do that sort of thing?"

Tom Notting, a neighbor three houses over from the Smith family mentioned changes he'd seen in the boy recently. "He used to come over fairly often to look at my model trains," Notting, a 64-year-old retired railroad worker said. "But since his mom's stroke, he stuck pretty close to home. He quit coming around much. When he did come to visit, he was pretty quiet and didn't stay long."

Tenants in the apartment complex where Emily Cater recently moved said they didn't know the missing woman well.

"She just moved here," said Tawnia Ballow, 19, who lives with a roommate two doors down from Cater's now vacant apartment. "I'd see her go out for a run just about every day. She was quiet, kept to herself. Seemed sort of sad."

Something about the story niggles in the back of my mind. Of course with people vanishing for no good reason, there's plenty of room for all sorts of niggling. I refold the paper and toss it back on the passenger seat.

My watch says it's been thirteen minutes since I called the tow service. The driver won't be here for at least another seventeen.

Time drags when you're anticipating evil dogs.

I check my mirrors, look out all the windows. The coast is clear, no pun intended. There's not even any traffic on this quiet, dead-end street. Not a single car has driven by since I ran out of gas. Most people in the sparsely populated neighborhood are probably at work, their kids in school.

My stomach rumbles, startling me, the sound too close to the throaty growl of a dog. I haven't eaten anything today. Haven't had much of an appetite the past several days, since Grandma died. I still have that energy bar I bought at the market.

I feel like a contestant on survivor – the one banished to Exile Island. Add a baby, a fog bank, a pack of wild dogs. Give me very little food, a flat fountain pop as my only fluid and only my wits to keep us alive.

Very dramatic.

Yeah, Grandma. Isn't it though? I unwrap the energy bar and take little nibbles. It's fairly unappetizing, the taste hovering somewhere between cardboard, tree bark and whipped air. But I need to eat. I have to keep my milk supply steady. Breast milk is the only nourishment I have to offer my baby girl on this deserted island inside my SUV. "And don't say a word, Grandma."

I have enough to worry about without taking ribbing from my dead grandmother: What if the tow truck driver can't find me? What if he doesn't come? He could be trying to call me now, and not be able to get through on my cell phone.

I really am on a deserted island. Surrounded by fog and gravel, instead of water and sand. Lurking dogs instead of circling sharks.

But stranded and surrounded by danger just the same.

Part Three: The Killings

Chapter Thirteen

Wednesday, 1:22 PM

Kevin had to get out of his office, had to get away from the eyes in the photographs of the three missing persons. He felt so helpless with these cases and staring at the victims' faces wasn't doing him any good.

A strong cup of hot coffee was what he needed.

He rounded a hallway corner and literally bumped into Sharon Brown. "Excuse me," he said, brushing imaginary lint off the front of his shirt. "Didn't mean to plow into you like that."

"No problem," Sharon said with a suggestive smile. The intrusion of her personal space didn't seem to phase her at all.

Of course it wouldn't. She wanted him to enter her space, didn't she? Kevin noticed now that she was back at the station, her shirt was fully buttoned. Made him feel positive the cleavage shot earlier had been for his benefit. He sincerely doubted Sharon had been trying to attract LeRoy Swank, the homeless man who found the boot.

"Going for coffee?" she asked.

"Yep."

"I just made a fresh pot."

"Great. Thanks." Kevin ran a hand over his sandy hair. Sharon seemed to be over her little snit from earlier. She was a short-tempered female and didn't much pique his sexual interest, but even he had to admit, no one in the department made a better cup of coffee.

Kevin mumbled a goodbye and followed the fresh-perked aroma down the hall and into the break room.

Buzz was there, standing in front of a vending machine, a puzzled look on his face.

"I wondered what happened to you," Kevin said as he poured himself a generous mug of steaming coffee from the glass carafe.

"I can't get this damned machine to give me my juice."

Did he detect a bit of a whine in Buzz's voice? Kevin hid a smile. Buzz was a brilliant detective, but technology baffled him. Digital cameras, computers, DVD players and apparently, even vending machines.

Kevin studied the machine. "Let's see…" He looked at the change-due amount. "Here's the problem." He pulled a dime out of his pocket and dropped it into the coin slot.

Buzz looked sheepish. He punched B9 for a bottle of orange juice and grabbed it out of the tray as soon as it dropped. He jabbed the bottle of juice near Kevin's face. "If you tell anyone about this…"

Kevin held his hands in the air, trying not to chuckle. "Hey, don't point that thing at me. I'm not saying anything." He leaned close to Buzz's ear and said in a confidential voice. "That is, I'm not saying anything unless you try to fix me up with Sharon again."

It was Buzz's turn to hold up his hands in surrender. "Okay, okay. Deal."

Kevin stood up tall and grinned. Excellent. He'd taken care of that little issue. And it only cost him a dime. Cheap at a thousand times the price.

"Hey, I'm going to call the vanishing vics' families again. Check on possible connections," Kevin said. "Gym memberships. Clubs and organizations. That sort of thing."

"Good idea," Buzz replied. "I'll be right there, give you a hand with that."

Kevin carried the mug of coffee back to his office. He was surprised to see a red number two flashing on his answering machine. Step out of the office for a minute, and poof! instant popularity. He grinned and hit the playback button.

"This is Cindy Termaine from the National Curiosity."

Great. It was a damn tabloid reporter.

"I understand there's been another Roseland disappearance. Chief Donning told me you were one of the detectives on the case."

Kevin frowned. He'd have to be sure and personally thank the chief for that later.

"Please call me at your earliest convenience." The reporter left a toll-free 800 number.

As if he'd be calling her back. He recognized the name – she was the same reporter who wrote about John Whitmore and his aliens. The last thing he needed was a pulp-gossip reporter sticking her nose in his cases, inventing ridiculous scenarios and making Roseland look like a town full of idiots. Again. It was bad enough the crime-beat reporter from the Roseland News called twice a day asking for updates, not to mention the endless calls from local television news stations, the national news, and yesterday, from a couple of TV talk shows filmed on the east coast. The Roseland Police Department didn't need or want all this media attention. He hit the delete button.

The next message made his breath vapor lock inside his windpipe. It was from Dianne, and her voice sounded far away and heavy with fear.

Kevin didn't even take time to scribble a note for Buzz. He grabbed his coat and rushed out of the station.

Chapter Fourteen

Wednesday, 1:38 PM

    I know I'm not thinking rationally, but what if the tow truck driver really doesn't come? What if he runs out of gas, or has a flat tire and has to call for assistance himself? And then what if he gets his gas or tire situation taken care of and just goes on home to his wife and kids and forgets all about me?

    The temperature is dropping. It's getting chilly inside the Blazer. A few more hours and the sun will sink beyond the ocean and plunge Megan and me into total darkness. Goosebumps pop out along my neck and arms. Since the motor won't start, I can't use my heater. I reach back over my seat and tuck the Pooh blanket more securely around Megan.

    That deserted island feeling sneaks up again, so I decide to take stock in what I have on hand. Popping open the glove box, I find the passenger registration, proof of insurance, the Blazer owner's manual, a small pocketknife and a book of matches.

    Inside my purse is a partial pack of chewing gum, mascara, and a tube of lip gloss. Besides the assorted credit, library, and store club cards, I have the $178 in cash in my wallet. My clients from the last senior portrait photo shoot I did paid in cash.

    Packed in the diaper bag are disposable diapers and baby wipes, a teething ring, an extra outfit for Megan, diaper rash ointment, a thermometer and liquid infant Tylenol. I've also got my camera and an extra, charged battery.

So, I can start a fire, chew some gum, and touch up my makeup. Wonderful. Oh, and I can change Megan's diaper, which I'll do when she wakes up.

Look on the bright side.

Okay, Grandma. The bright side.... If – or should I say when? – the dogs find me, I can jab small holes in their hides with the pocket knife. That should really tick them off. And I could build a fire if I had to. Of course I wouldn't want to step outside the Blazer to build one. Not with the possibility of the dogs being around.

I wonder if they're scared of fire, if it would keep them at bay the way a campfire does with wild animals.

After rifling through all my belongings, my thumb throbs. I could drink some of the infant Tylenol. I grab it out of the diaper bag and read the label. The dose is measured by weight. I'd need…let's see…about two bottles for a single dose. No sense in wasting the one bottle I've got. I hate to have to think this way, but if one of the dogs bites Megan, she'll need it.

What I wouldn't give to wake up now, and find this was all a bad dream. Everything from Grandma's death to the encounter with the abnormal dogs. The situation feels out of control. I don't enjoy the feeling.

I have my digital camera, if the dogs show up again, I'll record images of them. At least it'll prove to me they are real and I'm not a banana out on a limb.

Do bananas grow on limbs?

I don't know, Grandma. Does it matter? If the dogs do come sniffing around and I use the flash on the camera, maybe it'll startle them into leaving.

You're kidding, right?

Okay, it's a long shot, but worth a try. I've got to do something to convince myself I'm not helpless against the dog pack.

I go back to assessing my belongings. I eye the folded newspaper on the passenger seat. I could use it for extra warmth if I had to. Not only as fire starter, but as a blanket. Picking up the paper again, I find comfort in its bulk, its weight, its crinkly paperness.

The Blazer seats themselves have possibilities. I think about the thick foam padding I know is beneath the fabric covering. I watched a survival show once on the educational channel about how a stranded couple survived a long walk in subzero temperatures and three feet of snow. They made big, squishy snowshoes out of the foam from their bench seat, and used the wiring under the dash as lashings and bindings. If I remember right, the couple had a baby with them too.

It's not snowing, Dianne.

No, Grandma. But the fog is getting heavier by the minute. Best to be ready for anything.

Done taking inventory of my survival items, I'm feeling a little better about my situation.

I check the windows and mirrors again for rising steam in the distance, sinewy shadows, red beams of light. I see none of those things. Of course with the thick-as-clam-chowder fog, the dogs could be as near as half a block on any side of me and I wouldn't know it.

But I won't think about that right now.

I check on Megan. She's still sleeping peacefully. According to my watch, I've been waiting here for nineteen minutes.

I've still got a possible eleven minute wait ahead of me. Maybe longer. I make one last obligatory sweep of the mirrors and am satisfied the dogs aren't nearby. I haven't seen them since back on the highway, before I passed the last batch of vehicles and turned onto Otis Street. Maybe I truly lost them.

I can hope.

Hope is good.

Maybe there never were any dogs. How sure am I that I wasn't just seeing things? I try to move my swollen ankle and bend my injured thumb. "Ouch."

I'm very sure. There were definitely dogs.

I twist around and check Megan one more time. She's out. Rosy lips parted, little hands relaxed, chest moving up and down in perfect rhythm. I face forward, lean my head back against the headrest. Maybe I could grab a little nap too.

Uh-huh, sure.

Hey, it's worth a try. I recline my seat, unfold the newspaper, spread it across my lap and close my eyes. A catnap will make the time go by faster. I squiggle deeper into my seat, looking for the perfect comfort position. Ah, yes. There it is.

My eyelids pop open. What if I doze off and the tow truck driver happens by just then and misses me in this fog?

Oh, for heaven's sake, he's not going to miss you.

Probably true, Grandma. Besides, I'd wake up, wouldn't I? Tow trucks are just that – trucks. They are big and noisy and even in my sleep, I'd hear one go rumbling by. I close my eyes again, but I'm so on edge every little noise has me reacting like a Mexican-jumping bean: Traffic a couple blocks back; a distant siren; a barking dog.

A barking dog?

No. Please. Not the dogs.

Chapter Fifteen

Wednesday, 1:45 PM

I strain my ears to listen. The barking again. Is it getting closer?

Something else. In the distance. A crunching sound. What is that?

I check my mirrors. Search outside the windows. But the fog is so dense now, I can't make out anything further than three or four feet beyond my vehicle.

The crunching is getting louder. Closer. My heart jumps into my throat. Perspiration dampens my palms. Is it the dogs?

I search my rearview mirror. Only thick white air. Nothing else.

Wait. What's this? A light. Drawing closer. No, make that two lights. And still the crunching sound. Wet crunching.

Tires over a rain-soaked gravel road.

My heart settles back down. It's an approaching vehicle, although not loud enough or heavy enough to be a tow truck. It crunches to a halt behind me. A door opens and closes. Footsteps.

Who could it be?

What if it's the Roseland serial killer come to grab Megan and me? My heart beats staccato again.

The footfalls draw nearer. I press the door-lock button. It's already locked.

Not daring to breathe, I stare straight ahead. I don't want to make eye contact until I know who it is and what they want.

A dark form appears at my window. I can see it with my peripheral vision. I continue to look straight in front of me.

The form bends at the waist. A face appears, so close that the person's breath clouds the glass. My heart pounds harder.

"Excuse me, Ma'am. Do you need some assistance?"

The pattern of my heartbeats change from stark fear to something lighter, giddier; like the slap of a child's salt-water sandals running over hard-packed sand. "Kevin!" Am I ever glad to see him. I can't roll down my window without power, so I fling open the door.

It catches him in the shin.

"Ouch!"

"Sorry. Are you okay?"

Kevin holds his lower leg and groans.

"Oh, Kevin. I'm so sorry."

"It's…fine…really," he says through clenched teeth. He lets go of his leg, straightens with a grimace and forces a smile. "Injuries are expected in the line of duty."

Duty? Is that how he thinks of me now, as a duty?

"Are you alright?" he asks. "I just stepped away from my desk for a minute. That's when you called. You sounded scared."

Damn skippy I was scared. Still am. I glance in all three mirrors. The dogs and their red, glowing eyes are nowhere in sight. I don't want Kevin thinking of me as a nut case, so I don't bring up the dogs.

I feel safer with a cop nearby, although sitting here with my door ajar and Kevin standing outside in the open still makes me jittery. I keep my right hand in my lap, tucked under the newspaper so he won't see the bloody napkins wrapped around my thumb. "I'm okay. I ran out of gas. Stupid, I know."

Don't beat yourself up.

"It happens to people all the time," Kevin says, as if agreeing with Grandma. "I don't have a gas can with me, but I'll go get one and fill it. You and Megan can ride along so you don't have to wait here in the cold."

As I suspected, Kevin is a big enough man to push aside his wounded pride and still help me.

"Besides, I don't want you getting hit if someone drives up too fast. With this fog, I couldn't see your SUV until I was right on top of you."

Kevin on top of me. Now that conjures up all sorts of erotic images. My face heats. I clear my throat. "Thanks for the offer, but there's a tow service on the way."

I should tell him about the dogs.

"No problem." Kevin crinkles his chin and looks deep into my eyes. "You sure everything's alright?"

"Well, there are these d…"

Kevin's cell rings. He pulls the phone from its holder on his belt, glances on the screen.

Deja-vu from this morning snaps at me.

Kevin holds his hand over the mouthpiece of the phone. "I'm sorry, I've got to go. You're positive you're alright?"

I look up into Kevin's familiar gold-brown eyes. "I'm okay." At this precise moment, with him standing guard, I really mean it.

Kevin turns to leave. He stops. Hesitates. Spins back around. He leans down into my open doorway and kisses me full on the mouth. His lips are warm and firm against mine.

"Oh," I say when he draws away. "What was that for?" My lips tingle where his lips touched mine.

"For luck." Kevin vanishes behind me into the mist. His headlights spear into the fog then disappear as he turns his patrol car around and speeds away.

Kevin knows I don't believe in luck. But the kiss was nice. The lip tingling spreads, sending pleasant ripples through my body.

Very nice.

I firmly close the driver's door against any possible dogs. Lock it against any possible serial killers. I study my watch, do some quick math. It's been twenty-six minutes since I called the towing service. The driver should be here any time.

The aftermath of Kevin's kiss still vibrates along my skin. What made him kiss me?

You know.

Know what, Grandma?

Why he kissed you.

No I don't. Not really.

What were you fantasizing about earlier?

I chuckle. You mean the silly knight-in-shining-armor scenario?

Grandma doesn't answer.

Kevin wasn't wearing armor or riding a black horse just now, but he would have rescued me if I'd let him – and if he hadn't gotten called away. Again. I settle back into my seat. It's almost too bad I'm not playing the dating game. There would be a certain thrill in dating a real knight. The thought makes me smile.

I peek back at Megan. She's still asleep. Maybe I can grab that catnap now too. I readjust the newspaper over my lap. I see why homeless people use newspaper as blankets. The paper really holds in body heat. One more scan of the mirrors shows nothing unusual in the surrounding fog. I let my head fall back against the headrest and close my eyes.

The affects of Kevin's kiss linger. My body quietly hums, like after receiving a deep-tissue massage. I close my eyes and breathe deeper, enjoying the fingers of relaxation.

A horrendous smell fills the inside of my vehicle.

Sulfur!

My eyes fly open. "Do you smell that, Megan?" I jerk around in my seat to check. The putrid smell didn't wake her.

I test the air, like a hound scenting a fox, but now the aging pine-tree car freshener hanging from my mirror and salty sea brine are the only odors I can detect. Did I imagine the smell?

"Mommy might be losing her mind, baby. But don't worry, no matter how crazy mommy might get, she'll always take good care of you."

I search out the windows. I can't see a thing through this blasted fog.

The air around me once more thickens with the stench of rotten eggs.

Sweat trickles between my breasts and pools in my navel.

Something lightly squeaks at my window. Like a wet finger drawn along the rim of a drinking glass. Rhythmic puffs of white fan across the glass.

It takes me a moment to wrap my mind around it.

"Mother of God!"

It's a dog's nose pressed against the glass, steaming it up. The sulfur of his breath eeks in past the window seals. The dog tries to wedge his claws in there too, where the glass and the sheet metal of the door meet. His wet, shiny black toenails rake at the glass. Catch in the rubber seal.

The dog is going to force down my window.

Trying not to panic, I snatch up my cell. My fingers tremble. I jiggle the phone. Smack it against the dash – it worked so well before. This time the case breaks in two. Dumbly, I stare at the pieces of cell phone rattling together in the palm of my quivering hand.

The black dog throws himself against the window.

An incredible pressure rises inside my ears. Something similar to panic, only louder. The pieces of phone slip through my fingers and fall to the floor.

A rumbling grates behind me. Tires crunch in the gravel. The tow truck? A big diesel motor growls. Yes. It's got to be the tow truck. Thank you, God. I've never felt so happy to hear anything in my life.

The black dog drops to all fours. He slinks off into the fog.

But what about the driver? At least one dog is out there. Somewhere. I can still smell him. My neck muscles bunch like knots in a rope. My whole body trembles.

The tow truck rumbles past me. The driver pulls in front of my Blazer. I can see the rear end of his red and white truck, but I can't make out the cab through the fog. A door squeaks open. Footfalls head my way. A large human body appears beside my SUV. I wish I could just roll the power window down. I ease the door open instead, careful not to crack the driver in the shin.

He stoops over. "Good afternoon, young lady. Name's Mel. I understand you need some gas." His voice echoes, like he's talking through a long cardboard tube, but I don't think it's his voice that's weird, I think it's me – a stress-induced hearing problem on my end.

"B-b-b-be careful." My jaw vibrates like a set clacking wind-up teeth. "W-w-watch out for the d-d-dogs." My own voice sounds hollow inside my ears.

"Dogs?" Mel looks around. "I don't see no dogs." He furrows his brow. "You all right, missy?"

"Th-th-they're out there. C-c-can't you smell them?" I'm beyond caring if this man thinks I'm crazy. I don't want him getting hurt.

"I'm not sure what you're talking about. I don't smell nothing, except the diesel fumes from my truck. Heh-heh," he chuckles. This guy's not going to believe a word I say about the dogs. It won't do any good to warn him further. Mel pulls his shirtfront over his nose. "Pee-yew. Heh-heh-heh."

It's such a funny sight – a big, bald, paunchy, middle-aged man using his blue work shirt as a filter from his own truck's exhaust. If I wasn't so stressed out, I'd chuckle along with him.

"Were you headed home when you ran out of gas?"

"N-no. I was going to my grandma's."

"She live around here close?"

"Yes." I hesitate. "I mean she did. She passed away Monday."

My neck and shoulder muscles clench tighter. But thankfully no dog pounces out of the mist. The sulfur smell dissipates. Or is it just overpowered by exhaust fumes?

"Gee, kid. That's too bad." Droplets of moisture gather on the driver's head, giving it a moist, pink sheen.

Why doesn't he wear a hat?

"I lost my great uncle a couple weeks ago." He shakes his head. A few beads of water fly off.

"Oh. Sorry to hear that. I know how hard it is." I cup a hand over my nose to filter the diesel fumes. They really do stink. But at least I can't smell the dog anymore. I twist around to tent the blanket over Megan's face.

"Let me go get your gas and I'll shut off the truck."

I nod and quickly close my door. Still no sign of the dog, but I'm not taking chances. Could I have imagined it? On my window, there's a track, like a big snail crawled across the glass. Only this is no mollusk trail. This mark is from a dog's nose. My teeth begin to rattle again.

Mel lumbers out of sight, soon returning with a five-gallon gas can.

"B-be careful," I say. But either Mel is choosing selective hearing, or he really didn't hear me. "Please, be careful," I whisper.

My closed truck door doesn't phase him. He keeps talking, only louder. "Yeah, me and Uncle Don were close." I nod, watching him through my side mirror. He unscrews my gas cap and glugs unleaded into the tank. "He took me fishing a lot when I was a kid. Spent more time with me than my own dad did."

A slight trace of diesel fumes linger inside my Blazer, but no sulfur pierces the air. Maybe the noise of the truck motor scared the dog away for good.

Don't bet on it. The dogs of fear are still out there. Be careful.

Be careful.

Grandma's warning is the same as that uttered by the tattooed cashier earlier today at the market. A chill slides down my spinal column.

Outside, Mel yaks away. "...had a stroke and died in his sleep. Eighty two years old and still going strong till the end. Nice way to go, but man do I miss that guy." Mel finishes pouring the gas, then tosses the empty can in the back of his truck. "Be right back. Gotta fill out the paperwork," he hollers as he heads toward the cab. The fog swallows his big body. The truck door squeals open and shut.

I spend the next few minutes sniffing the air, in semi-panicked, teeth-clacking mode.

Mel returns to my Blazer. With a groan he hoists a foot onto the front tire. He uses his knee as a writing surface to finish the form and sign it. How can he stand there, so nonchalant, right out in the open? The tension in my neck atrophies my shoulders.

Mel tears out the receipt. The paper makes a dull, dead sound as it separates from his invoice book. Mel hands me a yellow copy with a huge, grease-stained hand.

I write a check for the exorbitant fee – glad I happened to have my checkbook along with me. After signing it with a shaky signature, I tear the check out slowly while thinking how many bags of groceries this would buy. I open the door a crack and force myself to hand him the payment.

Mel tips an imaginary hat and says, "It may take a few tries to get 'er started. The electric fuel pump has to prime and send enough fuel through the injection system."

He's talking mechanical Yiddish, but I nod anyway. He seems like a nice man – charges too much, but then he's just doing his job. He may not even be the one who sets the prices. And let's face it, he saved my butt. "Thank you." I fasten my seatbelt, more than ready to start my vehicle and get out of here.

"I'll stick around, make sure she starts." He gives me a nod and lumbers towards his truck.

Three large shadows slide out of the fog bank surrounding us. Mel spins to face them, his expression one of complete surprise. The biggest, darkest shadow leaps for Mel's neck. Mel throws up an arm, hitting the dog in the chest and knocking him back.

The brown and the gray dogs each grab one of Mel's legs and pull, yanking him off his feet. He lands on his back. With an "oof" the air leaves his lungs. He struggles to draw a breath.

The black dog rips at Mel's throat. Blood spurts from the ragged hole. Mel opens his mouth to scream. The sound comes out as a terrified gurgle.

My scream pierces the sulfur-thickened air inside my Blazer. Megan joins me with wails of her own.

"Go away, get out of here!" I shout through my window. "Leave him alone."

But the dogs are relentless.

I grab my cell phone and press the two sides of the case together. I shake it, bang it, plead with it. I've got to make a call. Got to get the police here. The paramedics. Get Mel some help. But I can't make the phone work again.

Maybe I can scare the dogs away. I lean on my steering wheel, blasting the horn. The dogs don't hesitate from their carnage. They don't even glance up from their prey.

Their prey. Oh my God.

I look back at my crying baby. We're next.

I can't make myself get out to try to help poor Mel. I won't leave Megan alone inside the Blazer. I can't strand her – motherless if the dogs maul me. What could I do to help Mel anyway? Wing my purse at the dogs like in the parking lot? I don't think that would help here at all.

Mel tries to help himself. He swings meaty fists at the dogs. One ham-sized hand catches the black alongside the head.

Everything seems to happen in slow motion.

The black dog retreats only a moment before leaping on top of Mel's chest. It sinks three-inch canines into the soft, bloody flesh of Mel's throat.

It's as if I'm trapped inside a theatre, restrained against my will and forced to watch a horror movie flicker across the big screen. I can't breathe. I unfasten my seatbelt so I can draw a breath.

What can I do? I'm not Rambo. I'm not a cop, a soldier or a sniper. I'm a photographer.

That's it! I whip my camera out of the bag, snatch off the lens cap and aim through the windshield. I don't pay attention to composition or framing, I just press the motorized shutter button and shoot shoot shoot. I'm not going for award-winning pictures here. I'm gathering evidence.

Mel kicks thick-soled boots at the dogs tearing into his legs. The animals hold on strong. As the black tightens his strangle hold on Mel's jugular, the man's thrashing weakens.

The black dog releases his grip for a moment. He turns to stare at me with eyes full of fire. The beast's face and chest are soaked with dark blood, his yellow fangs stained red. He's wearing that maniacal grin.

I drop my camera and scream. Megan wails. Mel swings a feeble punch at the black. The dog bites into the man's neck again. Releases his grip. Finds a new hold and clamps down tight.

Helpless, I watch as Mel's struggles slow. Then stop altogether. His head rolls to one side. His eyes stare at what he can no longer see.

The black releases Mel's neck and looks around. The dog's bloody jaw drops open and he pants. Red saliva strings to the ground. He takes one of Mel's forearms in his mouth. The gray and brown each grab hold of a leg and the huge dogs drag the man away, disappearing off the right side of the road into the mist.

The two Chihuahuas dash from the fogbank. With darting pink tongues, they lap up every last trace of blood.

My vision grows bright and out of focus like an over-exposed photograph. I can't faint. Not here. Not now. But I can't put my head between my knees. The steering wheel is in the way. I duck over the console as far as I can and bow my head.

My whole body quakes.

I can use Grandma's phone and call the police from her house. Maybe Mel just passed out. Maybe he's not really dead. Maybe the paramedics can get to him, save him before the dogs finish him off. But even as I think these things, I know none of them are true.

Megan's cries are high-pitched and seem to come from much further away than the back seat. I can barely hear her over the chattering of my teeth. I'm shaking so badly all over, there's no way I can drive up the coast and clear across town to my own apartment. Hopefully, I can make it safely as far as Grandma's.

The dogs are out there. Hidden in the fog. Chewing on the nice tow truck driver, ripping into his flesh. Licking at his eyes, biting off his fingers. A shudder racks its way through my body.

What if the dogs come back for us? Try again to get inside. Claw me, bite me, tear into my throat? Or worse, what if they push past me to the backseat and get to Megan? To her tender little body? They'd rip her apart in an instant.

A groan roils from my throat.

We have to get out of here. We have to get away from the killer dogs, and get inside Grandma's house. I have to get Megan to safety.

My hands are shaking so violently that I have to use both hands to turn the key. When I finally manage, it takes three tries before the motor roars to a start. I jam the transmission into gear and take off, quickly before the dogs pause from what they're doing and see me leave.

I pass the red and white tow truck abandoned alongside the dead-end road, drive the six blocks to Grandma's and pull into the driveway. Dark, dried rose hips cling to the thorny bushes. The pair of Japanese maples look dismal without their leaves. Dormant. Dead.

I put the Blazer in park, hesitating before turning off the motor – a hard thing to make myself do in light of how hard starting the damn rig has been today. Twisting in my seat, I unbuckle Megan. I don't want to get out to do it and leave myself vulnerable to the dogs. But soon I'll have to climb from the safety of the vehicle and dash to the house.

Before the dogs get here. Before they come after us again.

What do they want with us anyway? Why would they follow us all the way from the newspaper office? And if it's me or Megan they wanted, why did they kill Mel?

The fog has turned into serious rain now. It pounds on the roof, metallic and loud. I lift Megan over the seat; grab the newspaper from the passenger side.

I don't bother to grab anything else. All that matters now is getting my baby inside to safety.

I jump from the Blazer with Megan in my arms; shut the door with a hip. Holding the newspaper over Megan's head, I jog with her up the sidewalk to the house.

A dog barks.

The noise sends a jolt of terror through my system. The deep bark sounds again. I let out my breath. It's Grandma's lab, Bubba, acting the macho guard dog.

I have a key to the house on my key ring. In record time I'm inside the side door. Recognizing who I am, Bubba's barks change to excited yips. I hear him flap through the dog door from the backyard into the attached garage.

I hit the wall switch near the door, but the overhead light doesn't come on. "What now?" I walk into the kitchen and try the lights in there. Nothing. "Wonderful." Mom must have ordered the power shut off. Nice of her to let me know.

That's okay. I'm not going to let this minor set back trip me up. I'll make a few calls – get the cops here, the paramedics for poor Mel. Call Kevin to come give Megan and me a lift. My nerves are so jangled, I'm in no condition to drive back across town. I pick my way around the front room furniture to the phone, an old, black rotary-dial model.

Grandma didn't surf the technology wave.

Very funny, Dianne.

"Sorry Grandma. But you know it's true." Picking up the handset, I stick a clammy index finger in the round circle above the number nine, ready to speed dial – as fast as you can speed dial a rotary phone – but there's no dial tone. I press the handset button a couple times. Dead air. "Oh, no." Don't tell me Mom already had the phone service disconnected too.

"Thanks a lot, Mom." I slam down the receiver.

Don't be angry at Chenille. She was just trying to help.

"Yeah, well, lotta help she is." No power. No phone. And no way I'm stepping outside with Megan to get back in my Blazer to go somewhere else with lights and phone service. The dogs could show up any minute.

But they're not here now. And we are. I might as well make the best of a bad situation. I have to stay busy. Keep my hands moving. Keep my mind occupied so I won't think about what the dogs did to Mel…. My shoulder muscles clench, my teeth start rattling. Nope. Can't even go there.

First things first. Bubba. I need to feed Bubba.

I creak open the door between the kitchen and garage. Bubba is waiting on the other side. He pants and stares at me. I slam the door in his face.

Chapter Sixteen

Wednesday, 1:51 PM

Road rage. Hoo-boy.

Kevin flipped on his lights and drove as fast as he dared through the heavy afternoon fog. Since the Portland profiler had created a personality outline of Roseland's assumed serial killer, Chief Donning took road rage calls very seriously, sending a barrage of officers after every reported offender. Road rage incidents were the only leads the department had on the vanishing vic cases – weak leads though they might be. Still, Kevin hated getting called away from Dianne – for the second time today – especially when she and her baby were stranded like that.

Dianne.

Kevin's body still buzzed with the after affects of the spontaneous kiss. He wasn't sure what had made him decide to kiss her. He wasn't positive she'd approved. Then again, she hadn't put up a fight. In fact, she'd kissed him back. Maybe he still had a chance with her after all.

His nerve endings buzzed harder. He hoped there was a chance.

Like the others before this one, the road rage incident turned out to be just that – road rage, nothing more. A young, hothead driver cut another driver off on a corner after the first driver passed him. The two motorists exchanged a few choice words, some obscene hand gestures and here Kevin was, on the scene of two red-faced, male individuals, both snapping at each other like fiddler crabs in a turf war.

Kevin talked to the drivers, calmed them down. Took down both their names and ran their plates and license numbers. In no time, Kevin determined neither road-rage guy was Roseland's serial killer. At least not according to the big-city expert's profile. The youngest driver was sloppily dressed – dirty loafers, baggy shorts, wrinkled T-shirt. The inside of the older guy's car was a jumble of fast-food wrappers, mismatched socks and unopened mail. The interior of his Toyota smelled like an old gym bag.

Another officer on site wrote the younger hothead a ticket for reckless driving and gave the older hothead a verbal warning. The scene broke up and everyone disbursed.

Back inside his own car, Kevin's thoughts returned to Dianne, stranded alongside a dead-end road, her baby sleeping in the backseat. He'd wanted to rescue her – fill her tank with gas, take her in his arms and soothe away her troubles. She wasn't having a good week. Hell, she wasn't having a good year.

She'll go home to the flowers I sent. That should help cheer her up.

Had she found the bouquet yet? He wasn't far from Dianne's apartment. Curiosity got the best of him. Feeling a little like a stalker again, he cruised by her place. There was no Blazer in her parking slot. She must still be at Adelle's. What did she say she had to do there? Maybe she didn't say.

On Dianne's stoop, a bright red and yellow bouquet in a pretty vase nestled against the front door. The florist had done a nice job.

What woman wouldn't love going home to that?

With a smile, Kevin headed back to the station. He had a couple more hours and a few loose ends to tie up before calling it a day.

***

Wednesday, 2:36 PM

My heart's pounding like a jackhammer. It's saying, "Don't trust dogs."

My head's saying, "For heaven's sake Dianne, it's Bubba." I have to feed him. The evilness of the feral dogs isn't his fault. I reach for the knob of the door separating Megan and me from the old chocolate lab. My fingers feel numb, tingly. My dog-bit thumb aches. I pull my hand back.

I've got Megan in my arms. I can't take the chance with any dog around my baby. Not after what I just saw the pack of dogs do to Mel.

I'll lie Megan down first. I can't feed and water Bubba with only one hand anyway. I tread down the hall to the spare room – my old room – and lay Megan on the bed. I form a safety pen around her with pillows, in case she suddenly learns to roll over.

Megan waves her arms and coos. She's all happy, wet diaper and all. Shoot, I forgot to grab a spare from the diaper bag to change her. Thank goodness for disposable diapers and their ability to absorb three-billion times their own weight. I'll worry about the diaper later. I'm glad she's not prone to diaper rash. Right now, I need to feed Bubba. Poor dog probably thinks he's starving.

I trudge back through the kitchen to the garage door. On the other side of the door, a big dog waits.

It's only Bubba.

I know it's only Bubba. Good old Bubba. Remember when we got him, Grandma? I was still in high school. He was such a clumsy, doofy pup. I called him Super-Bubba. I'd joke that his super power was the ability to keep his intelligence hidden.

Bubba's super power has always been very strong.

Yes, Dianne. Now go feed the dog.

"Okay, okay." Grandma never did appreciate the humor of my Super-Bubba jokes.

"It's only Bubba. It's only Bubba, Super-Bubba," I chant, reaching for the garage doorknob. Bloody memories of torn flesh and gurgling screams flash through my mind. A deep, twisting sob chokes me. My damp palm slips on the knob. It takes a second try to open the door.

Bubba stares at me again. A shaft of light pierces through the rain and into the west-side garage window. Bubba's eyes glint red.

My breath catches in my chest.

Bubba turns his head away from the light source and his eyes change from red to warm liquid brown. He makes a happy little whining sound and wags his entire back end.

Relief floods through me. It was just the way the light struck his eyes for a moment. Good Bubba. Good dog.

"Hi boy," I yell it so the old, nearly deaf dog can hear me. "Are you hungry?"

Bubba's front legs leave the garage floor several times, his claws making joyful clicks each time they touch down on the cement floor. I take his ecstatic hopping as a definite yes. I pluck his food and water dish from the corner of the garage where I used to have a darkroom set up. When I switched to digital photography, I tore it down. It took up a lot of room and I didn't need it anymore.

Bubba tries to follow me back inside the house, but I close the door firmly in his face. "Sorry boy," I tell him. No dog is getting anywhere near Megan right now. Not even Bubba.

I rinse and fill the water dish, dump dry kibbles in the bowl and carry both back out to the garage. As soon as I set down the dishes, Bubba buries his pink-brown nose in the food. I give him a couple pats on the back and leave him to devour his supper.

On my way back inside I scoop up an armload of newspapers and grab a couple empty boxes. As long as I'm here, I may as well do some packing. Mom's already turned off Grandma's utilities, I'm sure she'll list Grandma's house in lightening-fast time too. So, it will need packing up and cleaning out. Besides, I've got to do something to keep occupied until I figure out my next move.

One thing's for certain – I'm not leaving the sanctuary of this house to dash to my Blazer and drive somewhere else. My little blue SUV may be only 15 yards away, but it might as well be parked in another lifetime.

I wish now I'd grabbed the diaper bag before I carried Megan in the house, because there's no way I'm going to leave my baby to retrieve the bag. And I'm certainly not going to carry Megan outside with me to get it either. Not with evil, murdering dogs lurking six blocks away. A shiver shoots up my spine.

It looks like Megan and I are in for the night here. And it's not as if anyone's going to miss us either. If something happens, if we get into trouble here, no one will know where we are. Except for Kevin. But he's not going to know if we don't show up back home to our apartment. No one expects us any place at a certain time this evening, or anytime tomorrow for Thanksgiving.

I've still got Grandma's obituary to turn in to the paper. It's in the Blazer, too, along with Megan's diapers, my purse, and my camera…with the photos I shot of the dogs attacking Mel.

Panic mixes with stomach acid. It rises, burning my esophagus.

I swallow the bile. "Keep busy," I tell myself. "Do something useful to make the time pass."

I wander around the house for a few moments, trying to decide what to pack first. The light is dim in here with no electricity. When the sun sinks behind the Pacific in a couple hours, it will be pitch black. I set down the paper and boxes and dig through the bottom junk drawer in the kitchen. I locate a flashlight. Grandma has kept one there since I was a kid. She used to let me use it to go on backyard safari and night-crawler hunts.

If I explored outside around her house today, I'm afraid I'd encounter wild creatures much more ferocious than worms, ladybugs and robins.

I try to shove the feral dogs out of my head. I grip the flashlight in my fist, which sends a jab of pain through my thumb. Okay, first thing I should do is clean out my wounds and get proper bandages on them. I pick up the newspaper and empty boxes and head down the hall. I deposit the packing supplies inside the door of the spare bedroom where Megan is happily gazing at the ceiling and then head for the bathroom.

I get out first-aide supplies. When I try to remove the blood-soaked napkin wrapped around my thumb, it stubbornly sticks. I pour peroxide over the remaining bits of napkin. The cold solution foams and bubbles. I rinse the last of the napkin down the sink, not caring at this point if it clogs up the plumbing. Gingerly, I cleanse the ragged wound with soap and water. As much as I hate to admit it, the bite definitely needs stitches. It's as though the little Chihuahua's teeth were made of razor blades. I slather on some anti-biotic ointment and tape a square of gauze around my thumb.

Now to take care of my ankle, which still aches with a dull throb. I pull up my pants leg, almost afraid to look. The puncture wounds are tiny. They never did bleed much. My ankle has swelled to nearly twice its normal size. I can just imagine the rabies germs dancing through my system, partying through my blood stream, tossing confetti as they urge my body to produce frothing saliva. I lay down a towel and pour copious amounts of hydrogen peroxide over my entire lower leg. But peroxide won't kill rabies germs, will it? I snatch the rubbing alcohol out of the medicine cabinet and douse my ankle with it for good measure.

"Take that you stinkin' germs."

I forgot how much rubbing alcohol stings. My howl of pain pierces the air. And echoes.

What the heck? Grandma's bathroom never had echo acoustics before. I strain, listening for any other sound.

I hear Bubba flap out through his doggy door to the backyard. He must have finished his supper. There are no other sounds.

I've got a second package of gauze half opened when all hell breaks loose.

Chapter Seventeen

Wednesday, 3:45 PM

Snarls, growls and banging noises come from the backyard.

Megan! Forgetting my wounds, I drop the rubbing alcohol and rush from the bathroom to the spare room. I snatch up my baby and hold her tight.

The dogfight grows louder. Fiercer. Bodies slam against the house. A dog yips in pain.

Bubba? No! Not good old Bubba.

I dash up the hall to the kitchen and stare out the window over the sink. What I see sinks my heart.

Bubba faces the black dog. His chocolate-colored hackles stand straight up along the ridge of his spine. He draws back his top lip, showing his pink inner mouth and the canines worn short from years of packing a tennis ball in his mouth.

The black's eyes glow like rubies. He crouches, his entire body tense, ready to spring. The grey and the brindle brown watch from the yard edge, tongues lolling, eyes aglow.

This isn't fair. Bubba is a family pet. He doesn't know how to fight. These dogs will tear him apart. How did they get in through the six-foot chain-link fence anyway? A flood of helplessness spreads over me. It's a feeling becoming all too familiar today.

The black pounces. He knocks Bubba to the ground. They scrabble, teeth flashing, each trying to gain access to the other's throat. The brown and the gray dogs slink around the two rolling in the grass. Bubba breaks free from under the black and charges the other two beasts, driving them back. Blood covers Bubba's muzzle. I'm not sure if it's his or the black's.

The grey and the brindle both bare their yellow teeth.

Bubba backs up towards the corner where the garage and cyclone fence meet. What is he doing? "No, Bubba, don't corner yourself," I yell, but he can't hear me. Or, if he does hear me, he doesn't understand. He continues creeping backwards towards the dog-door flap.

Oh my God. The doggy door!

Bubba's trying to keep the feral dogs out of the garage. Away from us. Bubba is trying to protect his family.

"Oh, Bubba." I lock the door between the kitchen and the garage. "I'm so sorry I can't help you." The tears streaming down my face partially blind me. I dislodge a chair from under the dining room table, slide it across the linoleum to the garage door and jam it under the knob.

The dogs have easy access to the garage. I have to keep them out of the house.

A new burst of snarls breaks out. I hurry back to the window. I don't want to watch, but I have to know what's happening. Bubba and the black are both standing upright on their hind legs, clawing with their front paws to keep the other at a distance. They look like fanged, furry boxers. Their teeth rip at one another's pelts. Tufts of fur fly.

"You go, Bubba!"

As if he heard me, Bubba puts in an extra surge of effort. He lunges at the black, knocks him onto his back and closes his jaws around the evil dog's throat.

I can almost feel the black's warm flesh in my own teeth; can almost taste the copper of his blood. A huge, satisfied shudder convulses down my back. The feeling of satisfaction both thrills and repulses me.

The black dog struggles beneath Bubba's hold, writhing and twisting to regain his footing. The gray and the brindle brown slink in like coyotes. The brown sinks his fangs into Bubba's neck and tries to yank him off the black. The gray grabs one of Bubba's rear legs in his teeth and tugs. Bubba whines in pain, but refuses to let go of the black's throat.

The bite wounds on my thumb and ankle throb with empathy for the faithful old chocolate Lab.

The gray and the brindle pull harder. Together their strength is too much for even Super Bubba. With a sharp cry, Bubba lets go of the black and twists to slash at the two enemies flanking him. He bites at the gray dog, opening a long wound along the side of his face. The gray yipes, lets go for a moment then finds a new grip on Bubba's back foot. Bubba twists and turns, but he can't reach the brown with his teeth.

The black struggles to his feet. He shakes his head. His eyes change from dark rubies to furious balls of fire. He pounces at Bubba, clamps down on his throat, and pulls the chocolate lab's upper body down to the ground.

Bubba fights till the end.

When his struggles are over the three evil dogs release their hold. They squint their eyes. Their blood-stained tongues loll. In and out. In and out.

A strangled sob surfaces from inside me. I hug Megan tighter. The black raises his head. He makes eye contact with me through the window. The red light in his eyes pulsates, as though driven by the angry beat of his heart.

I choke back a scream.

The three evil dogs push their way through the dog door into the garage.

I run down the hallway to the safety of my old room and slam the door shut. I pull the shades. Lie Megan on the bed in her corral of pillows. I have to block the door with something, in case the dogs get inside the house. There's not much left in this room anymore. A bed. A bookshelf. A shadow box on the wall housing dusty salt and pepper shakers. A few plastic totes filled with who-knows-what.

The dogs are at the garage door. They claw and whine, like pampered pets wanting inside to enjoy the comfort of their family's presence.

Boy, do I know better.

I grasp both sides of the bookshelf, try to push it, pull it towards the door. It barely budges.

The dogs scratch harder. One howls. Another joins in, then a third, followed by yips from the tiny dogs. Where were the Chihuahuas during the fight? I think of them licking up Mel's blood. Now they are probably lapping up Bubba's.

My body trembles.

I have to get the bookcase in front of the door before the dogs get inside the house and come after Megan and me.

I hurl books off the shelf. One shelf cleared. Two. Four. Five. Mounds of books litter the floor at my feet. I grasp the bookshelf and tug it through the piles of paperbacks, across the gold carpet to block the door.

"There." I stand back and look at my handy work. "That ought to keep them out, Megan."

But I doubt the truth of the words before they even leave my lips.

I pick Megan up off the bed and jounce her in place while I listen. All I hear is silence.

Too much silence.

The silence stretches for two minutes. Sweat trickles down the back of my neck. Three minutes of silence. Four. Five, The perspiration gathers at the small of my back. Six minutes.

Megan fusses. No. She can't make noise now. We can't draw attention to ourselves, or give away our location. I sit on the edge of the bed, fumble with my bra and stick a boob in Megan's mouth to quiet her. She's probably not really hungry. Which is good since I can't relax anyway, and it takes a bit for my milk to let down.

Dianne Harris, human pacifier.

Six minutes pass. Seven minutes. Eight. An eerie silence settles. Or nearly so. The only sounds are Megan's suckling and gentle rain hitting the roof. How many times have I been lulled to sleep by the rain, in this very house, in this very room? I feel as pacified for a moment as the baby drifting to sleep at my breast.

I check my watch. Eleven minutes since I last heard a scratch at the garage door. The dogs must be gone. At least for a while, I hope.

I tuck my breast away. Now I'm thirsty. And I have to pee. But there is no way I'm leaving this room.

"Keep busy. Keep busy," I whisper, looking around for something constructive to do. I could pack the books, but I don't want to lie Megan down. I like the comfort of her warm little body in the crook of my arm. One-handed, I load mystery novels into the empty boxes. Books are a snap to pack. In no time, I've filled two boxes.

I need something more challenging to occupy my brain, to keep it focused off the dogs, and away from how badly I need to use the restroom.

I pull a skunk saltshaker down from the shadow box, lay it on the bed, reach for the matching peppershaker and wrap them both in a wad of newspaper – definitely a challenge using only one hand.

Carefully, I take down a set of green shakers shaped like John Deere tractors. I grab a couple more sections of newspaper.

Something hits the window.

A bird?

I tuck the newspaper under the arm holding Megan and peek through the blinds, expecting to see a still, feathered form lying on the ground below the window.

Instead, a pair of red eyes set in a bloodied black face glare up at me.

The dog pulls his lips back into that maniacal grin I'm becoming all too familiar with. Bubba's blood stains his fangs. A chocolate-colored tuft of fur clings between his front teeth. The scent of sulfur rises hot in the air.

I gasp and choke.

The black dog raises a paw and thumps it on the window.

I snatch my fingers from between the Venetian blinds. The slats snap shut. "Holy shit," is all I can manage to say.

I back away from the window until my legs hit the bed. My knees go out from under me and I plop down hard on the mattress. The dog throws itself against the window. The thud of his body makes my stomach churn.

I stand on wobbly legs and back towards the door. The black smashes against the window again. This time there is another sound. A creaking.

The glass is ready to give.

I have to get Megan out of here. I yank the bookshelf away from the door, wrenching my shoulder in the process. Flinging open the door, I shove the bookshelf into the hallway, amazed at my own burst of strength. The sound of cracking glass follows the dog's next impact against the window. I slam the bedroom door shut and wedge the bookshelf against it. I lean against the hallway wall, trying to catch my breath. My shoulder burns from the one-armed exertion.

I don't know where to hide. I'm not sure where we'll be safe.

Outside, a howl, followed by a duo of yips.

There's a big dog breaking through the bedroom window, another big dog and two little ones still outside. Where's the fifth dog?

Something thumps in the kitchen.

Chapter Eighteen

Wednesday, 3:29 PM

One of the killer dogs is in the house!

The splintering sound of breaking glass comes from the other side of the bedroom door.

Now two red-eyed killers are inside.

I can't breathe. Can't swallow. Can't think. My feet won't move up the hallway.

Make them move. This is no time to freeze. Show no fear.

No fear, Grandma? You've got to be kidding. But you're right about one thing, I can't just stand here. I'm a sitting duck. Can a sitting duck stand? I laugh. Nervous. High-pitched. Insane. The crazed laughter jars me out of my paralyzed state. I reach down and grab a handful of my pant leg. Lift. Set a foot on the carpet in front of me.

The action triggers my body's muscle memory and I sprint for the nearest room, the laundry room, kitty corner across the hall. I dash through the doorway, quickly and quietly shutting the door behind me.

Bumping noises come from inside the house. Now a crash, as if a vase were just knocked to the floor.

How did the dog get inside? Did it get in through the garage? Did I leave the front door ajar? No, I wouldn't have done that. Would I?

A dog howls. From the living room. The sound startles Megan awake. She starts crying.

"It's okay, sweet pie." I whisper, jiggling her, rocking her, trying to keep her quiet, trying in vain to calm my own nerves. "The bad dogs can't get us in here."

I wish I felt sure of that. But I don't. Apparently, Megan doesn't feel too sure either. She keeps crying. I look down at the red-faced infant squalling in my arms.

A single tear rolls off the tip of my nose and splashes onto Megan's cheek.

It's me and her against the world.

This is no time to play the drama queen, Dianne. Think. Act. Do something.

Right, Grandma. Do something. Anything.

One-handed, I start hurling things in front of the door. But there isn't much of anything in this room with any weight to it, only laundry baskets, a plastic stacking utility shelf, a footstool, an ironing board. I pile it all against the door.

Something rustles in the bushes outside. Branches scrape against the house. The noise sounds like it's coming from outside, under the utility sink window.

From the hallway, claws rake against the utility door.

Holy mother of God. I've barricaded Megan and myself inside a room. And every exit is blocked by a red-eyed killer.

Oh, Grandma, what have I done?

***

Wednesday, 2:43 PM

Kevin didn't stay put in his office for long. He was in and out twice more to check into nearby road rage incidents – both false leads in the vanishing vic cases. The result was a mound of paperwork. He did as much of it as he could tolerate for one afternoon before heading out the door. The rest could wait until morning.

He had a couple errands to run before going home. After dropping the sympathy card for Dianne at the post office, he drove to a department store.

Kevin walked out of the store holding a giant teddy bear. Unlike the flowers, this gift he'd deliver to Dianne – well, actually to her baby – in person. He hoped it wasn't too much. Too pushy. He didn't want her to think he was stalking her or anything.

Good grief, McCoffey, are you kidding? She won't think you're stalking her. When she ran out of gas, who did she call for help? She called you, didn't she, before she even called the towing service. What does that tell you? She still has feelings for you, that's what. You sent her a card and flowers because her grandmother passed away. Now you're delivering a belated baby gift. Nothing wrong with that.

Talking himself into it, he drove towards Dianne's apartment, a tan teddy bear with a bright red bow riding shotgun.

He hated mentally taking his work with him, but he couldn't help it. During the drive to Dianne's, he kept mulling over the vanishing vic cases and the recent personal history of each one who'd disappeared:

Daniel Archer's daughter died of cancer.

Emily Cater had suffered through her husband's extramarital affairs. Then the philandering husband served her with divorce papers she didn't want. Next, he kicked her out of their home. She had to start over, when all she'd wanted was to save her marriage.

And according to family members, young Radley Smith's mother had turned inward since her stroke. Darker. The brain damage had changed her personality, made her do things she'd never have done before. She'd gotten three facial piercings and a tattoo of a snake around one wrist. Rumor had it that she'd started using meth. She was no longer the same mother little Radley had always known and loved.

Kevin felt sorry for each of the three victims. Now he felt sorry for their families. They'd all had nasty hands dealt to them, even before the blow of grief when their loved ones went missing.

They'd all had nasty hands dealt to them. It was something that tied them all together...

...Wait a minute, was the killer/kidnapper striking only people down on their luck? How would the killer know which people were suffering? Granted, the

Roseland Community News had splashed the Archer girl's story all over the front page, but the other two family's stories just quietly unfolded.

Kevin turned onto Daffodil Lane. He cruised into the apartment complex lot where Dianne lived. There was no Blazer in her parking slot. The bouquet he'd sent her earlier that day still waited on the stoop. He figured Dianne would've been home by now. No sense leaving the teddy bear by her door too, out in the fog to get wet and ruined or stolen. He was pleasantly surprised that no one had swiped the flowers – at least not so far.

Where was Dianne anyway? A ghost of foreboding whispered him a tuneless melody. He tried to shake off the sense of dread. *She's probably still at her grandma's house. No big deal. There's probably a lot of paperwork she needs to tend to – the will, death certificates, life insurance, bill paying, all that.*

He'd go to the gym, catch a workout and check back by Dianne's apartment later. If she still wasn't home, he'd let himself worry then.

He cruised north towards the gym. His thoughts wandered back to Dianne. Shoot, his thoughts had never really left Dianne all day. Not since he'd seen her that morning at the market and she'd told him her grandma had passed.

She's really down on her luck right now….

"Shit!"

Kevin made a sharp U turn. It was against regulations to use flashing lights when off duty, but he flipped on the red and blue strobes anyway and whipped his way through the thick fog and around traffic, the gym forgotten.

Part Four: The Escape

Chapter Nineteen

Wednesday, 3:33 PM

There's got to be a way out!

My glance dashes from the utility room door to the window to the ceiling. I look at the trap door in the ceiling above the dryer. "Not every escape route is blocked, Megan," I say with relief. "We can go up, into the attic."

Once, out of curiosity years ago, I climbed a stepladder and peeked through that trap door. There was nothing but spiders, cobwebs and darkness. A creepy feeling winds down my back. Oh, how I do detest spiders.

Snarls and clawing noises come from the hallway side of the utility room door.

I detest red-eyed killer dogs even more than spiders. Cob-web infested darkness here we come.

I'm still holding Megan, but I work one-handed to grab the footstool out of the jumbled pile in front of the door. It undermines the pyramid. The clothesbaskets and ironing board clatter to the floor. I don't waste time piling them back up. I was only fooling myself thinking they'd keep the dog – or dogs – out of the room anyway. With a foot I nudge the stool over to the sink. "Ouch." It's painful to put all my weight on my injured leg. Cautiously, I climb from the stool, onto the sink ledge, to the top of the dryer. No easy feat while injured and holding a baby. I stretch one hand up and slide back the attic door.

"Hang on, Megan. Mommy has to put you up here, where it's dark." And creepy. And full of spiders.

A loud, metallic *dong* rifles through the air. I almost wet myself. A gunshot? Who would shoot at us? Maybe they're shooting at the dogs, but we're in the line of fire. The gunshot makes me move even quicker. I shuffle-slide my feet along the dryer top until I'm directly under the attic opening so I can shove Megan up inside. I have to get her to safety, away from the dogs and the whizzing bullets.

The *dong* pierces the air again. I feel a vibration under me and look down.

The sound is the metal dryer lid, denting and un-denting under my weight. How stupid do I feel?

Stretching up on tip toes, I reach into the gaping ceiling hole. I grope around to make sure there are no rats lurking close by. No big, hairy spiders. Nothing sharp. Making sure it's safe for Megan.

Nothing warm or furry crawls over my hand. I lift Megan over my head. Something flutters to my feet. I gasp, was that a bat? I'm almost afraid to look and see what dropped. Curiosity gets the best of me. But when I glance down I see it's just a piece of newspaper. I'd forgotten it was still tucked under my arm from when I was packing Grandma's knick knacks.

I lift Megan higher and nestle her inside the attic, as far in as I can reach. As an after thought, I pick up the newspaper sections and shove them in alongside Megan. She starts crying again, in earnest.

"Shhhh-shhh, baby. Mama's right here."

Now I have to get up inside the attic with Megan.

How am I going to do that? Especially with the shoulder I wrenched when I yanked the bookcase into the hall.

I clench my fingers inside the opening and try to pull myself up. No way. Even without a sprained shoulder, I simply don't have the upper body strength. Megan's wails reverberate from inside the attic. "Hang on, sweet pie. Mama will be there in a minute." At least I hope Mama can be there in a minute. What I need is a boost.

I hop off the dryer to the floor and grab the footstool.

From the hallway comes the ripping sound of splintering wood.

No way. The dog is tearing its way through the door.

I toss the footstool onto the dryer and clamber back on top. Megan is screaming now. The clawing at the door grows louder. The dog must already be through the first layer of the hollow-core door.

I climb onto the step stool, grasp inside the attic opening and try pulling myself up. A pain stabs through my thumb, shoots up my arm and arrows through my sore shoulder.

"Ow. Shit." I let myself back down.

This is no time to be a baby, Dianne.

Sheesh, Grandma, give me a break. A dog bit me, okay? And I about pulled my shoulder out of the socket moving that shelf a minute ago. I'm experiencing some pain here.

You will be hurting a helluva lot worse if you don't get your butt up in that attic.

There's another splintering crash from the hallway and a fist-size hole appears in the door.

You are so right, Grandma.

A bloody snout pokes through the hole. Opens its jaw. Teeth rip at the wood.

"Holy…" I renew my efforts to hoist myself into the attic, ignoring the bolts of pain shooting up my arm and across my back.

The dog claws at the door, enlarging the hole. He pokes his splotchy brown head through and stares at me with glinting ruby eyes. He pulls back his top lip and growls.

The scent of sulfur fills the room, like smoke bombs on the fourth of July.

I jump and pull myself up at the same time. My feet are only five inches off the top of the dryer. But hey, I'm five inches closer to my baby.

The dog yanks his head back out the hole in the door. He rips and claws a bigger opening and pushes his head through again. A brindle-brown body follows.

The dog leaps over the items littering the floor, jumps against the dryer and snaps at my ankles. Saliva flies from his bloody lips. Flecks of red slime stick to my jeans.

I pull harder, gaining another two inches of elevation. My arms tremble.

I can't do this.

The dog jumps and snaps at me again. I can feel his hot, demon breath through my pants.

Come on, Dianne. Pull.

Believe me, Grandma, I'm pulling. I lift myself another inch. In PE class at school, I could do only one chin-up. That's all I need now, just one. A good one. If I can get my elbows wedged up inside the attic space, I should be able to pull the rest of my body up and in.

The dog leaps at me again. His teeth close on my pants leg. He tugs, making me lose what progress I'd made. "Let go of me!" I kick at the dog. Make-clog-to-snout contact. Once. Twice. He releases my jeans.

A ruckus comes from the hall. Something crashes against the wall outside the laundry room.

Did the bookshelf I shoved against the spare room door fall?

With all my might I lift myself, regaining a few inches.

A hairy black head pushes through the hole in the door. Red, unblinking eyes stare at me.

Oh, God. No. The black dog is here too.

Chapter Twenty

Wednesday, 3:42 PM

The black dog's neck and shoulders follows his head and then he plunges into the utility room. The hair on his face and chest is wet and shiny with fresh blood. The metallic scent mingles with the stench of rotten eggs. I gag. It's all I can do not to puke.

The brown leaps and snaps at my ankles. The black snarls and leaps at the brown's throat.

They're fighting over me. Over who wins the right to kill me.

I have to get myself into the attic while they're distracted. I pull up with everything I've got. The pressure in my face is intense with the effort. I grit my teeth and pull harder.

The brown challenges the black. Then, apparently thinking better of it, he drops to all four paws and cowers. Apparently, the black is still reigning leader. He jumps at me, knocking hard against the dryer. It sounds like a bongo drum. His teeth graze my leg before he drops.

For a moment I think his teeth against my leg made the hollow drum sound, as though I am the tin woodman. My calf burns where his teeth raked my skin.

The black gathers himself for another leap. Terror and fresh pain give me a new burst of strength. I flail-kick at the dog's head. I kick and kick and pull until I can wedge my elbows into the opening.

Megan lets loose with a new bout of screams. The noise works the dogs into a bigger frenzy. They try to leap onto the dryer. Their claws scrabble and slip against the metal. Their bodies twist in midair and fall back to the floor.

I pull and squirm until my chest rests on the attic floor. It's hard to catch my breath, but I'm almost there. If I can just pull my legs up before one of the rabid beasts gets hold of them… .

The dogs pummel against the dryer again. Their bodies make a loud, tinny thud. One of them barks savagely. His sulfur breath blows up my pant leg. It burns, hot and acidic.

I draw my legs the rest of the way up and inside the attic. Below, the dogs continue to jump and grapple against the dryer, trying to gain a foothold on the slippery surface but failing. I slide the wooden trap door in the attic floor back into place. The door muffles the sound of the dogs. I run my hands over Megan, making sure there are no spiders on her. I wrap an arm around her torso.

My whole body quakes.

When my breath comes more even, my heart rate has settled, and my limbs stop trembling so hard, I tuck Megan under my left arm, tight against my body and start crawling. Around a stack of boxes, and across the plywood sheets laying over the rafters. I could stand up in here if I stooped over, but I don't think my wobbly legs would support me right now. I pull myself along with one elbow, pushing with my legs and feet toward the tiny, western facing window.

It seems to take forever to inch across the length of the attic but it's like a magnet is sucking me through the layer of dust towards the only light source.

The loud tinny thumps in the laundry room slow. Quiet. Stop all together. Good. Maybe the dogs gave up. Maybe they'll go away now.

Don't bet on it.

Not to worry, Grandma. I'm not betting on anything today.

By the time I've covered half the distance from the attic door to the window,

Megan has stopped crying. When I get out of this, I'll know how to calm her down when she's fussy – jam her under an arm and alligator crawl across the floor.

When I get out of this? More like *if* I get out of this. How in the world am I going to get out of this?

Reaching the window, I sit up and peer out. I can barely see through the years of accumulated grime and cobwebs coating the glass. I'm hoping the webs are as old as they look and contain no living spiders or squirming egg cases. The thought makes my skin crawl. If I had a dust cloth, I could at least wipe off the worst of the dirt.

I brush at a spot on the floor with one hand and lie Megan under the window. I want to check her diaper. I'm sure it's wet, but is it messy too? She fusses when I put her down. The thumps and bumps in the laundry room start in again. The noises grow louder, more frantic. What, do the dogs have sonar hearing or something? Any little sound sets them off? I take Megan back up into my arms. I need to keep her quiet. I want the dogs to lose interest in us and go away.

Forever.

Silently, I spin around so I can lean against the outside wall. I rock my upper body. After a few minutes, Megan drifts off to sleep.

Outside, a howl. Followed by another. And another. Then a chorus of high-pitched yips. Although I offer them no standing ovation, the dogs give an encore performance. Same howls. Same yips. But farther away.

They're leaving! The dogs are leaving!

Don't count your chickens before they hatch.

Chickens, Grandma? We're talking dogs here. Can't you hear them? *THEY ARE LEAVING.*

If I could stand up and do a cheer, I'd consider it. But seeing as how the ceiling's too low to stand up in here, I have three throbbing dog-bite wounds, an injured shoulder, and a baby sleeping on me, I don't jump up and cheer. Besides, I still have to pee something fierce. My bladder probably wouldn't handle much bouncing.

I lie Megan down on the semi-dusted spot on the floor. I stretch out my legs and yank up both pant legs. My ankle is still swollen nearly double in size. There's a four-inch welt running down that same leg where the black's teeth raked it. At least his teeth didn't break the skin. If any of the dogs have rabies, it's definitely the black one. He's an evil, angry, feral, rabid dog if ever I saw one.

I don't want to think about rabies right now. I want to think about getting out of here. Getting back to my quiet, normal life of taking photographs and raising my daughter.

I need a plan because I can't get out the way I got in. I can't make the drop to the top of the dryer while holding a baby. If I left Megan in the attic, then jumped down, what if I couldn't reach up high enough to get her back out? What if the dogs came back right then and attacked me? I can't leave Megan to starve to death, alone in a dark attic if something were to happen to me. The dogs may not really be gone. They've come back before. More than once. I need a solid plan and a fallback plan too.

If I had some old sheets, I could tear them into strips, tie them into an escape ladder and climb down. Then I'd have two routes of escape – one out the window and one through the trap door. I eye the boxes piled near the attic entrance. Maybe there are some sheets, or old clothing packed away in the boxes. The light is starting to fail. I had better get busy before it's too dark to see. Megan's still crashed, content to slumber on the floor.

I bend-over walk to the boxes. Open the flaps and peer inside. Vinyl record albums in one – Abba, The Carpenters, Elvis – thick old 78s of Bing Crosby and Frank Sinatra in another. I could wing them at the dogs like Frisbees.

Here boy, here, wanna play?

Uh-huh, right.

I try the other boxes: Dishes and assorted kitchen utensils; tin wind-up toys – hey, aren't those collectible? Wonder if they'd fetch enough on eBay to pay the tow service bill.

Stay focused, Dianne.

Sorry, Grandma. You're right. I'll think about eBay and antique toys later. Besides, it's not like Mel can cash my check now anyway. Oh God, poor Mel. Think of something else, Dianne. Focus on what you're looking for.

I rip at the flaps of the last box, but it contains no sheets, no blankets and no clothing either. Inside are old, framed portraits. Beautiful black and whites and sepia shots of people I don't recognize. The composition and lighting of the shots is amazing. These aren't typical, old-time sourpuss, man sitting, woman standing poses. These are truly artistic.

Was there another photographer in the family, Grandma? Who are these people?

Our ancestors, Dianne. A person's legacy lives on after they're dead. We're never really gone.

Wow, Grandma. That was profound.

Yes. That is me. Profound Adelle.

I can't help chuckling. Grandma's sense of humor is definitely not dead.

The newspaper.

Huh? The newspaper? Oh, yeah.

I'd almost forgotten about the sections of paper I stuffed up inside the attic before I climbed up. It's not going to get me and Megan out of the attic, but I could use it to wipe off the grimy window, help let in the last traces of light before the sun disappears. It's setting fast. I snatch up the paper and stoop-walk back to Megan.

She's still sleeping. Good. I wad up a piece of the newspaper and dry buff the glass. It makes an eerie scratching noise, like dog claws against a car window, but it knocks off the biggest chunks of dirt and lets in a bit more light. At least for a few minutes more, I hope.

I hear no thumping from below. No barking in the backyard. No scrabbling claws. Maybe it's really over. Maybe the dogs really are gone this time.

As if on cue, a dog barks in the distance. Whether it's one of the red-eyed dogs or someone's pet, my body still reacts with a jolt and a shudder.

"It's just you and me babe," I say to Megan. And you, Grandma. I take one of Megan's hands in mine. Her skin is cool to the touch. Whatever heat had risen from the house is quickly being replaced by chilled, autumn afternoon sea air. I remember how the newspaper kept me warm when I spread it across my lap while waiting for the tow truck driver.

Mel. Poor, poor Mel. That terrified look in his eyes as he tried to beat off the dogs haunts me. The newspaper quivers in my hand. Don't think about it now. You couldn't help him. Don't think about it. You'll just make yourself crazy.

I unfold a couple sections of paper to cover Megan. A front-page photo catches my attention. The woman somehow looks familiar. I set that chunk of paper aside, cover Megan, and pick the newspaper section back up. Tilting it to catch the faltering light, I study the grainy photograph.

Forlorn is the only word I can think of to describe the woman. I look closer. It's the cashier that waited on me this morning at the speedy mart.

The headlines above the photo read:

Boy Mysteriously Disappears

I scan the story, although I read it thoroughly three weeks ago when it first came out.

… The boy's family has recently been dealt a one-two punch. Young Radley Smith's mother, Arlene Smith, suffered a stroke three months before the boy's disappearance.

I think back several hours ago to the cahier's sullenness. The limp-wristed way she closed the cash drawer. The clumsy manner in which she tossed the change into my hand. The dull look in her eyes. The lop-sided mouth and how it had all seemed somehow familiar. The pieces clunk in place like an awkward wooden puzzle.

The cashier reminded me of Grandpa Austin after his stroke fifteen years ago. Today at noon, my mind wouldn't make the leap from young woman to old man to link the stroke connection. Now, by 4:12 in the afternoon, circumstances have forced my mind into making all sorts of unbelievable leaps.

I think back to the cashier's hollow warning, "Be careful."

Did she mean be careful of the dogs? How could she have known? A shiver creeps up my arms and shoulders and rattles inside my skull. She couldn't have known, that's ridiculous. Of course, this whole day has been ridiculous.

The sun sinks behind the trees. With trepidation, I watch it glow the sky red and orange, then turn pink fading into yellow before it vanishes beyond the horizon.

Megan and I are plunged into complete darkness.

A dog howls from some distance away. Another answers, closer. Where is the third big dog?

It doesn't take long for my question to be answered.

A third howl sounds from the backyard.

Wednesday, 4:14 PM

Chapter Twenty-One

I had hoped the dogs left for good. Apparently, they were waiting for the cover of darkness before returning.

To finish off what they started.

I scoot closer to Megan until my outer thigh rests against her body. I settle against the wall. There's not much else I can do. Even if the dogs hadn't come back, I can't climb down out of the attic in the dark. There's no electricity. I can't see a thing. I can't chance slipping, falling and hurting Megan.

Like it or not, we're stuck up here with the dust and the spiders for the night.

I spread newspaper over my legs and try to get comfortable. My plan now is to stay as quiet as possible, and hope the dogs will lose interest and leave to prowl the night somewhere else.

Somewhere far, far away, like somewhere over the rainbow and beyond.

I hear the sound of tinkling glass followed by a loud thump. So much for over the rainbow. A whimper climbs out of my throat. The noise wakes Megan and she fusses. "No, sweet pie," I whisper in her ear. "You have to be quiet." I pick her up, snuggle her against me.

Downstairs, the noises increase. A loud crash – the sound of a door thrown open against a wall. From outside comes a hollow thud, similar to when the dogs threw themselves against the dryer. I look through the window, but of course, I can't see a thing through the blackness, except the dim outline of Grandma's tool shed next to the garage.

Another metallic *thud* resonates through the night air.

Why would dogs throw themselves against a tool shed?

Claws screech metal. It's the same sound the gray dog's claws made when he scaled to the top of my Blazer in the newspaper lot.

It can't be. A dog can't climb a metal building, can it? No way.

Again, claws scrape on tin. The sound is a thousand times worse than fingernails raked across a chalkboard.

Why would a dog want to scale a tool shed? Is it some sort of canine version of king of the hill? That's ridiculous.

I hear a *thump*, then scrabbling claws, like a dog landing and recovering its balance after a leap. The noises come from the direction of the garage. Nearby, another leaping *thud*, then the sound of loping footfalls above me, followed by clawing. Digging. Tearing.

Realization hits me like a blow to the kidneys.

There's a dog on the roof. And it's trying to rip through the shingles.

The scraping and clawing grows more desperate. I picture the brown dog as he looked earlier at the utility room door, splintering his way through the wood, shoving first his bloody muzzle, then his head, followed by his entire body through the jagged opening.

I bite my bottom lip and choke back the scream threatening to burst free. I don't want to rouse Megan. I don't want her to hear my panic. And I don't want my screams or Megan's cries to send the dog above me into a more desperate frenzy.

I lean back harder against the wall, pressing my spine and shoulder blades into the beams until my back aches, using the pain to force my thoughts away from the dogs. Especially from the one digging its way inside the dark attic where Megan and I helplessly wait.

Who says you are helpless?

Look around, Grandma. We're like rabbits in a snare here. We can't escape.

Then defend yourself.

With what?

Grandma doesn't answer.

Grandma? Hello? I could really use some help here. Defend myself with what?

Grandma doesn't come up with any brilliant ideas. Or if she does, she chooses not to voice them aloud inside my head.

I look around, as much good as it does me. I can't see my hand in front of my face.

Something slides down the roof, catches in the gutter.

A shingle.

Nearby, I hear panting. No, the dog can't be in the attic already. It's only torn off one shingle so far. Right?

Again the panting. It comes steady now. Rapid. Close. So close it sounds like it's in my own head. The scratching above me sounds farther away as my mind takes a trip through time and space. The panting grows louder. My breathing grows shallower. Can't catch my breath. I feel dizzy and lightheaded. It takes me a moment to realize what's happening. I'm hyperventilating. The panting is coming from me.

Get ahold of yourself, Dianne. Big breath in, blow it all out.

I do as Grandma suggests, trying to gain control of my panic-induced breathing. I wish I had a paper bag to breathe into, like I've seen done on TV sitcoms. Breathe in. Breathe out. In, slowly. Out. The dizziness begins to pass. My fuzzy brain makes the trip back to our own galaxy and begins to function again. It's so dark, I can't see the sleeping baby in my arms, but I nestle her closer and feel her warm breath against my cheek, which clears my head and brings me back to the moment.

Where was I? Escape. Protection. Weapons. The boxes near the entrance… . I do a quick mental inventory of the contents – framed photos, kitchen junk, old records, tin toys.

I've got an idea.

First, I have to free up my hands. Carefully, I lie Megan down and pull a couple sheets of newspaper over her with as little rustle as possible. Next, I crouch-walk towards the trap door. I trail my uninjured hand overhead across the exposed beams to guide me, shuddering at the clumps of cobwebs that pass through my fingers. I stretch a foot out in front of me, tapping my toes like a blind man taps his red-tipped cane.

A chilly sweat pops out on my forehead and under the hair on the back of my neck. I pause to swipe at a line of moisture trickling near my eye. I wobble, thrown off balance by the swiping motion, by the darkness, and by a case of plain, old-fashioned jangled nerves.

Something skitters over my knuckles. I squeal like a little girl. I hate spiders.

The noise excites the dog on the roof. He scratches and chews harder. Another piece of shingle slides down the roof, followed by another. And another.

Megan stirs and fusses.

I pivot and quickly toe-tap my way back to my baby. I can't leave her alone any longer.

Above, near the window, comes the sound of splintering wood. The dog is already through the layer of three-tab roofing. Why did I leave Megan over there, unattended? I should have brought her with me.

I grope faster through the musty darkness, through the creepy cobwebs.

Megan stops crying long enough to cough. It's a throaty, raspy little sound. Is she getting sick? She's never sick. But then she's spent too long in a wet diaper and now she's lying exposed to drafts inside an attic. It wouldn't be surprising if she came down with pneumonia. I must be the world's worst mother. With my toe in front of me, guiding me along the false plywood floor, I work my way closer to my poor, neglected baby.

Overhead, the clawing grows louder as the dog digs his way through the next layer of roof.

I swallow my panic. I can't start hyperventilating again. I need my lungs, brain and body to all be working in harmony so I can get to Megan and protect her.

Her coughs and cries are nearer now. I'm almost there. A few more taps with my toe, another clump of cobwebs through my fingers…and I'm there.

I kneel, wrap an arm around Megan and bury my face in her neck. "Shhhh, little one. Mama's here." I need to get her away from this area. The dog is directly overhead, scheduled to poke a blood-covered face through the ceiling any second.

Alligator crawling seems the safest mode of transportation with Megan in tow. I don't dare try to stand up and walk with her in the dark. One wrong step off a plywood sheet and I'd plunge a leg through the insulation and sub-flooring – a human drumstick for any dog lurking below.

I creep along with Megan towards the boxes and the attic doorway. It seems the most logical escape route. When it comes time, I'd rather drop six feet onto the dryer in the pitch-blackness than leap twelve feet out the window, in the dark, to the ground.

When it comes time…. A knot grips my intestines and squeezes.

Do not borrow trouble.

You're kidding, right Grandma? Today I don't have to borrow trouble – it freely presents itself.

Dust stirs as I wriggle through it, retracing my path. It makes me sneeze. Megan coughs, dry and croupy. I hug her tighter, kiss the top of her head. I have to keep crawling, keep reaching out with my free hand to feel in front of me. I have to get Megan to the escape hatch in the attic floor before the dog tears its way in through the roof.

***

Wednesday 4:35 PM

Kevin veered onto the Pacific Coast Highway. The fog lifted. So did his spirits, ever so slightly, as he increased his speed to eighty-five miles per hour without worry of blindly driving over a cliff and plunging into the ocean. After only a couple miles of decent visibility, the fog huddled back to ground level. Kevin let up on the accelerator and hit the steering wheel with the flat of his hand. "Damn!" He ran the hand back over his short hair.

I have to find Dianne. I have to get to her before the killer does.

His gut spasmed painfully several times. The pain sent an icy blade of premonition slicing through his heart. He'd felt the clenching and unclenching stomach spasms before. He knew what they were.

They were the pulsing warning signals of time running out.

Wednesday, 4:36 PM

Chapter Twenty-Two

My only chance to protect Megan and myself is to reach the boxes of cast-off items, and the attic door just beyond, before the dog above us chews his way through the ceiling and attacks.

The panic gripping my insides is becoming as familiar as the roar of the sea.

I hold Megan tighter to my chest, propping my upper body off the floor with an elbow to keep her out of the dust. I pull with my elbows, push and kick with my legs and feet to propel us forward through the darkness.

Overhead and behind me, the sound of the dog's clawing changes from scrabbling on sandpaper, to toenails on wood. He's through the shingles. He's reached the plywood section of the roof. His claws shred at one laminated layer after another.

I crawl faster, trying not to think of rodents, spiders, or the canine reciprocating saw above us. Rolling to one side so I won't smash Megan, I stretch and grope through the air with my free hand. I feel for the boxes – my landmark in the darkness. My fingers brush air. I run my hand along the plywood beneath me, testing for the edge of the makeshift floor, making sure I am centered. I don't want to venture off the edge and punch an arm or leg between the rafters.

What I wouldn't give for a flashlight.

I must be almost there. I hope I'm almost there. It's getting hard to breathe.

The dust is thick, laced with rodent urine. I struggle with a bout of nausea at the thought. Megan erupts with a fit of coughing. Breathing in mouse filth can't be good for her health.

The ripping and tearing on the roof grows methodical, as if the dog is clawing to the beat of a metronome.

Ridiculous.

Megan coughs again. The sound is pitiful. I brush my lips across her head and whisper into her hair. "Hang on, sweet pie. We'll be there soon." I hope I'm not lying. I have no idea how far we have yet to crawl. The darkness surrounding us is complete.

A deafening crack of splintering wood echoes inside the attic chamber. A gust of moist, salt-laced air enters.

The dog has broken through the roof!

I wriggle forward what I estimate to be another yard, roll onto my side and desperately feel the area in front of me. My fingers brush something solid. I inch forward, stretch again, rap my fingers against the object. I swallow the urge to whoop with victory. We have made it to the boxes, which means we are at the attic door.

The dog overhead snarls. I smell him, pungent and repulsive. He goes back to ripping and tearing. He's enlarging the hole. Soon his head, then his body will push through the ceiling. But Megan and I will be long gone. Darkness and all, we'll drop onto the dryer, dash through the house and out to the Blazer. We'll be out the driveway and on the road before the climbing, digging, stinking, sulfurous dog even realizes we're gone.

I scoot around the boxes until my fingers touch the lip of the trap door. I sit up and slide the door back a few inches. The scent of lavender, old linen and lingering memories rushes up from the body of the house. "Grandma."

It feels as if she is sitting right here beside me. I reach out a hand to touch her shoulder, but, of course, my hand touches nothing. The Grandma scent mingles with attic dust, fresh sea air and sulfur.

A big dog howls from the distance. Another answers from the backyard.

No! Now two of the dogs have come back. I have to move fast. And I have to be silent. How can I drop to the dryer without making any noise? It will cave in the top and pong like cannon fire.

A tinkle of glass comes from inside the house. The landing *thump* of a large body, followed by a growl.

One of the dogs is in the house.

Is it the dog from the roof? I strain to listen for sounds overhead. I don't hear any. I cock my head toward the hole in the roof, trying to listen over the pounding of my heart. At ceiling level, two circles glow red.

The dog on the roof is poking his head through the ceiling. That means the dog inside the house below us is a different dog.

I hear the friction of a furry hide rubbing against ragged wood. The dog inside the house below is shoving his way through the laundry room door. Something falls with a clatter to the utility room floor, followed by the sound of scrabbling claws against hollow metal. I peer through the attic opening, down into inky blackness. Two glowing orbs bounce like super balls in perfect synchronization, leaving red tracers in the dark.

The dog is trying to jump onto the dryer.

Overhead, a howl pierces the night. The dog beneath us stops bounding. He closes his eyes and answers his pack mate with a drawn-out howl. The roof dog starts up his scraping, clawing, ripping again., making the hole bigger. Big enough to fit his whole body through.

Like at the newspaper office, I'm surrounded. Well, not quite. There's still the attic window. But no way will I be able to crawl back to the window before the dog finishes tearing through the roof. I've seen how fast one can chew through a double-layered door. A roof can't take too much longer. Besides, even if I could get

Megan to the window in time, how would I escape to the ground? I can't jump.

Not two stories. Not with a baby, in the dark.

The dog on the roof pauses. He howls again. Long. Low. Plaintive. An answering howl comes from the backyard.

The backyard? That means all three big dogs are here. We truly are surrounded.

A pulsing throb of panic fills my head. I can't will away the bloody vision of the dogs ripping at Mel, tearing into his throat, strangling the life from his body. And Bubba. Poor, sweet, stupid old Bubba. All he was trying to do was protect his family and the evil dogs shredded him.

I can't will the horror out of my head because I know I am next. And after they're done with me, the dogs will tear into Megan.

A metallic taste fills my mouth. The taste of terror.

I can only keep the dogs distracted and away from Megan for so long. I can lay down my life, but that won't save her in the end, will it? I have to fight. I square my shoulders. And I have to win.

I need a plan. I need weapons. But most of all, I need courage.

You have courage, Dianne. Don't you know that by now?

You might be right, Grandma. Maybe I do have courage. Now, if I can just figure out what to do with it.

In the dark, I fumble with the flaps on top of a box, using only one hand. No way am I putting Megan down to free the other hand. The first box contains the old 78 records. I pull out a handful of the thick, heavy albums, stack them on the floor beside me and grope for the next box.

The noise above us ceases. Two spots of red glow overhead. Disappear. There's more clawing and splintering, then the red eyes reappear, glowing deeper down through the attic ceiling.

The hole is already big enough for the dog to shove his head and neck through. The eyes vanish once more and the ripping of wood resumes.

I have to hurry hurry hurry.

The next box contains the vinyl records. The Elvis albums might fetch a few dollars, but as weapons they're worthless. I scoot that box aside, and peek down through the open slit in the trap-door. The set of eyes below me continues to leave vertical red tracers. The dog throws his body against the dryer with greater force. His claws scrabble and screech against the metal. The glowing super balls stop bouncing. Now they are only a few feet below me.

The dog is on top of the dryer.

I shove at the attic door. I have to shut the trap door to keep the dog from forcing his way into the attic. I push at the door with my feet. It slides across the hole, but I don't hear the satisfying thunk of it settling securely into place.

There's no time to worry about the unseated door. Overhead, the red eyes poke down further into the attic. There's the unmistakable scraping of a pelt against broken wood. A yip, a whine.

Good, I hope the dog rips his hide wide open on a roofing nail and dies of gangrene. Again, I hear the scraping. The eyes shine yet lower into the attic.

The dog has almost squeezed through the opening. He will soon push his way in.

My pulse thuds inside my brain. I can't think. What should I do? What can I do? They're coming after me. They're going to get us.

What do they want with me? What did I ever do to them? I don't want to deal with this pack of dogs anymore. I just want them to go away.

I close my eyes and pray. It's the only way I can get through the next few seconds without having a panic attack. I pray as I've never prayed before. I beg God for safety. Ask him to send someone to help us. But most of all, I fervently pray for the dogs to drop dead like three-day-old flies.

When I open my eyes, God has not extinguished the double red orbs above me. He has not slayed the dog scrabbling on top of the dryer below. And I am angry. At God. At Matt and Grandma for dying. At Mom and Dad for leaving me. At Kevin for not coming to check on us. To help us. To rescue us.

Use your anger. Gather it together and use it.

Use it for what?

Use your anger to fight your fear, to fight the dogs.

I'm tired of fighting. I can't beat them. There are too many. They are too strong, too demonic. I don't want to fight.

We all must fight for what we love.

Megan squirms in my arms and in that instant I know Grandma is right. I can't give up without a fight. I am all Megan has – the only thing between her and the dogs. Between life and death. I hold her small body firm against my own, reach my free hand inside the box behind the records, feeling for a weapon. My fingers close around the handle of a frying pan. Classic. I'll bean the dogs over the head like Wilma Flintstone might bonk Fred. Yeah, great idea, I chastise myself. I pull the pan out anyway and drop it beside the stack of 78s. I reach back inside the box.

The dog shoves the rest of the way through the roof, and drops with a whump. Its eyes glow three feet from the attic floor. I suck in a sulfur-tinged breath of courage.

We all must fight for what we love.

Grandma's words connect me to what's real. What's important. What life is all about.

The dog's claws tick on the floor as it snuffles along. Apparently, his red eyes don't work as flashlights. He has to seek me out with his nose.

Beams of white cut through the darkness. Maybe I was wrong about the dog's eyes. A dense panic presses against my chest, threatening to choke off my air supply.

I reach back inside the box.

The dog's sniffing grows closer. He raises his head. The white lights move over the dog's body and throw a hackled-beast shadow puppet along the far wall. The shadow is eerie, surreal. It holds its tail stiff, carried straight out from his body like a wolf on the hunt.

I scream.

The shadow wolf leaps. Inside the box, my hand fists around the handle of a kitchen utensil. I pull it out, hoping it's not a serving spoon or a ladle, and press my fist holding the handle firm against my sternum. The light swings to the wall behind me, passes over the object in my hand, reflects off the double metal tines of the meat fork pointing straight out from my body. I have a split second to dodge slightly to the right, tuck Megan out of the path of the advancing dog. The dog lands, full force onto the fork and falls, trapping my left arm and leg under it's big body. The fork handle quivers in my fist. I gasp and release it.

The dog tries to stagger to his feet. The gash on his face from his fight with Bubba breaks open and seeps blood. I yank my arm from beneath him. The dog's claws rake my leg as I pull it out from under him. The dog crumples to the attic floor.

But he is not dead. His breathing comes in ragged gasps.

The utility-room dog bounds up and down as if the dryer were a metal trampoline. His head bangs against the trap door. He lets out a frenzied snarl.

The window. I have to get to the window and get us the hell out of here.

The beams of light still shine inside the dingy attic space. The dog's red eyes have disappeared. Are they closed? If so, where is the light coming from?

Outside, a rumbling.

"Dianne!"

Did someone call my name? Grandma, was that you?

"Dianne, where are you?"

It's a deep voice. Male. Southern accent. Kevin? Can it really be Kevin?

"Dianne!"

"Kevin? Kevin! We're up here."

"Up where?"

"The attic."

"Hang tight. I'll get a ladder."

"Be careful," I yell. Please, please be careful.

The rumbling I hear must be the motor of Kevin's car. It's his headlights throwing freaky shadows among the rafters. At least it's not pitch black up here anymore. I'm so glad he found us. What made him come looking? I'll think about that later, right now I have to get us to the window so we can get out of here. I stand up and sling Megan in my left arm. The dog lies on his side, directly in our path, the fork protruding from his chest. I don't want to take Megan anywhere near the injured dog, but there is no plywood flooring on the other side of the attic. There is no way around him. I have to go over him.

The dog's eyes are closed. He whines deep in his throat. It sounds like Lassie. For the briefest moment, I feel pity for him.

I lift my foot, poised in midair to step over him. The dog's eyes fly open and burn red. I gasp. He growls. My sympathy vanishes. He is not Lassie, he is Cujo – rabid, deviant and murdering. I step over him. He rears up his head like a cobra and snaps at my leg. I squeal and hop on one foot to avoid his teeth. My other foot catches the fork handle. The dog whimpers with pain and I almost feel sorry for him again.

Almost.

He tries to rise to his feet. I take aim and give the fork another kick. This time on purpose. The gray yips and collapses.

He won't stay down long, I'm sure of that.

I bend at the waist and walk as quickly as possible through the low attic, patting a hand overhead, across the beams. I have to reach the window. This time I hardly feel the mats of cobwebs snagging in my fingers. If a spider crawls over my hand, I don't notice.

Behind me, the gray writhes and twists, trying to regain his footing. Below, the dog on the dryer leaps and beats his head on the lop-sided attic door. I hear the door shift, slide open a bit.

Hurry, Kevin. Oh, please hurry. Before it's too late.

Wednesday, 5:02 PM

Chapter Twenty-Three

What was Dianne doing in the attic, Kevin puzzled. Did she climb up there to escape the killer? Maybe the killer was up there with her now, threatening her, torturing her, attacking. He'd heard the panic in her voice when she'd shouted out her location. He had to move fast.

He shined his flashlight on the cyclone fence, locating the gate. Adelle probably stored a ladder in the tool shed behind the garage. He shoved through the gate, scanned the yard with his Mag Lite and stopped short.

Adelle's dog lie dead. His flesh torn, his chocolate pelt bloodstained. *The killer was here. He'd killed already. And now Dianne and her baby could be next.*

Kevin's blood ran frigid. He hoped he wasn't too late. "Hold on, sweetheart. I'm on my way." He doubted if Dianne could hear him, but he had to shout the words aloud. He dashed to the metal tool shed, wrenched open the door and peered inside. *No ladder.* "Hell." *Maybe in the garage.*

The back garage door was locked. He tried kicking it in, but it wouldn't budge. He had to hurry. He needed something to ram against the door, or a tool to pry it open. Maybe there was a crow bar in the tool shed.

From the attic came a piercing scream.

"Dianne? Dianne, are you all right?" She didn't answer him. Kevin's gut spasmed. He was wasting precious time. He beamed his flashlight along the garage exterior, looking for a window, or any other way in. Spotting the dog door, he dropped to his belly and pushed his arms and head through the rubber flap. He'd laugh at the picture he must make, if the situation weren't so dire. His shoulders got hung up, but he twisted and managed to shove and wriggle his way through the opening. Kevin's father, a twenty-year veteran on the New Orleans Police Force at the time of his death, used to say, "Being a hero isn't always pretty."

You were right about that, Dad.

Inside the garage, against the far wall, leaned an extension ladder. "Yes!" Kevin flipped a wall switch, but the beam of his Maglite remained the only light. No power. That meant the automatic garage door wouldn't open either.

There's a killer in the attic with the woman I love. The seconds ticked inside Kevin's head like a time bomb.

He strode to the door, pulled on the chain to trip the release, and shoved the door up. He grabbed the ladder and shuffled with it along the fence to the house, struggling with the flashlight, trying to hold the beam steady enough to see the ground in front of his feet. In the side yard, to his right, the bobbing light picked up a double set of red reflectors. They seemed to shift.

An odd place for reflectors. By the time he could maneuver the ladder and the light back towards the reflectors, the red spots were gone. *My imagination is playing tricks.*

He extended the ladder, clunked it against the house under the attic window, and then hesitated. Ladders were not his forte. Ladders meant height. Height meant fear – paralyzing fear. For a moment, he was twelve again, peering over the edge of a cliff at the still form of his father, his acrophobia in full swing.

His gut knotted painfully. He didn't really need to climb up to the attic, did he? He'd stay on the ground and steady the ladder so Dianne could climb down to safety. Problem solved.

He beamed up the light. Dianne's face appeared in the window. She held her baby securely in her arms. He'd never felt more joy at the simple sight of two people in his life.

"Are you all right? Can you climb down the ladder?"

"Be careful." Dianne mouthed and glanced over her shoulder.

"Dianne? What's wrong?"

Her face looked stricken, pale. Apparently, she hadn't heard what he'd asked her. She looked back into the attic again.

"Are you able to climb down?" Kevin hollered up.

Dianne faced the window and struggled to open it. Her movements were jerky. Panicked. Useless. "I c-c-can't get it open."

What was scaring her? *The killer really is in the attic with her, coming after her.* Kevin drew his sidearm, held it up at his side, barrel pointed at the dark sky.

"Is someone up there with you?"

"W-w-watch out."

Fear of heights be damned, Kevin had to shag his ass up to the attic to help Dianne. He reholstered his weapon. He couldn't climb a ladder while holding both a gun and a flashlight. He wasn't sure he could make himself climb a ladder at all. He drew in a steadying breath, grabbed the ladder with his free hand and put a foot on the first rung. *Here goes nothing.*

"Kevin, watch out."

"Watch out for what?" *Why does she keep saying that?* Approaching footsteps fell in the wet grass. Before Kevin had a chance to shine the light in the direction of the footfalls, he felt a painful pressure on his ankle. "Ow! Damn!"

What was that? He swung the light at his feet. The beam raked across a shaggy brown body. A dog? A dog was biting him? Where did the damn dog come from? Kevin shook his leg to free it from the dog's grip, but the canine wouldn't release its hold on his ankle. It rolled its eyes to look up at Kevin. They burned like chunks of hot coal through the dark, damp air.

"Holy shit!" In his five years of police work, he'd seen all sorts of disturbing

things – abuse, bloody violence, junkies – but he'd never seen anything like those eyes before. He brought the flashlight down hard on top of the dog's skull.

The dog unlocked his hold. It whimpered before it bared sharp, yellowed fangs, and snarled.

Something ancient and primal wafted up to Kevin's nostrils – a mineral hot spring, seething and burbling from deep in the earth. He scrambled up the ladder, his acrophobia replaced by a new fear. A fear of the unknown. The set of red eyes still seared into his brain.

No wonder Dianne was panicked.

But why would she be so frightened of a dog that was outside? Was there someone, or some*thing* up there in the attic with her too?

Wednesday, 5:04 PM

Chapter Twenty-Four

I hunker over with Megan tucked firmly in my arm, trying to concentrate on planting one foot in front of the other. Trying to think of what lies ahead of me – Kevin, a ladder, an escape, safety. Trying not to think of what lies behind me – a pissed off, injured dog, who's trying to struggle to his feet and kill us. And a second dog, determined to bounce his way into the attic to help with the attack.

I can no longer hear the clicking of sharp claws on top of the dryer. Maybe that dog lost interest and left. The wounded gray is definitely still here. He's clawing at the floor, trying to propel his way over to us. He's also moaning, growling and snarling – basically letting me know he's going to get revenge against me for stabbing him. Soon he'll regain his footing, probably super-power heal in a matter of seconds, then pounce into the middle of my back.

Ridiculous.

Ridiculous? Grandma, that's my line. But you're right. Everything about these creatures is ridiculous, and unbelievably believable.

I hug Megan tighter, stumble over the last several feet of dimly lit attic floor, and reach the window. I see the beam of Kevin's flashlight moving around in the backyard. I want to call to him, shout out a warning, but I don't dare. Noise tends to rile the dogs. The last thing I need is for the dog behind me and the one below me to get more worked up.

Be careful, Kevin. The dog from the utility room could be outside now. Waiting. Watching. Stalking you.

The seconds drag their feet like hours.

Hurry with the ladder, Kevin. Please, hurry.

A set of red, glowing eyes shine on the ground below. We're still surrounded, with no safe escape route. Maybe Kevin will shoot the dog on the ground, then we can climb down the ladder, run for a vehicle and peel the hell out of here.

Behind me, the gray stretches out his front legs and pushes his hind-end up in the air, like a puppy wanting to frolic and play. But this is no pup, and he has no innocent puppy games on his mind. He pulls his lips back over discolored fangs, opens his jaw, and hisses. A cloud of putrid sulfur expels from the dog's mouth, stirring the attic dust into airborne particles, which float like ashes in the white slash of the headlight beams. The unbelievable stench is almost more than I can bear.

I scream, long and loud.

The dog tries to propel his body forward with his back legs, but he is too weak. He falls back to the floor.

I take seven more running, stumbling steps, and I am there. I reach out an arm and fall against the window frame. We made it.

At least we made it this far.

I hear a familiar noise. A creaking. Metal against rusted metal. The garage door. Grandma keeps the ladder in the garage. A beam of light bobs below. Kevin's coming! He's on his way to rescue us. My knight with shining flashlight. My heartbeat speeds.

The aluminum extension ladder rattles when he clunks it against the house. He aims the light up into my face. I've never felt happier to be temporarily blinded. But I can still see the burning red eyes of a dog in the yard near Kevin's feet. Are the eyes really there, or is my mind fooling with me?

"Be careful," I mouth.

I glance back into the depths of the attic. The injured gray dog rises awkwardly to his feet. I have to get Megan out the window before the monster can reach us. I try to open the window, but it won't slide up. The gray lifts his body and staggers in our direction. I can't tear my eyes away from his hypnotic, ruby stare. He's moving closer. Closer. The only sounds I can hear is that of his dragging paws across the attic floor, and the thudding of my own heart.

I try the window again, but it's stuck. Jammed. Painted shut. "I c-c-can't get it open." I whack on the frame with a fist until my hand aches.

Two red spots shine below, near Kevin, like flares on a dark, empty road. "Kevin, watch out."

I keep my back turned to the injured attic dog, protecting Megan with my body. I scoot away from the window. When the dog attacks me, I don't want the force of his weight to push us through the glass, knock us to the ground and into the jaws of the dog waiting below. I close my eyes and brace myself for when the gray's big body slams us into the wall.

The window bursts with a deafening crash. Glass flies. I turn my face aside and shield Megan. Shards spray my shoulder, pelt the side of my head. Did the gray just shove us through the window? I felt neither the fall nor the landing. I pat myself on the shoulder, feel down my arm. I'm still in one piece. Megan seems fine. Bits of glass litter the attic floor. No, it wasn't the gray dog who broke the window – the glass broke inward, not outward.

Realization cold-cocks me. The dog outside must have climbed the ladder and broken through the window. What happened to Kevin? What did the dog do to Kevin? I sit perfectly still, waiting for the inevitable stench of sulfur to drift in through the window frame. Waiting for fangs to sink into my flesh.

But neither comes.

I open my eyes, expecting a dog's blood-spattered body to push through the empty window frame. Instead, I see a flashlight, gripped in a big, familiar hand. The Maglite makes a circular motion and knocks the clinging shards of glass tinkling to the floor. The flashlight drops. A pistol barrel appears through the frame.

"You alright?" Kevin pokes his face in, scans the room, his sidearm at the ready.

Tears spring to my eyes at the sight of him. He made it. He's here. He's safe. He'll see the gray dog. He'll shoot the gray dog. Gray dog will fall down dead. I cover Megan's ears with my hands, try to squeeze my own eardrums shut.

No gunfire ricochets through the attic. Why doesn't he shoot?

"Shoot it!"

"Shoot what?"

I open my eyes, but can't bear to look behind me. "The dog." I jab a thumb over my shoulder, squeeze my eyes shut again. I can't force myself to look at the beast with his red eyes and the fork I jabbed into him still poking from his chest. As much as I hate the freaky, climbing, hissing dog, I don't want to watch him suffer or die. I've witnessed enough death.

"Dianne, there's nothing there."

"Yes there is. C-c-can't you see his red eyes?"

"No."

"You d-d-don't believe me, d-d-do you?" I knew he'd think I was crazy. I knew it. Maybe he's right. Maybe I am crazy. Maybe this whole thing, the whole day, has been a hallucination. A mirage. A flashback trip on LSD.

Except I never did LSD.

The bite wounds on my thumb, ankle, and leg throb, reminding me I'm not delusional. "It's not my imagination," I insist. I'm still tensed, waiting for the dog's weight to pummel against my back. I force my eyes open and turn to look back in the attic for myself.

There's nothing there. No injured dog. No glowing eyes. "He's gone." I snatch up the flashlight Kevin dropped and rake the beam across the entire attic.

The trap door is ajar.

The dog must have slipped down through the door when I had my back turned.

"You don't believe me do you?" Having Kevin think me sane seems vastly important at the moment.

"I do believe you." Kevin pushes his torso in through the broken window. "I saw it with my own eyes. I felt it with my own ankle."

What does he mean? Did the dog bite him? How did I miss that? I must have been watching the gray stagger to his feet and start after me. I guess I was a little distracted.

Kevin uses his shirtsleeve to brush the glass to one side. He pulls his lower body and legs through the window frame, knee walks over to me and Megan. He drops the hand with the gun to his side, and lays his other palm against my face. He gazes deep into my eyes. His hand is warm, comforting, strong. "I'm so glad to see you," he says. "Are you sure you're alright?"

I nod, tears of relief threatening again.

"And the baby?"

"She's okay."

"How did a dog get up in the attic with you?"

I point to the hole in the ceiling.

Kevin shakes his head. "You have got to be kidding me."

"No. And the dog that bit you was trying to get in through the attic door just a few minutes ago." I thrust my chin towards the partially opened trap door. "There."

"I'll take care of that." Kevin stands, bends at the waist, and hustles towards the trapdoor.

Outside comes the unmistakable sound of dog claws against metal. "What the…" I poke my head out through the missing window. I wouldn't believe it, if I wasn't seeing it with my own eyes: The gray is climbing the ladder. With each step, the wooden fork handle taps against a rung and the dog whimpers, but the pain doesn't stop him. He keeps climbing.

I gasp. "Kevin….the dog."

"What?" He's made it to the other side of the attic. He's wrestling with the heavy trap door.

"It's c-c-climbing the ladder."

"Huh?." With a solid *thunk* Kevin settles the door into place. He rushes back towards us, but the dog is closer. It's going to reach Megan and me before Kevin does.

The gray pulls himself up another rung.

I shove at the ladder with one hand. It barely budges. "Hurry, Kevin." but I know he won't make it back to us in time to help. This is something I have to take care of myself. I need both hands.

The dog climbs another rung. The wooden fork handle ticks against the aluminum ladder. The dog lets out a painful, anger-filled growl. The sulfur of his breath stagnates the salt-tinged air.

I lie Megan on the floor. She coughs. I ache to grab her back into my arms, but I can't. Not yet. First I have to get rid of this vile, stinking dog. I push at the ladder, use all my strength. It starts to fall away from the house. The dog shows his fangs, grapples with his paws, leans forward. The ladder pauses in midair before it clanks back against the house. This dog must weigh one-fifty. Which means it outweighs me by about 15 pounds.

The gray regains his balance and climbs two more rungs. The sulfur smell intensifies. I breathe through my mouth. The scent lands on my tongue, polluting my taste buds. It makes me gag.

Only one more rung and the gray will be at the window, then in, and it's over for all three of us.

Kevin is only two-thirds of the way back across the attic. The dog will be inside and on top of me before Kevin can get here.

Kevin takes two giant stooped-over strides and throws himself down onto his belly. He slides through the glass to the window like a baseball player sliding home. He holds his arms up and out in front of him and hits the ladder full force with his palms.

The ladder is falling. But so is Kevin. The forward motion carries his upper body out the window. He's going to tumble to the ground along with the injured dog.

"Kevin!" I've got to stop his fall. I grab hold of his legs, one in each hand, and plunk down hard on my butt. I brace with my feet against the wall, one on each side of the window frame. The momentum of Kevin's weight lifts me part way onto my feet. I push with my legs, pull with my arms. Kevin's body stops with a sharp jerk.

The ladder clatters to the ground. Shots pierce the night.

"Hell, I missed."

Megan wails.

"Kevin, I can't hold on much longer."

"Okay, baby."

Baby? As inappropriate as it is to feel warm and fuzzy with Kevin hanging upside down out the window, me holding onto him with all my might and Megan lying in a layer of dust, coughing, I still feel warm and fuzzy. But dang, Kevin is heavy. He's thin, but he's tall and he's solid muscle.

My grip slips. I picture him landing in a broken heap near the fallen ladder and my old familiar friend, Panic starts to take hold of me again. "Kevin…" My arms quiver, my strained shoulder burns, my injured thumb throbs.

Somehow Kevin pushes his way backwards against the side of the house until he's crawled with his hands back inside the attic. I throw myself into his embrace and shower his face with kisses. The comforting scent of his after shave settles around me.

"Whoa." He chuckles. "I'm going to have to rescue damsels in distress more often." He re-holsters his gun.

I stiffen. I didn't kiss him because he'd rescued me. I kissed him because I was glad he didn't plummet head first to the ground. "Hey, who just rescued who here? Besides, look around, you goof. I'm not exactly rescued yet."

"True," he brushes at dust and bits of glass on his shirtfront, "but you're as good as rescued. I'm just working out the details." He leans my way and kisses me full on the mouth. A long, deep, juicy kiss that leaves my bells ringing even after I pull away. My face heats. I'm glad the light's dim up here so Kevin can't see me blush. I pick up Megan, hoping the action will mask my pleasure and embarrassment. Megan's cries immediately quiet.

Outside, something thumps against the tool shed. A jolt of panic replaces the kiss-induced buzz "What about the dogs? What should we do?"

Kevin and I both peer out the window opening. Two sets of red eyes glow from the dark, shadowy outskirts of the yard. A canine form slinks in front of the sedan's headlights, throwing a wolf shadow-puppet along the attic walls again.

Kevin whips out his sidearm, points it out the window frame and fires a shot. One of the headlights explodes with a *pop* and our light source diminishes by half. "Ah, nuts. I hit the headlight. That'll be a fun one to explain to the chief."

He tracks the dogs' eyes with the barrel of his gun, fires five more shots. The noise is phenomenal inside the attic chamber. Megan wails. The two sets of burning embers travel to the backyard. Kevin fires another round. The eyes move further away.

"Missed again. I swear I hit both of them directly in the heart, multiple times. What are they, phantom dogs from hell?"

I envision the dogs chugging after me like steam locomotives through the mist, the black dog ripping into Mel's flesh, the evil sulfur hiss of the injured gray. I shudder. "You have no idea."

"I'll call for some backup." Kevin reaches for the cell phone case on his belt. The case is empty. "Where's my phone?" He shines the flashlight on the floor around the window and along the path he took to the trap door. No cell phone lays in the dust.

Megan coughs.

"I must have dropped it."

"Probably when you were hanging upside down out the window."

"Yep. Shit."

Kevin is quiet. Megan coughs again, breaking the silence. I cuddle her closer to my body.

"I think we'll tackle the dogs in the morning, when we can see," Kevin says.

The light in the attic has dimmed considerably since he shot out one of the headlights. "You m-m-mean spend the night? Up here? Together?" I have fantasized about a sleepover reunion between me and Kevin, sure, but the settings in my fantasies are far more romantic than a dusty, spider-infested attic.

Sometimes reality really does bite.

Besides, it's not only the spiders that bother me. A vision of the brown dog chewing through the utility room door, his eyes bouncing up to the dryer in the dark niggles at me. The gray clawing through the roof, his body hovering over mine before plunging himself onto the meat fork sets my teeth on edge. The same dog, pulling his injured body up the ladder, meat fork clinking on each rung gives me a bad case of the jitters.

"I don't want to stay up here." My voice sounds childish and whiny. I feel like a five-year-old, with imaginary crocodiles under my bed. Only this time the sharp-toothed monsters aren't make-believe. "What if the dogs climb up on the roof again and come in through the hole?"

Chapter Twenty-Five

Wednesday, 5:50 PM

"I'll sit guard," Kevin says.

"What if I fall asleep? What if you fall asleep and the dogs come back and shove aside the attic door? Or, like I mentioned before, what if they climb onto the roof and squeeze in through the hole? Huh, what then?" I hold Megan tight to stop my trembling, but my legs and arms, hands and fingers continue to quiver.

Kevin takes my hand. He notices my thumb wrapped in blood-soaked gauze for the first time. "What happened here?"

"One of the dogs bit me."

"I thought you said you were alright."

"I am alright." But I think about the possibility of rabies, and even as I say the words, I wonder if they're true.

"Are you hurt anywhere else?"

I nod. "But I'm alright."

"Where are you hurt? Let me see."

I shift Megan so I have a free hand. With shaking fingers I lift up my pants leg, show him the swollen ankle and the welts on my calf from the black's teeth.

Kevin lets out a low whistle. "That ankle looks serious. We need to get you to a doctor."

And face a long needle poked eight inches into my belly button? No thanks. "It'll wait till morning. You're right. As much as I hate the thought of spending another minute in this attic, it's the safest place right now." I push my pant leg back down. Kevin got bit too. If I have to get rabies shots, so will he. Mean as it might be, I'm slightly comforted by the thought. At least I won't have to go through the treatments alone.

How pathetic am I?

I change the subject. "I sure wish I'd grabbed the diaper bag out of my Blazer. Poor Megan hasn't had a diaper change since I left my apartment this morning."

"Let's take care of that." Kevin undoes the top button of his shirt.

What is he doing?

He slips a couple more buttons out of their holes.

Why is he unbuttoning his shirt?

He's wearing a white, sleeveless tee under his blue dress shirt. It clings to his chest in a very appealing way. He removes the tank. As he moves, his bare muscles dip and swim in the dim light. I can smell the male musk of his skin, mingled with deodorant, faint traces of soap, and his intoxicating aftershave. I long to lay my head on his chest and run my fingers through the dusting of dark golden hair. He's sprouted more hair on his chest since the last time I saw him shirtless six years ago.

Kevin hands me his tank. I snap back to planet earth. "Uh, thanks."

"You're welcome." He picks up his dress shirt, preparing to pull it back on.

The light and shadows play over his biceps, triceps and cheekbones. If I had my camera I could capture the beauty of his masculine lines. I watch him put first one arm and then the other into the sleeves. It's like a sensuous, reverse strip tease.

"Er, Kevin?"

"Yes?"

He eases buttons through their holes, once more covering his body.

Nonchalantly, I swipe the back of my hand over my lips, in case there's any drool. "Why did you give me your shirt?"

"You said you wanted to change the baby and you didn't have a diaper."

"Oh. Uh, yeah." Duh.

He gives me that quizzical look again. "Sure you're alright?"

"I think so." At least I thought I was all right until I saw him half naked. I've got a baby to raise. I don't need a man to complicate things. I don't need a man. I don't need a man. I don't need a man.

Who says you don't need a man?

Grandma, you're not helping here.

Well, really Dianne. What makes you think a good man – the right man – can't help you raise Megan?

"I don't know."

Did I say that in my out-loud voice? Kevin gives me a quizzical look. Oops, guess I did say it out loud.

Can I really trust him Grandma? How many times can I let the same man break my heart? I can't let him hurt Megan too.

He was young.

So was I, but it still hurt like crazy.

He'll learn.

What will he learn? And when will he learn it?

Everything that matters. Be patient.

Patient? I've been waiting six years for an explanation from him that I've never gotten, and you're telling me to be patient?

As if reading my mind, Kevin says, "I'll keep you and Megan safe. Trust me."

I want to trust him. What choice do I have? He's all I've got right now to help me keep Megan safe. Him and Grandma. And I'm not sure Grandma's reasoning is exactly spot-on since she's gotten dead.

Kevin brushes at the floor, making sure it's free of glass. I lie Megan down in the dusted spot, unsnap her pink romper and remove her saturated diaper. I fold and twist Kevin's shirt into a rough diaper shape. With his help, I knot it at Megan's hips. It's not pretty, and I wish for a pair of old-fashioned plastic pants, but the cotton tank alone will have to do. I refasten her jumper, pick her up and snuggle her close. At least she's dry now. It must be a lot more comfortable for her. I wish there was a bathroom up here. I still have to pee something fierce.

The rumbling motor of Kevin's car falters, sputters and dies.

I look at Kevin. "What...?"

"Out of gas. I knew it was getting low. I didn't want to take the time to stop and fill up. I just wanted to find you."

"What made you come looking for us?"

"Well...um, I...sent you flowers...in memory of your grandma, but when you didn't take them in off your front step, I figured you hadn't been home. With all the disappearances around town lately, I got worried."

"That reminds me..." I pick up the section of newspaper with the old story about the missing boy and his family. I hand the paper to Kevin. "Isn't this the cashier from the market? The one you were talking with this morning?"

"Yes. Arlene Smith."

"She didn't have the snake tattoo or facial piercings when this picture was taken."

"She got those shortly after her son disappeared."

"I wonder why."

"Anger, I think, confusion. She'd had a stroke, lost partial use of one side of her body. The stroke caused some brain damage. Then her son vanished."

I remember Grandma's words that morning: "Don't judge a book by its cover."

I look at Megan resting in my arms. If anything ever happened to her I'd probably do some dark, uncharacteristic things too. "Poor woman. I don't blame her for being angry." I refold the paper and set it aside.

From some distance away, a dog howls. A shiver the size of California wrestles along my backbone. Kevin stiffens, sits up straighter, his muscles taut as if he's ready to pounce.

"They're not close," I say.

Kevin nods.

"She warned me this morning."

"Who warned you?" Kevin asks. "About what?"

"The cashier. Looking back, I think she was warning me about the dogs."

Kevin gently pulls me and Megan closer to him. "Tell me about the dogs."

I settle in closer, lean my head on his shoulder. "What do you want to know?"

"Did you notice their eyes?"

"How could I not notice? It's the first thing I noticed. The second thing was the way they smell."

"Yeah, they stink. And not like typical dog either. It's more like rotten eggs."

I nod. "Or matches. They smell like sulfur." Like something from the bowels of the earth. I don't want to talk about the dogs – I don't want to relive the day. Yet if I don't talk it out, I'm afraid I'll go ballistic. I take a deep breath. "They killed Grandma's dog. They killed Bubba." I can't force myself to tell him about Mel. Not yet.

"I'm sorry."

I nod, but don't say anything.

"He seemed like a dog with a kind soul." Kevin knew Bubba from when we used to date.

I don't say anything.

"Are you alright?" Kevin asks. His arm around me tightens.

"I was just thinking about something Pastor McCann told me years ago."

"What was that?"

"When I was ten, I asked him if my cat, Amanda, would go to heaven when she died."

"What did he tell you?"

I pause, squeeze my eyes shut to avoid tears. "He said animals don't have souls." I hesitate and swallow the tears building in my throat. "He said animals don't go to heaven."

"Did you believe him?"

"I didn't want to, but I figured the pastor had a special "in" with God. I figured he must know what he was talking about. His words crushed me. I decided right then and there, if there was no miracle strong enough to get my sweet kitty through the gates of heaven, there were no miracles at all. Except for people going to heaven – I couldn't make myself not believe in that – but as far as luck, deja-vu, ESP, all that supernatural stuff, I refused to believe any of it after that day."

"I've often wondered about that. You're the only person I know who doesn't believe in luck."

"Now you know why."

"Pastor McCann is a good man, but he's only a man. He doesn't know everything."

"But he showed me a Bible verse to back it up."

The Bible is God's love letter, different in meaning for each of us. Listen to your own heart for the answers. Each person's truth is their own.

There she goes again. Grandma, the philosopher.

I study Kevin's face. He looks like his thoughts are far away, but there's no evidence he heard the voice of a ghost. Or a spirit. Or an angel – whatever Grandma is now.

While he's not paying attention, I study his features. Even half-shadowed, he's a handsome man, his chin and jaw line strong and masculine. What would've happened to me and Megan if he hadn't gotten here when he did? Goose bumps pop out on my arms. I lean against his chest.

"You know something? I think I do now," I say.

Kevin lays his arm over my shoulder and nuzzles my hair. "Mmmm…? You think you do what now?"

"Believe in luck, you goof."

"That's the second time you've called me a goof tonight. I might start getting a complex if you keep it up."

I pull away and give him a playful punch on the arm. "Kind of like the complex you gave me after you dumped me three separate times?"

Kevin rests his chin on the top of my head. "I'm sorry, Dianne. I really am.

I don't know why I did that." His voice is full of regret. "I was a fool. A goof. Whatever you want to call me, it's what I was. "

"You're wonderful, that's what you are." I may not totally trust Kevin, but I don't want him feeling guilty about those lousy breakups years ago. Not now. Not after he just saved our lives. So I change the subject, swing the conversation back to Bubba.

"Bubba was a good, loyal dog. I'm going to miss him. He gave his life to protect Megan and me. No one can convince me he didn't have a soul."

I lean back into Kevin again. "And you coming along when you did? No one can tell me there's no such thing as miracles either. You are my miracle." Megan stretches in my arms and yawns like a little bird. I smile down at her. "You and this baby girl."

"You've always been my miracle, Dianne. I've missed you so much." Kevin tips my chin. His lips meet mine. For a moment, I bask in the closeness of his face, his body, his scent. Then I pull away.

"What?" Kevin tries to draw me back to him.

I don't let him. "There's more."

"More what, calling me a goof?"

"No. More about the dogs." It's time to tell him the whole story. I can't keep kissing him and pretending away the vision of the dogs ripping into Mel. Kevin's a detective. He needs to know. I suck in a shaky breath. Hold it for a moment. Let it out with a river of words: "They killed a man. I watched it happen. I couldn't do anything to stop them." I can't do anything to stop the tears rushing down my cheeks either. I choke back a sob. "All I did was sit there inside my rig and snap pictures. The dogs drug his body away and lapped up every drop of blood."

"Who was the man?"

"The tow-truck driver. His name was Mel."

"My God, Dianne, how long have the dogs been after you?"

"All day. I saw the first one at the market, right before I ran into you."

"Why didn't you say anything?"

"At first I thought I must be imagining the red eyes. I started to tell you when I was waiting for the tow truck, but you got a phone call and had to leave. Besides, I didn't want you to think I was crazy."

"Too late. I've always thought you were crazy." Kevin squeezes my shoulders.

"Very funny."

"You know I'm kidding – just trying to make you feel better."

"It's not working. Kevin, I'm scared. Why are the dogs after us? What did I ever do to them?"

"You didn't do anything, but you've had a run of bad luck. I know how you feel about the concept of luck, so let me rephrase that – you've had a series of unfortunate events."

"What does that have to do with anything?"

"I'm not sure, but maybe the dogs feed off misfortune."

"That sounds pretty far-fetched." And then I remember. "Wait a minute. Mel was reminiscing about the great uncle he'd lost recently," my voice catches, "right before the dogs attacked him."

Kevin holds me tight. "Could be the dogs who took Arlene Smith's son."

"His mom had her stroke a few months before he disappeared…"

"Uh-huh."

"…and didn't the sanitation driver recently lose a child to cancer?"

"Yes, a daughter. Leukemia."

"What about the jogger? Emily, wasn't it ? She was my same age."

"Her husband had an affair, filed for divorce and kicked her out of their home."

"Ouch."

"Could be the dogs who got all three of the vanishing vics."

"Four. Don't forget Mel."

"Right. Four."

We are both silent for a while before Kevin says, "We've been looking for a two-legged serial killer. Never in a million years did we suspect killer dogs."

"I don't want to be next. I can't let the dogs get to Megan."

"Don't worry. I'll keep you both safe."

I think of his bullets, unable to stop the dogs. How is he planning to protect us?

The lone headlight on his car dims. Fades. Extinguishes. We are plunged into complete blackness.

Chapter Twenty-Six

Wednesday, 6:48 PM

Kevin clicks on the flashlight. He beams it out through the attic window opening, scans the yard, then shines the light up through the hole in the roof. No red eyes appear. No sulfur stench drifts into the attic. He clicks off the flashlight. "We'd best conserve the batteries. Why don't you try to get some sleep?"

"I can't." I wipe at the tears drying on my face. I do feel slightly better after telling Kevin about Mel.

"Why not? I told you, I'll keep watch."

"It's not that. Well, it's partly that, but it's also…" I'm not sure why I'm so embarrassed about this, "…I have to go to the bathroom. Bad."

"How bad?"

"Really bad."

"You're going to have to go up here, you know."

"I know. There's some pots and pans in the boxes over by the attic door. I could use one of those."

"As long as you don't use that pan to cook dinner for me." Kevin jokes. He clicks the flashlight back on.

I put a hand on a hip, which doesn't have the effect I was going for since I'm sitting down. "What makes you think I'm going to cook for you?"

"Well, you know, since I rescued you and all," Kevin lays the southern accent on thick. He used to do that when I was upset, to make me smile. "I figure you'll want to do something nice to thank me. A little fried chicken and corn bread, some okra. Maybe some rice and red beans."

The mention of food, even slimy food like okra, reminds me how little I've eaten today. My stomach grumbles a complaint. "You figure that, do you? How about if we discuss a home-cooked meal later, *after* you've actually gotten us down out of here, and *after* I've peed. Right now if you'd be so kind as to hold Megan and shine the flashlight over yonder," I mimic his drawl, "I'll meander that way and fetch a pot to piss in."

Kevin chuckles. He takes Megan from me and shines the light towards the boxes and the trap door.

I start across the attic floor. It feels like a journey of a million steps. I hate to leave Megan, even under Kevin's watchful eye. Whenever I leave Megan today, even for a minute, the dogs show up. If my eyeballs weren't floating, I wouldn't leave her now. I shuffle as fast as I can towards the boxes, trying to convince myself I have nothing to worry about. Kevin's here. He's got a gun. But either he's a horrible shot, or bullets simply won't kill these dogs.

Maybe they're like werewolves and we'll have to drive a stake through their hearts. I must have gotten that meat fork pretty close to the gray's heart. But doesn't a werewolf spike have to be made of pure silver or something? Doesn't matter. They're not werewolves. At least I don't think they are. Besides, I stabbed the gray. He's the climber, and now he's injured. Surely, he can't get all the way to the roof with a fork protruding from his body. And the ladder's laying on the ground, so he can't climb that. Unless the dogs can walk straight up a house, they can't get in through the window. As for the trap door? Kevin shut that tight. I watched him. I heard it thunk into place.

I'm halfway across the attic floor. I glance back at Kevin and Megan. He gives me a nod. I trundle the rest of the way to the boxes. Reaching them, I drop to my knees and dig around inside the one containing the kitchen items. I pull out a deep, aluminum pot. My bladder is so full I hope I can hold it long enough to unfasten my pants. I fumble with the snap, dance around.

"You gonna make it?"

I'm ready to burst, and he's laughing at me. "Just turn your head, will you? I don't need an audience."

"Don't look, Megan, your mommy has to piddle."

"I'm not a dog." I snap, thinking of the rabies I may be carrying.

"I didn't call you a dog."

"Puppies piddle. Women pee." I slide down my zipper. Kevin is gentleman enough to turn his head away. I whip down my pants, squat over the pot and let it flow. It's all I can do not to moan with relief.

A dog howls from the backyard.

I cut off my urine in midstream to listen. Another dog answers from under the attic window. I jerk up my pants. I have to get back to Megan. I don't bother to refasten my jeans, I scurry back towards Kevin and my baby.

Kevin swings the flashlight beam away from my path and points it out the window.

"Kevin!" I whisper. I can't see a thing in front of me now.

"Sorry." He aims the light back at my feet. "I had to see where they were. They're right under the window. They're both out there."

"Shhhh." He's talking too loud. Doesn't he understand noises rile them?

"Hurry. I need you to take Megan."

The dogs scratch and leap against the house. What's their plan now? Are they going to claw footholds in the siding? My legs are suddenly too weak to hold me. I drop to all fours and crawl. It feels like I'm a football field away from Megan. My knees ache from the rough wooden floor.

"Hurry, Dianne."

"I'm hurrying." I give more rev to my crawl, but it still seems like I'm moving in slow motion, like a wind-up toy with worn-out gears. My unfastened pants are slipping down off my rear end. Great. Another bit of comedy at my expense to amuse Kevin.

The dogs dig at the vinyl siding. The noise is deafening. I cover the last two yards and snatch Megan out of Kevin's arm. "Cover her ears," he says and points the flashlight and his semi-automatic out the window. He fires a few rounds before the pistol makes a hollow click. "Damn." Kevin drops out the empty clip and rams in a new one.

I brave a peek out the window. The dogs have scattered and are retreating. Kevin points the gun at their backsides and squeezes off more rounds. The dogs keep running. I don't hear any yelps of pain.

I yank up my pants and try to fasten them with one hand. It doesn't work.

"No way," Kevin insists. "There is no way I could completely miss them. I'm a proven marksman. I've won trophies. I couldn't miss that big a target at such close range."

"Maybe you didn't miss."

"What are you suggesting?"

"I don't know. They're not normal dogs."

"I can see that. But if bullets won't kill them, what will?"

I shake my head. "I don't know. Stabbing them with a meat fork doesn't kill them either. At least the sound of the shots scared them away. For a while. But they'll be back." That hopeless, helpless feeling squashes onto my shoulders like a concrete slab. "They always come back."

The gunfire frightened Megan too. She's crying. Probably getting hungry again. "I'm going to nurse her." I usually nurse in private, but these are special circumstances. Besides, I just peed in front of Kevin. And he's seen all my fun parts years ago. Why act modest now?

"Do you need the light?"

"Just for a minute." I fumble with my clothing. Once Megan latches onto a nipple I say, "Okay, you can turn it off."

"Easy for you to say." Kevin's voice is husky.

The sight of my lactating breast and big old honkin' nipple turns him on? That's kind of sweet.

"Dianne?"

"Hmmm?"

"You're beautiful."

"Thank you." I'm glad it's dark so Kevin can't see the flush heating my cheeks.

When Megan's had enough milk, I readjust my clothing and lean back against Kevin. His body is hard, like my own personal rock. He brushes a kiss across my hairline. "Do you think you can sleep now?"

I shrug. I don't want to speak and ruin the moment, or wake Megan. She's had a tough day. We've all had a tough day.

I close my eyes. I hear a whimper. It's the gray dog. He's right beside me. I bat at him with my fists. He ducks my blows. He lays a paw on my shoulder and shakes me.

"Wake up, Dianne."

The gray can talk?

"You're thrashing."

My lids fly open. Instead of fiery red eyes glaring at me, friendly golden-brown eyes gaze into mine. "Oh, good. It's just you."

"Just me? Thanks a lot."

"I didn't mean it like that. I had a nightmare – one of the dogs was here, beside me. I tried to hit him, but he started talking."

Dark shadows rim Kevin's eyes, but they still twinkle back at me with amusement. "What did he say?"

"I don't know. You woke me up." I yawn. Reality trickles into place and I recall yesterday's events. I also remember today's a holiday. "Happy Thanksgiving."

"Back at you, babe. How do you feel?"

Babe? Nice. How do I feel? My neck's stiff, my shoulder and knee ache and the dog bites on my thumb and ankle throb. But what good does it do to complain? "I'm okay. Hey, it's not pitch black anymore. I can see you."

"Yep, imagine that. It's dawn."

"I slept all night?" I sit up, rub my eyes and check on Megan. She's still asleep on my lap.

"If you could call it that. You tossed and turned and moaned a lot."

I run the fingers of my good hand through my tangled hair, wishing for a comb, a warm, wet washcloth and a toothbrush. "Sorry about that."

"No, it's alright. It kind of turned me on."

I smile and shake my head. Men. Such charmingly simple creatures.

"And you left your pants undone, so I had my way with you while you were sleeping."

"Oh, you are a funny man," I say it with sarcasm, but I can't help grinning. "Did you stay awake all night?"

"I told you I would." He sounds offended. Cranky from lack of sleep, I suppose.

"The dogs didn't come back?"

"No sign of them. Let's get out of here. No sense spending Thanksgiving Day in an attic. I'll go out and hold the ladder."

Kevin checks the rounds in his gun – for all the good non-dog killing bullets will do him. He crosses the attic, pushes aside the door and drops to the dryer. He settles the trap door back into place. I hear him drop to the utility room floor, walk through the house and exit out the garage.

The sun rises orange, trying its mightiest to burn through the morning fog. I can barely make Kevin out through the mist as he turns his back and relieves himself behind the tool shed. When he's finished his business, he crosses the yard to the ladder, heaves it up and clunks it back against the house.

"Ready?" he asks.

"Just about."

"Would you drop me the flashlight before you climb down?"

"Sure." I retrieve the Maglight and release it over Kevin's head. He catches it and sets it on the ground. "Okay, we're coming down." Carefully, I lie Megan on the floor near the window. She wakes up and fusses. "Just a minute, baby. We're going to get out of here." I snap and zip my jeans, turn around, back out the window and start down the ladder. It wobbles and clanks. "Are you holding it?"

"Yes. I'm holding it." Kevin sounds exasperated. It must be exhausting being a hero 24/7.

"Hold it tight, I have to get Megan now." I lean against the ladder and reach inside the attic for the baby. "Ready, sweet pie? Hold still for Mommy." I sling her in one arm, hoping she doesn't squirm and kick. Slowly, step after step, I make my way down.

I'm halfway to the ground. So far, so good. Megan's holding still. I shift her so I can use the fingertips of the hand holding her to sort of balance myself against the ladder.

"You're almost there," Kevin says, "two more rungs." I feel his hand on the back of my thigh to help steady me.

I step down, stretching a toe for the final step. The black dog lunges out of the mist and snatches Megan from my arms.

Part Five: The Edge

Chapter Twenty-Seven

Thursday, 7:22 AM

The black beast lopes off into the mist, Megan's pink romper clenched between his teeth. Megan flails her arms. Her shrill cries pierce the frigid morning air.

Kevin draws his pistol and aims it at the retreating dog. I wait for the shot. None comes.

"Shoot!" I scream.

"I can't. I might hit Megan." He lowers his gun and tears down the road after the dog. The ball of each foot twists as he launches forward for the next step. He leaves behind a trail of half foot prints in the damp gravel.

The dog and Megan's pink jumper vanish into the November morning mist.

Soon Kevin will disappear too.

I try to follow, but I can't. My legs have turned to Jell-O. Everything around me grows white – like a photograph overexposed in bright sunlight. Then the grass, the sky, and Grandma's house all dull, darken, fade to black.

***

Thursday, 7:23 AM

In high-school track, Kevin was a short-distance runner. As an adult, he competed in the Hero Olympics every year. He always placed high in the sprint heats against other public servants – cops and firefighters – but today he was no match for the black dog.

The speeding beast soon gained enough distance that Kevin lost sight of it in the dim fog. For a few seconds he could still see Megan's outfit, like a bright pink beacon in the dawning light. Then it too vanished.

Kevin pushed on anyway, running until his chest burned and his breath came in raspy blows. He ran for the baby's life. He ran for Dianne. He ran to prove his own self worth.

He'd promised to keep Dianne and her baby safe, but he'd failed.

He had to find the dog, rescue Megan, and get her safely back to Dianne. Not only for Dianne's sake. Not only for the baby. But for himself – for the sake of his own pride and for a shot at a future with them both.

After several minutes with no glimpse of the elusive dog, he decided he couldn't keep running after something he couldn't see. It didn't make sense. He stopped to check for tracks. The cold morning air burned his over-worked lungs. The gravel and the earth were wet, the shoulder of the road muddy – perfect tracking weather. But there were no paw prints, no bent grass, no bruised vegetation. No sign whatsoever that a dog ran through this way, although he knew one had. He'd watched it with his own eyes, followed it with his own flying feet. How could there be no tracks, no sign to follow?

He backtracked a few yards to check for his own footprints. There they were, half footprints from running fast on the balls of his feet. Where were the dog's tracks? He ran on ahead, but at a slower jog now so he could scan the ground as he went.

If he couldn't find the trail, if he didn't get Megan back…or if he reached the dog too late…how would Dianne cope? She'd lost a husband, then a grandmother, now her child – it could push her over the edge. Dianne was strong, but three heavy blows in rapid succession could plow under even the strongest person.

He slowed once more then pulled up to examine the ground. Nothing. He backtracked again and scanned the road, the shoulder, a nearby yard. Still no sign of paw prints. For all he knew, the dog might circle back around to pick Dianne off, too. He couldn't leave her unattended any longer. If he lost Dianne, especially now, after they'd finally reconnected, it would push him over the edge. He needed backup. He needed help from search and rescue. He needed to give authorities a heads-up about the missing child so they could broadcast an amber alert.

Kevin turned around and sprinted back the way he'd come.

When he reached the yard of Adelle's house, he spotted Dianne, crumpled near the foot of the ladder. Was he too late? Had one or more of the dogs doubled back and attacked her?

***

Thursday, 7:40 AM

Something touches my cheek. I blink and look up into a set of eyes. It all comes flooding back – THE DOGS. The baby-snatching killer dogs. I scream. Then I realize it isn't a dog's face so close to mine, it's Kevin's face. It's him patting me on the cheek.

"Dianne? Dianne, are you alright?"

The horrible reality of what has happened comes crashing down on me with tsunami force. "Megan. Oh, God. Megan."

"Come on, let's get you to your feet."

I pull my legs up to my chest and hug them there, rocking slightly back and forth. "No, I can't." I want to stay in the fetal position with my eyes closed until I wake up from this hellish nightmare.

"You can, Dianne, and you will. We need to find Megan, and I need your help."

I moan, unfurl my legs, and with Kevin's help, unwillingly stagger to my feet. From thighs down, my legs are numb. My vision and brain feel overcast. Only one thing fills my mind: The dark shadow of a dog, loping away into the mist, my baby's romper gripped in his jaws.

The same set of jaws that tore apart a grown man's throat.

The ground rises up to catch me. A keening wail explodes from my chest. The sound is followed by a series of high-pitched mewls.

Are those noises coming from me?

I have never felt so out of control of my own limbs and vocal chords.

Kevin grips my shoulders, and yanks me to my feet. His face is concerned, but stern. Determination fills his eyes. "Dianne. I know you're upset. You have every right to be, but moaning and screaming and rolling on the ground will not get Megan back. I need your help."

His last four words slap me like a douse of ice water to the face. "How can I help? Where did the dog take my baby? What if we can't find her?" I think of what the dogs did to Mel. "What if they k-k-k…" I can't even make myself say it. I can't draw in any oxygen.

Kevin grabs me, kisses me. I struggle to breathe, push him away, draw in a giant breath. "What are you doing?"

"Making you live."

"I don't want you kissing me right now. You said you'd keep us safe. I thought we could depend on you. I should know better than to depend on you."

Kevin's expression changes from worried, to hurt, to resolved. "Yell. Scream. Call me names if you want. You have every right to be pissed off. Just don't go comatose on me."

Kevin takes my hand. "I'm calling for back up. Come with me. I want to be able to see you, keep you near." He leads me to his car. He throws something big and tan from the front seat to the back, holds the passenger door open, assists me inside and closes the door. He calls dispatch on his radio.

His voice sounds deep and garbled, far away. My mind won't make sense of his words. Then my brain tunes in and I hear him say, "Roger that. Out."

Kevin opens my door, grabs my arm and pulls me from the car. "Help's on the way. Start looking for tracks. We need to pick up the dog's trail."

We search for paw prints around the foot of the ladder. We find Kevin's cell phone face down in the mud. He wipes it on his pants and puts it back into the case on his belt. We find no dog tracks.

"How can there be no sign? Dogs would have to leave tracks in this mud," Kevin looks up from the ground. "Where else do you remember seeing the dogs?"

I pause, trying to get my brain shifted from neutral into a working gear. "Two of them came in through the spare bedroom window."

"Show me. Maybe we can start there."

I lead Kevin to the window of my old room. He's been here before. He used to toss pebbles at the glass, wake me at midnight, so we could whisper forbidden teenage conversations of love in the dark. He and I round the corner of the house. The window lays shattered on the ground.

"Alright. There should be blood, tufts of hair, paw prints here for sure," Kevin mutters. He searches the area around the window. Inspects the branches of the nearby rhododendron bush. "Nothing. How can there be nothing?" He darts me a look, like it's my fault.

I shrug. I can't explain it. I can't make any sense of these evil dogs.

"You said they followed you from the newspaper office, right?"

I nod. The vision of three chugging puffs of steam fills my thoughts. I shake my head to rid the memory.

"Is that a yes, or a no?"

God, he's getting testy. I'm the one who should be testy here. I'm the one with the missing child. "Yes," I snap.

"If the dogs ran that far along pavement and gravel…" Kevin is thinking out loud, "…the pads of their feet would be raw and bleeding."

But there are no bloody tracks. There is nothing. It's like looking for an invisible needle in an invisible haystack.

Kevin and I continue to search for clues or tracks, without finding either. We're not alone for long. Within twenty minutes, Grandma's yard is chaos. Roseland police officers, state troopers and Lincoln County deputies – a couple of them leading harnessed police dogs – arrive on the scene. SWAT team officers dressed in black haul in a huge trailer and set it up as a command center. Officers barricade the area with yellow crime-scene tape and police cars. The red and blue lights strobe through the fog.

A woman officer in a dark blue uniform comes up behind me, firmly grips my elbow, and tries to guide me in the direction of the command station. "Come with me, please," she says.

Panic fills my chest. "No!" I yell and try to yank my arm from her grasp. I don't want to sit inside a trailer, answering a zillion questions. And I don't want a woman cop with a bad bleach job and too much eye makeup trying to console me. I want to keep looking for Megan. I turn to Kevin, using my eyes to plead my case.

"Sharon," he says, "this is Dianne. She's a close friend of mine. Thank you, but she'll stay with me. Dianne, this is my co-worker Officer Sharon Brown."

Sharon glares at me, glares at Kevin. She drops my arm and jounces back to command central.

Interesting energy between those two, but I don't have brain space at the moment to analyze it.

The two officers with the German shepherds begin scouting through Grandma's yard. The tan and black dogs dash back and forth, noses to the ground. The dogs resemble low-slung, hip-dropped wolves. I try to study their faces. The animals' eyes border on obsession, but, thank God, I see no red glow.

Volunteer searchers arrive close on the heels of law enforcement. A dozen or so teenage explorer scouts. Seven members of a four-wheel drive club and countless community members eager to be of assistance. My head reels at the amount of bodies all here to help us find Megan. How did they all find out about this? Do they all have police scanners, or was there already a news flash on the TV? It's Thanksgiving too. These people had to leave their families to help us. I feel humbled and grateful, but not comforted.

I won't feel comforted until Megan is safe in my arms.

Ken Donning, the Roseland chief of police, strides over to speak with Kevin. Kevin holds up a finger and turns to me. He leads me by the hand outside of the taped area. "Wait here," Kevin says. "I have to brief them. I'll be back soon. Don't move, or I'll sic Sharon on you."

I don't like his bossy tone, or his threat. This is my grandmother's property. Who does he think he is? Who do any of them think they are, telling me where I can and can't stand? It's my baby who's missing here. I throw Kevin a dagger look.

"Please," he says.

Better. Nicer. "Okay, okay. I'll stay put." I sure as hell don't want to get trapped with Officer Sharon inside the command station.

From my designated area on the outskirts of Grandma's driveway, I watch, baffled, as the drivers of three pickups pulling horse trailers park along the shoulder of the road. Three women and two men, all wearing cowboy hats, boots and badges, unload and saddle up their five mounts in a matter of minutes.

A dark brown mare lowers her head and snorts. A cloud of vapor escapes her nostrils and rises into the air. My muscles involuntarily tense as I wait for the scent of sulfur. Frantically, I scan the horse's pupils for traces of red. But the mare's eyes are a calm, gentle brown. No sulfur stench burns through the air.

Sharon stands with a group of other officers. They huddle like football players near the ladder leading to the attic. She glances at me twice. Her glances are not friendly. Do she and Kevin have a past? Or is she hoping for a future with him? As upset as I am at Kevin for letting the dog snatch Megan, jealously lances my heart.

Ridiculous. I don't need Kevin. I don't need any man. I have a baby to raise.

A baby. Oh, God, Megan. My Megan. What is that dog doing to you?

Tears well in my eyes and run hot down my face. Sharon glares my way again, but at the sight of my tears, her expression changes. Hard determination glints in her eyes. It's similar to the transformation I watched take place on Kevin's face earlier. Sharon gives me a confident nod. She has just gone from scorned woman into full-blown cop mode.

Was she born with an ingrained sense to uphold law and order? Does it over-power the normal female jealousy/nesting instincts? I have never before comprehended a woman's desire to be a cop, but in a flash, I almost understand her need to serve and protect. I give her a return nod and brush away my tears. I know she will put her personal feelings aside now and do everything she can to find Megan.

The door of the command trailer swings open and Kevin trots down the three iron steps. He crosses the yard to me, and thrusts a chin at the horses and riders. "I see the posse's arrived."

"I wondered who they were."

"They're volunteers through the sheriff's office. Generally they do wilderness search and rescue, but when a child's missing, every available body shows up."

"What did you tell them in there?"

"Everything you told me, plus everything I saw for myself. No doubt they'll think we're both crazy when they can't locate any tracks either."

"But if they can't find any tracks, how are they going to find the dogs? How will they ever find Megan?"

"We've got the best-trained search and rescue teams here. If anyone can track those dogs, it will be these folks."

"But what if…"

"They'll comb the entire neighborhood. Send crews door to door. If anyone has seen or heard the dogs this morning, we'll soon know about it." Kevin grabs my hand. "I've got an idea." He guides me firmly but gently towards my Blazer. "My car's got a dead battery. We'll have to take yours." He opens the passenger door and helps me inside, as if I am an invalid. "Are the keys in here somewhere?"

I nod. "They're in my purse. But Kevin, we can't leave. We have to stay and find her."

"The others will still be looking around here. We're just going… somewhere else."

Chapter Twenty-Eight

Thursday, 9:03 AM

"We can't give up," I insist. "We have to keep looking for Megan."

"We're not giving up," Kevin says. "Not at all. I need you to trust me on this, okay?"

I look into his familiar gold irises. A feeling of homesickness washes over me. He takes my hand, gives it a firm squeeze. My stomach clenches into a painful knot. "Okay," I say.

But it's not okay. Nothing is okay. If I don't get Megan back safe and sound, nothing will ever be okay again.

"Find the keys for me, would you? I'll be right back." He jumps out of the Blazer and slams the door. He ducks under the police tape, sprints to his car, opens the door and sticks his head inside. He rummages through the backseat.

I dig through my purse. My hand trembles. It's like Deja-vu at the parking lot yesterday when the dogs were after me and I couldn't find my keys to get inside my Blazer. That was only yesterday? It feels like a lifetime ago.

Kevin returns, tosses something into the back of the Blazer and crawls into the driver's seat. I'm still desperately trying to locate the keys. He takes the bag from my fumbling fingers, reaches inside and pulls out my key ring on the first try. Figures. He inserts a key into the ignition. The motor fires right up. Figures again. A woman's car never acts up when there's a man at the wheel.

Kevin eases out of the driveway, but there are rigs parked all over, blocking the road. He pushes the four-wheel-drive button and steers the SUV down through a sloping ditch, then back up onto the gravel road, leaving the surreal scene behind us. I glance in the side mirror. Sniffing police dogs, snorting horses and bustling, uniformed officers fill Grandma's yard, trampling her grass and her flower beds.

I'm sorry, Grandma.

Don't be. It's not your fault. They're just doing their job. Besides, you don't really think I care about stuff like trampled flowers anymore, do you?

I guess not.

Kevin drives west on Otis Street. We meet a white van with the local news station logo emblazoned on the side. "Great. A news team. Just what we don't need," Kevin remarks. "Thank God we got out of there when we did, or our faces would be splashed all over the TV news tonight."

Once we hit the highway, he steers south.

Why are we headed south, towards town? "Where are we going?"

"We're going to visit someone who may be able to help us."

Visiting? We're going visiting? I want to fight the ridiculous idea, but I am mentally drained and exhausted. I have little fight left in me. I lay my head back and let my mind go numb. Numbing myself is the only way I can cope. The scenery blurs past my window, obscured. The sea-blown pines hold out ghostly arms in the fog, as though pointing the way.

Kevin turns onto Center Street, motors up several blocks and stops in front of a signpost. The wooden sign swings in the wind. It reads, "FORTUNES TOLD".

I've traveled past this sign hundreds of times over the years – with my mother, my grandmother, on the school bus, in my own rig – but the same itchy curiosity doesn't tug at me today as I look at the two swinging words. Today the tug feels closer to death.

I look over at Kevin, incredulous. What is he thinking? "Oh, no. I'm not going in there. What's wrong with you? A dog steals my baby and you bring me to a crazy con-artist?"

Kevin lays a hand on my knee. "You said you'd trust me, Dianne. I know this is hard for you, but just try to keep an open mind, okay? For me. For Megan." He doesn't sound one-hundred percent sure himself.

With trembling fingers, I push a wayward lock of hair out of my face. I don't want to be here. I want to go back to Grandma's and help search for Megan. But what choice do I have? It's not as if I can kick Kevin out of my vehicle, slide behind the wheel and burn rubber out of here. I'm in no condition to drive. I'd wreck for sure, probably kill myself, maybe maim or kill others. I could hitch a ride back to Grandma's, I guess, or call a cab. But I hate depending on strangers. What if I couldn't catch a ride? What if the dogs found me while I was standing alongside the road?....What if they.... What if.... Megan....

A fresh burst of tears stream down my face. I feel angry at my weakness and swipe at the tears with my sleeve. I've cried so much in the past eighteen hours I'm surprised I'm not dehydrated. A dizzy spell passes over me, messing with my vision. The fortuneteller's sign seems to loom larger, beckoning me to come inside. Maybe I am dehydrated.

Kevin bends over the console and gently places a kiss on my cheek and another on my forehead. I suddenly find it hard to argue.

He steps from the SUV, circles in front of the vehicle and opens my door. "Come on, sweetheart," he says.

I'm not your sweetheart.

Don't fight it.

Don't fight what, Grandma?

Grandma doesn't answer. I pause several seconds before climbing out of the Blazer onto the cracked sidewalk. I can't believe I'm standing here, in front of the crazy fortuneteller's peach-colored cottage, actually contemplating going inside.

"Are you coming?" Kevin asks, his voice filled with patient frustration.

"No. This is a mistake." I turn to crawl back into the familiar interior of my SUV. Kevin grasps my hand and pulls hard.

"Dianne, we have to save Megan, and to save her we have to find her. Delta may be able to help. Please, let's give it a try."

Delta? Is that the fake fortuneteller's name? And Kevin knows this why?

In spite of my better judgment, I allow him to lead me up the walk to the purple front door. A welcome sign with toll-painted baby robins hangs above the doorbell. The effect is benign and almost comforting.

The woman who answers Kevin's ring is fiftyish, round-faced and large-breasted – motherly looking. When I've seen her around town, I've avoided direct eye contact. Today I look into her eyes. They're the same shade of aquamarine as her sweater set. Her slacks are tan, her hair shoulder length. She must use hair dye because I see no streaks of gray in her dark hair. "Welcome. I'm Delta. Please come in."

Kevin and I step over the threshold, into the world of false claims and woo-woo. Is he actually going to pay this woman money? She'll never see a cent of my hard-earned cash. I refuse to help support a rip-off artist, even one who rips off mainly tourists.

Delta gestures, palm up, to a choice of mismatched wooden chairs circling an oak table. "Please. Have a seat."

They are ordinary-looking chairs. The table is nothing unusual. I can't imagine anyone predicting "secrets of the future" around this table. Or around any other table for that matter.

"I think I've made a mistake," I say, spinning to dash out the door.

"I can feel your pain," Delta says.

What kind of hokey line is that? The room is cool, but sweat beads pop up under my bangs. "Good. I'm tired of feeling it."

Delta smiles. At least she has a sense of humor. "Let me help you," she says, touching my shoulder. I stiffen. I don't like strangers touching me, especially a stranger as notoriously strange as this one.

She whisks her hand off my shoulder. "Just a moment, please," she says and disappears into another room. I wonder if the crazy woman will come back wielding a knife, a gun, or a fireplace poker, and put an end to my misery.

Kevin pulls a chair out near where I'm standing and waits for me to sit. I lower myself down, perching on the edge of the chair, ready to take flight if the fortuneteller does anything over-the-top weird, or turns the least bit threatening.

Kevin takes a seat to my left. He stretches his long legs under the table and slouches, dwarfing the ladder-back chair under his tall lank. He looks exhausted. I feel the same way, but I don't want to relax. Not now. I have to stay alert. I can't let down my guard. It's hard to say what this Delta woman may do next.

All these years, I'd pictured flickering black candles, sage smoke and burning incense within these walls. But I smell none of those things. There are no beaded curtains, no drapes of dark fabric. Instead, Delta's cottage is all about light and air and color. With orange and yellow curtains, a batik happy-face wall hanging and hand-lettered inspirational plaques such as: "Discover Your Inner Beauty" and "Believe" and "God Loves the Whole World, Not Just Our Little Corner." Steel-drum reggae softly pumps into the room. A fresh citrus scent invites me to relax.

It's working. A little. I'm starting to get over my initial heebie jeebies of being inside the fortuneteller's house. My instincts try to tell me to trust this woman. But instinct is a funny thing, not always explainable and in my experience, not always reliable. I'm saving opinion on the crazy lady until I know more about her.

Delta glides silently back into the parlor. She carries a rolled-up mat and a brown Yahtzee cup. You have to be kidding. Yahtzee? At a time like this? She unfurls the mat and lays it flat on the table. It's white with a large black circle painted roughly in the center. It looks like a target, or a primitive dartboard. What sort of black-magic prop is this?

Delta tips the cup upside down on the table, lifts it up and off. I pull back, expecting something eerie, like spiders – possibly with glowing red eyes – to scuttle out from under the cup. But only a pile of eight, inanimate, un-glowing dice lay on the table before me. They are typical dice – white with black dots.

"Pick up the dice," she says.

Kinda bossy, isn't she. "What?" I try playing dumb. I don't want to touch this whacked-out woman's dice.

"Pick them up." Her voice is assertive, like one of my high school softball coaches. But I am no longer in high school. I make my own choices now and I choose to get in my vehicle, go back to Grandma's and look harder for my baby.

"No. This has gone too far already. We're wasting precious time here. I'm leaving." I start to rise from my chair. "Come on, Kevin. Let's go."

"Dianne," Kevin says, "do it." His voice is flat and assertive, plus he's got that hardcore cop-look in his eye, the one that shouts, "Drop your weapon, or I'll shoot!"

I glance over at the Glock holstered on his duty belt. I know he won't really shoot me. Slowly, warily, I sit back down and pick up the dice anyway. My fingers tremble. All this hocus-pocus crap is giving me the jitters.

"Now throw them," Delta says.

I see the black dog's sharp teeth, his red eyes, the bloody saliva stringing from his tongue. Into the mist, I see him loping off with Megan's pink jumper clenched in his fangs. I hear my own wails of terror pierce the foggy air.

All the pent-up rage at the feral dog swells from inside me and I hurl the dice across the room. They ping off a lampshade, the wall, and a framed photo of a smiling young woman.

"Dianne," Kevin says, covering my hand with his. "When Delta told you to throw the dice, I don't think that's what she meant."

"That's exactly what I meant," Delta said. She reaches in her front pants pocket, pulls out eight more dice, and sets them on the table. "But I want you to pick up this set and roll them on the mat in front of you."

I scoop them up, feeling more cooperative, and strangely more at ease after sending the last dice zinging across the room. I give these eight a good Yahtzee-worthy cup shake and tumble them onto the mat. Two threes, a four and a six stay inside the circle. A two, a six, and two fives land outside of it. I'm glad we're not really playing Yahtzee. This roll would suck.

Delta studies the dice and says, "You are concerned about your child."

I feel the blood leave my face. Kevin and I didn't tell her why we came here. How does she know my fear is for my child? Does it show on my face? "How could you know that?"

She holds up a hand and closes her eyes. "Shhh. I can see you are not a believer."

How can she see anything? Her eyes are closed.

"But sometimes, Dianne, even you have to admit there are things that cannot be explained." Delta pauses as though waiting for my reaction. I have none to give her. I am too busy trying to remember when I told her my name.

"What is your greatest fear?" she asks.

"Who, mine?" I play dumb again.

"Both of you, yes. You go first. It is Dianne, is it not?"

I nod and swallow the lump of uncertainty lodged in my throat. I'm positive I didn't mention my name. "My greatest fear…"

"Go deep within yourself. Be as honest as you can." Delta says. "This is important."

I think about Megan, alone somewhere with the dogs. I think of Mom, Dad, Matt and Grandma.

"Do not be worried to feel your fear. This man is with you."

This man was with me when the dog stole my baby too. A lot of help he was. I try to make my features neutral. Kevin reaches under the table and tries to take my hand. I pull it away.

"Close your eyes," Delta says. "Block out everything around you, except the love you feel for this man, and the love he feels for you. It is your strength. Your truth." It almost sounds like something Grandma would say.

Why does everyone seem to be on Kevin's side? First Grandma, now this wacky fortuneteller woman. The guy broke my heart three separate times. Then he promised to keep me and Megan safe, but he didn't. How can I count on him to be my strength or my truth?

Delta shifts slightly in her chair, away from me, as if to give me some space and privacy. "Now say it aloud. Your deepest fear."

"Out loud?" It's bad enough just being here, in the Roseland crazy lady's house, *thinking* about my greatest fear. Now she expects me to put it into words? Out loud, in front of both her and Kevin? I don't think I can do it.

"Speaking of what frightens you will make it smaller," Delta says.

Smaller is not always good. It was a small dog that bit my thumb, and small dogs who lapped up Mel's blood. But it was a big dog who stole my baby. The face of the huge black beast fills my thoughts: His menacing smile; his wolf-like confidence; his three-inch fangs. I decide smaller is definitely the lesser of two evils.

Speak it and it will become smaller.

Okay. Here goes nothing. The moment of truth. I wipe my sweaty palms on my jeans and swallow hard. "I'm afraid everyone I'm close to will die or leave me."

Kevin takes my hand and gives it a squeeze.

Yeah, thanks, buddy. You dumping me three times didn't help ease the pain of Dad leaving, or Mom moving away. It didn't help me last year when Matt got killed. Or three days ago when Grandma died. And it doesn't help now, after you let a wild dog steal Megan away from me. I choke on a sob.

"Good," Delta says cheerfully, as if I'm her favorite student, and I just scored an A-plus on a pop quiz. "Admitting your grief is hard."

Grief? She thinks my biggest fear is grief?

"Now, Kevin. It is your turn. Close your eyes. Go deep within yourself. Feel the strength of your love for this woman and her love for you."

Love? What I'm feeling for Kevin right at the moment is closer to loathing.

"When you are ready," Delta says, "state your greatest fear aloud."

Kevin closes his eyes, but remains silent.

"In this world there are only two emotions," Delta says. "Love and fear. Love is all things good. Fear is all things evil. To eradicate evil from your life, you must face the thing which frightens you most."

How wise that sounds. And as strange as it seems, sitting in this bright little lemon-orange room, with eight dice on the table in front of us and a smiley face wall hanging behind us, it almost makes perfect sense.

Kevin groans, his eyes still closed. His eyeballs jiggle behind his eyelids as if he is experiencing REM sleep. My heart rate rises to meet an unknown dread. What's going through his mind to make him react like this?

***

Thursday, 9:49 AM

He was twelve again, on vacation with his family in the Pacific Northwest. He and his father had hiked in to a high-mountain lake to fish. His father stepped close to the edge of a cliff and the rocky footing gave way. Kevin watched, helplessly, as his father toppled over the edge.

"Dad!" He ran to the spot where his father had slid out of sight. Peering over, Kevin saw his dad, lying still on a ledge ten yards down.

Below his father's form, the cliff sheered and dropped at least another ninety feet. Kevin backed away and sank to the ground. He hugged his knees to his chest and rocked back and forth. He had no rope. They'd hiked in with only their fishing poles and some tackle. His dad parked their rental car at the trailhead, three miles away. With his mind's eye, Kevin searched the trunk of the Ford, searched the back seat. He couldn't remember seeing any rope. What should he do? He went to the cliff edge and peeked over again. His father hadn't moved.

"Dad? Can you hear me? Dad, are you alright?"

No answer.

Fear of heights or not, Kevin had to get down to his dad. There was no other choice. He took in the distance from himself to his father, from the ledge to the bottom of the canyon. In his mind, he measured – ten yards to his father, another thirty to the bottom of the canyon.

Kevin tried to take a breath. Tried to gather his thoughts, but his lungs wouldn't expand. They felt scorched, as though he'd run a marathon through a forest fire. His vision swam. Blurred. Darkened. His heart hummed like a two-stroke engine. The pumping of his own blood pressure rang like a smoke alarm inside his ear canals.

His fear of heights drove him back from the edge, away from his father.

He could do nothing.

He waited as near his father as he could until help came. But it was hours before more hikers happened along. And it seemed hours beyond that until a mountain search and rescue crew arrived with their climbing gear. By the time the rescuers repelled down the cliff, his father's heart beat no more.

Kevin could have done something to help him. He could have climbed down, slid down, tried to fashion a rope out of vines, or from his own clothing. He'd rolled the possibilities over in his mind a million times. But at the time it really mattered, he didn't do any of those possibilities. He didn't do anything. He let his father die, thirty feet from him.

He would never forgive himself.

***

A small groan slips from Kevin's lips. Beneath his lids, his eyes continue to race back and forth. His chin wrinkles in concentration. I've seen this pained expression on Kevin's face before – he's thinking about his father. He will never quit beating himself up over what happened, even though it wasn't his fault. Seeing him relive it makes my stomach ache.

"Kevin, are you okay?" I ask.

He moans again and opens his eyes. The whites are bloodshot, the pupils dilated. Stark, naked fear crawls in their golden depths. I grab his hand with both of mine and hold it tight under the table against my outer thigh.

"Are you ready, Kevin?" Delta asks.

He nods, opens his mouth, shuts it again. Finally, he says, "My greatest fear is that I won't be able to take care of those I love most."

Like a flash out of the blue, a jolt of understanding hits me. Six years I've waited for this revelation – Kevin didn't dump me all those times because he feared commitment. He dumped me because he worried he wouldn't be able to take care of me, or save me if I was in danger.

But yesterday, and again today, he did save me. We saved each other.

Now I desperately need his help to save my daughter.

"There are demons that live in each of us," Delta says. "Their names are fear. By facing your fears, you have conquered the worst of your demons."

I close my eyes and cringe, waiting for her to slap her palm against my forehead and shout, "Out demons, out."

Instead, she moves to the front door and swings it open. "Go now, where the dark tangles live. Find the child."

It all sounds so wise, so spiritual. And so damn confusing.

"Dark tangles?" I ask. "What do you mean by dark tangles? And where do they live?"

I knew we couldn't count on this supernatural, black magic, mumbo-jumbo bullshit to find Megan. Panic rises from my stomach, into my chest cavity, to the back of my tongue where I can taste it, dark and dank and bitter.

"Your fears will lead you," Delta assures me.

Wonderful. A bunch of fearful demons will lead us to a dark, snarly place where a crazed dog has my baby. And I have no idea where we're going, or what we'll find when we get there. Can this get any worse? I slouch in my chair and knock my forehead on the table.

But apparently Kevin isn't going to allow me time to properly despair. He grabs hold of my arm and tugs, jerking me to my feet. He drags me through Delta's front door and out to the Blazer. He opens the passenger side, places a firm hand on top of my head, and pushes me into the seat as though I am a handcuffed prisoner.

Which, without Megan, is exactly what I am.

"Let's find her," Kevin says. "Let's get Megan back." There's a powerful new strength in his voice. A shiver spreads gentle warmth through my body. For the first time since the dog snatched Megan, I feel a thread of hope mingling with the dread.

***

Thursday, 10:02 AM

Kevin raced the Blazer through town as though he was in high-speed pursuit. "I have one stop to make." He lurched into the parking lot of a hardware store, leaped from the Blazer, swung through the storefront door.

"Rope?" he asked the man behind the cash register.

"End of aisle five."

Kevin grabbed the first package of sturdy-looking rope he found, and returned to the front counter. Tossing thirty bucks at the cashier, he didn't wait for change or a receipt. He dashed back out the doors to the Blazer, which he'd left running. He threw the coil of rope on the floor at Dianne's feet, pausing only long enough to brush a lock of hair from her face, look into her eyes and say, "It'll be alright," before he jammed the Chevy into gear and sped south down the coast highway.

Towards the spot he feared most.

Chapter Twenty-Nine

Thursday, 10:11 AM

The ocean was choppy, dotted with white caps. Kevin felt thankful for the sea wind pushing the dense wall of fog inland, out of his path – the path which lead to "The Heights," a rocky cliff wall where local young people liked to congregate.

Before his promotion to detective, while still working patrol, Kevin had to often shoo teenagers away from The Heights, especially during the warm summer months. Amateur rock climbers caught thrills by repelling over the steep cliff and climbing back to the top. Besides the danger of such inexperienced play, The Heights was on private property, belonging to an elderly, church going widow, who didn't much care for trespassers. She didn't like the drinking they did, the trash they left behind, or the liability their activities posed.

He couldn't blame her. After all, it was her property.

Time after time, Kevin had driven to the top of the cliff and chased away the kids. Each time he did so, he had to fight the flood of memories that splashed over him like battery acid. Each time he'd forced himself to peer over the edge, to make sure the last of the young people were off the rock face and safely on their way.

Repeatedly he'd tacked up "No Trespassing" signs, wondering each time why he bothered. Within a week, someone came along behind him and tore down the signs.

But today was different. Today his fears all but vanished. Today he had no time for painful memories or remorse. Today only two things mattered: The woman beside him and the rescue mission ahead of him.

Kevin whipped off the highway, onto a gravel road headed east and up, away from the sea. He reached over to pull Dianne's seat belt taut. "Hang on." He laid a palm on her leg for a moment before gripping the steering wheel with both hands.

He was glad he was driving Dianne's little SUV and not the police sedan. Her rig was equipped with four-wheel drive, which he engaged with the push of a button. He took a deep breath and gunned the motor. The road was rough, narrow and steep. The Blazer lurched and rocked, the front end squeaking in protest.

Dianne's head cracked against the passenger window.

"You alright?" Kevin heard the concern in his own voice.

Dianne held a hand to her head and nodded. But she didn't look alright. Not at all. She looked like a zombie – her color pale, her eyes blank. *She's in shock.* Shock was a dangerous state for the human body. If she went into deep shock, her system might shut down completely. He wished there was something he could do for her, but there wasn't. He was doing everything within his power to help her. To save her. To save her baby.

Reaching the high landing of the dead-end road, Kevin was relieved to see no other vehicles. This was no time to have to deal with trespassing, drunk, daredevil kids. He threw the car into park, grabbed the rope from under Dianne's feet and jumped out. He ripped open the plastic packaging, but his stomach sunk when he shook out the coiled rope.

It didn't look long enough.

It would *have* to be long enough.

Approaching the edge of the cliff, Kevin peered over. He sucked in his breath and backed away, searching for a sturdy object to use to anchor the rope. The only objects solid enough within three or four yards of the cliff were a boulder, or a scrubby, wind-twisted pine.

The big rock was closest to the drop off. To conserve rope, Kevin chose it over the tree. He secured one end of the rope around the big rock with a knot he'd learned during search-and-rescue drills. The other end of the line he knotted around his waist. He backed to the steep drop off. Without giving himself a chance to change his mind, he let himself over the edge. He hardly noticed the rope biting into his palms.

Bracing with his feet and legs to take some of the pressure off his hands and arms, he lowered himself bit-by-bit. An image of his father's crumpled body lying on a rocky outcropping shot through his mind. He shoved it aside. He couldn't keep living in the past. Now is what counted. Dianne depended on him. She'd put her trust in him to find her baby.

He wasn't going to let Dianne down. Not again. Not ever again.

He stole a quick glance up. Dianne stood gazing over the edge, her hands clasped tightly in front of her. What was she feeling? Terror? Worry? Resolve? The firm-lipped expression on her face was hard to read.

Kevin turned his attention back to his descent. From talking to the young people who used to hang out around here, he knew that in the face of the rocky wall was a cave.

The cave was his destination.

Hand-over-hand he let himself down. His arms shook as the muscles cramped and spasmed. He tried not to think about the pain, how far he had yet to go, or how far he'd fall should his rope snap in two.

The rope lurched. So did his stomach.

"Kevin!" Dianne yelled. "The rock is moving!"

He nodded and continued down, keeping his movements as steady and smooth as possible so he wouldn't dislodge the boulder further. What else could he do? Stopping wouldn't help, his weight would still hang on the rope attached to the rock. Trying to climb back up would cause jerking. That would definitely bring the boulder crashing down on top of him. Besides, his clenching gut was urging him to reach the cave.

Before it was too late.

The motor of Dianne's Blazer roared to a start. Gravel ground under the tires. The sound drew dangerously close to the edge of the cliff. Bits of rock and dirt rained over his head and shoulders. He tried to duck aside. Did Dianne mean to drive over the cliff? Was her mental state that desperate?

"Hey, what are you doing up there?"

He got no answer. Another shower of gravel and soil peppered him. Dread jabbed at his intestines.

The engine stopped. A car door opened and closed. Footsteps tromped to the edge. Dianne's face appeared above him. "I moved the Blazer in front of the boulder. It shouldn't go anywhere now."

A jet of relief flushed through his system. "Good thinking." Why had he doubted her? Why hadn't he thought of inching the Blazer to the cliff edge and attaching the rope onto the vehicle? Oh well. No turning back now.

He lowered himself the last few feet and dropped to the narrow cave ledge. The rock shelf was uneven and he threw out his arms to steady himself as he landed.

The cave must be there, behind those blackberries. Kevin slashed at the tangled vines with his feet. The thorns tore at his pant legs, clawed at his flesh. He buried his face in the crook of an arm and pushed his way through the entrance, jerking the last couple feet of slack rope, still tied around his waist, along with him.

The cavern smelled dank and musty. It was black as the inside of an alligator's belly. It took a few moments for Kevin to orient himself. He stretched his arms out on either side, his biceps quivering from exhaustion from lowering his weight down the cliff. The fingertips of both hands brushed against the damp rocks. Roughly eight feet across at the entrance. Did it get narrower as it got deeper?

"Megan?" His voice echoed off the walls, bounced back from the end of the cave. From the way the sound reverberated, Kevin guessed the cave opened wider towards the back, forming a keyhole shape. He shuffled deeper inside. His foot caught something and sent it flying. The object made a tinny, metallic sound when it landed. Probably a beer can left behind by an underage drinker.

From deep within the bowels of the hillside, a dog growled. Low and menacing.

Kevin drew his gun.

A baby cried.

"Megan!" Dianne shouted down. "Oh, Kevin. She's here. She's alive. Is she okay?"

"I don't know. She's in a cave." Dianne hadn't mentioned hearing the dog growl, so he didn't bring it up. Dianne had enough to worry about already. "I can't see a damn thing in here."

How was he going to rescue the baby if he couldn't get past the dogs? It's not like he could shoot the bastards. He couldn't even see them – not that bullets seemed to kill them anyway. He couldn't see Megan either. If he fired at the dogs, he might hit the baby with a stray bullet, or hit her with one that ricocheted off the cave walls. Besides, bullets hadn't stopped the dogs last night, why would today be any different?

The baby cried out again. Shrill this time. He had to do something fast. He didn't like the sound of those cries. Why hadn't he thought to bring his flashlight?

"Can you get to her?" Dianne sounded desperate.

Of course she sounded desperate. Her baby daughter was halfway down a cliff, inside a cave. And she didn't even know the worst of it yet. She didn't know the dogs were in there too, snarling and standing guard over her baby. At least Dianne wasn't zombied anymore. Seeing her in that state disturbed him more than hearing her voice desperate with worry.

"Oh, Kevin, please hurry."

He didn't answer, afraid if he did his voice would trigger a dog attack.

Another mini avalanche peppered the blackberry bushes and the ledge outside the cave. He didn't like Dianne standing so close to the edge like that, especially not with her in such a panicky state of mind. What if the ground collapsed under her feet and she fell off the cliff. Like his father?

He couldn't lose her. Not again. Especially not the same way he'd lost his dad. He had to grab Megan and get back up to Dianne.

He groped his way further into the cave. Six inches…feeling with his fingertips over the rock and soil walls…a foot…over the tangle of tree roots jutting into the cave…eighteen inches. He couldn't touch both sides of the cave wall at the same time anymore. His guess had been correct. The cave widened as it deepened.

A warning growl vibrated through the cavern.

What was he going to do when he reached the dogs, or when they reached him? They'd attack without mercy. The same way they'd attacked the tow truck driver, and Adelle's dog. Kevin knew he'd have to depend on his combat training and sheer instincts.

He crept along the right wall, calculating as he went. Twenty inches…twenty three…twenty six. The rope grew taut around his waist. End of the trail. He extended an arm out in front of himself, waved it around, expecting any moment to feel jaws clamp onto his hand.

He touched nothing. No sharp fangs or dog pelt. No soft baby clothing. No back cave wall.

He was out of rope, and he couldn't reach far enough to retrieve the baby. He had to get the rope undone around his waist. But without the rope, he'd have no safety net. If the dogs attacked him – correction, *when* the dogs attacked him, for it seemed a certainty – they could knock him out the cave entrance and over the ledge.

He had to take the chance.

He fumbled with the knot at his waist. His fingers seemed extra thick today and clumsy. It didn't help that he was working by brail.

"Damn."

Several feet away, a throaty growl vibrated through the hair on the back of Kevin's neck.

His fingers flew at the knot. His weight on the line had tightened it. In his haste to get down to the cave, he must have used the wrong knot, not the easy-to-release hitch he'd learned years ago. Had he tied the same knot around the boulder? He hoped so, then at least he wouldn't have to worry about that end coming undone and plunging him to his death on the way back up.

If he made it back up.

He couldn't let himself think that way. He gave it one more gallant effort, tried to get the rope to his mouth so he could use his teeth. He imagined the fit his mother would throw if she saw him trying to use the teeth she'd spent a small orthodontic fortune on to untie a rope. She'd scraped and saved to pay for his braces, on a single parent's income.

He had to get to Megan, but the knot wouldn't budge. He doubted he could untie it even if he could get it to his mouth and use his straight white choppers, which he couldn't.

He needed Dianne's help. She'd been through a lifetime of tragedy in the past year, a second lifetime's worth of despair since dawn. Would she be able to help him? Was she up to it? He hated himself for what he was about to ask of her.

Another snarl rumbled through the cave. He backed to the entrance and struggled through the brambles until he stood once more outside the cave on the narrow ledge. He quickly scanned the blackberry patch for tufts of dog hair – evidence – before he pulled the two feet of rope out through the sticker bushes and shook it slack.

He tipped his head back to look up at Dianne. "I need your help."

She nodded. "Anything."

***

Thursday, 11:08 AM

I'll do anything to help save my baby.

"I need my flashlight and gloves from the back seat." Kevin's voice holds an edge of determination.

"Okay." I'm glad to do something, anything to help rescue Megan. I dash to the car, grab the flashlight and a pair of yellow leather gloves, and return to the edge of the cliff. "Do you want me to drop them down to you?"

"Uh…no. If I miss, we're up shit creek."

"Then what do you want me to do with this stuff?"

"I want you to bring it down to me."

"Huh?" I'm not a mountain climber. Has he lost his mind? "You want this stuff hand delivered?"

"Yes."

"I can drop the gloves and flashlight right to you. I was a pitcher, remember? I have good aim." I think of how my aim was off in the newspaper office parking lot yesterday when I lobbed my purse at the dogs, but I don't dwell on it. Today is a new day. I line the Mag up with the top of Kevin's head, ready to release.... "I'll drop the flashlight first."

Kevin shakes his head. He doesn't hold out his hands. If I go ahead and drop the Mag anyway, It'll clunk him a good one. I heft the flashlight in my hands. It's heavy. If I beaned him on the head with it, it could knock him out cold. "Hold out your hands."

"Dianne, listen, I wouldn't ask you to do this unless it was necessary. It's necessary. I need you to put on the gloves and bring the flashlight down to me."

Fear grips my insides and squeezes. Me? Scale down the wall of a cliff? I want to say no. "O-o-okay," I say instead. After all, Megan is down there.

You'd give your life for her.

Damn tootin', Grandma. I would. I suck in a deep breath. "Wh-what do I do?"

"Tuck the flashlight into the waistband of your jeans."

I stick the Mag in my pants. It looks like a giant black dong, ready for action. The head brushes under my breasts. I don't mean to, but I giggle. Hysterically. When I'm nervous, I laugh at the stupidest things. I hate that about myself.

"Dianne?"

"Sorry. It's just that I feel like a real man with this thing sticking out of my pants."

"Tuck it in the back waistband." Kevin's using his cop voice. Obviously, he doesn't see the humor. I pull the flashlight out of the front of my jeans and re-tuck it at the small of my back.

"Okay." Another snicker slips out. I am so pathetic.

"Back yourself to the edge like I did. Grab the rope with both hands."

I back up and stoop over to pick up the rope. "Okay."

"You're going to have to lower yourself down."

I look over the sheer drop-off at Kevin, and beyond. If I miss the ledge, I'll topple all the way to the bottom. I'm not that good at judging distance in feet or yards, I just know it's a long way down.

"I don't think I can do it."

"Yes, you can."

You can do it.

My own personal cheering section.

"What if I can't hang on? What if I fall?" What if I make Megan an orphan?

"Then I'll catch you."

"Kevin, I'm scared."

"There'd be something wrong with you if you weren't scared." Kevin looks up into my face. "You have to trust me." Even from this distance I can see his earnestness.

Three times he dumped me and broke my heart. This morning he let a vicious, feral dog grab my baby. But he ignored his fear of heights and climbed up to Grandma's attic to save Megan and me. And just now, he battled his fear again to repel down to save Megan. That's courage. That's a knight in shining armor. Minus the armor. And without the horse, of course.

Horse of course. That's funny. A giggle slips from between my lips. A horse would get in the way right now. Pooping all over. Stomping and pawing and acting all spooked around the cliff.

Dianne, quit with the babbling thoughts and the immature giggling and get on with it. Megan needs you. Kevin needs your help.

Yes, Grandma. You're right. I switch off the mental comedy riff.

"Okay. I trust you." I say to Kevin, and lower myself over the edge.

The rope slips in my hands. I feel the burn through the gloves and fight the instinct to let go. My body spins. I glance down. Kevin is standing directly below me, pulling the slack in the rope taut. He's trying to stop me from spinning, but it isn't working. I spin on the rope like a garden spider on a strand of web. Gross. I hate spiders. I don't want to be like a spider. My head hits a protruding rock. Again, I fight the urge to let go of the rope, this time because I want to press a palm against my head, like after I cracked it against the Blazer window on the way up here.

At this rate, I'll wind up with serious brain damage before the day is over.

"Use your feet! Brace yourself with your legs."

I twirl. Face the cliff. Flail with my legs, kick the rock wall and swing out into nothingness.

"Slow down, Dianne. Focus. Try again."

I try to control my movements, kick less violently. I manage to catch the cliff with one foot, praying my clog stays on. My arms tremble with the effort to support myself. "I can't hold on!" I picture Kevin squashed flat under one-hundred and thirty-four pounds of my dead weight.

"Yes you can!"

You can do it.

The rope burns my hands. No, Grandma, I can't.

Think about Megan. She needs you, honey. Kevin needs you too.

Good old Grandma – philosopher and match maker. She always did like Kevin. I slip another twelve inches down the rope. That's another foot closer to Megan, right?

Right.

I catch the side of the rocky cliff with my other foot. "Ouch." Hand-over-hand I lower myself. I can't believe I'm doing this. I sucked at rope climbing in gym class. Yet here I am, cliff walking down to the two surviving people who mean the most to me. I can't wait to hold Megan in my arms. I wouldn't mind feeling Kevin's strong arms around me either.

"Good job," he says. "You're almost there."

I don't want to look down. It makes me dizzy. So, I just keep creeping, slipping, holding my eyes straight forward. Hand-over-hand. Foot-over-foot. Rock after jutting cliff rock.

"Okay. You can let go now."

"Let go?" Is he crazy? I thought of letting go a couple times on the way down. Now all I want to do is hang on for dear life.

"Yeah, honey. Let go and drop."

What's with everyone calling me honey all of a sudden? First Grandma, now Kevin.

I still can't let go.

"I'm here. I'll catch you."

Carefully I lower my feet from their grip on the cliff. Kevin grabs my ankles. Holds me steady. Guides me to the perfect place to drop.

"Let go now."

"What if I knock you over the edge?"

"Don't worry. You won't."

I drop and land on a loose rock. "Ow!" I twist my ankle, lose my balance and crash hard into Kevin.

"Oof!" he says, right before he starts to fall.

Chapter Thirty

Thursday, 11:35 AM

Oof? Oh, no. It was the same noise Mel made when the black dog knocked him down. Right before the dog ripped open his throat.

"Kevin!" I'm trying to regain both my footing and my balance on the narrow cliff ledge.

Like watching the dogs attack the tow truck driver, this scene seems to unfold in slow-motion cinema. Kevin flails his arms for a moment, almost righting his balance before he falls backwards over the ledge.

It's a short fall. The rope around his waist jerks tight, leaving him hanging horizontal. He spins on the end of the line. His head hammers against a big rock.

I watch with horror as blood spreads through his sandy hair, pooling inside his ear before running back out, pouring a strand of liquid red honey to the bottom of the ravine.

"Kevin!" I scream, belly crawling as close to the edge as I dare before reaching for the rope. For a moment, I am torn between rushing into the cave to grab my baby, or staying here to help Kevin.

As much as I want to hold Megan right this instant, I can't leave Kevin here, dangling and bleeding. I grasp the rope, try to steady it and stop him from spinning and swinging. "Kevin?"

He doesn't answer. His eyes are closed. He isn't moving.

No no no. He can't be…dead…can he?

"Kevin?"

Inside the dark cave, a dog growls.

A dog? Kevin didn't say anything about a dog. I was thinking hoping praying the black brought Megan to the cave and left her alone here. Are Mel and the other three missing persons in there with the dog too? A convulsive shiver winds down my backbone. A second growl echoes, throaty and fierce.

"Kevin! Wake up!" Oh, holy shittin' mother of God. "WAKE UP! The dogs are here! Inside the cave. With Megan."

But Kevin doesn't wake up. How can he wake up when I've killed him?

The oxygen in the air grows thin. My vision blurs.

Dianne, don't you dare faint.

Saved by the Grandma. I shake my head, rise on my knees so I can put my face between them and get some blood flow going back to my brain. I won't be any use to Megan, or Kevin, if I pass out. And chances are good if I pass out, I'll fall over the edge, too.

The dizzy spell starts to pass. What am I going to do now? I can't just leave Kevin dangling here, arms splayed, neck bent back, head dripping blood. And I certainly can't leave Megan in a dark cave with a murdering dog. Did the same dog growl twice, or are there two dogs? Where are the others? Are they still at the top of the cliff? Will they plunge over the side of the cliff to the ledge and attack me from behind the minute I enter the cave?

Even as I thank my lucky stars that Megan is alive, I wonder why the dogs didn't kill her. Maybe they felt a paternal pack instinct and wanted to raise her as their own? Like the wolf pack raised Mowgli in the Jungle Book.

Ridiculous. I'll let these mangy dogs keep Megan over my dead body.

Getting dead is one of my three biggest fears at the moment. Megan getting killed, and Kevin already being dead are the others.

I take another look at Kevin, suspended over the ravine. His body gently swings in the breeze, but he makes no movements on his own accord. No grimace. No twitching fingers. Nothing. His eyes are still closed.

The rope cutting into his waist would cause severe pain if he were conscious. But at least the line is holding him. I lie back down on my belly, lean over the edge, grasp the rope with both hands and pull as hard as I can. Kevin's body budges a couple inches. My own slips a few inches farther over the ledge. Beneath me a chunk of soil breaks free, raining debris onto Kevin's midsection, and narrowing the ledge by another three inches.

I belly crawl backwards like a lizard in reverse. There is no way I can pull Kevin up, not even the three feet to the ledge. I'm physically spent from the climb down. My arms and legs are still trembling with fatigue.

As long as Kevin's rope holds, he isn't going anywhere. At least the bleeding from his head wound has slowed. Wait a minute. Does that mean his heart has quit pumping? Is he really, truly dead?

Everyone I love either dies or leaves me – both my biggest fear and the unarguable pattern of my life.

Even Megan left me.

But only for a little while. And not by her own choice.

Megan is all I have left. I swallow the sob threatening to suffocate me.

Dogs or no dogs, I have to save my baby. I have to get her back. I need her and she needs me. I yank the flashlight from the back of my pants, click it on and shove through the briars into the cave.

The air is heavy, dank and laced with the stench of sulfur. I barely think about how many spiders must reside in here as I skim the light over the walls and ceiling. The beam picks out six pairs of eyes at the back of the cave. Five sets burn hot red – three at waist height, two at shin level. The last pair, low to the ground, illuminate warmly.

Normal eyes. Human.

"Megan!" her name rolls from my tongue and fills my mouth with love. It's followed by the bitter aftertaste of fear.

All five dogs are here too.

One of them snarls and moves towards me. I freeze. Fight the urge to flee. I can't run. Can't leave Megan here with the dogs. Where would I go anyway? Over the ledge and into the ravine, that's where. I'm not a rock climber. I can't scale the cliff face without a rope. And Kevin's got a monopoly on the rope at the moment.

Kevin. Oh, poor Kevin.

I can't think about him right now. I need to focus on Megan. I force my feet to shuffle ahead, closer to the back of the cave. Closer to my child.

And closer to the dogs.

I keep the light directed at their eyes. My plan – if you can call it a plan – is to temporarily blind them while I grab Megan.

Two sets of eyes move towards me.

Closer.

I stand my ground. A burst of anger fills me with courage. How dare these stinking dogs drag a helpless baby into a damp, dank, musty cave? "Come on you mangy assholes. Give me what you got."

I brace my legs for the attack.

The brown dog leaps for me, followed closely by the gray. I swing the flashlight hard, as if I'm batting runners home. The Maglite hits the brown in the head, catches the gray upside the face on the backswing. Both dogs drop.

Damn. You're good.

Thank you, Grandma. I got my game back.

I step over the furry bodies, towards Megan. Towards the black dog and the two ankle biters. I'm thankful the missing person's bodies aren't in here to have to step over. I'm afraid that would be more than I could mentally handle.

The black stands guard in front of Megan. Hackles raised, lip lifted in that maniacal grin I detest. I keep the strong beam of light focused directly into his seething red eyes.

"You son of a bitch. If you think you can take my baby from me and keep her…" I take a giant stride forward, "…you've got another think coming." I lift the Maglite over my head and bring it down hard on top of the dog's skull.

With a single, pitiful whine, the black sinks to the ground.

I snatch up Megan, lift her as high as I can with one arm, out of harm's way of the injured dogs. I shine the light around my feet, then behind me. The three big dogs lie where they fell. But where did the two Chihuahuas go?

Kevin!

The little dogs could be out on the ledge. They could be gnawing through Kevin's rope for all I know. I wouldn't put it past them. And they've got Megan and me right where they want us – trapped in the back of a dark cave. My fingers grip the flashlight tighter. I squeeze Megan closer to my body, kiss the top of her head. "Hang on, sweet pie."

I step over the bodies of the brown and the gray dogs, stumble over the rough cave floor, shove through the briars. The mid-day light shocks my pupils.

I don't see the little dogs.

Megan blinks her eyes at the sudden brightness too. Her clothing is dirty, but I don't see any blood on her. Her eyes are clear and bright. She shows no signs of fever, and so far she hasn't done any more raspy coughing like she did in the attic.

I snuggle her close to my chest and kiss her soft, round cheek. "Megan. I love you so much." She waves her tiny hands and kicks her feet, and I know she loves me too.

She nuzzles at my neck. Poor babe is hungry.

I peer over the ledge at Kevin. He's still suspended, like a knocked-out Spiderman dressed in blue and gray instead of blue and red. "Kevin?" No response. I can't stand seeing him like this. Below him lies the narrow ravine. Somehow the small dogs must have gotten down there and high-tailed it out of sight. I can think of no other logical explanation for their disappearance.

But how did they get off the ledge and down there? I scan the rock wall face. No way they went up. Maybe they have a secret passageway through the cliff. Maybe their toe pads are sticky, like tree frog feet.

Frog feet? You call that a logical explanation?

No, Grandma. I don't. There is nothing logical about this. How would you explain it? The tiny mutts simply vanished, into the salty air.

Grandma doesn't offer a better explanation.

I sit, cross-legged on the narrow ledge and gaze into Megan's face, still amazed the dogs didn't devour her. I lift my sweater, push aside my bra, cuddle Megan close to a breast while I stroke her wispy hair. "Thank you, God," I pray aloud while Megan nurses. "Thank you for sparing my baby." I draw in a long, trembly breath. "I could still use more help, if you don't mind."

This ordeal isn't over yet. The little dogs are still around, somewhere close. There are still three big dogs in the cave. Injured, but not necessarily dead. And we may have a very long wait ahead until someone happens to find us. I'm positive all available search and rescue crews are still combing the area around Grandma's house, looking for Megan. No one will know we found her, or know to come here to look for us, rescue us, pull Kevin's body up to the top of the cliff.

I wipe at a tear. The moment is so bittersweet. I got Megan back, but I lost Kevin. Brave, kind-hearted, handsome Kevin.

My first love. My last love. My only true love.

I swipe at another tear and focus my attention on Megan. Can she really be unharmed? While she tugs greedily at my nipple, I unsnap her romper and push it aside, inspecting her pudgy body for dog bites or scratches. I work quickly so she won't get chilled in the cool air. When I don't find a single mark on her, I breathe a sigh of relief and refasten her pink jumper. I can hardly believe it. The dogs didn't injure her at all.

My maternal concern doesn't slow her feeding. She continues to nurse greedily, making little satisfied grunting noises. I hope her grunts don't alert the dogs. I'm praying the dogs are dead, but in reality, I probably just knocked them out. When they wake up they'll have headaches the size of the Pacific, and I don't imagine they'll be in the best of moods.

Megan makes a funny sound, one I've never heard her make before – a low-pitched groan. "Megan?" I look down, astonished. She groans again. I've never heard a three-month-old make a guttural sound like that. Maybe she isn't unharmed after all. Maybe the dogs infected her with rabies. Or possessed her. Maybe she's suffering from internal injuries.

But Megan continues to suckle, one tiny, perfect hand resting on the upper curve of my breast. For one fleeing moment, I feel a sense of perfect happiness before a rustling noise jars me back to reality.

The rustling comes from the mouth of the cave. I look from Megan's innocent face into the red-eyed glare of the black dog. He shoves his way through the briars, flanked closely by the brown and the gray. I have a brief moment of satisfaction when I notice the meat fork still protrudes from the gray's chest.

The black slinks closer. A growl rumbles in his throat. His wicked eyes blaze. I hold my breath, clutch Megan tighter to my chest and struggle to my feet. I have to face them. I have to fight. I can't run. There's no one to help me. But what about Megan? What do I do with her? I pop my nipple out of her mouth, but I don't dare set her down. The dogs would be on her in an instant. How can I ward them off while holding a baby?

Before I have a chance to work through my own questions, the black lunges forward and sinks his teeth into my leg.

Chapter Thirty-One

Thursday, 12:29 PM

I flail at the black dog, pick up the Mag Lite and strike at him, but I can't make solid contact. I'm afraid to bend over to reach the dog – I can't let Megan get that close to it.

The dog sinks his teeth deeper into my calf muscle. I scream in pain and fear as he tugs me towards the edge of the cliff. I hold Megan tight and hop on one foot to keep from falling over backwards. If the dog gets me on my back, I'm a goner for sure, and so is Megan. The black pulls harder on my leg. The pain is excruciating. I pull against him. Fight. Swing the flashlight, trying to make contact with his skull, his nose, any part of him.

Megan lets out another one of those horrid, un-baby-like moans.

It takes a moment to register. Of course they're not baby-like. The moans aren't coming from Megan. They're coming from below us.

The noise distracts the dog too. The black lets go of my leg, and I fall backwards onto my butt. The dog looks over the ledge. Out of my peripheral vision, I catch movement. The rope is wiggling. Is it a dog making the rope move…or can it be…"Kevin!" I butt-scoot a few inches closer to the edge so I can peer over.

Kevin's eyelids flutter open and he raises a hand to gingerly touch the bloodied spot on the side of his head. He moans again.

"Oh, Kevin. You're not dead."

"Uh-uh," he groans, "being dead couldn't hurt this much."

The black dog acts confused for a moment, as though not sure which person to attack. I take advantage of the opportunity by hefting a rock in my right fist and letting it fly. The rock makes contact with the black's snout. He yipes in surprise. I pick up another rock and throw it. Then another. As fast as I can, one-handed, I pick up rocks and pummel the dogs. I am a human pitching machine. I am relentless. I have one boob exposed and bobbing in the breeze.

The black hesitates. Cowers. Backs towards the ledge. Then I watch something unbelievable: One by one, the four big dogs slip over the side of the cliff and vanish. Into thin air.

Wait a minute. Four? The last dog to disappear I've never seen before. It's light-colored, nearly transparent. I shake my head to clear it. I've been through a lot lately. I must have imagined the last ghostly white dog.

A fearless feeling of peace settles over me.

They're gone now, Dianne, for good. You don't need to worry anymore.

I believe you're right, Grandma.

I tuck my breast away and lie Megan on the most rock-free patch of the ledge I can find, and as far away from the edge as possible. She cries with indignation.

Her wails blend with Kevin's moans. The sound is the most beautiful two-part harmony I've ever heard.

I crawl to where Kevin hangs.

"What happened?" He grabs at the rope to pull himself into an upright position.

"You…you sort of fell." If he can't remember what happened, why do I need to 'fess up to knocking him off?

He snorts, as if to say, 'duh'. "I figured that much."

"No need to get testy with me. We can talk about it later. Right now let's get you up."

Kevin nods, which brings another groan. He raises a hand to his head again, pulls it away and looks at the sticky dark blood covering his palm. "My head."

"Yeah, you rapped it a good one on a rock. Can you try to pull yourself up? I'll help you, but I can't do it by myself, I already tried."

Kevin rakes at the rocky outcrop, gets a finger hold between the rocks and tries to lift himself. I sit, bend my knees, brace with my feet and pull on the rope. I don't hardly notice the pain in my ankle, leg or thumb, or the blood that oozes down my calf into my sock.

Together we manage to inch him up. He claws his way back onto the ledge and lies there on his belly for a few minutes, breathing hard. I throw myself on top of him and hug my body tight to his back.

He groans. "I love you, sweetheart, but I can't breathe."

"Sorry." I sit up. "I'm just so happy you're alive."

Kevin's breathing comes evenly now. "I'm happy I'm alive too."

"Your head's bleeding again."

"I'm all right." He looks around, his eyes resting on the baby lying nearby. "You got Megan back. Is she hurt?"

"Seems fine. I can't find a scratch on her."

"The dogs!" Kevin draws his gun. "Where are they? Still in the cave?"

"They're gone." The ghostly white dog flashes through my mind, but I don't mention it. What's the point? They're gone.

"Where did they go?"

"I don't know. I hit them with the flashlight inside the cave. They fell. Then they came out here. The black one attacked me, so I threw rocks and they…they disappeared. Vanished over the side of the cliff. Just like that. I can't explain how I know. I just know they're gone. Really gone."

With a wince, Kevin re-holsters his gun. His palms are raw from rope burn. "Some things can't be explained."

Yesterday morning I would have snorted and said, "Ridiculous." Today, aloud I say, "Amen to that."

Kevin raises an eyebrow and shoots me a surprised look. The eyebrow lift must have shot some pain through his head. He grimaces and touches the wound again. His fingers come away bright red.

"We've got to get that bleeding stopped."

"Let's just get you and that baby off this ledge and away from the dogs. We'll worry about my head later."

"Shhh." I'm already peeling off my sweater to get to the stretchy tank top underneath.

"Dianne, really, I'm fine."

"None of us are getting off this cliff if you black out again. I can't get Megan to the top without you." This is no time for Kevin's macho-male attitude. It's also no time for modesty. I pull off the tank and feel my nipples stand at chilly attention through the fabric of my bra. Kevin's eyes light up. Sheesh. Even with a nasty head wound the guy is still all randy male. A warm flush spreads across my cheeks, through my breasts and down between my thighs. Guess I'm not so different. In a female way, I mean.

I brush my libido aside and crawl the two steps on my knees to Kevin. "Duck your head." I'm all business now. He drags his eyes from my boobs and gives me a wry grin. As he tucks his chin to his chest, his cheek grazes one of my nipples. Heat seers through my breast and spreads down through my body. I suck in a rapid breath.

I'm not sure if it's Kevin's head wound or the nipple contact that causes him to groan.

Trying to ignore the vibrations pulsing low in my abdomen, I wrap my tank around his head. Immediately a bright red spot stains the white fabric. "This might hurt."

Kevin lifts his chin so my nipple is even with his mouth. "Even if the pain kills me, I could die right here, a happy man." He parts his lips. I can feel his breath hot on my breast. Then he kisses the fabric-covered nipple.

I can't help smiling, although this is no time for fooling around. Kevin's lost a lot of blood. I've got to get the wound staunched. "Hold still," I tell him.

He takes his lips off my breast. He grits his teeth as I knot the shirt tight around his head. I lean back to admire my handiwork. With his gun and bloody head band, he looks like some sort of bad-ass commando.

It turns me on. A lot.

I am so pathetic.

"Where was I?" he asks. "Oh yes, I remember…I was right here…" He takes my nipple in his mouth and tongues it through the fabric. My groans mingle with his and I grab his head, hug it with both arms and hold it close.

"Ow. Careful with my head."

"Oh. Sorry." I'm so glad to have him here, warm and alive, I got carried away. I drop my hands to his shoulders.

I lower my face to his and he kisses me. All the years of pent-up yearning are in this kiss. Love and relief fill me with warmth. Megan's safe. Kevin didn't die.

The pattern of your life is about to change.

Thanks, Grandma. I think you may be right. No offense, but would you mind leaving us alone now? This is sort of a private moment, and I feel funny thinking about you watching.

Goodbye, Dianne. I love you. I will see you again one day.

Bye, Grandma, love you too.

Kevin thrusts his tongue in my mouth and I return the favor, momentarily lost in the primal sport of tongue fencing.

Wait a minute. Grandma? I just wanted you to go away while we're…while we're…well, until later. Okay?

You do not need me anymore, Dianne.

Yes I do.

I pull my tongue back inside my own mouth, but keep sliding my lips around on Kevin's, so he won't suspect I'm carrying on a silent conversation with my dead grandmother.

I'll always need you, Grandma.

You will always have me. I will always be with you.

Okay, that's a relief. I feel Grandma's presence slip away. I'm glad she's not hanging out, watching. How wrong would that be?

I parry my tongue with Kevin's again. He doesn't seem to suspect anything out of the ordinary. Although even without my dead grandmother talking to me, Kevin and me kissing on a narrow ledge, halfway down a cliff is definitely out of the ordinary. Add the fact that we're both injured, and rabid dogs are lurking around somewhere nearby makes the whole thing just downright weird. Funny though, given the circumstances leading up to this moment, what Kevin and I are doing feels perfectly natural.

Kevin reaches behind me, unclasps my bra and pushes the straps off my shoulders. My breasts spring free. He lets out a groan. I'm nearly positive it's not pain that made him groan this time.

I slip the lacy bra off my arms, over my hands and give it a fling. Kevin caresses my skin with his fingertips. He's careful not to touch his raw, rope-burned palms to my flesh. His fingers are big and calloused and each touch resurrects a sweet memory.

He rubs the tips of my breasts with his thumbs. I close my eyes. My breath comes faster. When I open my eyes, he's looking into my face. His eyes smolder. He stoops to draw a nipple into his mouth, the sensation very different than Megan's suckling.

Megan! She got so quiet. I need to check on her.

"Hold that thought," I tell Kevin. I pull my nipple from his mouth, snatch my sweater off the ground and crawl the couple feet to Megan. She's busy waving her arms and studying cloud formations. She smiles and coos when she sees me. I touch her cheek, cover her with my sweater and crawl on my knees back to Kevin.

"I missed you." His voice is thick.

"You knew I'd come crawling back."

"I didn't know if you would, but I was hoping."

I smile, press my forehead to his and whisper, "Now where were we?"

"We were right here. On a ledge in the middle of nowhere. Together, where we belong."

I wrap my arms around him and lay my head on his chest. I can hear the comforting thump of his heart.

"I love you," he says.

"I love you back."

"Look at me for a minute." He takes my shoulders and gently pushes me away so he can see into my eyes.

"Okay." I look back into his amber eyes. A hundred miracles shine in their depths, sparkling with a thousand unspoken promises I know he'll never break again.

"There's something I want to ask you."

"Shoot."

He gives me a lopsided grin, and says in his charming southern drawl. "Never say shoot to a man with a loaded gun."

I glance at Kevin's sidearm, then down at the growing bulge in his slacks and giggle. I'm not sure which loaded gun he's referring to.

Kevin grips my shoulders a little tighter. A little too tight. "Dianne?"

He's suddenly turned all serious cop-like on me. What's up with that? "Yes?"

Kevin's chin wrinkles. He hesitates. What happened to the light-hearted, lusty mood he was in a minute ago? "Will you be my wife?"

Wow. I didn't see that coming. Did Kevin, the confirmed bachelor, the man of no long-term commitments just ask me to marry him?

I shake my head to clear my ears. Maybe I got cliff debris in them. "I'm not sure I heard you right. I thought for a minute there you asked me to marry you."

Kevin's face is still serious. He nods. "I did."

I'm speechless. Literally. I can't make my lips form words and my tongue's gone numb.

"Aren't you going to answer me?"

What am I doing? I'm half-naked, on the side of a cliff, seriously considering taking a man up on a marriage proposal. What about my resolve not to date until Megan is grown? Remarrying doesn't fit into my plans either. Blended families don't work, do they? Kevin is not Megan's father. What about that?

Would Megan's biological father have scaled up to a rooftop, then down a cliff to save his baby daughter? Maybe. But maybe not. Matt was more bravado than action.

Kevin is more action than talk.

I like action. Action is good. I'd like to be a part of this man's action for the rest of my life. Starting right now.

"Yes," I say. "I'll be your wife." The words break a dam inside me. All the fear and grief, hope and love I've felt in my lifetime wells to the surface and pours down my cheeks.

Kevin pulls me into his arms and waits quietly until my tears ebb. Almost as rapidly as it started, the salt-water flood is over. I take in a big lungful of air and let out a quivery sigh. I feel drained, but cleansed.

Kevin rains little kisses all over my face, nibbles away the clinging tears. He lifts his face so we can look into one another's eyes. I'm glad I don't see pity in his. Instead they are filled with love. "You alright?" he asks.

I nod.

"Sure?"

I nod again.

"Did you really mean it when you said you'd be my wife?"

"I meant it."

"In that case, you've made me the happiest man…" Kevin looks around, "…on this whole cliff."

"That's not saying much since you're the only man on this whole cliff!" I give him a playful punch.

He flails his arms like he's falling backwards over the edge.

"Not funny," I pout. I'm thinking he remembers now that I'm the one who knocked him off the first time and I pout harder.

"Come here, sweetheart. I'm just playing with you." Kevin pulls me to him and wraps his strong arms around me.

It feels like home.

He bends down for another kiss. "Speaking of playing…"

One kiss leads to another. Soon we are kicking free of our jeans and underwear. Kevin leaves his shirt on since the rope is still tied around his waist. We don't want to give him any more rope burns.

Making love on a narrow ledge high above a sheer drop off is not as easy as it may sound. But where there's a will…

"Maybe if you straighten your legs out in front of you," I suggest.

Kevin stretches out his long legs. They reach nearly the length of the ledge. His legs aren't the only things sticking straight out. His naked gun bobs in the breeze. As much as I want my body next to his and to feel him inside me, the ridiculousness of the situation suddenly hits me and I start giggling.

"I'm sorry," I gasp, trying to gain control of myself.

Kevin looks down at himself. Looks at our surroundings. Looks at me. Immediately he gets the same sense of hilarity and starts laughing too.

We cling to each other and laugh until my side aches. When our laughter settles, I'm happy to see his gun is still loaded and ready for action.

His thoughts are running nearly parallel with mine. "Care for a ride, ma'am?"

I nod. The giggling didn't cool my jets either. If anything, it made me feel more relaxed, even sexier.

"Climb on up here in the saddle my cowgirl."

I'm still giggling, a little, but I swipe at my tears of laughter and straddle him. I lay a lip lock on his mouth and slowly slide down onto his bobbing gun until he's all the way inside me. Our laughter is quickly replaced with moans of pleasure.

"I love you," I whisper against his neck as I ease up and down.

He raises his hips off the ground, driving himself deeper inside me. "Not as much as I love you."

"Bet me."

"Anything you want."

"This," I say. "Lots more of this."

I lift and plunge. Lift and plunge. Faster. Deeper. I look down at our bodies mingling, watch him glide in and out of me. The sight pushes me over the edge.

Well, not literally.

"I'm going to explode," I pant as the blood pounds through every inch of my body.

"I'm right behind you, baby," Kevin says.

A pleasure bomb bursts deep inside me, sending tingling fingers of explosives through every nerve ending.

I don't stay straddled atop Kevin very long. The rocks are digging into my knees, and I'm sure they're digging into Kevin's backside, sitting buck naked on top of them like that. I kiss him and climb off, slowly, so I don't knock either of us off the cliff.

Carefully, we pull our underwear and pants back on, taking turns so our elbows don't send the other flying. "Have you seen my bra?"

"You mean that lacy white number you were wearing earlier?" Kevin gives me a lopsided grin.

"That would be the one."

"Haven't seen it for awhile."

I venture a peek over the ledge. Twenty feet below, draped over a jutting tree root hangs my bra. I point and giggle. Kevin looks over and laughs. "Oops," he says. "Did you want me to go get that for you?"

I know he's kidding, but the thought still gives me a gut jolt. "Don't you dare even think about it." No way do I want to see Kevin dangling over the ravine again.

Megan is still snuggled under my sweater, waving at the sky. "Excuse me young lady, but may I wear your blanket?" Megan doesn't object, so I whisk my sweater off her and pull it over my head. I hope the weave is tight enough to keep my nipples from popping through. Although both Kevin and Megan might appreciate that, for varying reasons. I look down at my chest. The girls are cooperating and staying under wraps. I'm so glad I'm not prone to milk leakage.

I check Megan's makeshift, T-shirt diaper. It's wet, but there's nothing I can do about it here. There are spare diapers in the Blazer....

Kevin stretches his arms over his head. Working out the kinks, I guess. I admire the slender strength of his long body.

My fiancé.

"What now?" I'd pay ten bucks for a deck of cards to pass the time until help arrives. Strip poker springs to mind. I wouldn't even mind losing. Getting naked with Kevin all over again sounds like a marvelous way to pass the time.

"Now we climb back to the top."

Part Six: The Truth

Chapter Thirty-Two

Thursday, 12:54 PM

Climb to the top of the cliff, with one rope, a baby, and both of us injured? "Huh?" Is Kevin serious? "With your head wound? What about Megan? How will we get her up?"

"Ah, my lovely, doubting Dianne."

How did he guess I sometimes call myself doubting Dianne? It rattles me a little. "Very funny. Let's be serious."

"I am serious. I've got a plan."

A plan is good, if it's a good plan. If it's not a good plan, it's worse than no plan at all. "I have a plan too."

"Yeah?" Kevin looks genuinely interested. "You first."

"We call for help on your cell phone."

"The Heights is a dead zone for most cell signals." Kevin pulls his phone out of its holster and checks the screen. "Nope, sorry. No bars." He re-holsters the phone. "What's your plan now?"

"We wait here until help arrives."

"You know how long that could be? Every available body is searching for that baby in your arms. No one will come looking for us until tomorrow. And that's best case scenario."

I don't want to climb the cliff, especially not while carrying Megan. I want someone to hoist us up. Kevin can't do it, he's too worn out. He got no sleep last night, he's injured and now, thanks in part to me and my animal urges and inability to say no to him, he's physically drained.

I feel a little smile tilt my lips. "I'm okay with tomorrow," I say. "We spent last night in an attic. We could spend tonight on a cliff ledge. It will give us a story to tell Megan when she's older."

"We'll have plenty of stories to tell Megan." There's an impatient edge to Kevin's voice. "I don't want you and her spending the night out here. We have no diapers. No blankets." Kevin's gaze sweeps my chest. He cocks an eyebrow. "And I can tell you're already cold."

I ignore that last comment. I don't have time for sexual innuendos right now, I'm busy fighting my case. "We could sleep in the cave." The thought of cuddling with Kevin and Megan in a damp cave sounds a lot more appealing than trying to drag my tired butt, along with my baby, up a steep rock wall.

"What if the dogs come back?" Kevin points out.

The dogs.

I can't say I'd forgotten about the dogs – I don't imagine I'll ever forget about the dogs – and I can't put it into words, exactly, but I feel calm now when I think about them. "The dogs aren't coming back."

"How do you know?"

"I'm not sure." I think of Grandma's words: *They're gone now, Dianne, for good. You don't need to worry anymore.* "I just do."

"I hope you're right, but I'm not taking any chances. I don't want us sleeping here tonight."

What is with him? He wasn't too worried just a bit ago when we were naked and doing the wild thing out here in the open. All I want to do is rest here and wait. Is that too much to ask? I decide to appeal my case one last time. "Kevin, I'm worn out. You're injured. Let's just hang tight, right here, until someone shows up. They'll call for the fire department and those guys will have us up in no time."

Kevin's chin wrinkles. "*The fire department?* You really don't trust me to keep you and Megan safe, do you?"

An ah-ha moment beans me alongside the head like a can of creamed corn. That's what this is about. At Delta's house, Kevin said, "My greatest fear is that I won't be able to take care of those I love most." Getting us safely up this cliff is important to him. Integral to our relationship. Imperative to our future together.

Kevin has always needed to be a hero. Now he needs to be our hero.

I need him to be our hero too. "I trust you," I say, and I mean it.

Kevin's chin smoothes out and his expression lightens. "Here's my plan…"

So, I strip off Megan's romper and the tank top/diaper, then redress her in only the romper. Together Kevin and I fashion the versatile, wet T-shirt into a sling, which Kevin wears over one shoulder and under one arm, leaving his hands free to climb the cliff. Once the baby hammock is securely knotted, I tuck Megan inside.

I wait on the ledge, watching Kevin scale back up to the real world with my baby. I stand directly under them. If they fall, I want to pad their landing, or topple over with them. I don't want to get left behind. Not ever again.

An image of a stooped, silver-haired Kevin with a permanent chin crease enters my head. Okay, aging and death are an inevitable part of life, and someday Kevin will die. But I pray it doesn't happen for a long, long time. And then I hope God sees fit that we die peacefully together. He is and always will be the love of my life.

It's a lot slower going for Kevin to climb the cliff than it was for him to repel down. But even injured, packing a baby and harboring a fear of heights, Kevin climbs with sure-footed strength.

He'll make a great dad. Maybe we'll have more kids. I picture a golden-haired baby boy with a crooked grin and a dimple in his chin. I touch my abdomen and smile. Kevin and I didn't use protection. Could be a baby boy sprouting in here already.

Kevin grows smaller above me. It's as though I'm watching through a dream filter. I am going to be Kevin's wife. Megan is going to have a father. We are going to be a whole, happy family.

Amazing how fast life can do a three-sixty. Even while you're busy clinging onto the side of a cliff.

I think about Grandma. Although I've heard her voice off and on the past two days, I still miss her like crazy. But I know it will be all right without her. I'll be okay.

What do you think about all this, Grandma? Kevin and I are going to be married.

I'm surprised when Grandma doesn't answer. She's always been so fond of Kevin.

Kevin and Megan disappear over the top. I'm up next. There's the small pocket knife in the glove compartment of the Blazer. The plan is, Kevin will cut the rope from his waist, toss down the line and help pull me up.

My palms grow damp thinking about the ascent ahead of me. Besides, silly as it sounds, I'm feeling melancholy at leaving this ledge. Our ledge. The place where Kevin and I reconnected physically, where he asked me to marry him. He was my first love. My third love. And now, my last love. But now there's nothing left for me down here except memories. I'll take those up with me. My whole world is waiting for me at the top.

I can do it. I have to do it – my family needs me.

"Ready?" Kevin yells.

I rub my hands on my jeans. "As ready as I'll ever be."

He snakes down the rope. I catch the end, wrap it around my middle, knot it once. Twice. Three times – just to be on the safe side. I grip the rope with both hands, brace a foot on the side of the cliff, give Kevin a nod and start climbing.

My arms immediately tremble against the strain on my upper body. Vibrations travel down the rope and tingle my hands. I imagine the quivering to be like sound waves of Kevin's strength and love for me.

The song "Stairway to Heaven" pops into my head. I let it play. Thank goodness it's a long song, because my journey is a slow one, even with Kevin helping pull me up.

Step after grueling step I cliff walk up, up, up. The muscles in my arms cramp and burn. My leg injuries throb. The new bite wounds on my calf start seeping blood again. I push the pain aside and think about what awaits me at the end of this rope – the rest of my life, and the two people who matter most.

When I finally make it to the top, Kevin grabs my forearms and pulls me up over the edge and onto firm footing. My legs give out and my knees buckle. Kevin catches me before I hit the ground. "You alright?" he asks.

I try to catch enough breath to speak. "Never better," I pant. "You and Megan?"

"Never better." He smiles and kisses me.

I lean against him, waiting for my heart rate to slow, waiting for my rubbery arms and legs to change back to flesh and bone. When I've regained a bit of strength, I step away from Kevin and stand on my own two feet.

"Ready?" He asks.

"Are you okay to drive?"

"Hell, yeah. If I can rock climb carrying a baby, I can drive."

Okay, typical male response. "I was worried about your head."

He gives me a crooked grin. "Funny, you're not the first person to worry about my head."

I'm glad he's lightened up. "I meant the head wound, wise guy."

He touches his head and winces. "It's tender, but I think I'll live."

I hope so. I hope you live for a very, very long time.

He hands Megan over to me. I lie her in the backseat of the Blazer, slip her out of the dirty jumper, mop at her with a wet wipe, tape on a fresh diaper and dress her in the spare two-piece outfit from the diaper bag. She's still a little dirty, but not bad considering what she's been through the past couple of days. I'm still amazed there's not a single bite or scratch on her. I kiss her, nuzzle her neck, and buckle her into the car seat.

Kevin climbs behind the wheel, fires up the motor. "Where to, ma'am?"

I want him to get that head wound looked at right away. "Let's go straight to the hospital."

"You sure? Don't you want to get cleaned up first? Give Megan a bath?"

Sheesh, are all men babies about going to the Doctor? Matt was the same way. I decide to appeal to Kevin's budding paternal side: "No. I want to get Megan checked out first thing."

He looks over at me and nods. "You've got a few injuries that need looked at too."

And possibly rabies. I've tried to avoid thinking about the disease and the needles-in-the-belly-button, pit-of-the-stomach panic that accompanies it. Of course, a dog bit Kevin too when he was climbing the ladder to the attic. But I'll let a doctor be the one to break the horrific news of navel injections to him.

Kevin throws the truck into gear, turns it around and aims it down the steep, bumpy road.

I wiggle my swollen ankle, touch the spot on my head that I cracked against the cliff, inspect the dog bite on my thumb. The climb back up broke open the thumb wound. The shredded gauze it's wrapped in is bright red. The inside of my sock feels warm and squishy from the blood oozing from the fresh bite wounds on my leg. As much as I detest needles, I can't argue with Kevin – I may need a few stitches here and there. But my battle wounds are nothing compared to the gash on the side of his head.

"How are we going to explain our injuries?" Kevin asks. "They'll never believe us, you know."

"Who?"

"Anyone. Everyone. The doctors. My co-workers. The chief. My mother."

"If I hadn't lived through it, I wouldn't believe us."

Kevin shakes his head. "Me neither. I've seen some strange things in my life, but those dogs beat all." His chin wrinkles.

There is something more on his mind. "What?" I ask.

"Oh, I was just wondering how I was going to explain to the families of the four missing people how their loved ones probably died."

"That's a tough one. They'll probably either think you're nuts, or that you're making up some bizarre story just to close the cases."

Kevin shakes his head. "I don't think even my partner, Buzz, will believe me. He's kind of like you – or how you used to be – he doesn't believe things he can't explain."

"Are you going to try?"

"Try?"

"To explain?"

"I don't know. Buzz wasn't born in the deep south. He didn't see shamans in action, using voodoo dolls and bending energy to heal people." Kevin rapped his index finger on the steering wheel. He takes a hand off the wheel and runs it back over his hair. "Buzz was taught to depend on facts. With these dogs, there are no facts. No evidence at all, except our wounds. The dogs left no tracks, no blood. I even checked the blackberry bushes in front of the cave. Couldn't find a single tuft of fur. If normal dogs pushed through briars like that, they'd lose clumps of hair."

"Wait a minute!" I twist around and grab my camera bag from the backseat. "I took photos."

"That's right. You mentioned that last night."

I pull out my Canon and scan through my images on the digital screen. The most recent shots make me feel physically ill – Mel, covered with blood, his mouth open in a silent scream. His fists wave in the air as the black dog rips at his throat. His legs are torn and bleeding. But where are the other two dogs? All three big dogs were attacking when I took these photos. I dial through the images again, trying not to look at Mel's tortured face. There is no long-haired gray dog and no brindled brown anywhere in the frames.

"There's only one dog in these pictures."

"One is better than none, as far as evidence goes."

"I suppose that's true," I admit. But still, I'm puzzled.

"Back on the cliff, didn't you say the dogs just vanished?"

I nod. "Into thin air."

"Like the victims."

"Exactly."

"Hoo-boy."

"You can say that again."

We've reached the bottom of the rocky lane.

"I should get cell reception here," Kevin says, "I need to let the department know we found Megan, and she's safe." Kevin pulls out his phone and makes the call. With the cell to his ear, he swings the SUV onto the Pacific Highway and heads north, back towards civilization. Not really fair that cops are allowed to talk on their cell phones while driving, unlike regular Oregon citizens.

"Chief? McCoffey here. We found the baby. She's alive. Seems to be in good shape. The search teams can stand down." Kevin pauses. "No, the dogs are still on the loose. I'm taking the baby and her mother to the hospital to get them checked out. Then I'll drive them home. I'll call and fill you in with the details after that. I'll be in tomorrow for briefing. I'll fill out the report then, too." A pause. "Thank you, sir."

Kevin ends the call and turns onto Seaside Boulevard, which leads to the hospital. To our left, the ocean sparkles blue, immense and mysterious.

"You know, I thank God for this with all my heart, and I probably shouldn't even question it," I swallow the knot that catches in my throat, "but why do you suppose the dogs spared Megan?"

"I don't know." Kevin drums his fingers on the steering wheel. "But I know someone who might."

We look at one another. "Delta," we say in unison.

***

Thursday, 2:28 PM

When the receptionist at the emergency room asks what we're there for, Kevin and I exchange a look. We decided on the way here not to go into details. "We were attacked by dogs," I say, and leave it at that. No sense trying to explain the past twenty-six hours, and having the hospital staff think us insane. As Kevin pointed out earlier, we don't want child welfare or mental-health agencies poking their governmental noses into our lives.

The receptionist ushers us into a tiny triage room where a male nurse gives our injuries a quick check. The nurse asks a few more questions. We give vague answers. He thrusts forms at us to fill out. When we're finished with the paperwork, he escorts us to the back of the building to an exam room. We wait there for a doctor.

I help myself to the wet wipes on the counter. First I finish cleaning Megan's face and hands, then Kevin and I mop at the dirt on our own exposed skin. When we're finished with our pseudo sponge baths, we wait. And wait some more. Why does a visit to the emergency room take so blasted long? EMERGENCY – the word itself suggests hustle, people, HUSTLE.

Finally, someone raps on the door. A willowy woman enters. "Hi, I'm Doctor Asbury." She shakes our hands. "Let's get you three fixed up and on your way, shall we?" She flips through our charts, peers over the top of the clipboard. "Dog attack, was it?"

"Yes, ma'am," Kevin says.

The doctor raises an eyebrow. Glances through the charts again. I brace myself for a barrage of questions. "Undress the baby and lie her on the exam table, please." The doctor gives Megan a quick but thorough once over before announcing, "I can't find anything wrong with this beautiful baby." I breathe a huge sigh of relief. I like this doctor.

Next she tends to Kevin. She cuts off the makeshift shirt-bandage from around his head. As much as I want Kevin's head wound taken care of, when the doc tosses the bloody shirt into the hazardous waste bin, I can't help thinking, 'there goes my sexy commando man.' Dr. Asbury cleans the gash before ordering X-rays.

While Kevin's off getting pictures taken of his head, the doctor looks at my injuries.

"You need stitches in those thumb and leg wounds," she says. I hold Megan close while Dr. Asbury gives me shots in the thumb and both legs. "We'll give that a few minutes to numb the areas."

After the numbness kicks in, she sews up the bites. I look away as she works, fussing with Megan's clothing to avoid sight of the needle.

"How are you doing?" She glances up from her work.

"I'm feeling light-headed."

The doctor nods, as if she sees needle-phobia every day. "Lie back on the table. Remember to breathe."

I try to breathe normally through the rest of the procedure, hugging Megan against my torso, feeling like a bigger baby than she is.

After Dr. Asbury finishes her handiwork – six stitches in my thumb, eleven in the leg the black bit on the cliff ledge – she cleans the bite on my ankle. "There you are. All patched up. Was the dog that bit you vaccinated for rabies?"

This is the part I've been most dreading. But I need to tell her the truth. "More than one dog bit me. And I don't know if they were vaccinated."

She nods.

Why is she nodding? What does that mean? "Will I have to have shots?"

"Depends."

Come on doc, I need more information here. "Depends on what?"

"Do you know who owns the animals that bit you?"

Owns? Ha! No one owns those beasts. I just shake my head.

"Do you have access to the animals?"

I must give her a puzzled look because she says, "Can you, or the authorities, catch the dogs so they can be contained and observed for ten days?"

Even the authorities can't capture bullet-proof creatures who slip over the sides of cliffs and vanish into thin air. "I doubt it. They were sort of…" I search the ceiling, as if I'm going to find the right word to describe the murdering, red-eyed dogs etched there, "…feral."

The doctor frowns. "That's not good."

You can say that again.

"I'll alert the dog pound as soon as we finish up here. Someone needs to get those dogs off the street before they hurt others."

Amen to that. Big time.

"Let me ask you one more question. Did the dogs exhibit normal behavior?"

I think of the way they chugged after me like red-eyed demon diesel engines through town and down the highway. I picture the gray climbing my Blazer, onto the roof of Grandma's house. Then up a ladder with a meat fork protruding from his chest. I remember the black's maniacal grin before he crashed through my old bedroom window. The ripping sound of wood as the brindled brown tore a passage through the laundry room door. I close my eyes and Mel's terror-filled face, his jagged and bloodied throat flickers behind my eyelids. My breath snags in my chest and my pulse rate hastens.

As much as I fear needles poked into my belly, there is no way I can stretch the truth far enough to say the dogs acted normal. I shake my head. "No."

"In that case, we'll give you an injection at the site of the entry wound, or wounds in your situation, and then you'll have to have a series of shots."

"Through the navel?" Saying the words out loud nearly gives me a coronary.

Chapter Thirty-Three

Thursday, 3:54 PM

The doctor chuckles, as if the question about injections through my navel is the punch line to some sort of sick and twisted physician's joke.

Yeah doc, real funny. Not.

"No," she says, still smiling. "You won't have to get shots through the navel."

Thank the good Lord for small miracles.

"You'll need a series of five injections, along with a couple of boosters, given in the shoulder muscle. We'll start the series today."

"Oh." I let out a huge breath. Five additional shots is not great, but much better than even one needle jabbed into my stomach.

"Did the dogs also bite your husband?"

My husband? Oh, of course. She means Kevin. A fuzzy feeling warms my insides. "We're not married. Yet. But yes, Kevin got bit too."

The doctor sends a nurse scurrying to gather our vaccines.

Kevin comes back from X-ray, and Dr. Asbury cleans up the wound on his ankle. It requires nine stitches. I turn my head while she does the job. She uses some sort of glue to seal the gash on his head. Just as she's finishing, a technician delivers Kevin's X-rays. Our doctor pokes the images into a light box on the wall. She takes a careful look. "No fractured skull, but I believe you've suffered a concussion – bruised your brain. You need to give that brain tissue time to heal. Take it easy for awhile. No strenuous activities for a couple of weeks."

Does that include making love? I hope not.

Kevin's mind is going in the same direction as mine. "By strenuous, do you… uh, mean no sex?" It's cute how he kind of stammers.

The doctor is professional though. I can hardly detect a smile. "Nothing jarring," is all she says.

Nothing jarring? Okay. I envision long, slow, passionate love-making sessions. I can definitely live with that. Judging by the pleased look on Kevin's face, he can live with it too.

The doctor cleans the rope burns on Kevin's palms and wraps them in gauze.

Someone raps on the door. The nurse slips in through the door, wielding a tray filled with syringes and vials filled with what I assume is dog anti-venom.

Dr. Asbury explains the rabies preventative procedure to Kevin.

"Who want to go first?" she asks.

"Shoot me, doc," Kevin says. He takes the injections like a tough guy.

When it's my turn, I'm not as tough. But considering I've already surpassed my needle quota for the day – no, make that for the whole year – I don't think I do too bad. I have to put my head between my knees to get through it. But having Kevin here, with his hand on my thigh definitely helps.

"Where to now?" Kevin asks as we leave the hospital.

It's after five and already dark. The parking lot is well lit, but I hug Megan close, keeping a close watch on the shadowed outer edges of the tarmac, checking for any signs of red, glowing eyes. I notice Kevin is keeping a watchful eye between the cars too.

"I need to board up the window at Grandma's. Secure the house." Even if it is dark. Even if the dogs do happen to come back. I must honor Grandma by taking care of her property. And her faithful friend. "I have to bury Bubba." My voice catches.

"We'll do it together."

I give him a tired smile. "Thank you."

Kevin rubs his hand lightly over my shoulder blades. His touch skips goose bumps down my arms.

After the three of us are buckled inside the Blazer, I lay my head back against the passenger side headrest and relax. In a way I haven't relaxed in six years.

The motion of the car immediately puts Megan to sleep. We travel the rest of the distance to Grandma's in comfortable silence. Scenes from the past two days start to flicker through my mind like an old-time, silent picture show. I shut down the projector. I don't want the images haunting me. Reaching across the seat, I place a hand on Kevin's forearm. The smile he gives me is full of the future.

The headlights illuminate the trampled grass and a yard filled with muddy tire ruts as Kevin swings the Blazer into Grandma's driveway. "What a mess," I say. Crime scene tape still surrounds the place. I climb out, lift Megan from her car seat and hold her close.

"Is it okay to cross the tape?" I ask Kevin.

Kevin leaves the Blazer running with the headlights aimed at the garage. He steps from the vehicle. "Sure. We found Megan. I'm surprised an officer didn't rip it down. Maybe one of the agencies is still hoping to find some sign of the dogs." Kevin snorts. "Best of luck to whoever they send back to look."

"You're a detective. Won't it be you?"

"I hope not. This is outside city limits. It's really county jurisdiction. But since you first sighted the dogs inside the city before they followed you here, that makes it our case too. It would be a waste of my time to look for sign. Those dogs are like phantoms. No tracks. No scat. No hair, no blood."

Talking about the dogs, while standing exposed with Megan in the chilled night air is making me edgy. At least there's no fog tonight to add to the eeriness.

"Shit," Kevin says.

My heart races. "What?"

"I almost stepped in some."

"Some what?"

"Some horse shit." He chuckles.

"Geez, you scared me. I thought you saw one of the dogs." If he were close enough I'd give him a punch on the arm.

"I thought you said the dogs were gone."

"I did. But how can I be a hundred-percent sure?" My own doubt makes me nervous, so I change the subject. "We're going to need some light. I think there's a couple lanterns and some kerosene on the back shelf." I thrust my chin toward the garage. The door is still open from when Kevin fetched the ladder yesterday afternoon. Only yesterday? It seems like half a lifetime ago. So much has happened and changed for us in the past twenty-four hours.

Kevin clicks on the Maglite. I follow him into the garage. We locate the camping equipment in the back corner and pull down lanterns and fuel from a top shelf. I hold the flashlight while Kevin fills the lanterns and lights them. I hand him back the Mag and take a lantern. "I'm going inside to get Megan settled."

"I'll start digging a hole."

I nod. Poor old Bubba.

I grab the diaper bag out of the Blazer and turn off the headlights. No sense in having two vehicles with dead batteries. At the side door into the house, I grip Megan a little tighter before turning the knob. The last time I entered here, I stepped into a living nightmare. But no scratching or scuffling noises come from inside the house. No premonition prickles the back of my neck. I open the door, and let out a sigh when the scent of lavender, instead of sulfur greets me.

"I think they're really gone, Grandma."

Grandma doesn't reply.

I lie Megan on the couch to change her diaper. I wish I could shower and change my own dirty clothes. My skin feels oily, gritty and gross. Hot water would be a dream. If the power was still on, Kevin and I could each take showers. On second thought, make that singular. We could go green. Conserve water. Shower with a friend. The image of Kevin and my body, together, naked and streaming with soapy water sends jets of pleasant anticipation coursing to my toes.

But instead of a sexy duel shower, I make due with a quick baby-wipe sponge bath. I still feel grungy, but not as gross. At least now I smell like fresh baby lotion.

Baby lotion and Kevin.

Memories of our naked moments on the cliff ledge linger. I can't help smiling.

I settle back on the couch to nurse Megan, still marveling that she's unscathed after her ordeal with the dogs. Shoot, I haven't heard a single cough out of her since we were stuck in the attic. Last night I'd thought she was getting sick, but it must have just been from the thick attic dust.

Through the dining room, I can see out the kitchen window to the backyard. Kevin's lantern-illuminated head and upper torso bob into view with each shovel full of dirt he lifts out of the hole.

As much as I'm dreading it, I need to get out there and help him.

Where shall I put Megan? With the broken window in my old room, I can't leave her in there. The fog has burned off, but the air outside is still damp and cold.

I decide to put her in Grandma's room – it faces the backyard. I'll leave the shades open so I can periodically shine the flashlight in to check on her while we work. I carry Megan down the hall, pausing before the splintered laundry room door. I half expect a bloody, brindled-brown muzzle to shove through the gaping hole and snarl at us. But no dog snout appears.

In Grandma's room, I smooth my hand over the double-wedding-ring-pattern quilt on her bed. She hand-quilted it over forty years ago. A few of the blocks are frayed at the edges where the tiny stitches have lifted and the material has started to give. But it's still a work of art. A family heirloom.

"I miss you Grandma." I lie Megan down on the bed. Maybe someday Megan's own baby will sleep on the quilt. Like the connecting rings in the pattern, the circle of life never ends.

I kiss Megan on the forehead and cover her with a blanket. I form a pillow barricade around her little body before I slip out of the room and out the back door.

Grabbing a shovel from the tool shed, I join Kevin. Side-by-side, we jab our blades into the earth. With each scoop, we dig the grave a little deeper.

Nearby lies Bubba's body. Ripped, muddy, blood-caked and still. Oh, Bubba. Tears fill my eyes, blinding me. I swipe at them impatiently.

Kevin stops digging for a moment. He folds his hands over the end of his shovel handle and watches me. "I can take care of this," he says.

"Thanks, but I need to help." It's true. It's time I faced the circle of life – and death – head on. I stab the shovel back into the ground, sniffling back the brine burning my throat.

Even with his rope-torn hands, Kevin shovels two scoops to my one. In no time we've dug a gaping hole. I hustle to Grandma's bedroom window, hold the lantern high and peer in at Megan. She's sleeping. No dogs have snuck in to accost her. Kevin walks with me to the garage to find an old sheet. I carry it to the back yard and start to wrap it around the old chocolate lab.

"Wait." I stop what I'm doing. "Since the red-eyed dogs killed Bubba. Does the crime lab need any DNA samples or anything before we bury him?"

Kevin shakes his head. "I told them the dogs killed Bubba. Any samples they needed, they already took."

We wrap the sheet around the old chocolate Labrador, then lower his stiff body into the ground.

Raining the first few shovelfuls of dirt on top of Bubba is the hardest. After that, the work goes quickly. We pitch the last of the disturbed soil over the hole and tamp at the mound with our shovel heads.

"I'd like to say a few words," I tell Kevin.

He nods and leans on his shovel.

I've never before given a eulogy. I bow my head. Draw in a shaky breath. "Bubba was a good dog. He was loyal and kind. A happy-go-lucky soul always up for a game of fetch. Bubba loved his family. And though he was gentle, he fiercely protected those he loved."

My voice breaks. I have to pause to gain composure. "He gave his life to protect us."

He wasn't perfect, I almost say. Once he ran away and forgot about us. But I realize I'm no longer reminiscing about Bubba. Now I'm actually thinking about my dad.

"He's gone, but I'll never forget him. Goodbye, Bubba."

Goodbye Dad.

"Goodbye," Kevin mutters and brushes at the corner of an eye, as if there's a speck of dirt in it. Such a tough guy. He's not fooling me, I know he was wiping at a tear. Could he be thinking about his own father?

Kevin motions me over. He tosses his shovel aside, folds me into his arms and hugs me close. We stand like that for awhile. His chin on my head, my head on his chest. His heart beats a steady *whump-thump, whump-thump* under my cheek. His breath warms the top of my head.

"Shall we?" Kevin asks, breaking my trance.

"Mmmm? Shall we what?"

"Finish up."

"Oh, right." Unwillingly, I step from his embrace.

We walk hand-in-hand to the tool shed where we find a sheet of plywood, a hammer and a can of nails. I hold the wood while Kevin nails it in place over the broken bedroom window. It's a temporary fix, but it will work until I can arrange for someone to replace that window and the one in the attic. I'll also have a contractor patch the hole in the roof as soon as possible and replace the laundry room door. I'll crawl up in the attic myself in a day or two and empty the pot I peed in and get the boxes down. Then Mom can list the house with a realtor.

The thought of strangers living in Grandma's house makes me want to sit down and bawl. But I've shed plenty enough tears lately.

After we put away the tools, Kevin uses the Blazer's battery to jump start his car. He grabs a gas can from the garage and dumps gas in the tank of his police sedan. We decide to convoy back to my apartment. I lead the way in my Blazer. Megan coos from her infant seat in back. Kevin follows in his undercover car. I sneak peeks in my rearview mirror. Usually it's unnerving to have a cop follow me, but today it gives me tingling thrills.

I don't think that's so pathetic.

I was surprised when Kevin wanted to go to my apartment first instead of his. I figured he'd at least want a change of clean clothes, but he insisted we go straight to my place.

I understand why when I pull into the lot at the end of Daffodil Lane and park directly in front of my apartment door. The flowers he'd mentioned last evening are gorgeous – a bouquet of roses and carnations, still looking florist-fresh waiting there on the stoop.

I cast a sly glance towards Kevin, who's just pulling into the visitor slot next to my Blazer. I leap from my truck, pluck Megan from the back seat, take the two front steps in a single bound and snatch the tiny envelope from amidst the poufs of baby's breath. I tear open the seal.

The card says, "I'm sorry about the loss of your Grandma, Dianne, but she will always be with you."

If he only knew how true that really is.

The card is signed, "My love will always be with you too, Kevin."

He steps from his car. I beam him a smile. He flashes one back.

His head and shoulders disappear as he stoops to rummage around in the backseat of his car. When he reappears, he's got a giant teddy bear in his arms. What is he up to now? I admire his tall, lean physique as he strides over the strip of grass and up the sidewalk. I tip my face up to his and he kisses me, slow and firm.

My heartbeat quickens and my knees wobble. "Someone sent me flowers."

Kevin shifts the teddy bear in his arm, as if holding it puts him outside his comfort zone.

"Oh yeah? Who?"

"A secret admirer."

"Should I be jealous?"

"Mmmm, maybe. He's tall, kind, handsome and brave."

"I'll kick his butt."

I laugh. "You'd look funny doing it. Especially while you're holding that bear.

Besides, you're not supposed to do anything jarring. Kicking yourself in the butt would definitely be jarring."

"Guess you have a point there." He gives me his wry, lopsided grin. "How do you like the flowers?"

"They're wonderful. The man who sent them is even better."

Kevin's eyes twinkle. He kisses me again.

We're getting married. I must be the luckiest woman alive.

When we part from the kiss I ask, "Who's this?" and give the stuffed bear a pat on the belly.

"Oh, right. Where are my manners? Dianne, I'd like you to meet my new partner, Teddy."

I grip one of the bear's plush paws in my fingertips. "Nice to meet you, Teddy. Where were you hiding? We could have used your help earlier today, when we were stuck on a cliff."

Kevin wrinkles his chin.

I raise up on my tip toes to kiss him.

He stiffens and pulls away.

"What?" Was it something I said? What did I say? Two seconds ago we were joking around, kissing and having fun.

"I know you were kidding just now. At least I hope you were. But I think we did alright on that cliff without any help."

Oh, that. Me and my big mouth. I didn't mean to poke a hole in Kevin's fragile, one-hundred-percent-male ego. I forgot how important it is to his self-worth – his capability to take care of us.

"You're right, honey. I was only kidding. Megan and I couldn't have asked for a more competent rescuer. Or a more handsome one." I throw that last compliment in for extra brownie points. "No offense, Teddy. But I'm attracted to tall and clean shaven, not short and hairy." I stretch up to meet Kevin's lips with mine again. This time he doesn't pull away. "I love you," I say.

Kevin seems to relax. "I love you, too." He holds the bear out to Megan with his bandage-wrapped hands. The bear is three times her size. "And this is for you, young lady." Megan waves her arms and kicks her feet. We both laugh.

"I think she likes it," I say.

I unlock my apartment door, "I'll fix us something to eat. I'm starving."

"Maybe a quick bite. But I can't stay long."

I turn my face so he won't see my disappointment. I was hoping he'd spend the night.

"I have to get home. I've got a dinner date."

"Oh?" Jealousy pricks my every nerve. I keep my back to Kevin while I get out a vase, fill it with water and arrange the bouquet of roses inside. He sent me flowers, for crying out loud. He asked me to marry him. What's he doing going on a date? What made me think I could ever trust him?

"Her name's Sophelia."

"Sophelia?" Sounds French. And slutty.

"Mmm-hmmm."

Oooh, I don't like the way his 'mmm-hmmm' sounds.

"She has long, black hair."

Definitely a French bimbo – I'll bet she doesn't even shave her legs. Or her armpits. She probably doesn't wear deodorant either. What a disgusting, hairy slut.

I don't get it. He has a fiancé now. I know the whole commitment thing between us literally happened overnight, but still, why doesn't he just call and cancel his "date"?

"You can use my phone to cancel." I try to keep the emotion out of my voice.

Apparently I am not successful. Kevin grabs my shoulders and turns me to face him. "You're jealous."

"Well, duh." I can't bring myself to look at his face. "What are you doing having a date?"

"Sweetheart, I'm teasing you."

I look up into his eyes. They're twinkling like crazy.

"Sophelia's my cat."

"Oh." I feel really stupid and embarrassed. So I punch him.

"Ouch." He rubs his bicep, pretending to seriously be injured. "Guess I had that one coming."

"You bet you did."

I stick Megan in her wind-up swing and fix ham and cheese sandwiches for me and Kevin – two for him, one for me. I scoop a handful of potato chips onto each plate and plunk a dill pickle on the side. I pour two big glasses of milk and carry the meal to the table. We dig in like we haven't eaten in a week.

"A cat, huh?" I ask between bites.

Kevin feigns to the right. "You're not going to punch me again, are you?" He laughs.

"Very funny. No, I'm not going to punch you again. At least not this second. Do you have a dog too?" My feelings about dogs right now are mixed. I all ready miss Bubba, but the black dog's evil red eyes and yellow fangs may haunt me forever.

"No dog." Kevin inhales the rest of his second sandwich and pushes away from the table. "Well, I'm going to be on my way. Feed my cat. Shower. Get some shuteye. I have to head into the station first thing in the morning for debriefing. And then I'll have a mountain of paperwork to do. Thanks for the food. Happy Thanksgiving. We should have eaten turkey sandwiches."

"Ingrate," I say.

Kevin stoops to kiss me, then he's out the door.

"When will I see you again?" I ask. But he's already pulled the door closed behind him.

Just as tears of exhaustion, frustration and doubt start to prick the back of my eyes, Kevin opens the door again, sticks his head in and says, "I love you, baby. I'll call you tomorrow. Wanna go out to dinner when I get off work?"

"Sounds great," I say.

I wouldn't stop the huge smile that spreads across my face if I could.

Chapter Thirty-Four

Thursday, 7:50 PM

After I wash the dishes, I give Megan a quick bath in the kitchen sink, dress her in footie sleepers, nurse her and tuck her in her crib for the night. Then it's my turn to get cleaned up. Hot water has never felt so glorious. I let the water from the showerhead beat against my aching muscles until my skin turns red and the hot water turns tepid.

As I step from the shower, I remember the senior photos that need editing. I could work on them now – but a bone-tired weariness settles into my joints. I towel off, blow dry my hair, brush my teeth, pull on a nightgown and crawl into bed.

My body is exhausted, but my mind races through the day's events. It's been a Thanksgiving I'll never forget: My baby was abducted by an evil red-eyed dog. I went into the fortuneteller's house – a place I swore I'd never set foot. The fortuneteller told us where to find Megan, and she was right. Kevin faced his fear of heights for us. Again. I scaled down a cliff. I thought Kevin died. I fought the dogs and got Megan back. One of the dogs bit me. Again. The dogs vanished, hopefully forever. Kevin came back to life. He proposed to me. I accepted. Kevin and I did the wild thing on a narrow ledge on the side of a cliff. We got ourselves and Megan back up the cliff. We went to the hospital where we got patched up, stitched up and injected with needles.

No one else except Kevin, Grandma and Delta the fortuneteller would possibly believe such a story.

It was a Thanksgiving without turkey and trimmings, without a big family gathered around a food-laden table. But I still have so, so much to be thankful for today. I have my daughter back, safe and sound and sleeping in the next room. I once more have Kevin in my life. This time forever. I miss Grandma, but at least now I know she will always be with me. And I once more believe in miracles.

I didn't make it to the soup kitchen to help serve the less fortunate. Maybe next Thanksgiving Kevin and I can serve there together. Tomorrow is Friday and the holiday will be over. Tomorrow life should feel almost normal. Tomorrow I'll work on the photos. Tomorrow I'll see Kevin again. Tomorrow I'll… .

…I'll beat the dogs off with a stick. Then we'll scale the cliff. But Megan's trapped in the cave. The rope's frayed. It won't hold me. It won't hold Kevin.

The dogs close in around me, snarling, drooling, their eyes red as molten steel, their yellow fangs razor sharp. Bloody foam flies from their muzzles. Red flecks of saliva stick to my arms and face.

"Megan!" I bolt upright, drenched in sweat. I swing my feet to the floor and stumble down the hall, mentally punching at the fading images.

Megan's eyes are closed. She lies perfectly still. Is she breathing? I don't see her chest moving. "Megan? Megan?" I scoop her out of her crib. "Megan?"

She stirs in my arms, blinks her eyes and cries with startled indignation. I let out a huge sigh of relief, hug her close, breathe in the clean, baby-fresh scent of her skin and hair.

"Sorry to wake you, little one. There's someplace we need to go."

I nurse her. Get us both dressed. Brush my teeth, run a comb through my hair, gather it back into a quick pony tail. Slap a little makeup on my cheeks, lips, eyes. Make a cup of instant coffee. Pour it into a travel mug. Glance at the microwave clock: 7:18. I hope it's not too early.

Tough shit if it is. I need answers.

I burst out my front door, Megan in my arms. Determination gives spring to my step.

A blast of wind stings my face and I drape a blanket over Megan's head. After I've strapped her into her car seat, I fire up the Blazer and drive north.

I'm surprisingly calm, considering what I'm about to do.

In eight minutes, I reach my destination. I climb out of the SUV, unload Megan and take a couple of deep, cleansing breaths. The air is fresh off the sea. No sulfur tarnishes the scent.

The sign near the sidewalk hangs from chains and eye hooks, the hardware rusted from the constant salt air. I give the creaking sign a wide berth. Ducking my head against the pelting wind and pulling Megan's blanket up over her face, I trudge up the front walk to the cottage. My knuckles sting after the three sharp raps I give the door. I study my sneakers while I wait.

When Delta opens the door, she doesn't say "Hello," or "Come in." She doesn't ask, "What can I help you with?" She just steps back and says, "I expected you."

She's dressed in pink. Her face glows, as though freshly scrubbed. Her lipstick and eye makeup is carefully applied. It's as if she did, indeed, know I would show up at her door first thing this morning.

I don't know exactly how to greet her, so I don't say anything. I just walk myself on inside her little house as though I'm not the least bit nervous. I hold Megan with one arm and inspect the fingernails of my other hand, waiting for Delta to ask me what I want. But she doesn't ask. She just looks at me. I can feel her eyes. She's not staring exactly, just looking. Searching. Waiting. I shift my weight, start to fidget. I'm not sure how to begin.

I have this woman to thank for finding Megan. I owe her my baby's life – her and Kevin. And Grandma. I was abrupt with Delta when I was here before. I don't want to act rude this time. But how to ask what I came here to ask without coming across as bitchy?

"Not that I'm a skeptic…" I blurt. But of course I am a skeptic. A lifetime of skepticism doesn't disappear overnight. I'm not fooling myself and I have a strong hunch I'm not fooling the fortuneteller either.

Delta shoots me a look that says my hunch is right.

"Okay, okay," I back pedal, "I am a skeptic. Not about all of it…something was obviously at work here. You knew things…" This is the part that rattles me. I draw a deep breath and plunge, "…but how did you know, uh, what you knew, just from looking at eight dice thrown at random onto a painted circle?"

"I only knew what you told me."

"That's what I'm asking. That's why I'm here – because I didn't tell you anything."

A smile tiptoes across Delta's painted pink lips. "Ah, but you did."

"What do you mean, I did?"

Delta raises an eyebrow and gives me a slow chin nod. "Would you like to sit down?"

I shake my head. "Thank you, no." I only intend to stay long enough to slake my curiosity, then I'm outa here. Delta seems like a nice enough woman and I do feel bad for judging her so harshly all these years, but this whole "fortunetelling" thing still gives me the creeping willies.

"You told me everything I needed to know," Delta continues.

"I didn't tell you anything." I repeat, waiting to see what she'll say. She doesn't say a word, so I keep talking, "Yet you still knew…things. Things you couldn't have known. My baby was missing. You knew where we could find her. I mean, you even knew my name for crying out loud. I'm sure I never told you my name. I want to know how you did that. How you guessed all that stuff." It was definitely more than a con-artist parlor trick. I drum my fingers on the oak table.

"The questions and answers were obvious."

This woman can be so frustrating. "I deserve a straight-up answer. You're talking in riddles."

"Life is a riddle." The smile vanishes from Delta's lips like smoke.

I heave an exaggerated sigh. "See, there you go again. I ask a simple question…"

Delta pulls a chair out from the table. She brushes her long pink skirt smooth over her bottom and takes a seat. She gestures for me to do the same. "And I gave you a simple answer. But it is not the answer you expected."

Pulling out a chair, I join Delta at the table. "I expect the truth." One thing I've recently learned is the truth can take a while. I plan to park myself right here until I get it.

"Look inside yourself for that."

"Riddles again…." I utter under my breath, quietly so she won't hear me.

"How do you solve a riddle?"

Besides her unexplainable "psychic" abilities, Delta also has exceptional hearing. I make full-on eye contact. Maybe I can stare her into submission. It didn't work day before yesterday when I tried staring down the dogs, but I'm willing to give it another shot today with Delta.

Unblinking, Delta' eyes lock with mine. I glance away. So much for the stare down.

"How do you solve a riddle?" she repeats, an air of authority crisps her voice.

It's starting to feel like I'm trapped inside Batman's cave having a conversation with the Riddler. And I'm finding it damn annoying. Delta may have exceptional hearing, amazing insight, superior knowledge – I don't care what sort of super-hero powers she possesses – I just want honest answers to my questions. This fortune-teller, mumbo-jumbo, beat-around-the-bush, cryptic talk is getting on my nerves.

"Well, I've never been good at solving riddles," I admit. "But maybe I'd have half a chance if I had some clues to work with."

"Exactly."

I let out another huge sigh. "What do you mean by 'exactly?' "

"When you and Kevin were here that day, you gave me clues."

This woman constantly makes me fight the urge to roll my eyes.. "How did I give you clues? I hardly said anything that day."

"Clues do not have to be spoken."

This conversation is getting nowhere fast. I seriously consider pushing up from the table, stomping out the door and slamming it behind me.

"Your body language is telling me much right now."

"Oh, yeah?" I sit back in my chair. I'd cross my arms and huff if I wasn't holding Megan. I can't cross my arms, but I can still let out a huff. So I do. "Like what?"

"Like you are about to leave, because you do not feel as if your questions are being answered. And you will make a lot of noise while leaving to prove your point."

Wow, she's good. I sit forward, deciding to fight fire with fire. I'll answer her with questions. Only questions. Play her with her own game. See how she likes it. "What point would I be trying to prove?"

"That you are exasperated."

"That, I am." I shift in my chair again, then remember my question-asking strategy. "Why am I exasperated?"

"And you blame me for your feelings of frustration," Delta continues as though I never asked a question, "because you do not understand how something can be unexplainable, yet still be true."

Coming from her, that was a damn long sentence. She pauses, as if she's used up her word quota for the next sixty seconds. Finally she says, "Relax please, Dianne."

I stiffen my spine. "I am relaxed." There she goes calling me by name again. Who ever told her my name? I sure as hell didn't, and neither did Kevin.

"Take off your coat. Would you like a cup of tea?"

"Why, do you want to read my tea leaves? I didn't bring any money with me to pay for a 'reading.' " I couldn't afford a reading, even if I'd asked for one. As Grandma used to say, 'You can't squeeze blood from a turnip.'

"No charge today. Refreshments are free, and I do not read tea leaves. Just consider us two acquaintances, having a friendly chat."

Anything worthwhile takes awhile. Another one of Grandma's favorite sayings. Nodding, I say, "Okay. A cup of tea sounds nice." I've already resolved myself to staying here until I get the answers I seek. At this rate, that'll take me into next week. I'll need some fluid intake during that time to keep from dehydrating.

Delta slips from the room. While she bangs about in the kitchen, I take the opportunity to really look around her front parlor. A bright border of yellow and orange poppies tops the walls. Framed floral prints hang in groupings of threes. I turn in my chair and check out the décor behind me. A pie cabinet is filled with ruby glass.

My mind flashes back to the dogs' glowing ruby eyes.

I gasp.

But my fear is ridiculous. This red is collectible glassware, not dog eyes. Still, I am uneasy knowing the ruby red dishes are behind me. I turn sideways in my chair, so I can keep a peripheral eye on the shelves of glassware.

When Delta pops back in, I'm glad to see her. If anyone can ward away evil glassware spirits, it would be her. She carries a tray. Steam rises from two mugs. She sets the tray in the middle of the small table. I choose a packet of spearmint tea from an assortment in a small basket. Delta chooses black decaf. I stir in two cubes of sugar while waiting for the tea to steep.

She smoothes the back of her skirt and sits across from me. She drops the tea bag into her cup. Then, leaning her forearms on the table, Delta hits me with a real whammy:

"I could not tell a thing by the numbers on the dice."

"Huh?" She kind of hit me out of left field with that admission. I'm not playing stupid now. I truly feel dumber than a box of rocks.

"Just like a few minutes ago, you were ready to leave, and I knew."

I nod.

"The day your baby went missing, I studied your body language."

"That's all there is to 'fortune telling?' Body language?" I shake my head. Amazing. Even I can read body language. Maybe photography is the wrong business to be in. Wonder what a fortunetelling session pays? I can see my own lettered wooden sign now, curbside and swinging in the breeze like Delta's. Only mine would say: "Dianne the Magnificent" or something like that, and below, on the second line it would say, "Let me read your mind – only $49.95 a pop." Then at the very bottom, in teeny tiny print, it would say, "Tourist rate: $79.95."

"No. There is much more."

So much for striking it rich just by studying people's posture. I knew it was too good to be true. "Explain it to me. Please."

"Not everything can be explained."

Here we go with the damn riddles again. This time, I can't stop my eyes from rolling. "Try me."

Delta leans my way. There, see, I can read her body language. She's telling me she's interested in me and she has something significant to say. "Dianne, you recently lost people important to you."

"See, how could you know that?"

"Is that not true?"

"It is true." I catch myself speaking without contractions, like Delta.

"You were grieving. You are still. Although not nearly so much."

"Okay. That's also true. So?"

"You were locking up your grief and your memories of those who left you. The memories of your grandmother. Her voice. Trapped inside you."

Okay, now this is getting downright freaky. How could she know I've been hearing Grandma's voice? "How could you possibly know that?"

Delta is silent.

I want to shake her, rattle her cage the way she rattles mine. But I don't touch her. The thought of touching her terrifies me – physical contact may allow her to sip at the secrets of my soul.

I wiggle uncomfortably in my chair. "Why did you have me throw the dice?"

Delta says nothing. But that's okay. I still need to ask the question I've most wanted answered, but avoided because it gives me chills: "And what was the deal with the dogs?"

Again Delta sits quietly, as if sensing I am not finished yet. She's right. I'm not. "Were the dogs from this world? What did they want with me and Megan? And with the poor tow truck driver and with the others who disappeared? The dogs did take them, right?"

"You have many questions."

"I'm hoping you have many answers. Please don't tell me to 'look inside myself,' either. If you need money, I'll go home and get some." I start to push up from the chair. Two or three 20-dollar bills should coax her into giving me straight answers. I've got bills to pay, but I could take a credit-card draw. "I'll be back with some cash in about fifteen minutes."

"Sit." The demand catches me off guard. "Please." She adds firmly, with a palms-up gesture which lessons the harshness. A little. I remain seated.

"I had you throw the dice. Not to see the numbers, but to see the depth of your fear."

"Fear? Of throwing dice?" I wouldn't admit it out loud, but she was right. Those dice and the truth they might have revealed that day terrified me.

"Not fear of throwing. Fear of the unknown. Fear of loss and death. Fear of yourself."

I'm not sure if Delta pauses so that what she's said can soak into my thick skull, or so she can organize her thoughts. Straight forward answers, like the ones she's finally giving me, seem to be difficult for her to manage.

"And I wanted to gauge your anger," Delta finally says. She arches an eyebrow. "You had much that day."

Grandma had just died. I'd seen a man ripped apart. I'd watched Bubba get killed trying to protect me and Megan. To top it all off, a murdering dog stole my baby, and Kevin let it happen after he'd told me he'd protect us. Damn Skippy I had anger. But I don't say any of this. I just sit silently like Delta did a bit ago. A taste of her own medicine might do this woman good.

Seconds tick by. Delta nonchalantly sips her tea. The silent treatment doesn't seem to phase her. She takes another sip. Finally, she says, "Anger is a manifestation of fear." She says no more. Ten seconds. Fifteen. Twenty seconds of silence. I guess she's giving me time to absorb her words. "Fear is the root of all evil."

"I thought money was the root of all evil." I think of a Bible passage I've heard quoted my entire life, although off hand I can't think of the chapter name or verse number.

Delta gives me a puzzled look as though I am speaking Hebrew. Which in a translated, round-about way, I guess I am. I take advantage of her silence to try and process what she's just said: Anger is fear. Fear is evil.

I still believe the root of evil is money, but decide to let it slide. So now, back to the tough question. "What about the dogs?" I ask.

"The dogs were a manifestation of grief."

"I thought fear was evil. Now you're saying grief is evil? Those dogs were definitely evil."

Delta nods. "Grief is anger, which is fear turned inward." She speaks slowly as though the few words are a lot for me to comprehend.

She's right about that. "Let me get this straight," I say. "Grief is anger. Anger is fear. And fear is evil?"

"Yes, Dianne." She says this as though I am a first grader, questioning why the number two comes after the number three. "All negative emotions are fear."

"But why are we talking about fear in the first place?"

"You were angry. You were grieving. Anger and grief are fear. Fear nourished the dogs. Your fear made them bigger. Tougher. Meaner. More 'evil' as you put it."

"So, are you trying to tell me that the dogs 'fed' off my negative emotions? They 'fed' off my grief and anger and fear?"

"In a way." Delta nods again.

"In what way?"

"The dogs *were* your fear."

Wait a minute, that's what Grandma called them – "dogs of fear." Just before the dogs killed Mel. Why did they kill Mel?

I haven't mentioned Mel to Delta, so I don't ask that question, instead I voice another, "But if they were my fear, why did one of the dogs bite Kevin?"

"That fear – that *dog* – was also his fear, his grief."

"But there were more than one."

"Exactly."

"What do you mean by exactly?"

"For each of you there was one fear for one grief."

"But there were five dogs."

"For you, perhaps."

Okay, she's speaking in riddles again. Did I mention how much I hate riddles? I decide to step sideways with my line of questioning. "Why did the dogs spare my baby's life?"

"Your baby was not grieving. She was simply being. Babies are love. They carry no evil. There was nothing negative in your baby to drive the dogs to attack."

This isn't making sense. "Then why did a dog take her in the first place?"

"Your baby coming to harm is your greatest fear."

Uh, yeah okay, she's got me there.

"You forced yourself to face your greatest fear."

Forced myself? Delta says it as though I had a hand in the black dog snatching Megan. Never would I have made that happen. Not in a million years. Not if I could help it. Could I not help it?

None of this makes complete sense, but I'll try to puzzle it out later. Before I leave, I have two more questions.

"What made the dogs – my fear, as you call them – vanish?"

"Your positive emotions overpowered your negative emotions."

Which opens the floor wide open for my final question. "So if negative emotions are fear, what are positive emotions?"

Chapter Thirty-Five

Friday, 8:16 AM

"Love," Delta answers.

Is that a twinkle I see in the wise and serious fortuneteller's eyes?

"Love is the most powerful emotion of all," she says.

I don't understand everything Delta's told me, not really. I came to her for answers, yet I still have many questions. On the way back to my apartment, I mull over our conversation. Fear. Fear and love.

I think of Megan's big blue eyes, her chubby baby hands and feet, her fuzzy blonde hair. The way she gazes up at me as she nurses. The vanilla fragrance of her head. How her small body fits perfectly in my arms. The pride that wells inside me every time I think of her, look at her. Every time she smiles, or coos. The way I've loved her since the moment I felt the flutter of life inside my womb.

I think of Kevin, his big fingers gently caressing my skin. His laughing golden eyes and the way they soften when he looks at me. His clean-scented cologne. The concerned cleft in his chin. The courageous way he fought his fears for us. The way my heart swells and my stomach flutters when I think of him.

Delta claims all positive emotions are love. Now there's a truth I can totally understand.

***

Friday, 7:15 pm

Kevin takes Megan and me out to an Italian restaurant for dinner. Megan sits in her infant seat in the booth beside me. In a hushed voice, over my plate of lasagna, I ask Kevin how many red-eyed dogs he'd seen.

"Two, of course. The gray one that bit me and later climbed the ladder, and the black one that took Megan."

I must give him a funny look because he asks, "Why? Were there more?"

I nod. "There were five. Three big ones and two small ones." I don't mention the white dog I saw for a moment on the cliff before they all disappeared.

"Oh. Where were the rest of them?"

Inside me? Inside my head? I don't know how to answer his question, so I don't. "I went to see Delta today. She said the dogs were our grief, or our fears. But if that's true, why did I see five and you only saw two?"

"Grief, huh?" Kevin chews a bite of pasta and takes a drink of iced tea as though this notion of grief/fear-induced dogs is as easy to swallow as his meal. "I had grief over my dad."

"That's one."

"And…"

"Yes?"

"I had grief over you."

"Me? Why? I'm not dead."

"In a way you were. To me. I let you go, and I was afraid I would never get the chance to get you back."

As for me? I suppose one of "my" dogs was grief over losing Kevin, too. And losing my dad, my mom, my husband, and then Grandma. That's five. I'm glad when Kevin doesn't ask me to tick them off out loud. And I don't even try to figure out which personal grief corresponds with which dog. Really, what's the point?

***

Sunday, 2:05 PM

Grandma's service starts at two o'clock sharp at the Roseland Southern Baptist Church. As I suspected it would be, the church is packed. Kevin sits beside me with his hand on my knee. Halfway through the service, when Megan starts to squirm and fuss, Kevin takes her from me and stands in the aisle off to the side, jouncing her gently in his arms until she quiets.

He will make an excellent father.

After the service ends, Kevin asks, "Are you alright?"

I nod. I feel drained and sad. But I'm okay. I'll always miss the living, breathing Grandma, but I know, in a different form, I will always carry her with me.

Kevin hands Megan back. "I should get back to work, sweetheart. But if you need me to stay, I will."

"You go ahead. I have a few things to talk with Mom about anyway."

"You sure?"

I nod. "Yeah, I'm sure."

He kisses me softly, looks deep into my eyes. "I love you," he says.

"I don't think I'll ever get tired of hearing you say that."

"I love you," he whispers again before turning to leave.

I watch him go and think how lucky I am before joining the crowd of mourners in the reception hall. The church ladies spent all morning, and probably a good share of yesterday, preparing a full meal. I dish fruit salad, a roll and a spatula full of tamale pie on a plate and take a seat across the table from Mom and Gene. I hold Megan in my lap. Mom reaches over and takes my hand in hers.

"I'm sorry, Dianne," she says. "I know how close you and Mother were."

"I'm sorry too. For both of us." I pause. "I'm sorry for a lot of things, Mom."

She waves a hand and shakes her head as though whatever I'm talking about is no big thing.

But it is.

"Let's go outside. Take a walk," she suggests.

"Okay." I'm surprised, and curious about what she might have to say to me in private. We slip out the side door. It's a cool day, cloudy, but not bone-chilling. Megan kicks her feet with excitement when the breeze touches her face. Mom and I both chuckle. We stroll along the covered sidewalk that surrounds the building.

I'm the first to speak. "I'm sorry I didn't forgive you when you left."

"I'm sorry I left you."

Mom is not one to apologize. Even when she knows she's wrong. I am shocked into silence. It's a pleased silence.

"I'm so glad you're okay," she says. "When I heard you and Megan were attacked by dogs, I was beside myself with worry. I couldn't wait to see you both for myself, make sure you were alright." Fresh tears turn Mom's irises into miniature green seas.

If she only knew the whole truth about the dogs and how evil they really were… Maybe someday I'll tell her.

Then again, maybe I never will.

Right now I want to ask her a question I've meant to ask for years. "Why did Dad leave?"

I'd never let myself come right out and ask her before. She never wanted to talk about Dad. She always changed the subject if I brought up his name. But for the moment there is a strand of trust wavering like a mercury thread between us. This is the closest I've felt to Mom in years. I hope she feels it too.

Mom is silent. I wait for the inevitable twist she'll spin into our conversation, wringing it out into small talk about the weather, tomorrow's breakfast plans, or some other mundane subject. "He left after your baby brother died," she says.

My heart drops to my black pumps. This isn't the answer I anticipated. Not at all. I certainly wasn't braced for Mom to reveal a secret sibling. "I…I had a brother?"

The memory of a baby's cry sounds in my ears, tinny, hollow, far away, like a seventy-eight record on a wind-up phonograph. I close my eyes so I won't lose the sound. A dog's face – white, with red eyes – flashes among the shadows dappling the back of my lids.

"Yes."

"What happened to him?"

My mom is silent again. That harsh look she gets crosses her face. The one that says, "Dianne, you've crossed the line."

I don't take back my question. I just wait. What else can I do? He was my brother. I have a right to know. "I mean, how did he die?"

My mother still says nothing.

"I'm sorry to pry, Mom. But please tell me. Don't you think, after all these years, I have a right to know?"

After a few more silent moments, I guess Mom decides I do have the right. "He died of SIDS when he was four months old."

"Oh," is all I can say for a moment. A flashing memory of a chubby-faced baby boy zips through my mind, followed by a big, white dog face – a ghostly German shepherd. The dog's brown eyes begin to change to red.

No, not this again. My stomach clenches, sickens. "But, why didn't you ever tell me about him? I've never seen a picture of him or anything. What was his name?"

"His name was Seth." Saying the name seems to hurt her face like an impacted tooth.

My brother. "Seth," I say, letting the name roll in my mouth. I'm not an only child after all.

"I'm sorry I never told you. I couldn't talk about it, honey. It was too hard. I lost both my son and my husband in the same month."

Mom hasn't called me honey in…in I can't remember how long. "Why didn't Dad come back to us?"

"I don't think he could have lived with us without thinking about the baby everyday. He couldn't deal with it."

It seems grief has been nipping at my family's heels for years. "You couldn't deal with it either."

Mom doesn't say anything for a minute. "He had an even harder time than I did. He just shut down."

"Him leaving us wasn't the answer."

"Try to forgive him."

"Have you?"

"Yes, but it took a long time."

"How can you forget? He abandoned us."

"I didn't say I forgot what he did. I said I forgave him. There's a big difference."

We've walked two loops around the church already. We start into a third lap.

"Everyone makes mistakes," Mom says.

I can't believe she's writing off Dad's actions with three words. "We lost a member of our family, so Dad throws in the towel and disappears. What kind of a husband and father is that?" I ask.

"No one is perfect, Dianne."

There she goes again. My mother and her pat answers.

"I'd settle for decent. Responsible. Mature."

"Men like your Kevin don't grown on trees," Mom says, then mumbles. "Believe me. I looked for one like him for years."

I'll say she looked. For years she took close and very personal looks at anything single and male. "So why did you move away and leave me before I was out of school?"

"You know why, honey. Gene got an excellent job offer."

"Gene had a good job here, Mom. He adores you. He would've stayed if you'd asked him too. You know that."

Mom nods. "I guess I wanted to escape."

"You ran away."

"Isn't that the same thing?"

Realization settles on me like cold, misty dew. Mom couldn't start a new life surrounded by the empty memories of a dead son and a broken marriage.

"I just wanted to get away," Mom says, "make a fresh start. A new beginning…." her voice grows hushed, "…after I'd dated so many men here…I, well, I never want Gene to find out how many there had been."

"Yeah, what was with that?" I match Mom's quiet tones, although everyone else is still inside the church, eating and making funeral small-talk. It's not as if anyone can hear us. "That was a nightmare for me growing up. So many men in and out of our lives. Everyone talked about it. Even the kids at school teased me."

"I'm sorry." Mom stares off into the distance. "I was searching."

"For what?"

"For a love like I had with your dad."

"Did you find it?"

"No." Mom pauses. Looks away before she looks back at me. "I found something better."

"What?"

"A man who won't run away when things get tough."

For the first time in as long as I can remember, I feel true happiness for my mother. But I want her to answer one more question. "Where did Dad go?"

"I don't know. That question ate at me for years. I never heard from him again. I finally let go."

"He really did run away."

Mom nods.

"Did you ever look for him?"

Mom laughs. It's a helpless choking sound. "I filed a missing persons report. I was the biggest pest the Roseland Police Department has probably ever known. When I learned how to use the internet, I went online and searched hours at a time for him. For years I intended to hire a private investigator. But they're expensive. So, I scraped and saved. I almost had enough – he'd been gone for years by then – when it hit me. He doesn't want to be found. He's never coming back. Why should I scrape by and go without just to keep searching for him? Why should you go without, just so I can pay out hard-earned money to an investigator who may, or may not find him? What difference would it make if a private eye did find him? Your dad wasn't coming home. It just took me awhile to realize the obvious."

At Mom's words, coal red eyes burn like hot pokers into my brain. The ruby eyes are encased in the face of a white wolf.

Maybe Dad couldn't come home. Maybe his beasts of grief and fear didn't let him.

"I used the money I'd saved for so long and bought you a stereo and a new wardrobe. Remember? When you were a freshman?"

I nod and swallow back the lump building in my throat. I'd wanted a stereo of my own forever. And that year, I was among the best dressed girls in high school. I never realized what my mom went through to get me those clothes and that stereo. A brick of guilt clunks me over the head. I squeeze my eyes shut. I wonder what living hell my dad went through before he vanished.

"Shortly after that, I met Gene."

Mom finally met someone decent after she stopped grieving for a man who was never coming back. It took her over a dozen years to get over my Dad and move on with her life.

And I thought I was bad at dealing with grief. Now I know where I got it.

If a grief-manifested dog got my dad all those years ago, why didn't one take my mom?

How many years have red-eyed dogs been circling my family?

Mom and I pause behind the church. Megan coos. We are three generations of women, here, together, to put another generation to rest. Mom and I gaze over a small field, clumpy with sea grass. Megan babbles. It sounds like she's saying "Mama."

"Did she just say what I think she said?" Mom asks.

"It sure sounded like it." I hold Megan out so Mom and I can both look at her. We smile and admire her with awe as if she could be a female baby Einstein. Judging from her hair, which sticks up all over, she could be. I smooth the billowy blonde puff down with my fingertips. The breeze immediately lifts it back into genius mode. Mom and I both laugh.

The sound lingers, pitch-perfect, like the ending note to a beautiful piece of classical music.

Reluctantly, I remember why we're here, and feel obligated to join Grandma's friends inside the church.

"I should get Megan back inside where it's warm."

Mom reaches over and takes my hand. Hers feels small and helpless inside mine. I give it a squeeze. We walk in silence towards the front entrance. When we get close to the door she drops my hand. No public displays of affection, even with family. That's her motto. Oh well, Rome wasn't built in a day.

I think of the forgotten baby brother I barely knew. He was only a few weeks older than Megan is now when he died. The white dog's face flashes through my thoughts again. The beast draws back its lips in a snarl. It's teeth are long and yellow. It's eyes burn red-hot.

Oh no you don't. I swing a mental right hook at the dog. I'm not skirting around the wall of grief this time. I'm going directly through it, where no evil, grief-manifested dog can follow.

The dog's face fades and blurs. Only two pinpricks of red still glow in my mind.

A warning. A reminder not to let sorrow over rule love.

We go back inside to Grandma's reception and sit with Gene. I reach across the table and take his hand. "Thank you."

Gene looks surprised. "For what?" he asks.

"For making Mom happy."

He nods and gives me a wink.

***

Monday, 9:09 AM

The day after the service comes something else I've dreaded – the reading of the will. Mom, Gene and I sit in the stuffy little office of Grandma's attorney. The guy is ancient, his face a network of lines. I can't believe he's still practicing law, but Grandma trusted him. She used him for legal advice her entire adult life.

The wording of the will comes as no surprise. Mom inherits Grandma's house and meager bank accounts. She and I share Grandma's other belongings.

There are only a few special things I want: The double-wedding-ring quilt Grandma made; a plump Dutch girl cookie jar Grandma used to fill with homemade cookies; my old bed for Megan to sleep in when she's older; and the newly discovered box of black and white photos in the attic. The pictures of our ancestors. Other than those few items, I intend to let Mom take whatever she wants without a squabble. After all, Grandma Adelle was her mother.

I have just one favor to ask of Mom. "Could you wait a few weeks to list the house?"

Part Seven: The Rewards

Chapter Thirty-Six

That same Monday, and beyond

Mom agreed to postpone putting Grandma's house on the market. She also agreed to have the power turned back on. The next day, she and Gene flew home to Malaysia, only to turn around and fly back to Oregon six weeks later for me and Kevin's wedding.

Those six weeks were a flurry of activity. Besides a wedding to plan, Kevin and I had several more trips to the doctor's office for injections, so we wouldn't turn into slobbering, rabid beasts. Although since my last conversation with Delta, I've wondered if grief/anger manifested dogs could actually carry rabies.

Speaking of which, the authorities have still not found the dogs. With only our bite wounds and the photos of Mel as proof, I'm not sure what the people of Roseland thought of our story, what little they actually knew of it.

I printed out the photos and Kevin took them to the police station. The chief didn't release the photos to television news stations, the Roseland Daily News, the Associated Press, or to any of the gossip pulps for that matter. "Too graphic," he said. "And none of their business. It's an ongoing investigation."

Since our encounter with the dogs, no one else has vanished from Roseland.

The gossip pulps had a hey day with the whole thing, even without any killer-dog photos. For the span between Thanksgiving and Christmas, Kevin and I were followed by paparazzi, pestered by reporters, and propositioned by producers of sleazy television talk shows. We turned down all requests for interviews. I don't know how many times we said, "No comment." Commenting publicly on any of it would have made us seem like idiots.

After a few weeks, the hubbub died down and life in little Roseland by the sea went back to it's tourist-driven, slow-paced churn.

Photography-wise it was a busy season for me, too. During the end of November and the beginning of December, I took the last of my scheduled senior portraits. Due to word-of-mouth advertising and my flash-in-the-pan "fame," I also acquired a bunch of new customers who wanted family portraits taken for their Christmas cards and to give as gifts.

On the eighth of December, it snowed – a rare occurrence on the Oregon coast. Kevin and I scraped together the scant inch of snow in Grandma's front yard and built a snowman. I used a tripod and wireless remote to snap a family photo of Megan, Kevin and me standing around the little snowman for our own Christmas cards.

Megan and I had a nice, quiet Christmas with Kevin, his mom, and his sister and her family.

In the meantime, I continued to go through Grandma's things, boxing them up and labeling them as I went. I'm not sure what will become of all her stuff at this point. I can't fit it in Kevin's apartment, which is where we've decided to live after the wedding, on account of my apartment won't allow Sophelia – who is a nice, spayed black kitty, and not a smelly French slut at all. We'll live in Kevin's building until we can save enough to buy a house of our own. As for Grandma's belongings, Mom doesn't want the expense of shipping them to Asia. Yet neither of us is quite ready to let go of Grandma's things yet. For now, Kevin and I keep stacking filled cardboard boxes in the garage. I suppose we'll rent a storage unit until we decide what to do with all this stuff.

***

Kevin and I got married in Grandma's living room.

My dress was simple, off-white, mid-calf length with a fitted bodice. Gene walked me up the aisle. Asking him to give me away was the ultimate peace offering I could make to both him and Mom. Besides, blood or not, he is the only dad I have now, and he is Megan's only grandfather.

I carried a bouquet of yellow carnations and red roses. The same kind of flowers Kevin had delivered to my house on the day I first saw the evil dogs. The flowers were what ultimately led him to me. In a roundabout way, those flowers helped Kevin save mine and Megan's lives.

The wedding guest list and the ceremony were both short. After Kevin and I exchanged our vows, my new husband kissed me long and deep and slow. I could have melted right into the gold shag carpet.

After the kiss, we just gazed into one another's eyes until one of the guests cleared their throats, which brought a round of laughter and reminded us we weren't alone.

I felt Grandma's presence very strongly during the ceremony, although she managed to hold her tongue. After the vows and the throat clearing, a spot on my forehead grew warm, as if Grandma kissed me there. Then Grandma broke her silence.

Goodbye Dianne. You got yourself a good man.

Goodbye? You're not fooling me, Grandma. I know you'll be popping in to voice your opinion again soon.

Again? These are the only words I've said since moving to the other side.

Huh? What do you mean? You've talked to me a bunch.

No, dear.

Then who was it? It couldn't have just been my imagination. Could it? Grandma? Could it really?

But Grandma never answered me. She and her voice vanished then, forever. Well, not forever. I know I'll be with her again someday. And Kevin was right when he had the florist write, "She'll always be with you" on the card he had sent with that sympathy bouquet of roses and carnations. Grandma Adelle is a part of me. And nothing – not her death, not red-eyed dogs, and not even me thinking she was talking to me when maybe it was just me talking to myself – none of that can take her away from me.

When Kevin and I break our gaze and turn to look out at the guests, I am surprised to see how many sets of eyes brim with tears. A liquid, salty and sweet, burns at the back of my nose too.

It was fate that brought Kevin and me to this place. I never believed in fate before, but with Kevin standing beside me as my husband, holding my hand, loving me, I've never believed anything more in my life.

"Are you single ladies ready?" I turn my back to the crowded room, wait for the group of four unattached women to assemble behind me. With eyes closed, I toss the roses and carnations backwards over my shoulder. Delta seems first surprised and then flustered when she catches the bouquet.

I guess even fortunetellers can't predict everything.

After all my years of negative feelings aimed at Delta, I feel honored now to know her. I'm glad Kevin suggested we add her to our guest list. After all, it's because of her that we found Megan on Thanksgiving in the cave.

In the traditional manner, with his hand over mine, Kevin and I cut the untraditional German chocolate cake. It doesn't really go with the white champagne, but no one complains.

We open the gifts. Mom plays secretary and writes down who gave us which coffee pot, toaster or towel set.

I save the gift from Mom and Gene for last. My hand trembles as I carefully remove the gold ribbon and lacy-looking silver paper. Mom has never been good at gift shopping, but I'm determined to appreciate whatever's inside the box – even if it's hideous and I hate it. My new relationship with her is like a tender spring shoot. One wrong step will snap it off at ground level. If that happens, I'm afraid it may never regrow.

I remove the box lid, push back the tissue. Nestled at the bottom is an envelope.

"What's this?" I look at Mom.

"Open it," she says. Her face is flushed. Is she holding her breath?

It's a document envelope. Aged and yellowed. I open the flap, slip out a thick piece of paper, unfold it.

I gasp. I can't believe what I'm holding in my hands.

Kevin peers over my shoulder. "What is it, sweetheart?"

I'm so choked up I can't speak, I just hold the deed to Grandma's house up so he can see it too.

"Wow," he says. "Wow."

"Yeah. Wow is right." Tears spring to my eyes. "Thank you, Mom, Gene. I can't believe this."

"We want you and Kevin to live here. Raise your babies here. Keep the house in the family."

"It's…it's so much, Mom."

"Gene and I talked it over. We decided since we didn't pay for your wedding, we wanted to do this for you."

More than fine by me. I didn't want or need a big, expensive wedding anyway.

After the ceremony and reception, Mom and Gene head to the airport in their rental car to catch their overseas flight. We'll join them in Malaysia next week for our honeymoon. I've never been there. Neither has Kevin. So after talking it over we decided what the heck? We can take in the sights and have a free place to crash at night. Besides, Mom and Gene have lived there for eight years now. I'd like to see the country they call home. Shoot, I'd like to see the house they call home. Mom said when we get there, she and I can look through a box of old photos she kept of Seth. I'll get to see what my baby brother looked like. I hope she lets me keep one of the photographs to bring back with me.

A white dog flickers through my mind. I hurl mental boulders at him. His red eyes dim. Fade. Extinguish.

After the rest of the guests leave, Kevin and I gather up the plastic champagne glasses, paper plates and wadded-up wedding napkins scattered around the house. Around *our* house. I do a little 'Sound-of-Music' spin in the middle of the living room, which cracks Kevin up.

"It's ours," I say. "Can you believe it? Our very own house."

Before Kevin can answer, someone raps at the door, which about sends me into cardiac arrest. Even weeks after the episode with the dogs, I'm still jumpy. Besides I was just twirling around the room like an idiot, with the curtains wide open.

Kevin crosses to the door. "It's Buzz," he says back over his shoulder. "I'll be right back." He slips outside and pulls the door closed behind him.

Probably police business. Kevin has to keep his detective stuff secret, even from me. I tread down the hall to my old room – Megan's room now – to check on her. She's sleeping soundly – a blonde cherub inside a pillow corral. I return to the front room to finish gathering disposable wedding remnants.

Kevin opens the back door a crack and sticks his head through. "Dianne?"

"Yes?"

"Could you come out here for a second? There's something I want to show you."

I'm thinking, "Yeah, I've got something to show you too, but can't we wait to start the honeymoon until we're alone?" Buzz's car is still parked out front.

But I humor Kevin. Once out in the backyard, I can see the sparkle in his eye. He's holding both hands behind his back. He is definitely up to something.

"Come closer, sweetheart."

Since he acted the gentleman and didn't shove the first bite of wedding cake in my face, I'm expecting him to pull out a water pistol, or a can of whipped cream and let me have it. When he brings his hands from behind his back, I anticipate water or whipped cream and dodge to the right. But he's not holding anything to squirt or shoot at me. Instead, snuggled inside his palms is a big, golden fluff ball.

"What's this?" I ask.

"My wedding gift to you," he says. He holds the fluffy ball close to my face.

The fluff ball shifts and a tiny nose and two liquid brown eyes appear. I bend lower for a closer look. A tiny pink tongue flicks out and licks the tip of my nose.

My heart melts. "Oh, Kevin. It's adorable."

"So are you, baby."

I smile. Kevin kisses me. I hold out my hands to take the puppy. "Is it a boy ball of fluff or a girl?" I ask.

"A boy. Like Bubba."

"What should we name him?"

"Bubba Junior?"

"There can never be another Bubba," I say, picturing Bubba doing the doofie-dog dinner dance on his hind legs. Bubba, hackled and fighting the red-eyed dogs to protect us. "How about we just call him Junior?"

"Or BJ."

I try the name on for size. "BJ." The furry pup in my arms wags his plump tail. Kevin and I both laugh.

"He likes it," Kevin says.

"BJ it is then. Thank you. I couldn't have asked for a cuter wedding gift."

Buzz is standing discretely alongside the house, watching us. Kevin turns and gives his partner a thumbs up.

"Thanks for your part in this," I say to Buzz. "He's adorable."

"Who, Kevin? He's not that adorable," Buzz jokes. "But you're welcome."

Buzz's expression changes from that of a jokester to that of a serious detective. He pauses and looks down at his feet. "Do you, uh…do you know if Delta is seeing anyone?"

I have to work hard to suppress a smile. Delta *did* catch my bridal bouquet. But Buzz and Delta? Really? I never would have matched those two up. Kevin once said Buzz was like I used to be – no belief in much of anything he can't see or touch. Ah well, stranger things than Buzz and Delta getting together have happened. I think back over the past seven weeks. Much stranger things have definitely happened.

"I've never heard her mention a man in her life," I tell Buzz.

"Okay. Good to know," Buzz says, his expression lightening. "Catch you two lovebirds later." He gives us a wink and shows himself through the garage and out to his car.

Kevin and I look at each other and grin. Buzz and Delta. Now there's a true case of opposites attracting. I can't help shaking my head in disbelief. We take the puppy inside. I set him on the floor. He waddles along behind us as we finish straightening up, making us both laugh.

"Buzz offered to keep the pup while we're on our honeymoon," Kevin says.

"That's great. I was just wondering what we'd do with him while we're gone."

Kevin and I talk about how we'll arrange our furniture. Whose couch we'll keep, whose TV, whose stereo. We discuss updates we'd like to do to the house as we can afford them, starting with new flooring.

"It won't bother you to live here?" Kevin asks.

"No. This is a happy place for me."

"Even after what happened with the dogs? After what happened to Bubba?"

"Even after what happened," I assure him. Together, Kevin and I have unpacked and defeated our emotional baggage. We don't need to worry anymore about evil dogs hunting us down and ripping us to pieces.

The puppy discovers Kevin's feet. He romps at a shoelace and grips it in his teeth, pulling back with a squeaky growl and a shake of his head. The shoelace slips through his teeth. The pup tumbles. He gets up, looks around and takes a couple of high-stepping prances as though to say, "I meant to do that."

Kevin and I both laugh.

"The happy memories inside this house outweigh the evil-dog memories about a thousand and seventeen to one," I say. "Besides, I think between memories of Bubba and memories-yet-to-come with little BJ here, there will be plenty of happy-dog memories to counteract the bad ones."

I look at the golden retriever puppy at my feet. He looks up at me with soulful brown eyes.

Familiar brown eyes.

Bubba? Bubba, is that you in there?

Chapter Thirty-Seven

Saturday afternoon, early January

Looking at the golden retriever pup at my feet on Grandma's kitchen floor, I almost believe in reincarnation.

The fluffy puppy chases his tail. He catches it in his teeth and pulls himself over. He flails to regain his feet, looks up at me with liquid brown eyes and whimpers.

Yep. Bubba the Wonder Dog lives again.

After Kevin and I get the house back in order and Megan is down for her afternoon nap, I take the puppy out to the backyard and watch him frolic, chase his tail and stumble over his own feet.

I hear the back screen door bang shut. Kevin sneaks up behind me, wraps his arms around my waist and gently rubs my belly. He plants small kisses along the length of my neck, sending shivers skittering a path to my toes. My mom was sure right about one thing – men like Kevin don't grow on trees.

I turn around and meet his mouth with mine. "Wanna make a baby?" I murmur against his lips.

He pulls back, wearing a fake, flabbergasted look. "Are you propositioning me, ma'am?"

I laugh. "Yes, sir. I suppose I am."

"Well, forgive me if I'm mistaken, ma'am…" Kevin exaggerates his southern drawl. "…but I thought we already done went and made us a baby." He lays a big hand on my stomach. His laughing eyes soften.

A flush of warmth radiates from where his hand touches me. The warmth moves down. Lower. And lower. "Shut up, sir, and kiss me."

Sir obliges.

We part and gaze at each other. "I've heard practice makes perfect," he mutters before bending down for another kiss. When we come up for air, his voice is husky. "I'd be mighty happy to practice with you, ma'am." His eyes twinkle. In their warm, golden depths I see bottomless love.

He takes my hand and leads me inside the house, down the hall and into the master bedroom. *Our* bedroom now. I pull back Grandma's wedding ring quilt. Kevin flips on the clock radio. It's tuned to a country station. We undress each other to a George Strait song.

Kevin pulls me into his arms, right where I belong. Where I've always belonged. We slow dance around the room. Close, naked, and in love.

His baby maker is hard against my thigh, raring to practice. "Is that a pistol in your pocket?" I ask. "Oh, never mind. You're not wearing pockets."

Kevin dances me over to the king-size bed, dips me low over his arm, and lies me down. He stretches out beside me and runs a single, teasing finger up the inside of my leg. "I love you, Dianne."

He's amazing. Long, lean, handsome. Loving. And mine. I've never wanted him more in my life. I grin. "I know. You've always loved me."

"You…" He tickles me.

I draw my knees up to protect my most ticklish spots, but he doesn't let up. "You know what I want you to say."

"We're going to wake up Megan," I protest between gasping fits of giggles.

"Say it." He straddles my legs and holds his hands over my stomach in tickle position. "Say it."

Tears run down my cheeks and my jaw aches from laughing, "No. Don't. I can't take anymore."

"Say it."

"Uncle."

"Not that."

Kevin pins my arms over my head and starts making little tongue circles around my nipples.

"Mmmm," I moan. "I love you, too."

He smiles. "That's more like it." He lets my arms free. His tongue moves lower. And lower. And lower still. I groan with pleasure and my breathing comes in short gasps.

He stops what he's doing.

"More," I beg.

"You love me too…" he slips his index finger into his mouth to wet it and slides it inside me. "…and…"

"…and…" I say back, panting.

He moves his finger in and out, while rubbing my pleasure button with his thumb. I moan.

He pulls out his finger.

"Kevin, don't stop."

"…and…" he says.

I push up on one elbow, playing dumb. I know what he wants me to say, but I'm enjoying the game too much to say it. "And what?"

"You love me…and…" He playfully shoves me back down on the bed, runs the same index finger across my bottom lip and down my neck. He trails the damp finger over one of my breasts, around the nipple and down my stomach. He holds his finger poised over my mound and at the ready.

I lick my lips, tasting my own salt. I move my pelvis up against his hand, trying to convince him to continue.

"Well?" he asks. "How bad do you want my trigger finger, ma'am?"

I let out a groan. "You know how bad I want it. This is black mail," I complain. "And your point is…?"

I arch my hips. I want to feel more of his thrusting finger and rubbing thumb. But he doesn't thrust or rub. He just looks at me, a pained twinkle in his eyes. Grandma always said, "Pick your battles." This is one I know I won't win, don't want to win, even in fun. So I cave. "…and…I'll love you forever?"

A slow, deviant smile lights up his face. "Bingo. That wasn't so hard, was it?"

"No. But you're hard, and I want to feel your hardness inside me. Deep inside me."

"Patience, my sexy bride."

His bride. His sexy bride. I love the way that sounds. But I have run out of patience. My toes curl as he moves his index finger in and out, moves his thumb around, up, down, around and faster. It makes me whimper and wiggle and thrash. I close my eyes, riding the tide of passion to a current of release.

Before I can catch my breath, Kevin straddles me. The pistol he's packing is fully loaded. I can feel its hot barrel pressing hard against my stomach. He lifts his hips a few inches away from mine.

"Kevin…"

His big gun brushes my inner thigh. "Mmmm?"

"I've always loved you."

"I know." He smiles and reaches down to guide himself into me. The sight of his big fingers wrapped around his thick shaft nearly sends me into orbit. He slips only the very tip of his steel pistol inside my velvet holster, and holds it there. His chin wrinkles with the effort to keep still.

I arch my body to meet his, wanting to feel his firm smoothness glide way inside. He pushes himself half way in. Pulls back out.

I gasp. Where is he getting his self control? "Deeper, baby."

"Impatient little vixen, aren't you, ma'am?" he drawls, his teeth clenched, a look of sheer concentration etched across his face. He presses only the tip of himself inside my tender flesh and stops.

"Tease." I groan and grip his ass with both hands, trying to force him deeper inside me. But he's stronger than I am. I can't budge his hips.

"Is that what you want?"

"You know I do."

"Say it."

"I want it."

"How much do you want?"

"I want it all."

"I want it all too, sweetheart." He thrusts, hard and deep.

I cry out with surprise and delight.

He moves with firm, long, even strokes. The friction of his flat lower abs against my pelvis sends me sailing the sea of ecstasy again. I grip his hips tighter and bury my head in his chest to muffle my cries. I don't want to wake Megan. I'm not finished practicing yet.

Luckily, neither is Kevin.

He slows his thrusts, and meets my lips with a deep, wet kiss. He lowers his head to my breasts and takes one in his mouth, rolling my nipple around with his tongue as though it is a piece of exotic candy.

"You know Babe, we've got it all," Kevin says.

I moan and nod. I'm appreciative, but I'm in the mood for another orgasm, not conversation at the moment.

He covers my cheeks and eyelids with tiny kisses. He's still moving slowly in and out of me. I feel an avalanche building once more.

"Come with me," I beg.

He moves faster, groaning, stroking me from the inside out. His erection feels enormous. I slip over the edge. Farther. Over.

And then we both explode on a sea of light and waves and sensation.

This kind of practice, I'll never grow tired of.

"Come here, sweetheart," he says when we've both regained normal breathing patterns. "Cuddle with me."

With Kevin, the after-the-lovemaking is even better than the lovemaking itself. Well, maybe not exactly better, but good – tender, sweet, and wonderful. I snuggle into the crook of Kevin's arm, lay my head on his hard chest. My body is warm and tingly, pressed tight against his. Megan is sleeping safe and sound in the next room. Kevin's baby is growing inside me.

I feel an almost overwhelming amount of love flood over me, through me. I must be the luckiest woman alive.

I close my eyes and my mind flashes forward, as though I am Delta, the fortuneteller. I see our babies growing into toddlers. Children into adults. And Kevin, always Kevin, the foundation that makes my life complete.

I see the two of us as old people. Slow dancing. Holding wrinkled, age-spotted hands. Helping each other through our daily chores, through life's ups and downs.

I flash to the end.

I'm lying in a hospital bed and Kevin is at my side. Our middle-aged children and their children – our grandchildren – gather close. They speak in hushed voices, telling me it's all right to go. They love me. They'll remember me always.

I am not afraid.

Kevin interrupts my flash forward when he lifts me and rolls me on top of him. My breasts smash tight against his hard chest. He hugs me close. "You are the love of my life, Dianne," he says.

And then he kisses me. Deep and slow and forever.

Danita Cahill is a full-time, multi-published, award-winning freelance writer and photojournalist. She lived in the Pacific NW on a small Oregon farm with her husband, two sons and their animals – a horse, several cats and guinea pigs, a herd of alpacas, and two dogs – neither of which has red eyes. Danita is busy working on newspaper and magazine assignments and her next book.

To read more about miracles, visions and other amazing things, visit Danita's miracles blog at www.miracahills.wordpress.com. To see samples of Danita's photography, visit her photo blog at www.cahillphotojournalism.com.

Danita loves to hear from readers. You can find her on Facebook – Danita Shattuck Cahill – follow her on twitter @DanitaCahill or email her at: danita1363@gmail.com.

Made in the USA
Charleston, SC
09 December 2012